Curse of Russia

❧

Kate Valery

Order this book online at www.trafford.com
or email orders@trafford.com

Most Trafford titles are also available at major online book retailers.

Print information available on the last page.

ISBN: 978-1-4269-0162-1 (sc)
ISBN: 978-1-4269-3491-9 (e)

Trafford rev. 03/28/2022

 www.trafford.com

North America & international
toll-free: 844-688-6899 (USA & Canada)
fax: 812 355 4082

<u>To holy memory of :</u>
my mother Liudmila,
my Baba Sofia,
and my Great-Baba Ekaterina.

Acknowledgement

I want to thank **Camilla Gibb**, the world famous Canadian author, who taught me, inspired and gave me advice to write a book about my Russian childhood.

For editing this book I want to thank my dear friends and colleagues from the site FanStory.com, especially Abigail David, Johnny Carwash, Nor84, RajaSir, Raymond John, Topaz, and Witchykym.

The big thank you I want to say to my great helper in proofreading Mr. Noel Noren who had also an experience in living in Russia some times.

The greatest thank you I wish to send to professionals - writers, journalists and poets – and to my devoted readers who sent me their feed backs about my previous books **STOLEN** and **DEADLY PARADISE,** and mentally supported me.

All of the above great people gave me a chance to write my book **CURSE OF RUSSIA**.

Enjoy your reading, my dear ones, though it will be scary and sad at some places!

If you are a Russian,

And decided to write a thriller set in hell, you don't need to create a thing.

Being a Russian emigrant, just turn your mind back and describe your past.

Residing in Russia, just look around – and describe your present...

PREVIOUS BOOKS AUTHORED BY KATE VALERY:

STOLEN
Dorrance, Pittsburgh, PA, U.S.A
www.rosedogbookstore.com

DEADLY PARADISE
Trafford, Victoria, BC, Canada
trafford/07-0351

"*STOLEN* is an amazing, original and unique novel of intrigue, full of ecstasy and curious twists."

> **Liliia White**, author of the **POETRY FROM THE SKY**

"I even don't know what to say. I'm in shock. I hadn't ever read anything like **STOLEN** by Kate Valery. It's a very, very different, impressive and unusual book. I read it three days straight because I couldn't put it down."

> **Paula Wolchuk**, certified Canadian psychologist

"**STOLEN** offers us a plot that is extreme and unique. Kate Valery does a good job in revealing the internal workings of the characters. Overall **STOLEN** is a fascinating tale.
This love triangle story is full of outrageous jealousy, deceit, suicide, passion, and guilt. Some sex scenes are hot and intense...
Having been a victim of theft, will Nick become a stolen treasure himself?"

> **Inna Spice**, author of the short story anthology
> **QUENCH YOUR THIRST**
> www.SpiceMedia.ca

"**STOLEN** by Kate Valery is a serious literature that really struck a cord with me. Though, the true situation in East Germany was much worse than portrayed here. The book captures the essence of fear we all felt. I know; I've spent some years in prison there only uttering a few careless words..."

> **Kurt Berisch,** a political refugee
> from the former East Germany

"I cried while reading **DEADLY PARADISE**. It felt like the book was written about me..."

Ilona Zelinska, Polish journalist, immigrant in Canada

"I want to thank Kate Valery, author of the novel **DEADLY PARADISE**, for capturing my life story that really deserves to be in a book."

Ernst Zimmer, the Second World War emigrant from Germany

"The novel **DEADLY PARADISE** is a dramatic exploration of the forces at work when striving and exploitation meet behind the placid façade of a high-rise condominium. I want to say to the author, "Good for you!"

Erin Bouma, editor of **THE ENGLISH NEWSPAPER**

"In **DEADLY PARADISE** I liked hearing Nina describe the challenges of managing an apartment building. The writing has a good sense of suspense to it and tension pulling the narrative forward."

Writer's Digest 15th International S-P Book Award

Table of Contents

PART 1

ANCESTORS

I didn't want to write in this book about politics, the Communist regime, the Bolshevik Revolution, Russian Civil War or Lenin's terror. All these things are already quite well-known around the world.

But how could we, ordinary Russians, possibly escape them? Our flesh and blood were raised on politics, like bread-dough was raised by yeast.

Anyway, I'll try to avoid social events, as much as I can.

Chapter 1

THE BOAT ON THE POND

Our rooms were finished quite plainly. The furniture and the curtains were old and I have no memory of when they appeared in this suite. To me it seemed that they had been there forever.

On the top of our wardrobe had always rested an old suitcase; on top of a china board, under our beds and under the couch were stored the cardboard boxes which were filled with old things because the suite had no closet or storage space at all. Definitely, there was not even enough room for the three of us – my grandma (whom I called in Russian 'Baba'), my mom and me - three generations of women.

In addition, we had some furniture which the people I knew didn't posses – a piano and my mom's writing table. My friends and acquaintances – our neighbors, my classmates and their parents, our neighbors at the summer village where we rented a dacha, my mom's friends, my Baba's friends, our relatives – never wrote anything and never played the piano. They didn't need any pianos or desks but we did. And it made our two rooms much more cramped.

My mom and my Baba both played piano and began teaching me when I was six.

To tell the truth, for many years I didn't like it. It seemed boring to me and meant a lot of hard work to practice and I preferred to be lazy. I liked to create something new - but in learning the basics, there was no possibility to be creative – just drill, drill, drill. I did the monotonous short tunes, melodies and cords (sometimes only two or three notes at a time) which I had to repeat over and over again, pecking away like a woodpecker, with no thinking or imagination.

I wanted to run away and play with my toys, but there sat my Baba right next to me, watching me closely. So, I had no choice but to obediently keep on doing my piano drills, even though I had no heart for them.

While meaninglessly training my fingers, I usually searched the room, desperate to find something interesting to occupy my mind. I studied all the fretworks on our piano – in fact, right in front of my

3

nose; I studied the wallpaper pattern on the walls and memorized the swirls and designs.

Then, my scanning eyes slid upward and rested on the painting framed with antique gold that hung over my seat of torture. The edges of the frame also had a fretted look, but were really only stucco moldings shaped from alabaster. They were broken in some places and undercoat of white intruded on the supposed elegance. It didn't look very good and I suggested to my mom a couple of times that she restore the frame with some touches of gold paint.

Since it wasn't so important, my mom never got around to doing it. Sometimes, she was busy working, sometimes she couldn't find any gold paint in the stores (no wonder, it was barely possible to find something to eat, to say nothing of paint for an old frame). It was hopeless. So, I understood that the painting would be enclosed in a partially gilded frame to the end.

The painting itself captured a woeful scene. There was an over-grown dark pond, surrounded by weeping-willows whose branches hung down into the water and reflected on its smooth surface. An old boat was chained to a little wooden moorage. Strangely enough, the weather was sunny – as witnessed by the twinkling water dancing with sunbeams and the green and fresh grass on the moorage bank. But the brightness lived only in the corner, and the view was dominated by the inky water and mournful willows which created a doleful impression that stayed with the viewer.

The painting was obviously the same age as the sorry frame – its colors were dulled but, still, through the melancholy, it was clear that the painter possessed talent and captured landscapes very well.

In my teen years, I wasn't a big art connoisseur. I didn't like the old stuff and dreamed of something new. I'd always look for the chance to throw the old things in the garbage and to replace them with modern ones. At the same time, I'd always look for a way to escape my music lessons and tried to talk with my Baba about things other than my exercises.

One day, when I was possibly around fourteen, I asked my Baba, "Why is this old picture still here? It doesn't look good. Mama couldn't find the gold paint to fix the frame. Well, why don't we just throw it away?"

"You know, it's the only thing left to remember my mother by," Baba said. "She painted it..."

"Did you have a mother?" I asked surprised. I always knew that my Baba was raised by her father.

"Of course, everybody has a mother," she insisted. "Otherwise,

4

how could I appear in this world? She took off when I was three-years-old and my older sister, Anya, - four. My mom painted this landscape before leaving, but everything happened so suddenly that she had no time to finish it and she abandoned it on the easel right beside the pond. Later, my dad framed it and kept it to remember her."

"I'm sure I want to know the story," I begged. "I don't understand how she could leave two of her own little girls. Didn't she love you?"

"Well," Baba took a deep breath. "I myself don't know too much, just what my father told me about her. But anyway, hers is a special story. My parents got divorced in 1897. Nobody was divorced in the 19th century. There was no divorce in Russia but my parents applied for the Tsar's permission and they got it. Isn't it special?"

"Yes, it is," I nodded readily, craving the personal details of her narrative to end my tedious music lesson. "There must be something there. Tell me, Baba, please..."

...This afternoon Ekaterina walked down the hill to the pond in a nervous state. Dinner had just finished and it was disgusting. Not food, of course. It had been wonderful, as usual, but the situation was nearing the brink of a crisis. Her oversized mother-in-law, Stephanida, who rested on two chairs because of her size, was more loathsome than usual.

During the entire dinner, Stephanida had blamed their manager and leaseholder, Zbignev Pshesinsky; she shouted at the girls and even threatened them with her whip if they didn't eat well; she slapped the face of her maid, Marusya, because, in her opinion, some of the napkins weren't clean enough. She finally concluded that the whole mess at their estate, *Vysokoye,* was Ekaterina's fault.

"You're lazy! You're doing nothing!" Stephanida announced, addressing her daughter-in-law. "Just walking, reading, playing with the children, and painting! Do you think you're a princess?"

"I'm watching my girls and I'm nursing Xenia," Ekaterina protested but then realized that it was the last time she'd object. There was no point in trying to talk to this ridiculous, rude and uneducated woman; she would keep silence from now on.

"I nursed my ten children while ruling the whole estate when I was younger," Stephanida retorted, breathing heavily after the dinner and proudly lifting up her three chins. "My husband used to live in Warsaw because he was a professor there, at the university. He only came here for visits but I never went there. I was a country priest's daughter. I was a farm girl, and I ruled this estate alone. I gave birth to my children, pray and work hard. That's my life.

"We didn't have any leaseholders or managers in those days. I could handle everything that went on here – the fields, the harvest, the cattle, and dairy production. I was hardworking and full of energy. But you, Ekaterina, are only able to play the piano, paint landscapes and cry! I guess you think that your royal blood makes you special! No way, my dear! Actually, your ancestor wasn't really the child of an Empress, he was only a bastard! I don't understand how my smart Vladimir could marry you! He certainly was mistaken to have chosen you. He needed a wife, not a porcelain statue for his home."

Ekaterina burned with outrage, ready to defend herself. At that moment Zbignev squeezed her hand under the table and restrained her impulses. Then, he stood up.

"Well, Pani Stephanida," he uttered calmly, "thank you for a nice dinner. I have to go to work. Panenka Anya and Panenka Sonya, do you want to walk down to the pond and play with Marek?"

"Yes, we do!" the charming 3- and 4-year-old sisters clamored down from their high chairs, looking timidly at their grandma who was the obvious boss here. "Could we, Baba?"

"Go, go!" Stephanida peacefully waved her hand, drying her sweaty red face with a big cotton napkin. "I'm too busy and have too many things to do. You have your mother to take care of you."

The highest permission was gratefully received. The dinner concluded and everybody felt free to return to their usual routine. The maid, Marusya, still sniffing from being reproached, began to collect the dishes and clean the table.

"Let's make a picnic," Zbignev suggested to the little ones. The girls applauded and jumped up, grinning and making funny faces.

He took a plaid rug from the couch and hung it over his shoulder. Then he gathered some leftovers from the table, divided them between two little baskets and handed them to Anya and Sonya. "Are you ready to go?"

"Yes, yes, we're ready!"

"Okay," Zbignev took the girls' hands and walked toward the pond with them.

Ekaterina lifted her baby, Xenia, from the cradle, put some toys and clean swaddling clothes in a bag and followed them down the hill, carrying the child in her arms.

Zbignev is so amazing, she thought, - tall, strong, blond-haired, green-eyed, and handsome. He is also very kind and so patient. He knows perfectly well how to deal with Stephanida and how to manage any situation.

Ekaterina felt that her survival here depended totally on his wisdom and grace. If he weren't here, she would be long gone by now. This was not a summer for her, not vacation, not rest - but torture. She counted the days, waiting impatiently for her husband, Stephanida's son Vladimir's return from his business trip around Russia, when he would fetch her and the children. She felt really upset and anxious after this damn dinner and, even being on the banks of the pond, still couldn't completely relax.

Zbignev spread the rug out over the grass and turned to Ekaterina. "You settle down here," he said, smiling at her and holding her glance a bit longer than usual. "I'll go and call my wife and Marek to play with the girls."

"Thank you," she nodded and gracefully lowered herself onto the rug. She placed little Xenia in the shade and wrapped her baby with her scarf; then she pulled out the toys. Anya and Sonya fussed with the baskets, trying to serve the picnic. They grabbed the toys and started to play right away and soon everything quieted down. Ekaterina felt that she was finally able to relax, being left alone with her daughters.

She lay on her back, gazing up at the sky. It was bright, blue and bottomless. The curly clouds swam overhead, creating different pictures of snowy mountains, or sheepskins, or tufts of cotton. The bugs and flies were actively and invisibly buzzing around. A big azure dragonfly hung above the wild rosebushes beside her. Only the girls' laughter and chatter, along with the chirping of birds broke the stillness of the summery afternoon. She felt a blissful release.

However, there was still something missing in Ekaterina's quiet country life. She sensed its absence but couldn't quite put her finger on it. Now, while contemplating the changing sky, she understood what was lacking. She yearned for some intellectual stimulation, some work for her mind. She needed to do something, to study something, to create something – in some way to express her inner soul. It was impossibly boring to live like a vegetable – only to eat, sleep, walk, and watch the children.

Even Stephanida, who was working hard the full day, was a vegetable, too. Sure, she produced things like harvested crops and dairy products – with the labor of her workers, of course. But anyway, these all were material things. Though Stephanida was very religious and prayed many times a day, and walked to the church every Sunday, (didn't matter how tired or ill she was), there was nothing in her life

7

that could be considered creative, nothing intellectual, nothing that was born from the heart. She was uneducated and barely literate. She couldn't even read much of the Bible, to which she appealed all the time. As a consequence, Zbignev was hired to do all the paperwork for the estate.

Ekaterina clearly realized that this lack of creative output and soulful spirituality was exactly the thing which placed such an insurmountable barrier between the mother- and daughter-in-law. She had nothing to do here on this estate, in this company. She felt compelled to activate her creativity and liberate herself through it. It was her true vocation in life.

The realization appeared from the sky and in a moment revealed the truth. It put everything into perspective for her. Ekaterina felt acutely that she should follow the lead of her intuition. That's why she had started to paint some days ago. That's what she was guided to do. She had to be an artist.

Ekaterina sat up on the spread rug; arranged her dark brown curls with both hands and searched out her girls at play. Then she stood up, put on her white, lacy hat with long blue ribbons and walked toward her easel which stood waiting for her beside the pond since yesterday. It was her time to finish this landscape.

When Zbignev came back with his wife, Eva – a shy simple Polish farmer's daughter, and their 3-year-old son, Marek, Sonya and Anya ran, happily shrieking and squalling to greet their friends. Ekaterina and Eva gave each other a sisterly kiss and hug. Then Eva began to play with the children – she had a fondness toward them and was a natural at their games.

Ekaterina returned to her easel and Zbignev approached and stood beside her. He watched closely how she was painting.

"Did you take classes?" he asked after five minutes.

"Why are you asking?" she glanced at him, smiling. "Does my work look so unprofessional that you're not sure if I've been trained or not?"

"No," he laughed. "I didn't mean that. I'm just curious. I don't know much about art at all..."

"I did take classes one year, as a teenager, while I was studying at the Institute. But I had to drop them – my mom passed away; then, six months later, my dad also died. I had no money to pay for classes."

"I'm sorry to hear that," Zbignev noted sympathetically. "What happened to them?"

"Tuberculosis. Infection swept over the whole family. Seven of my siblings died, too, one by one. Only three of us survived: my elder brother Hermann - because he left for Russia to study much earlier; then me because I was living on campus at the Institute at the time, and last, my baby-sister Lily, who was born just before my mother went.

"Following mom's death, my dad, ill and desperate to care for Lily, married too quickly and unwisely. My stepmother turns out to be an evil woman. She hated me and Hermann and deliberately forced my dad to exclude both of us, his older children, from his will. My father died some months later, and she was left with Lily and inherited the house and all the money.

"Hermann and I were left with nothing. Zero. Actually, Hermann didn't need anything from her. He was already an engineer, with a good position at a metallurgical plant in the Russian city of Taganrog and made enough money for living. He even bought some equities from his plant and wrote me that he plans to buy more, later on. He made his career and I'm happy for him."

"Now I understand, why you ended up marrying Pan Vladimir," Zbignev thoughtfully commented, studying her face attentively. "Otherwise, it makes no sense. You're so beautiful and so much younger..."

"Yeah...Actually half his age – I was eighteen and he was thirty-six when we got married." Ekaterina sighed and paused to mix new colors on her palette. She added more black and dark brown to the green blob. Zbignev greedily followed each of her movements with his eyes.

"Your pond looks too sad," he observed sociably. "It seemed to me that you're using too many dark shades. Look, at the pond everything is much shinier. Are you doing it intentionally or is it the way you feel?"

"I don't know," Ekaterina shrugged. "Oh, no, I'm lying. Of course, I know. I feel sad... Very sad... I'm trapped. I don't know what to do and can't see an exit out of my tunnel."

"Exit? Tunnel? What are you talking about?"

"About my situation. I have already three children. What can I possibly look forward to in the future?"

"Your fourth little one!" Zbignev laughed.

"Exactly!" Ekaterina exclaimed, agitated. "Women are just baby machines! Like my mom was, like Stephanida was. I don't want that! I feel that I want to be a person, a creator, but not a machine!"

Her cheeks flushed with excitement, her dark blue eyes sparkled and Zbivnev was drawn to her passion. He couldn't help but think she would grow more and more attractive as she opened up her sensuality.

"But each child born is a created being," he objected in order to continue the sharing.

"That's not what I mean. A child is a biological creature of nature, but I'm talking about spiritual creatures, about creative works."

"Many women today are painting," Zbignev shrugged, "or writing books, or embroidering pictures in silk... You could combine your art with motherhood. I even read in a newspaper that one woman became a scientist in physics, somewhere in France or Germany. I don't see any problem with that."

"Okay, let's try you then. Would you want your Eva to begin attending university and become a scientist in physics?"

"Of course, not," Zbignev shook his head, grinning. "She doesn't want it, either. You can ask her yourself. Look over there. She is so happy playing with those four children. I'm sure that she would like have many of them by her own and make a big family instead."

"The most important thing is that Eva loves you. That's why she is happy with her family. I can't say I'm in the same boat."

With this, Ekaterina painted the old boat on the surface of the pond, then stopped suddenly and looked up at Zbigev questioningly.

"I'm always thinking about this boat," she declared. "It seems very old. Is it seaworthy at all? Could we possibly go boating today?"

"I guess so," Zbignev answered uncertainly. "I'll check it. Do you want to go out?"

"It would be amazing."

"Let's try... Honey," Zbignev waved to Eva, heading to the boat, "I'll boat a bit with Pani Ekaterina and you please stay with the children."

"We go boating, too, Papa," Marek, his head a crown of curls, responded excitedly and ran toward the boat.

"Me too! Me too!" Sonya and Anya shrieked, following him.

"Well," Zbignev squatted and opened his arms to catch them all. "Okay. I'll tell you what. We'll make one tour around the pond first - just to be sure the boat is safe. Then I'll come back to get you and we'll do a second round. How is that?"

"Good! Okay! Hurrah!" the children shouted, jumping around and trying to help Zbignev unlock the boat. The chain was very old and rusty and it was not an easy thing to do.

Finally, he succeeded; then he stepped into the boat and tried the oars. The rusty rowlocks squeaked from disuse.

"Well," he glanced at Ekaterina, "if you enjoy this ride, I would gladly oil them tomorrow and we can take her out every day. I would also clean the boat."

"Okay," she nodded her assent, took his hand to support herself and stepped with her refined white shoe onto the slippery and slimy planks of the boat bottom. The floor was damp and littered with rotting fallen leaves and neglected equipment because nobody had used the boat for years. But Ekaterina was brave enough to shift a few steps toward the back seat and settle down, cautiously lifting the lacy white hem of her blue skirt. Ignoring the caked mud in her chosen vessel, she extended her silk stocking ankles to get comfortable and smiled at Zbignev reassuringly and bid him to set sail, "Let's go, Pan!"

"You aren't put off by how dirty everything is?" he asked her in amazement.

"Not at all," she replied. "I've had enough of Stephanida's blame and abuse so I'm ready to do something drastic and bold."

"Well," Zbignev laughed, "let's do it, then."

He placed himself on the middle bench and started to row.

"Bye! Bye! Good ride, Mom! Good ride, Papa!" the little ones whooped from the bank, jumping, waving and blowing kisses to them.

Eva finally pulled the children from the waterside and proposed a race to determine the lucky child to win the next ride on the lake.

The boat glided smoothly along, though the rowlocks protested loudly and annoyingly, while the dark water splashed softly in response to the oars. Zbignev turned directly to the other side of the pond and, soon, Ekaterina could reach out and touch the low-hanging wiping-willow branches with her hand, moving them away from her face. The drooping green fronds kissed her cheeks and slapped her summer white bonnet banded in blue silk; the branches also played with the long ribbons trailing from her hat down over her lithe shoulders.

"Stop, Zbignev," she laughed, as she removed her bonnet and placed it on her lap. "I'm already caught in this jungle. I prefer to just rest. Let's sit and talk some."

"Okay," he nodded, smiling and feeling quite content that the situation was going exactly as he hoped it would. "I have one question for you..."he started, but floundered in uncertainty.

"What do you want to ask me?" Ekaterina queried her escort as she gazed at her hat. Her fingers twisted the band on it as she continued, "Is it something personal? I consider you a good friend and have nothing to hide. You can go on with your question."

"Is it true what Stephanida said today during dinner? Do you really have royal blood? Is one of your ancestors the Empress's son?"

"Is it so important?" she grinned. "I didn't expect that anything like that would matter to you. I don't really know. It's just a legend in our family. Do you want to hear it?"

He nodded expectantly.

"Well, in August 1763, the Empress Catherine the Great did visit the Baltic countries," Ekaterina began her narrative. "The tour went partly by land, and partly by sea. One Swedish naval officer fell in love with her and she had a short affair with him. This happened in the Estonian city of Piarnu, right on the Baltic Sea coast. In remembrance of the occasion, which seemed to be important to her, there was even built a little church. It might have been that the Empress was in love with him, too. Nobody knows.

"However, in nine months the twins were born – boys, whom she named Boris and August. At that time, women dressed in big, full skirts that often disguised pregnancies. It is possible that this kind of story was often repeated and the Empress produced many babies and usually gave them up for adoption. This pair – they were taken back to Piarnu, baptized at the same church and adopted by the Lutheran priest of the church who was childless. His name was Willy von Wilde. The twins received his family name which connects to me because my full maiden name was Ekaterina von Wilde."

"Is there any proof?" Zbignev asked, looking at her with excitement.

"With the boys, the Empress gave two vases of a very special pink crystal. On each vase is her own seal, written in gold – a big letter E. It's her initial. In Russian her name begins with E – *Ekaterina*. There is also a big Roman number *II* intertwined with the initial. It meant *Ekaterina the Second* - her true title in history.

"Boris died as a child, so August inherited both the vases. Later, he married a German woman from Poland and moved from Piarnu to Warsaw. His son, named Leon, was born around the year 1800. He was my grandpa – Leon von Wilde, who became a military doctor. August passed the vases to him.

"In turn, Leon left the vases to his son - my dad, Eugene von Wilde, who was born in 1836. He was a military doctor, as well.

"Then I was born in 1870. I inherited the vases from my dad because my elder brother, Hermann, refused to take them. Hermann set off traveling to Russia and crystal vases were not the best things to travel with. They could be easily broken. Next, I'll pass them on to my daughters, Anya and Sonya. Now, the vases are here with me. They are standing in the girls' bedroom on their bedside tables. Haven't you ever walk in the girls' bedroom and seen them there?"

"No, I haven't been there," Zbignev shook his head. "I've only been in the dining room of the house. However, to me those vases are proof enough. Actually, you're not far removed from royalty. August was your great-grandpa, right? Pretty close. And you look very much like the young Empress. I read that she was beautiful, with blue eyes and dark hair, straight nose and white skin..."

"This resemblance isn't very useful today and doesn't give me much happiness," Ekaterina objected. "Though, I was named after her. It might be that I'm like her in some way – I want to do something serious in my life. I couldn't rule the country like she did, of course, but I'm certainly capable of running my own life."

"But you're not free. You're subject to your husband's wishes."

"I know. We already discussed the possibility of my studying and he flatly said 'No!' We don't have much in common, though he is a nice man - quite the opposite of his mother. But I'll tell you a secret - I don't love my husband."

"Actually, it's not a secret," Zbignev smiled ironically. "Everybody knows that."

"I just had no choice," Ekaterina continued, ignoring his remark completely. "My step-mother was the same kind of horrible woman as Stephanida. She hated me. It was possible she would try to poison me to get rid of me, if I hadn't have taken the first marriage proposal I got after returning home from the Institute. Vladimir Diachan was her lawyer. He came to see her in connection with some papers and accidentally met me. That was it. He fell in love from his first look and the next day proposed me. Of course, my stepmother was happy and gave her blessing right away. We were wed within a week."

"It's unbelievably fast," Zbignev thoughtfully shook his head. "You didn't know him at all."

"Too fast, really. It was generous of him because I was extremely poor. I came into his home, wearing one dress and holding my two vases in my hands. That's it. Anyway, I was happy to leave my stepmother's house, but I didn't know that I was coming from the frying pan into the fire. Stephanida was waiting for me here. So, you see, I'm isolated, unhappy, and surrounded by hate. Though I've been married for five years, I don't even know what love is."

"I think you're wrong, here," Zbignev objected ardently. "Your husband loves you…"

"He travels too much. I don't see him often. When he's home, we're always arguing about something," Ekaterina retorted fast. "I can't reciprocate his kind of love."

"Your daughters love you…"

"That is different. You know that. I see only judgment around."

"Come on. You shouldn't take Stephanida seriously. Think about her like as if she were only bad weather. Nothing else. And may be… may be someone else loves you. But, you just don't know it."

"I know," she blushed, feeling an inner satisfaction to finally hear this from a young and handsome man.

"Ekaterina, you know, we're from different classes!" Zbignev started passionately. "I'm only a farmer's son, but I have education, and some money. If I weren't already married…"

"Stop it!" she exclaimed heatedly. "Stop, please! Your 'if'makes it all impossible! I could say the same. If I weren't married…"

"Well, what do you want?" he implored her.

"I want to leave *Vysokoye* tomorrow morning. Forever. I'll pick up my kids, pack my stuff and go to the train station. It is five kilometers away. Would you mind helping me and give us a ride?"

"I will. But where will you go?'

"To Warsaw."

"And then?"

"It doesn't matter. I'll figure out what to do next…"

"Ekaterina, tonight…" he leaned forward and took her hand.

At this moment they heard Eva shouting, calling her husband by his nickname, "Zbyshek! Where're you? The children are waiting to go!"

"Let's get out of these willows," Ekaterina whispered, "please, quickly, Zbyshek, faster. In God's name, let's go back!"

He took the oars and bit his lips. Ekaterina parted the leaves and the boat inched forward. Now, the whole panorama was in view – Stephanida was walking down the hill and spied them, as well.

"Boating?!" she exclaimed angrily, lifting up her fists and shaking them. Then she reached Eva and shouted at the young woman, "Are you a stupid idiot? Are you crazy? Why did you let your man go boating with her? She is a bitch! She will try to take him away, can't you see that?"

"Oh no," innocent Eva muttered, her terrified big eyes fixed on the distant boat.

"Zbyshek! Zbyshek!" the kids chanted, jumping and applauding. "Mommy! Mommy!" they waved their hands. Stephanida stood with her arms akimbo and watched them attentively, knitting her brows and breathing heavily with anger.

Zbignev rowed fast around the pond. Suddenly Ekaterina saw ahead of them what was hidden from him – an old crooked snag emerging from the water, but they were already upon it. Ekaterina only shrieked, "A snag!" and then a light crack snagged the boat hull, ripping the half-rotten planks. The black peaty water gushed inside the boat which slowly began to sinking.

"Don't worry! It's not deep!" Zbignev shouted to Ekaterina. He stood up, threw the oars away and grabbed her in his arms. In a second he was standing at the bottom of the pond, holding her. The water came up to his chest, so Ekaterina was buoyed by both the water and his clasp. She hugged Zbignev's neck in fright. He managed to step out of the boat and walked slowly toward the bank, carrying her in his arms. The shallow pond made it a mishap rather than a tragedy.

Ekaterina's hat, which she had put on her head, now fell off and floated on the pond. The spectators lining the bank yelled crazily for minutes and then fell silent, seeing that nobody was in danger. Then the kids began wailing for the lost of the boat.

Ekaterina put her head on Zbignev's shoulder. The water was cold and she felt feverish in her wet and dirty gown and shoes, destined now to be thrown into the garbage.

"I love you, Ekaterina," Zbignev whispered, turning his head and touching her cheek with his lips. "I'll come tonight..."

She closed her eyes and refused to answer his appeals. He continued walking slowly - it was difficult to walk in such slippery and mucky water, carrying a grown woman, though Ekaterina wasn't heavy and the water even lightened her modest weight.

"Look at this!" Stephanida shouted, spraying saliva in disgust as they emerged from the pond. "Are you an idiot, Zbignev? What did you think you were doing? Didn't you know that the boat was rotten? Thank God no children were on board! The pond is deep enough to drown them all! It was so stupid to go boating with my bitch of a daughter-in-law! Or are you ambitious? Her ancestor, Catherine the Great, slept with her soldiers and then raised them up to be generals! But you are wasting your time, I'm afraid. This Ekaterina has no power to even promote you to a lieutenant."

Zbignev's response was his usual tactic with his boss - he said nothing. He came out of the water and stood Ekaterina on the grassy shore as Eva rushed him, sobbing, and hanging on his neck, though he was soaking wet. Little Marek hugged his legs. Anya and Sonya ran to Ekaterina, but she was in such a state, that she needed to be alone for a while to recover. She turned away from her darlings and ran up the hill toward the house.

"Mommy, Mommy!" the girls shouted behind her, sobbing. Even the tiny Xenia was woken up and began to cry – rested, she was now hungry. Ekaterina blocked out everything around her, however, even her daughters. She continued running away, burning with shame and her ill-judged efforts and looked for a sanctuary to disappear into.

The girls followed her for a bit, but then reading her mood, stopped pursuing their retreating mother. Then, looking for comfort through their tear-smeared eyes sought out Grandma Stephanida and returned to her, grasping the folds of her large dark brown gown.

"Baba! Baba!" they both clasped her legs.

She bowed and petted their heads tenderly.

"My God! Poor kids! What a shame to have a mother like this! Don't cry, don't cry, my sweethearts! Your Baba will be with you! Let's go home. I'll wash you up and give you some milk with cookies." She grabbed the girls' hands and then turned to Eva, "You, silly you! Pick up Xenia and carry her home. This stupid bitch should nurse her whether she wants or not."

Eva cradled the baby in her arms; together, Zbignev and Marek picked up the rug, toys and stuff, so the picnic came to a sorry end and everyone trudged up the hill home.

In her rooms now, Ekaterina had already removed and disposed of her ruined clothes. She wrapped herself in a terry robe and was lying on her bed, her face buried in the pillows and receiving the anxious sobs coming from her offended psyche.

She was convinced that she had done nothing improper; she had no intention of flirting or cheating on her husband. She considered Zbignev as only a devoted friend, so shared with him her family problems, her hopes, and her anguish. She anticipated compassion and friendly support, but instead received an indecent proposal from a married man to sleep together before her departure. She felt totally humiliated and outraged by his vulgar suggestion in return for her confidences.

This weren't the first of these kinds of suggestive remarks from men around her, even before her early marriage - even in her teenage years. She always felt she was being slapped in the face after such distasteful encounters. She dreamed of a beautiful, pure love in her life, about holy feelings, about the deepest understanding of two souls. However, the men seemed only interested in her royal blood in order to brag later to their drinking buddies, of having slept with the Empress's great-great-granddaughter. All this would be, of course, accompanied by bawdy winks, hinting that Catherine the Great's famous nymphomania still ran in the family.

Ekaterina really regretted that she always truthfully told this family legend to her classmates, friends, relatives, and then, to her husband who passed it on to his mother, Stephanida. Her openness made her especially vulnerable to sarcastic, envious and cruel people who took great delight in tormenting and belittling her. Now, she'd received yet another slap from Zbignev, who she'd taken for a friend, but who had shown himself as the same crude adventurer as the other men. It was unbearable!

The soft knock on the door sobered Ekaterina. It was the maid, Marusya, who had already changed Xenia and brought the baby to her mother for nursing.

Holding the child at her breast, Ekaterina felt such sacred sweet warmth of her baby that this feeling pierced her heart movingly and she sensed her tears returning again. But she suppressed them and tried to hold herself in check. Her time of thinking and feeling had ended and now she must act.

Finishing the feeding, Ekaterina placed Xenia in her cradle. Then she wrote a note to her husband who would be returning home in some weeks and put it on his pillow in their bedroom.

"Vladimir," she wrote, "thank you for everything you've done for me. I was a devoted wife and tried to love you but I couldn't do it. Your mother turned my life into a hell and I couldn't take it anymore. Forgive me that I took the kids. God bless you. Ekaterina."

She dressed herself and fixed her hair, packed some things for the baby and herself into a small bag and walked to the girl's bedroom.

It was already nine o'clock and Anya and Sonya were peacefully sleeping in their beds after having milk with cookies and being washed by Stephanida. Ekaterina kissed them on their foreheads and whispered to them in turns, "Good night my sweetheart. Sweet dreams! Don't miss your mommy. I'll find a cab and pick you up tomorrow. But now I must go. I can't stay here anymore."

Ekaterina looked around the room helplessly. For sure, her two the little kids wouldn't be able to walk five kilometers to the train station. They also needed some things. Who would carry their bags? Her hands would be full with Xenia, who was already nine months old and quite heavy. It was not hard to carry her inside the house,

17

or even to the park, but five kilometers...It was almost impossible, however, Ekaterina was ready to do that in order to escape and avoid seeing either Zbignev or Stephanida tonight – or ever!

Her farewell glance fell on the Empress's vases on the bed-side tables. She had no plans to leave them behind. She came into Diachan's family carrying these vases; now she would leave the family carrying them away, plus her kids – all she earned during her five years of unhappy marriage. She'd pick up the vases and the girls tomorrow.

With these thoughts, Ekaterina left the girls' room, picked up the sleeping Xenia and her bag and tiptoed outside the main entrance to the house.

She walked through the park as fast as she could, breathing heavily from her burden and also from fear of detection and obstruction. But all seemed quiet. The big gate framed by two tall white pillars and an arch, was open as usual, and Ekaterina quietly slipped onto the country road, unnoticed by anyone.

In about half a kilometer she turned once more and found herself on the main cart-track which led to the train station. The well-used truck was dusty and rutted. Gravel and stones sometimes made her almost stumble as she progressed.

Sun had already begun to set, emblazoning the lower sky in red-orange, hanging above the yellow fields of wheat. Her artistic eye unconsciously grasped the beauty of the spectrum. It would be her last memory of *Vysokoye*. She would paint this picture – *The August's Sunset* - sometime later.

The evening was cooling, and she began regretting she hadn't worn her big warm shawl on her shoulders. The day had been so sunny and hot; she had completely forgotten that the evenings were usually chilly because it was already the middle of the August. She expected that she would walk fast and would be hot. However, in reality, she grew more and more tired with her burden and her steps slowed, so the cool evening air hit her. Her discomfort nearly brought tears to her eyes but she fought them and kept walking.

After an hour, she finally gave up and plopped on the grass next to the roadway. She put daughter Xenia down beside her to rest. But the grass was wet from the night-dew because the twilight had already finished and Ekaterina couldn't sit for long, chilled as she was. She rose and continued walking for the next fifteen minutes, then she suddenly heard the clatter of horses' hoofs behind her and realized with horror that these must be her pursuers. No one else would be traveling at night time.

She jumped aside and hid behind a big wild rosebush on the edge of a field. It was almost dark and her gray dress helped her blend in. As the horse and wagon rumbled by her, Ekaterina realized that it was Zbignev, urging the horse on.

What if he alone is looking for me? The terrified thought crossed her mind. Perhaps he had tried to climb to the balcony of my bedroom and discovered that Xenia and I were missing! He might even have read my message to Vladimir. Did he wake up Stephanida and everybody? Probably not, otherwise, he'd be hard pressed to explain why he had been in my bedroom at night? He must be the only person looking for me now. That's a relief, thanks God.

As the dust settled behind the wagon, Ekaterina took a deep breath, picked up Xenia in her arms and went on walking. She now kept to the edge of the road, in case Zbignev came back along this way from the station, where he would search for her in vain.

Half an hour later that was exactly what happened, but she successfully hid behind the bushes again. So Zbignev returned home empty-handed. He was visibly worried and Ekaterina felt satisfied with her little revenge on him. He had truly misjudged her as a desperate, lonely woman who would easily fall into his arms.

She came to the station about the midnight, knowing full well that the train to Warsaw would soon pull into the station. A telegraph officer in his booth was awake, so Ekaterina bought a one-way ticket and wired her father's old friend, Baron Peter Young von Altenburg that she would be arriving in the capitol the next morning.

Once on the train, she felt feverish and couldn't sleep all night because the rumble of the wheels loudly echoed the constant hammering within her temples. She was also busy nursing her daughter and changing her through the night.

"It seems to me that you have a high fever, child," Baron Peter said, meeting Ekaterina at the station in Warsaw and kissing her forehead. "Your cheeks are too red and hot. What happened to you? It was such a surprise to get your telegram out of the blue! Let me take Xenia. We'll go in my cab now."

"I'm so grateful to you, Peter," Ekaterina gave him a daughter's hug. He was twenty-five years older than she and had always taken an interest in her well-being. "The only thing I have to do immediately is to pick up my children from the estate and bring them here. I have left my husband forever and I'll file for divorce."

"Oh, my goodness! Ekaterina! What happened? Vladimir is not such a bad man!"

"I know, Pete, I'll tell you all about it later. Could we go and pick up my kids now?"

"Let's go to my home, first, settle down, and find wet-nurse for Xenia. You really need to have a good rest and be checked by a doctor before you go anywhere. You are not well. Remember, your family doesn't have the best health history. Then, tomorrow, or the day after tomorrow we'd go and pick up the little ones."

Ekaterina silently agreed, feeling exhausted and chilled and unable to stop her teeth from chattering.

"I fell into a pond this afternoon," she whispered and let the Baron take over, guiding her to cab.

Then, days later, she came to again and she was still in bed, surrounded by doctors and lawyers. She looked up to see her husband, Vladimir, in tears and a wet-nurse holding Xenia. They were saying something about papers and documents but her head was swimming. Then darkness returned. She didn't know then that Anya and Sonya had remained with Stephanida at the estate. There followed a period of convalescence: weeks in bed pursued by months at a Black Sea health treatment on the Crimean Peninsula, famous by its lung health-resorts. The cold and cough were finally gone. Thanks God, there was no tuberculosis. The divorce papers arrived. The Tsar decided as an exception - since there was no infidelity - that the divorce would be permitted. The children would stay where they were: Xenia with the mother, Anya and Sonya with the father.

Ekaterina cried sheds about her daughters. She applied for review of the decision many times but Tsar didn't change a thing. The girls and the Empress's vases were left with Vladimir Diachan's family.

A year later, Ekaterina married the old Baron and became the Baroness Young von Altenburg. Her new husband, Peter, was like a father for her. He was not in the best health and not sexually active, which was good for her – no more kids, finally. But he filled a need in her heart, as a best friend, sincerely caring for her and allowing her to attend university courses. She thrived and became a professional artist. She still didn't know the love of a man but she was able to express her feelings through her painting, and it was successful.

Ekaterina Young von Altenburg became a quite well-known European artist. Her paintings were shown in many exhibitions in Poland, Germany, France and Spain, and her famous *The Boat On The Pond* was bought by an art museum in France.

Her new husband provided her with a good life where she could do everything she wanted and didn't even need to take care of Xenia, who was raised mostly by the governesses and by old Peter. He had a special fondness toward the girl because he had not had any other children in his life. Ekaterina was thankful to him and became a devoted wife.

As First World War began, Xenia turned nineteen. She married a Pole, medical doctor Stanislav Sosnovsky, and they immigrated to America to escape the German troops who seized Warsaw.

Ekaterina and Peter chose not to leave Europe - its culture and artistic life. They moved to Ukraine, to the city of Kiev, and remained there for many years despite the Bolshevik Revolution.

...I slide my eyes up to the painting above my piano. "You said *The Boat On The Pond* was in the French Art Museum. Why is it here, Baba?"

"Ekaterina painted a second *The Boat On The Pond*, later, from memory, and it became famous. However, that was only the copy. This is the original...unfinished...that she left on her easel beside the pond in *Vysokoye.*"

"How did you learn about her later life?"

"I met her once, but that's another story," Baba spoke sternly, seeing that I'd try to escape my music exercises again.

"I'll play, I will, I will," I promised heatedly, "just one more question, please. Baba! Where are the Ekaterina's vases?!"

"We left them where they were – on the bedside tables beside our beds in *Vysokoye*. When we ran away to Russia in 1914, escaping from the Germans, my dad took my mom's first painting because he treasured it a lot – he did love her dearly his entire life. But we left the vases, guessing that they, anyway, would be broken during the rush and chaos of the evacuation."

"So, they were lost forever?"

"Not exactly. I saw one of them many years later."

"Where?" I looked at my Baba with big eyes. "Tell me, please."

"Next time. Play, now."

I conceded because it was obvious that Baba wouldn't change her mind.

"Very last question," I begged. "Are you sure that this family story was true?...I mean, about Catherine the Great? Your mom was really named Ekaterina after the Empress, wasn't she? And I was named after your mom, wasn't I?"

"You were named after both of them," my Baba confided in a whisper, putting her index finger to her lips. "But you're living in a communist country. Remember that and keep it a secret."

Chapter 2

THE RUG OF AN ARISTOCRAT

Every evening as I was falling asleep, I looked at it. It hung on the wall over my bed. It was my friend – the red carpet in a very flowery style, and, to me, covered with meaningless ornamental strokes, flowers and different shaped, multi-colored figures. There was something of black, and blue, and white, and a little green color in the lines of a tracery.

I've never wondered what it was, how come it was here, or to whom it belonged. It was the rug on the wall - my wall, in my world, and it had been there since forever and would remain forever, I was sure. I took it as a given, natural and absolutely necessary in my room - just as any child accepts their house or apartment as they find it. The doors, windows and floors are all here and that's that.

My rug was old. Age hadn't dulled the bright colors, but moths had eaten holes here and there. I used to insert my fingers in the holes and enjoy the sensation of the rough foundation fabric. I sometimes hid my treasures inside – beads, or ladybugs, or tiny pieces of paper, or flower petals. I thought of the openings as normal and natural, again. When I saw unblemished carpets at someone's home it seemed strange.

Why were the holes missing? I wondered. What was wrong? Something was clearly amiss. I found such carpets boring and unfinished. Maybe they only needed my assistance to create the proper holes?

I attempted to rectify the situation, but, fortunately, didn't quite master the technique.

I did like my rug. Many times I would lie in my bed, facing the wall. I don't know why but I felt at peace in this position, save and secure. If I turned my face outward, I felt the cool of the drafty air, the dark, scary emptiness that robbed me of my refuge. So, I turned back to the wall, to the rug, curled up my little body and instinctively, as an animal, returned to a realm of safety, feeling once more calm and protected.

I did play with my rug while sick. It's strange but I was ill most of my childhood and spent a lot of my time lying in bed and playing with the rug. It was my world. It was to me a geographic map, my atlas.

The lines were rivers or ocean coasts; the flowers were cities; the squares, triangles and rectangles were mountains, valleys, islands and gulfs. I traced them with my little finger and gave them names – Star Valley, or Sea of Blue Islands. It was a world of my imagination. It was fun.

I had just turned eleven when my mom decided that I was big enough to hear some prohibited things and keep it secret from others. She told me the story of the rug.

Vladimir even didn't know how he did it. It was easy. It was nothing. He just remained concealed behind a heavy, cherry-colored velvet curtain while soldiers left a theater box, pulling those apprehended with them. He waited a bit, all trembling, and then, he left the box as well, carefully checking for danger. He walked down the rounded corridor of the *Bolshoi* Theater, listening with horror as his shoes resounded on the polished wooden floor.

It was all quiet around him but he heard a distant noise – the hum of a throng, screams, yells, bangs, shots and shrieks, accompanied by shouted commands - somewhere in the direction of the main lobby. All the time his heart was pounding loud enough to drown out all the external uproar.

He was completely numb. His brain was almost paralyzed and suppressed by his only thought - to get well away from the theater building as soon as possible, and as far as possible!

Vladimir didn't know where his wife was. She was here, somewhere, at the theater, with a group of other leaders. She was a chief, too, though he was a regular member of the *Left S-R Party* – the banned, underground, communist opposition party. He was in a subordinate position to his wife.

They had managed to raise a large mutiny against Lenin, but, obviously now it seemed to Vladimir that they weren't successful. The *Bolshoi* Theater was surrounded and the Bolsheviks had taken it by storm using both soldiers and armed workers. It looked like there was no way out.

Vladimir couldn't even guess what had happened with his wife, and where she was at the moment. He only knew he should escape anyway he could. Otherwise, he wouldn't be able to help her.

Unconsciously, he opened a little door at the end of the corridor and found himself on the stairs of a fire-escape. What luck! He raced down three flights and entered a basement hall with many doors. Vladimir tried all of them and, surprisingly, found one unlocked, opened it and stole into a dim large room full of theater equipment.

It was hard to make anything out. Only the narrow cracks at the perimeter of a large outer door let in a few streams of light from the street lamps. They created a spooky atmosphere in the darkness but allowed him to see what was there.

Without thinking, Vladimir felt around him and discovered stage set trees and bushes made from cardboard or papier-mâché. There was also furniture – it wasn't long before he stumbled over some armchairs, small tea-tables and stools. One of them overturned and crashed loudly and he was sure someone knew he was there. But, luckily, the basement room was far removed from the upstairs drama and Vladimir thanked God that nobody could hear him.

He stood still momentarily and let the dust settle around him. Then boldly he continued his search, looking for a place to hide, opening some boxes on the shelves and some cabinet doors. Everywhere he looked spaces were crammed full and piled with layers of dust. It was clear that this room was seldom entered. It seemed to him to be something like quite neglected long-term storage.

The mustiness of the room made it hard to breath. Vladimir's trembling hands were wet with sweat because of his nervous tension. They became dirty as they groped the dusty and painted objects around him and also felt sticky. As he wiped his damp forehead, his fingers left smudges and spots on his face while his oiled and well-groomed hair curled and matted up. In the dark, it mattered little what he looked like and it was the last thing on his mind.

On one shelf he located a cardboard box filled with hats. Vladimir probed them, one by one, and rejected them. But then it dawned on him how useful one might be for his situation. He chose one shapeless peasant fur hat and put it on. There were several similar styles, probably costumes for a choir playing town's folks assembled on Red Square in the scene where the Tsar is crowned in the opera *Boris Godunov* by Mussorgsky. It was amazing - exactly what he needed at the moment.

He started hastily digging inside all the boxes and cabinets until, at last he found the other parts of the costumes – dark trousers and sheepskin jackets. He found no shoes, but Vladimir didn't need a pair. The trousers were long enough to cover his patent-leather shoes and hide them from sight.

Throwing his black evening suit into a box, Vladimir changed

24

and even took a papier-mâché rifle with wooden butt-stock from a cabinet full of prop weapons. Now he was ready to go out.

Before leaving the storage room, he checked the outside door, hoping that he might use it, but it was locked. His only exit was to return to the public floors and walk out the main door, past patrols of soldiers. It was truly dangerous, but he couldn't stay in the basement forever. He must go somewhere else, so he left.

In the hall, Vladimir glanced at his reflection in the mirrored wall. He looked awful – dirty, shabby, tousled, and slovenly, but that was his good luck. There was something a bit suspicious about him because his sooty face still looked too refined and intelligent for a Bolshevik soldier. Vladimir grimaced and tried to set an expression he could use to portray an angry vagabond. He wasn't a very good actor, but he had no choice and assured himself that he would probably not be noticed in all the hubbubs around the theater since there was nothing calling attention to him.

When Vladimir reached the main lobby entrance, he saw a great, rowdy crowd - many soldiers and workers scurrying in and out carrying weapons from rifles to homemade instruments, axes and pitchforks, even.

He couldn't understand why a small, insignificant detail caught his attention at the moment – the white marble floor was covered with grease and slush. He never had seen it look so dirty and he was shocked by it, even though more serious things were happening around. But a filthy, greasy floor at the *Bolshoi*! It perfectly represented the disaster going on in his country.

Shaking, Vladimir growled, "Aaaaah!" like a madman with an idiot's grimace on his face and ran among the crowd, holding his rifle with both hands in front of his stomach.

Finding himself outside, he slowed down, then circled the theater, pretending to be walking on patrol with his rifle. Nobody noticed him; there was nothing special in his look – he was just a regular proletarian. He was the only person who felt uncomfortable about his appearance.

The weather was foul – a cold, windy and slushy November evening, so garbed in his peasant costume he was able to keep warm. He had warned his wife that to take action on such a day was not so wise, but she only made fun of him, saying that their business depended on only the political weather of Moscow. Lenin had planned to visit the *Bolshoi* Theater that evening and they would arrest and charge him and seize control of Russia from the Bolsheviks.

Crazy woman, he thought about his wife. She led a circle of

twelve conspirators – her party bosses - who wanted to overthrow the Bolsheviks! How absurd! She is in too deep, too worked up! It's my fault. As a husband I should have forbid her to be involved. It might be better for her to stay at home and have children. But what am I thinking about!? It's too late now, anyway. It's all over and done. All hopes are dashed and the revolt has crashed...

Normally, Vladimir was a very kind, shy and intelligent man. He studied philology at the university and was interested only in science, languages and literature. He had little or no interest in politics and was more of a pacifist. But then he fell in love with Maria – a twenty-two-year-old university law student, public figure, who was beautiful and sensual. She was too devoted to her *Left S-R Party* which chose for Russia the free Western political model, based on private property. Maria even promised to marry him only if he would become a party member. He did, of course. Then came this big political coup attempt, and then...what now?

Now Vladimir moved quietly through the nearly empty city's streets. He quickly disposed of the toy rifle in a dark corner, since it felt silly and he had no need of it.

When he reached his small, rented room where they stayed temporary, his landlady, Anna Ivanovna, failed to recognize him. She was a widow of a major in the Tsar's guard unit and she was alarmed at this intruder.

"O, my God! Mr. Orlov, is it you!?" she exclaimed in excitement and then asked, "Where is Masha?" It was the Russian nickname for 'Maria', which they always used.

He just waved his hand nonchalantly.

The next morning the newspapers were full of horrible stories of the night's events. The city of Moscow buzzed with rumor and disbelief. It was announced that all the leaders of the rebellion had been executed on the spot, except for one plotter, Maria Orlova, who was found pregnant. Bolshevik regime, out of compassion, would await the baby's delivery before executing the mother.

Her expected child belongs to the Soviet people and he must live and become a builder of the Communist Future. He should be raised in a proper home and not by a counter-revolutionary who doesn't deserve to live, read the article.

The revelation was news to Vladimir. He was so glad that Masha was alive and safe for now, but he was dumbfounded to learn about her pregnancy. He couldn't understand why she had kept her pregnancy from him. He tossed and turned all night with worry. He couldn't sleep while she was locked up, carrying his child. He couldn't find the answer –why? He cried and felt helpless, sick and weak. The stress of his escape from the theater had taken its toll that fateful evening. He was limp and powerless.

Finally, Anna Ivanovna brought him a glass of hot lemon tea, put it on the table beside his bed and said strongly, "That's enough, Mr. Orlov. Shame on you! You should be a man. Don't you understand that Masha kept silence about her pregnancy because she was sure you would block her from participating in political activity with the child on the way? Can't you understand that? She is lucky your child saved her life. Go, and find a way to save her once again. You should rescue your family now, not only Masha but the coming child, as well. You'll never get the baby after Masha is killed. The Bolsheviks would raise and educate him themselves - and nothing is more horrible for a child than that. Even if you would go and claim your child, they'll kill you, as well. You have no choice – go and do something. And do it now!"

Vladimir hadn't expected such decisive urgings from this small old lady in ringlets of gray hair. She was strong-willed; she pushed him up and woke him to his plight. He drank her tea, listened to her and realized, step-by-step, what he had to do.

For the next few months, he scouted out Masha's whereabouts. She was transferred to some different cities because the jails everywhere were overcrowded, and prosecutors had difficulty to find a room for her. Her belly grew and was quite obvious by January. Her behavior was calm. She sat or rested quietly during her long days and didn't create any problems for the guards. So, the Bolsheviks relaxed their watch on their less-then-dangerous prisoner.

Finally, they placed Maria in the small old Russian city of Viatka and kept her, not in a prison cell, but locked up in a beautiful aristocratic mansion. It had been appropriated from the owner and now belonged to the proletariat. The mansion was transformed into a sort of prison, as well, because the regular jails were now full.

Vladimir moved to Viatka and spent his days observing Masha's elegant jail from a distance, trying not to be noticed by the guards. He continued wearing his peasant theater costume which served as a good disguise and gave him the possibility of walking around unnoticed. To the Bolsheviks guards, he seemed to be just a regular Russian proletarian among the crowds.

However, at any time he could be stopped for a document check by street patrols and this was risky because he lacked these papers. For sure, he would be arrested and shot right away without documents. If he were to show true identity papers, they would find a

27

wanted conspirator in their midst. Vladimir badly needed new documents and he was able to accomplish this at the local flea market.

It was a common practice in this period, so counterfeiters had a brisk trade going – they bought stolen passports and IDs cheaply from pickpockets; they also took documents from the corpses lying abandoned on the streets here and there - and then they sold the documents at the flea market in barter for valuables like jewelry, antiques, Tsar's gold coins, staples, vodka and tobacco.

Very little was still sacred and holy for the people at that time. Their mentality and spirituality was broken by the revolution five years earlier and the hardships they had endured. The certainties of the past were gone forever. The country was torn apart by a Civil War. Pure animal survival was the level most lived on.

Roaming the flea market daily, Vladimir met some people who were selling beautiful antique vases, silver goods and plate, pillows and blankets embroidered in silk. He asked an elderly women covered in a gray knit scarf where she got what she was selling, had a little chat with her, then gave her one golden Tsar's coin (thankful that he still had some left), and he got all the information he needed – he found out where to go to buy documents. The old woman even introduced him to the people who ran this business and he ordered two IDs for himself and Masha, hoping that she would be with him soon and would need it.

Vladimir also found out that most of the beautiful things on the market were ransacked from the aristocratic mansion on the hill. The former owner put his best foot forward to save his life and left all his belongings behind. Many people were now making their living on it. They would approach the guards, give them vodka (one or two bottles, depending on how many guards were on the shift) and got their permission to enter the mansion and to take some things. Then they sold these things at the flea market.

That was a mansion where Maria was imprisoned and locked in one of the rooms. That gave him the means to enter where he was searching!

The next evening, Vladimir showed up at the mansion loaded with two bottles of vodka and locksmith's tools in his pocket – all of these he bought at the same flea market.

It was February, quite cold and snowing. Three guards were sitting outside, in front of the main entrance of the mansion. They built a small bonfire, put some blankets from the mansion down on the snow and sat in a circle, crossing their feet and holding their rifles between their legs. They did talk loudly and laugh coarsely, sometimes jumping up, shoving each other and stomping to warm up themselves.

It was plain to see that they were young, uneducated and possibly inexperienced. They were just kids, fooled by the Bolsheviks and they deserved to be made a fool of once again. Having no other choice, Vladimir gave them bottles of vodka, chatted a bit and said that he wanted to enter the mansion and to take one rug.

The guards were eager to warm up and started to drink immediately right from the bottles. They jovially laughed, and told him that he could go and take any rug he wanted because there were a lot of them and, anyway, nobody needed them. Vladimir entered the mansion while soldiers continued drinking and completely forgot about him. It took him awhile to find the room where Maria was locked, to break the lock, to take a rug from the wall and to roll his pregnant wife up in it.

When he walked out, carrying the rolled rug over his shoulder, the guards were already very drunk. One was sleeping beside the fire and two others were sitting relaxed and mumbled something, swearing and giggling. They waved him farewell, and he turned to wave them back, wished them good night and walked away.

Some days later, Vladimir traded at the flea market for new identity papers for himself and Maria with different names on them and they left Viatka. They headed to the city of Petrograd where they got married once again in order to combine their new last names into one family name. Then they moved to Central Asia for a few months to hide their tracks, and finally ended up back in Moscow, in Anna Ivanovna's apartment, where their baby was born on May 16, 1923.

"Wow!" I said to my mom, excitedly, as she finished her narrative. The story seemed to me very much like my favorite adventure novels by Alexandre Dumas, Irving Washington, Walter Scott or Jules Verne, that I adored. "Are you sure it is true? I can't believe it! I couldn't even guess all that had happened. Was it my rug? This one?"

She nodded.

"And my last name...is it a false one? Not a real one?"

She nodded again.

It was already 1959 – Khrushchev's time. The time had passed when it was dangerous to have an aristocratic past. No one was then arrested because of that. So, I was able to learn about my real ancestors. Vladimir and Maria were my grandparents and their only baby was my father.

Chapter 3

THE SUITCASE FROM WARSAW

The suitcase was huge and very old. It was made from veneer and upholstered with a fabric which was glued to it with varnish. Many years ago its surface had probably been shiny, but by now had already lost any luster it had once had.

The suitcase corners were edged with brass clips. There were also two big brass locks on the lid and a large brass logo in the middle, as well. The metal had darkened with age. Nobody had ever polished it and dusky coating hid the florid antique letters on the logo that were of little interest to anyone.

The suitcase didn't strike me as special or in any way unusual. Seeing it every day, I got used to its appearance and didn't pay any attention to it, considering it as a casual thing. Actually, I had no other suitcases to compare it with, as it was only one in my life.

It usually rested on the top of our wardrobe, which was more than filled with three seasons of apparel for the three generation of woman sharing the flat: my Baba, my mom and me. So, naturally, Baba used the suitcase to store some of the out-of-season wear. Nothing was ever discarded; old things were always recycled and made use of.

Every spring, Baba would call the building caretaker, a Tatar named Shamil, who was never without his *valenki* (Russian felt boots) that he wore inside orange rubber galoshes. She paid him something for his help and he would retrieve the heavy overhead suitcase so she could unload and repack it once more.

Then a fantastic time for me would commence. We took out my old summer dresses, skirts and blouses which seemed new to me because I had already forgotten about them during the winter.

Baba asked me to try them on, one by one, and, in the process, measured my growth during the past year. Then she ripped their hems to lengthen them one more time. If they couldn't be lengthened, she resourcefully added a flounce of a different fabric. For this purpose, she usually cut out pieces from the clothes I'd recently overgrown and which deserved only to be used as hem extensions for my dresses for couple more years. There was almost nothing available in the shops and most people extended the life of their clothes. Otherwise, it was just about impossible to acquire something new for growing children.

While Baba was busy with this work, I was allowed to play with the suitcase. It was so huge that I couldn't suppress a wish to climb in, close the lid and to hide inside. I left only a narrow crack of the lid open to breathe through.

It felt miraculous in there. The suitcase was lined in white silk, studded with brass drawing pins. They sparkled in the gloom like magical stars. I did touch them with my little index finger, counted them, talked to them and called them names.

Inside, I was surrounded by the smell of naphthalene because over the summer months, Baba put strong moth balls in the case to protect our winter wools and furs. The scent penetrated the entire case and remained a permanent feature that stayed inside it forever. I liked it, however, because it added something new and exciting to my humdrum existence.

Then, we usually packed our winter clothes away into the suitcase and Baba called Shamyl again; this time to hoist it up on top of the wardrobe for another 5-6 months. It was a routine which repeated twice a year. A big girl now at age 12, I proposed to Baba that, instead of hiding in the suitcase, I wanted to clean and polish the brass.

I brought some tooth powder and my old cotton panties as a polishing cloth and began to rub the locks and the logo in the middle of the lid. Before long, the antique script became readable and I, who was already started to learn German at school and French at home, could make out the Latin letters.

"Murex & Mary-Lisa," I read. "Baba, what does it mean?"

"It was a very stylish, beautiful and expensive fashion store at Warsaw," she answered. "We usually bought our clothes there. One day, our ball dresses were delivered to us in this suitcase."

"Really?"

I looked at her suspiciously. I knew in theory that Poland was a part of Russia at that time, and that my Baba was born and raised there, in Warsaw - the capitol. But I couldn't believe in my heart that my Baba had ever been young and even well-dressed. And had she attend the balls, too? Like a princesses in a fairy tale? Like Cinderella? She was already a senior in her late 60s, stooped and gray-haired. Around the house she always wore her thick flannel robe. She didn't look anything like a princess to me. She was only

31

my Baba - cooking, taking care of our family, and standing for hours in endless lines in order to buy butter, meat, oranges, sunflower oil, or even bread.

"Mademoiselle Anya, Mademoiselle Sonya," their maid, a Polish woman named Josefova, shouted, waking them early in the morning. "There is a delivery from Murex & Mary-Lisa. Your dresses are here."

The girls – Sonya, 18, and Anya, 19, run excitedly downstairs, still tousle haired, and wearing their nightgowns. The Big Christmas Ball at the *Noble Assembly Hall of Warsaw* was being held that very evening and the girls had barely slept the night before from anxiety over their ordered dresses.

Josefova had already tipped the delivery man and he had left. In the middle of the entrance foyer now stood a bright shiny suitcase next to the fresh snowy footprints on the black-and-white tiled floor.

"O, my Goodness! It's such a snowy morning!" Josefova grumbled to prevent the girls from stepping in the cool puddles forming. "Let me wipe it first, Mademoiselles!"

But the sisters had already impatiently grabbed the suitcase and carried it together into the living room.

"Wait, wait, Mademoiselles," Josefova shouted, running after them. She tried in vain to catch the suitcase because the girls fiercely gripped it for dear life. All their dreams were locked inside that case so they refused to surrender it. It wasn't hard to handle, not heavy at all. How much could two gossamer dresses possibly weight? For brunette Anya, there was a sky blue evening gown trimmed with silver roses and for blonde Sonya, a dancing dress of shell pink with golden roses.

With sparkling eyes, flashed cheeks and happy shrieks, the girls unlocked the suitcase, pulled the gowns out and held them up to their bosoms to capture the magic. They paraded in front of the large mirrors most of the morning while Josefova tried to serve breakfast.

Their new high-heeled dancing slippers were prepared some days ago – silver for Anya and gold for Sonya. Now, only one small problem remained – to visit the hairdresser this afternoon and to have their hair done. It should be done in the same style – parted down the middle with a bun at the back of the head and long hanging tendrils on either side of the face. Colored roses would be intertwined with their shiny locks.

The ball tonight would be a special one for the popular sister duo. In addition to being a Christmas ball, there would also be a Grand Prize awarded for the best dancers of the Polish Mazurka – two tickets for the maiden cruise of the newly build transatlantic steamship, Titanic. Of course, both Sonya and Anya, along with their escorts, hoped to win it: Anya, with her fiancé, Lieutenant Nicolay Obolensky and Sonya with her beloved admirer Count Alexander Dedulin, the son of the Tsar's courtier.

Sonya and Alexander often took to the dance floor together but could also be found riding horses at least twice per week. Alexander was a true horseman and he taught Sonya to love the intelligent and noble-looking animals as much as he did. She gained experience and confidence in dealing with them and could even handle a light Russian carriage called a *droshky*.

Unlike her sister, Anya shied away from horses. When she was only 6-year-old she had an accidental fall from the horse on their estate, *Vysokoye*. The resulting injury had scared her forever.

But the sisters were undisputedly the best dancers in Warsaw and rivaled one another for supremacy, especially since only one would win the special prize this evening.

The ball promised to be especially exciting for Sonya. The night before she received a note brought by a delivery boy from Alexander reading: 'Dear Sonya, I really need to talk to you. It's very important! Sincerely yours. Alex.' She guessed that maybe Alexander would propose her and this thought both excited and agitated her, adding to her concerns about her dress and winning the special prize. She had even had a restless night of anxiety.

During their breakfast, the girls' father, Vladimir Diachan, joined them. He was bald, stubby and rotund, suggestive of a fairy tale dwarf. Yet, in spite of his loveable appearance he was highly respected in society – a royal lawyer with the rank of *Tayny sovetnik* (in Russian – The Secret Adviser). On the Russian Table of Ranks he held the highest civilian position, equivalent to a general in the military.

The girls loved him dearly. He was an excellent father, gentle, generous and indulgent towards them, possibly, because he was raising them as a single parent.

After the breakfast, a cab was called and Anya left for hairdresser escorted by Josefova. Sonya would go later because Vladimir Diachan wanted to speak to her in private first.

Sonya knew that her father quite often liked to talk to her heart-to-heart; she was his favorite daughter. He loved her much more that Anya, but tried not to show this in any way and always bought them absolutely equal presents, only in different colors. Shapely Anya with her huge blue eyes, fine skin and dark brown curly hair was much more beautiful, resembling their mother, Ekaterina. Slim Sonya, on the other hand, was green-eyes, fair-skinned blonde.

However, Sonya was brilliant and hardworking and truly shone at the Gymnasium. She often did the assigned homework twice – once for herself and again for her lazy sister who had little interest in studies. Anya was waiting only to marry, but Sonya planned to attend university courses and become a doctor. This was a challenging goal especially for women in those days.

His younger daughter's ambitions and scientific bent attracted Vladimir Diachan and drew him closer to Sonya and she unconsciously felt this deep in her heart.

She sat on the couch and looked questioningly at her father pacing the room. He locked his hands behind his back and uneasily walked to and fro.

"What's the matter, Papa?" Sonya asked having no idea what was agitating her father.

He stopped in front of her and pursed his lips, reluctant to began, then cleared his throat.

"I would like to know, my dear, what your relationship with Alexander is," he finally blurted out.

Sonya blushed. She was a bit confused but felt she had nothing to hide. Her father was her trustee and she had no secrets from him.

"I love him, Papa," she said simply. "And he loves me, as he admitted. He is not lying, it's true. I know that for sure. I would say that he is quite serious about me."

"I was not very pleasantly surprised some days ago," her father explained, "to hear from one of my assistants that Alexander was asking a number of personal questions about our family."

"I don't see anything wrong with that," Sonya objected. "I expect that he may propose to me soon. He only arrived here a few months ago from St. Petersburg to visit his sister. As he isn't from Warsaw, he may want to know more about us."

"Still, it's a bit suspicious to me," the senior Diachan went on. "He interested in my financial situation. That's what I really don't like. Of course, my assistants didn't give him any information. But why is he trying to get it? I find it very irregular. He is from a respected good family and his father is quite rich, as far as I know. What, do you suppose, it's all about?"

"May be I'm not rich enough for him?" Sonya guessed feeling offended. "I don't know, Papa. All I know is that Alexander is in love with me and money is not important to him. Our love is very beautiful and pure. I think we make a very good couple."

"I have quite a good position with an excellent salary," her father continued, not paying much attention to her comments, "but I did work hard my entire life to achieve it. You know, my father was a Warsaw University history, philosophy and philology professor. He received his Title of Nobility from the Tsar. But his father – my Grandpa - was a simple sexton, who was even illiterate. Both my father and I reached our respectful positions by our own efforts. We didn't inherit anything. We're intelligentsia; we're gentry but not silk-stockings. My father had ten children, so, even the farm *Vysokoe* he owned was divided ten ways. I have no other property except this suite and the tiny piece of the farm remaining. Nothing else!

"Our status is nowhere near the Dedulins. They own the dozens of factories, plants, hotels, ships, farms, estates and grounds. They've had them for many generations... for hundreds years. And his father is a courtier."

"But Alexander isn't of royal blood like I have!" Sonya exclaimed. "You told me that my mother is a descendant - fourth generation straight from Empress Catherine the Great!"

"None of that matters, my dear girl, if we're talking about money. Sometimes relations of the Tsar went bankrupt and ended in poverty. Then royal blood is of no help at all. We are now living in the twentieth century. It's already 1912 and money is the political currency today, more important than blood lineages. I'm just warning you because I love you. Be very careful with Alexander and find out what he wants before you completely trust him."

"Of course, Papa, I will," Sonya promised, being quite confident that she was very mature and wise. In all her eighteen years, she felt that her experience of life qualified her to judge such a situation. Maybe her father was blowing everything completely out of proportion. After all, nothing had happened yet, only the confirmation that Alexander was serious about her. The only problem, from her viewpoint, would be how to combine in the life of a young countess's marriage and university studies. But, if they relocated to St. Petersburg, near Alexander's family, she could attend university there – one of the best and oldest in Russia.

Her father was right to remind her of the year. Many new ideas about the position of women in society were springing up and circulating. Sonya had felt excited by some of them and hoped they would allow her to pursue her dreams to one day becoming a doctor.

At six o'clock the sisters, decked out in their new gowns, arrived at the ball. Their father stayed home since the loss of his wife had caused him to forswear public dances and trying to join in the festive atmosphere.

But his youthful daughters were bursting with life and thoroughly enjoyed the balls. The usual pre-ball fuss thrilled them. They really liked these preparations – people arriving, gathering in groups, the small talks, flirting while drinking champagne delivered on trays here and there by liveried servants. It was a good chance to mix with the beautiful people of Warsaw - and to be seen, as well.

The ballroom shimmered with light reflecting off the polished hardwood floor. Excitement hung in air like the crystal and candle ornaments filling the lush Christmas tree proudly occupying the corner next to the uniformed orchestra. As the hubbub dimmed, the musicians arrived, took their places, and began tuning up.

Anya and Sonya hurriedly shed their fur coats, hats and muffs along with their elegant winter boots and parked them with the loaded down doorman. In the ballroom lounge they quickly changed into their custom high-heeled dancing shoes and swept into the hall, trembling from happiness and chattering to each other.

Their best friend, Barbara Torchinsky, ran to met them as soon as they entered the room. They fondly called her by her Russian nickname - Varya. She was their classmate at the gymnasium, 18 and a half years old (falling between them in age), but she was already been married now for six months. Her husband, Earl Alexei Torchinsky, was forty years old, but this didn't make her into a serious and mature young woman. She remained the same excited young lady full of fun she had been, like the two sisters, and devoted to their close friendship.

Barbara had married in total ignorance of the realities of life, particularly her wedding night. Her mother had failed to prepare her at all for what to expect. When her new spouse began undressing her and made sexual overtures, Barbara in fright, shrank from him and escaped by climbing onto the large wardrobe in the room. She then spent the entire night there sitting and bemoaning her fate.

"You are such a terrible man!" she shouted, sobbing. "You are totally indecent! If I had known what kind of person you were... and so revolting, I would never have married you. I'll tell my mom!" she wailed.

Earl Alexei had no other choice but to be patient and let his naïve bride consult her mother the next morning about his 'disgusting behavior' and get, better late than never, the 'facts of life'. Barbara's mother was finally able to calm her down and convince her that sexual relations between man and wife were normal and acceptable. After a few days of parental consultations, Barbara, finally, agreed to allow her husband to touch her body. Surprisingly, she liked the experience very much and quickly became, after such a rocky beginning, a willing and satisfying wife in bed. They made a nice couple. Earl Alexei always took particular care of Anya and Sonya, driving them home after all the late evening balls.

The girls lacked a mother so Barbara was now in a position to secretly educate the sisters in the mysteries of sex as she herself, once an innocent, discovered them.

Now, at the Christmas Ball, Barbara herself hoped to compete for the Grand Prize, as well.

"Come on, come on, faster!" she exclaimed, taking their arms and whisking them along. "The music has already begun. First will be the Polonaise, then the Waltz, followed by two Cotillions and then – Mazurka. Thank God, we will have enough time to warm up before the competition. My husband Alexis refuses to dance and, instead, is playing cards. So, my partner will be my cousin Mikhail. Alexander and Nicolay are already here and have been searching high and low for you."

The two young dashing escorts soon found their beloveds and took them onto the dance floor. Tall and blonde Nicolay, decked out in his crisp white military uniform and stocky dark Alexander, dressed a black evening suit and white tie perfectly complimented the lively and lovely Anya and Sonya.

"Are you ready to win the prize tonight?" Lieutenant Obolensky asked Anya, holding her hand and lining for a Polonaise. "It would be a wonderful honeymoon trip for us, wouldn't it?"

"Oh, yes," she readily agreed. "I hope we will win. I think our only real competition will come from Sonya."

"Anyway, we'll do our best," her groom reassured her, following the line of solemn Polonaise gait.

"I got your urgent note last night," Sonya reported to Alexander as they took their places as well. "Does it mean something has happened? I couldn't help but worry."

"Not really," Alexander smiled to comfort her. "I had received a message from my father and was just a little shaken, that's all. I know it was wrong to alarm you that way. Please forgive me, dear. For now we should concentrate on our dancing. I really want us to win and I think you do, too. Later, we'll talk things over. All right?"

He smiled so charmingly and stared at her so lovingly that Sonya immediately felt reassured and could focus her mind and all her efforts to dancing.

More dances followed until the crowning event - the Mazurka - began.

The competition was organized quite well. The five-man jury had been appointed from among the parents of the young competitors and from the guests of the honor who were senior generals. Ten couples would dance the Polish favorite, one by one, in turn. The poor musicians would need to replay Mazurka over and over, but it promised to be great fun for spectators. Everyone looked forward to the festivities, heightened by the competition.

The Chair of the Noble Community offered a short speech. He described the rules which would be observed and explained the prizes - two tickets on the Titanic as well as two train tickets to reach the Southampton dock where the boarding would take place. In addition, the winners would receive a substantial check for spending money for the whole trip. Following the cheers and applause, the jury took up their posts on one side of the hall, while the dancers sat in a row of chairs on the other. The first couple was called, and the music started.

Sonya and Alexander were to dance sixth, so they had enough time to watch the others, to analyze their mistakes and to consult with each other in a whisper. They could decide how best to dance and what to avoid, which was lucky for them.

While waiting their turn, they held each other's hands and promised to love each other forever. These feelings inspired them. They glided onto the floor on a huge wave of enthusiasm and were, for sure, the best. The later couples had been waiting too long and had grown tired and annoyed, which lowered the artistic level of their performance. The jury voted unanimously for Sonya and Alexander.

The prize package was handed to Sonya, but it was expected, of course, that she and Alexander would be married before they left on the trip.

Following the ball, Barbara, her husband and Nicolay Obolensky drove Anya home, but Sonya refused to accompany them and said that she would walk with Alexander because they need to talk. She promised to come home a bit later.

"Be careful, it's quite cold and snowy," Anya kissed her good-bye, "I won't sleep and will wait up for you."

But Anya was so tired she couldn't stay awake. That's why, when a snowball hit her window just before dawn, she sat up, startled, rubbed her eyes and tried to see who it could be through the lacy frost that filmed the pane. So, Anya got up and blew a ring in the snow cover and scratched the ice with her beautiful fingernails. She was more than surprised to see her sister standing frozen there below in the snowdrifts under the street lamp.

"O, my goodness!" Anya exclaimed to herself. "The front door must be locked. What time could be? Morning already? Six o'clock!! Oh, Virgin Mary! I pray father and Josefova are sound asleep. If not, they'd be horrified! What a scandal! Jesus! Help us, please!"

Anya ran downstairs on her tiptoes, unlocked the door and let Sonya in.

"Quickly, quickly – get inside!" she pulled her lightheaded sister by her coat sleeve. "What happened? Where were you so long?" she demanded in a hushed voice, sweeping the snow from her shoulders.

Sonya looked pale and cold, her lips almost blue. She was shaking with a chill and her teeth were chattering. She could barely talk. Anya helped her to take away her coat and hat; then dragged Sonya upstairs to bed.

"Why?" she asked worriedly. "Why were you walking so late and got so chilled? It's terrible! Why didn't Alexander at least hire a cab to drive you home? I was sure you would only be walking for fifteen or twenty minutes, no more. You shouldn't have been out, at all!"

"It's over between Alexander and me," Sonya mumbled, her eyes refilling with tears.

"What?! It's impossible! Why? Why, Sonya?"

With shaking hands Sonya withdrew from her muff the envelope with the Grand Prize package and handed it to Anya. "Yes, it's all finished..." she stammered. "His father... insisted he come home to St. Petersburg... immediately... and marry there. He found for him a merchant's daughter whose dowry would be three million rubles. Alex doesn't want to, of course. He loves me... but he must listen to his father."

By now Sonya was suffocating from sobbing and couldn't continue. Soon her sobs turned into hacking coughs.

"Hold on!" her sister exclaimed. "Maybe we can still do something? Maybe you can elope right away, against his father... before his father even finds out?"

"Alex doesn't want that, and neither do I. It would be too humiliating for me, Anya. Alexander has betrayed me, although it wasn't easy for him. He helped me to win this prize like a thank you gift for my love. It's all so horrible! Like a nightmare!" she cried, burying her face in her sister's shoulder. "In spite of everything, I saw him off at the train station. I was generous enough to give him farewell hug because I still love him. He is already gone. His train to St. Petersburg departed at five in the morning... That's why I was so long..." Sonya broke into spastic coughing. "Now, I've decided, so my prize will not be in vain, that you and I should take the Titanic trip together. You'll go with me, instead of Alex, won't you?"

"O, my Gosh! How lucky I am!" Anya wholeheartedly hugged Sonya, tears streaming down her cheeks in amazement. She was torn, to be sure, by her conflicting compassion for her sister and the unexpected possibility of traveling trans-Atlantic with her on their dream trip. They stood, arms around each other, and crying joyfully, until finally Anya whispered, "You know, Sonya, it's funny, but we are almost ready for the trip. Let's take this beautiful suitcase from Murex & Mary-Lisa in which our dresses were delivered. We can start packing it tomorrow..."

Sonya couldn't answer because her fits of coughing overcame her and she covered her mouth with both hands. She still was very pale and continued sobbing and hacking almost breathlessly until, weak from effort, she hung unconscious in her sister's hands.

"Help! Help!" Anya screamed, lowered Sonya to the floor and ran to wake their father and Josefova.

...I looked at the suitcase and touched it in disbelief. That very suitcase was here, in my room. It hadn't sunk in the dark, deep, cold Atlantic on that fateful night. Then I looked at my Baba Sonya.

"How come?" I whispered, trembling with curiosity and dread. "I read that some women were saved from the Titanic, but surely no suitcases! So, how is it possible it is here?"

"You see," Baba laughed, "things sometimes have their own fate, too. The good fortune of this suitcase is to rest on our wardrobe now – instead of at the bottom of the sea.

"I had a bad case of pneumonia after my snowy walk that night with Alexander," she continued. "The deep nervous shock provoked my illness, as well. I ended up spending three and a half month in bed, nearly dying. So, we missed our trip. Anya wanted to go with Nicolay, but it was impossible because it was my ticket – I was the

Mazurka winner. For quite a long time, I felt very unhappy and anxious after that painful parting as I lost my first love so suddenly and shamefully. But in reality it was my good luck. I had been skating on thin ice - if it hadn't been such a cold night and I hadn't sent Alexander back to St. Petersburg, I would have been on the Titanic that fatal trip. And it's just possible you would never has appeared in this world and there would be no young lady today playing with that very memorable suitcase."

Chapter 4

THE BIRTHMARK

Wednesday evenings were a special time for us.

"Katya, please, eat faster," my Baba urged, watching me play with my mashed potatoes, "it's already time to call the neighbors to the toilet."

"You go, Mama. Go. I'll clear the table and wash the dishes," my mom said as Baba hobbled as fast as she could into the corridor and started knocking on each door, shouting, "Go to the toilet, everybody! It's toilet time! We're starting our baths!"

Really, it was far from an easy procedure to bath in the flat where we used to live. That was because eight families resided in the nine rooms and shared the kitchen and the bathroom. The lavatory was equipped with a small sink and a cold water faucet, lidless toilet and a gas-heated bathtub. Altogether, that meant that twenty people, including four children, shared these facilities.

Each family had their scheduled evening for baths, which meant that while one family was using the bathtub, the door was locked and everyone else was denied access to the toilet or the sink for the duration. It was actually possible to wash your hands in the communal kitchen, but no alternative was available. This created innumerable problems for the household, until a practical solution was found.

Since that development, a warning knock and call was send out before the bathroom could be occupied for the evening -"Use the toilet now. We will start bathing."

People were quite disciplined. They had no other choice but to line up in the corridor and enter to use the toilet, one by one. The entire procedure took about half an hour. After that, the bathroom could be engaged for the next two or three hours, so the scheduled family need not be disturbed by anybody.

The next step in the weekly ritual was that my Baba began to clean and disinfect the tub with chlorine and prepare everything for washing – a brick of stinky gray soap, thin waffle towels and regular cotton sheeting to wrap me in afterwards. My mom and I didn't even suspect that terrycloth towels and bathrobes existed in the world –

we have never seen them. My Baba Sonya had possibly known about them in her youth in Warsaw, before World War I, but she had no chance to use them here, in Russia. They simply couldn't be found in the shops.

Because the toilet had no lid, we used a piece of plywood to cover it so we could place our things off the floor. There wasn't any table or any counter at all in the tiny bathroom. There was no heating, either, so, my Baba, as a rule, sacrificed for us and was the one who took the first bath in the cold room in order to warm it up for us.

Then, she washed and disinfected the bathtub once again and refilled it with hot water for my mom. It was a good thing that both gas and water were very cheap in Russia then, so we could use as much as we wanted. I was always the last one to bath, after the room was the warmest. But I also had the right to join with my mom, to perch on the plank over the toilet, cushioned with towels, to scrub her pink back with a natural sponge, and to converse heart-to-heart with her.

This was a treat for me because my mom went out to work most days and I seldom had time to spend with her. I missed her terribly, even though my Baba was always with me. As dearly as I loved my grandmother and felt she was my best friend, my comforter and my refuge – she wasn't my mother. No one else can truly take the place of one's mother and I emotionally craved contact with her and grabbed at each opportunity to be near her. So bath time was usually our time to share.

We take advantage of this relaxed weekly time of sharing. I tell mom about school and my friends, the pictures I have drawn and the problems I am facing. I also report to her about what I have been reading and asked her my questions. She was always good at giving me advice. She tells me stories and fairytales. And together we play word games, brainteasers and puzzles of logic. We discuss the latest political developments and my mom's strongest interests, philosophy and astronomy. Even when I was quite small, she would find simple, clear and comprehensible explanations to help me grasp serious scientific concepts - and I did.

Those were, without a doubt, the richest moments of my childhood – the hours when my mother developed my brain and my mind, taught me through the games and stimulated my creative thinking. It was a total bliss for me - the greatest 'home school' where I learned much more than I ever did at school, college and university put together. My mom was an outstanding educator and she was amazingly talented.

Then, back to the bathroom, we would exchange places. She would dry and dress, again clean and disinfect the tub for me, and refill it once more with hot water. Next, she undressed me, placed me in the hot tub and scrubbed my back with the soapy sponge. Now, she rested on the toilet board as we continued our conversations.

One day, during bath time, my mom revealed a very unusual mole on her leg – big, pink and star-shaped.

"It's strange," she said. "You have the same mole, but on your wrist. What the interesting things are our genes! How do they operate in this twisted way?"

Of course, I knew my own mole very well. From my birth, it was on the right side of my right wrist – the same size as my pinky nail, light brown and star-shaped, as well. Being a baby, I didn't pay much attention at all. But as soon as I grew and started to explore my own body and its peculiarities, as every normal child does, I rediscovered my mole and began to scratch it. It seemed to me a little bug or piece of dirt. However, it didn't want to leave.

Later, I understood that it was part of me and not something external. I grew accustomed to it and, finally, almost indifferent.

"Does Baba have the same mole, too?" I inquired.

"No, she doesn't. Have you ever seen anyone with star-shaped moles like we have?" my mom asked.

I shook my head 'no'.

"It's uniquely ours," my mom said. "Mine was bright red when I was born, but now it's lost color and turned to light pink, almost beige. You know, it arose during very unusual circumstances. Did Baba ever tell you about it?"

Once more I shook my head, adding, "But I want to know." My eyes begged mom to tell me the story.

...Victor had just changed his white lieutenant's uniform and put on a regular shirt and pants, as he heard a strong banging on his door.

"Coming," he shouted, hung the uniform up into the wardrobe and walked to open the door. He was sure it was his landlady - an elderly woman, returned from the market. But damn fate! He was mistaken. Three Bolshevik soldiers, armed with automatic rifles, stood before him. If he had known, he never would have open up, but it was too late now.

"Greetings!" one soldier said. "We came to arrest Victor Demin, the Tsar's officer. Is that you?"

"No," Victor lied. "I'm his tenant, a worker. I'm renting the room here."

"Okay. Where is Mr. Demin?"

"He's not at home."

"Well, we'll wait here until he returns." They shoved Victor aside and entered boldly. He was unable to protest.

Victor felt quite feverish. His framed portrait - in damning uniform – lay directly ahead of the intruders, on the china shelf. His fluffy blonde hair, straight nose, big eyes and accurately trimmed beard were really recognizable. Luckily for him, the soldiers were slow to take notice of it.

But, if they decided to thoroughly search the place, they would easily spot it. Even though the photo was two years old, he looked much the same. Besides, his uniform was hanging right in the closet.

The evidence was totally damning. He must do something!

"Of course, guys," Victor spoke as hospitably as he could, "he's sure to come soon. Make yourself comfortable and wait." He gestured to the couch and deep leather armchairs. "I can offer you some refreshments." He took a bottle of vodka and four glasses from a kitchen shelf and put them on the table.

The soldiers sat down. The youngest of them grabbed the bottle right away, but the others weren't in a hurry and sternly looked around.

"Where are you working?" one of them asked Victor.

"At the Oil Mill." Thanks God, he knew the city of Rostov-on-Don well. He had been born here.

"What is your name?"

"Ivan Petrov."

"Show as your documents."

Victor put his hand into his pants pocket.

"O, shit!" he exclaimed pretending to be surprised. "They're not here. They must still be in my work-jacket. It's next door in my wardrobe. I'll be back in a minute."

Pretending to be calm, he slowly moved to the next room, then tiptoed one more room over, then raced out of the flat, to the owner's place, closing the door behind him. He opened the window to the garden, jumped out, and then – ran.

He ran like his life depended on it. He could have possibly won the World Championship or Olympic Games. It turned into a steeplechase, as he jumped over fences and ditches, climbed walls and trees, crawled under the heavy wooden gates with only the briefest breaks to catch his breath behind the high stacked woodpiles in backyards.

As he tore up the stairs into the third floor suite on Konkrinskaya Street, he looked horrible – all dirty, shirt hanging out, hair matted but eyes sparkling. He was almost breathless as he rang the bell.

Sonya, who was at this time 27, opened the door very much surprised.

"What happened?" she asked worriedly.

"They found out that I returned from the Army and came to arrest me... I can't go back to my home," Victor explained, breathing heavily. "I would never return there whether you like it or not, but I'll stay here and we can get married. It's fate."

The night before, he had proposed to Sonya but she had asked for a day to think about it. She really liked Victor, calling him fondly the Russian nickname Vitya. Her feelings were neither as passionate nor as romantic as for her first love, Alexander Dedulin, but now she was much more serious and mature. She had already known Victor for five years and found in him the most important quality of reliability and trustworthiness. Sonya was sure he would be a good husband; however, she resided with her father, Vladimir Diachan, who was very sick and lay in bed, paralyzed by a stroke for four years now.

Her father's illness had come suddenly. At the beginning of the year 1917, he was chosen as the best of the Tsar's lawyers and invited to a solemn celebration in St. Petersburg. There, the Tsar, in person, had handed him the award for serving 'Tsar and Motherland' – a chunky golden chain dangling a big golden cross studded with diamonds.

After the ceremony, Vladimir Diachan planned to stay in St. Petersburg another three months to complete some of his legal investigations. However, the unexpected February Revolution and abdication changed everything. In spite of the chaos and horror of the event, he stayed on in the capital quietly doing his business, hoping things would settle down and it would finally be possible to return home, to Rostov-on-Don. It had been his home for three years.

The Revolution broke his spirit and confused him. Just who should the State lawyers now serve? The new Provisional Government? Or the old law? It looked to him like the country was no longer governed by laws. He was surrounded by disaster, which Sonya's father tried to steer through without losing his balance.

At last, the train connections were all operating, so when Vladimir discovered it, he determined to set out for home. He left his hotel room, walked toward the train station to Moscow, where he could catch another south-bound coach to Rostov-on-Don. Russia was now Tsar-less, but still he proudly wore his award around his neck and the cross reached his navel. The valuable object was covered by the lapels of Diachan's wool spring coat.

He walked slowly, carrying his small suitcase and enjoying the warmth of the nice April day. As he approached closer to the train station, he saw more and more crowds on the streets. They were boisterous and noisy, pushing and shoving. Finally, he reached the big square in front of the station and could make no more progress through the wall of humanity. He was trapped in the middle of the crowd. In front of him was a huge iron-clad military vehicle.

Vladimir Diachan couldn't miss a short, slim, balding middle-aged man standing on the top of the car who haranguing his audience with political slogans and visions for the Russian State now that the Tsar had been overthrown. He strongly proclaimed that his Bolshevik Party - as representative of the Russian people - would take over power in Russia. It was obvious that this radical was well-educated and intelligent, but his aggressive manner and tone of grievance against traditional Russian values upset Vladimir. Yet, this orator had a mighty influence over the gathering and was very effective at arousing their sense of injustice. Diachan had never heard anything like it.

"Who is that?" he asked worker beside him who was participating in the crazy shouting, accompanying it with fervent applause and swinging his fists.

"It's Lenin! It's our leader!" the worker exclaimed happily and proudly. "He just returned from abroad to bring us our proletarian revolution in Russia! He promises that even kitchen maids can rule Russia! Then, my wife will be in power! I will be in power!"

"Do you really believe him?" Vladimir Diachan asked suspiciously. "I suspect he's the one who'll have the real power - not you! It's easy to see that he's a liar and only playing on the lowest instincts of the crowd to foment trouble."

Luckily for Vladimir, the worker had little interest in his observations; he was caught up in the mass ecstasy of the moment. Truth to tell, Diachan was more alarmed at the man's frenzied enthusiasm than by Lenin's speech. Without another word, he elbowed and shouldered his way through the crowd; then boarded his train home to Rostov-on-Don.

"What happened, Papa?" Sonya asked worriedly, seeing his pale and lifeless face as he entered the suite. "Did you get your award? You look miserable."

47

Her father dropped wearily onto the couch and said sharply, "The Russia we've all known is now dead, my dear daughter. The villains, dangerous villains, are on their way to the power in our land and the foolish masses are stirred up by them when they should be throwing them into prison. I'm afraid Russia is through! Forever!"

He covered his face with both hands and sobbed, all shaking, until he passed out. Frightened, Sonya called the doctor. It was a stroke. Vladimir Diachan was paralyzed and bedridden for the next four years.

Sonya nursed her father faithfully and took the burden on her weak and thin shoulders. She even sacrificed her education for him and left her Medical Institute where she had done two years of medical study. She was doing everything possible for her father. She tried not to worry him, to shield him from problems and troubles. So yesterday, after Victor's proposal, she wanted, at first, to discuss her possible marriage with her father and to consider the situation with him.

"Okay," Sonya shook her head in confusion. "Come on in, Vitya. Let's talk to papa."

The Diachan family had been in this flat for seven years now since the World War started. When Garman troops seized Europe and approached Warsaw, the staff and families of Warsaw University were swiftly evacuated to Rostov-on-Don in Southern Russia.

Father Diachan continued to share his home with his two daughters until, a year later Anya got married to Nicolay Obolensky. The newlyweds moved one block to another apartment, around the corner of Konkrinskaya Street. At present, Nicolay was at the front with the White Army in the Civil War raging in the Crimea while Anya remained at home. She already had three children: 5-year-old son Yura, 3-year-old Vera, and the baby Galya.

The Diachan apartment, where Sonya and her father lived, consisted of small corridor, kitchen, bathroom and two rooms – Sonya's and her dad's bedrooms. There was no living room at all, so Sonya and Victor entered from the narrow hallway straight to Vladimir Diachan's bedroom.

Her father lay on his bed, on top of his blankets, dressed in his pajamas and thick-striped robe. It was the terry robe he had brought from Warsaw and the very last one Sonya would see in Soviet Russia. Vladimir felt much better now, after years of being cared by his daughter; he even started to walk a bit with a cane - only to the washroom - and could sit for a short time at the table. Mostly he was supposed to lie on his bed.

"Papa," Sonya began, "please, forgive Vitya's appearance. He's just escaped from the Bolsheviks who came to arrest him an hour ago. We can offer him safety here. You and I discussed my possible marriage to him last night. Now, he is here to get your answer. Do you want to talk to him privately?"

"Yes, my dear, but I don't mind if you're present," her father replied. "Vitya and I have known each other a long time now and have nothing to hide from you. But children, can you come a little closer, please?"

Sonya and Victor approached her father. He took their hands, joined them, and blessed them with the sign of the cross.

"I'm blessing you, my dear ones," he said solemnly. "The only advice I can give you is to always yield to each other when you have a disagreement. That way you'll live a long and happy life. Believe me. I had experience. In my day, I was stubborn and unbending so, as a result, I lost my beloved wife and had to raise my two girls alone. It was a good lesson to me."

"Yes, Papa, I promise," Sonya said in a quavering voice, blinking back her tears.

"Yes, I promise," Victor repeated wholeheartedly. They kissed each other and then the old man on his cheeks.

Next morning, Victor shaved his beard and dyed his hair with black ink to change his appearance. He set out with Sonya to the municipal office to get married because there was no other way - all churches were closed and all priests imprisoned or killed.

The city hall had been bombed, half destroyed and half burnt. A strong smell of smoke wafted in the air. Nevertheless, most of it was still functioning. A young but plain and poorly-dressed secretary was sitting and smoking on an upturned rusty pail in the center of the hall. She was surrounded by the wreckage of smashed windows, splintered doors and broken furniture. In front of her stood a wooden box, also upside down, posing as a table. But, all the same, she had the authorized logbook, a thick pencil, and a little box containing an ink pad and official stamp – all to serve the people.

"Do you have a lot of work?" Victor asked.

"Yeah," she smirked.

"Does anyone register marriages or births?"

"Some..." she shrugged, "...but mostly – deaths."

"We need to do some legal business with you," Victor smiled. "We want to register our marriage."

"This is not the best time," the girl grinned huskily, and opened her logbook. "Okay," with great difficulty she wrote down their names. She was almost illiterate. "You're husband and wife now - the Demin's family," she declared. "But I have problem to give your actual marriage certificate because we don't have the forms available right now. In truth – we are out of paper! The building was bombed and everything was burnt. I just have a couple of pages from an old newspaper that are still usable. There're no pictures on them, only text, so I can write the marriage certificate over it for you. Later, you can come in and to exchange it for a regular certificate, if you like."

Sonya wanted to protest, sensing that her marriage was beginning on the wrong foot – no special dress, no witnesses, no champagne, no rings, no flowers, no guests, no congratulations and now, not even a proper marriage certificate. It was a very trying moment. But Victor nodded and said, "Well, please, do it."

I must support him, Sonya reflected on her promise to her father. She tried to calm down and nodded affirmatively, as well.

The girl tore off the piece of newspaper and printed across the top in black pencil – 'Marriage Certificate'; then she copied the names and details from her book onto the scrap of paper and recorded the date. Finally, she stamped it with her seal and handed it to Victor.

He looked closely at the stamp. It was possible to make out the words: Postov-on-Don, Soviet Municipal Government. It was their official document dated September 21, 1921. And it was completely free – the courtesy of the Bolsheviks.

This evening they had a spontaneous celebration in their apartment with guests – Vladimir Diachan and Anya with her children. Also attending were Barbara Torchinsky and her husband, since they, too had relocated to Rostov-on-Don, as Barbara's father, Sergey Pyshnovsky, was a chemistry professor at Warsaw University. Victor's family was represented by his two brothers – both engineering students at the Technological Institute.

Victor presented Sonya with a ring he had inherited from his mother and bouquet of lovely white chrysanthemums plucked from a neighbor's garden. His older brother, Boris, brought a bottle of champagne he had bought at the flea market from one of the workers at Rostov's Champagne Wine plant. It was common for employees at such a plant to steal some of the output to barter for their own survival. Most of the plant's production went directly to the tables of the Bolsheviks bosses and only leftovers went to the shops where they were stolen by shop assistants and sold under the counter. It was rare for champagne (and other luxuries) to be on sale in the shops.

Barbara gave Sonya her used cream-colored evening dress which still looked good and festive. Anya cooked the dinner – potatoes with mushrooms she had picked that morning in the riverside park -

served with flaxseed rye bread brought by Victor's younger brother, Basil.

So, they had a wedding celebration at least with kisses and congratulations, ring and flowers, guests and food. It was modest in scale, but good enough for the period of the Civil War. Finally, Sonya felt satisfied and really happy.

Next morning, Victor asked Sonya to give him what was left from her father's award – the gold links and big diamond cross. It was kept hidden under the mattress. Sonya removed the package wrapped in cloth, put it on the table and unwrapped it. The luster of the diamonds brilliantly lit the dim room. It looked like the sun had risen in all its glory.

After Bolshevik Revolution (which was carried out 6 months following Lenin's historic speech on the iron-clad military vehicle), the invalid Diachan had given his daughters permission to break the chain in order to sell the links. Sonya usually walked to flea market and bought bread for these single pieces of gold. To sell the whole thing would be very dangerous; it was too expensive and she would be killed while trying to sell it.

To keep the award in the house – even as a remembrance - wasn't safe, either. At any moment, Red Army soldiers could arrive unannounced, search the apartment, find the valuables and confiscate them 'on behalf of Revolution and the people'- but, in reality, they went straight into the Bolshevik bosses' pockets. Such stealing was officially sanctioned as 'expropriation', which hid its real meaning from the illiterate masses.

To loose such a valuable item this way was crazy. It would be much better to have something to eat from it, since their family had no real means of subsistence. Sonya sometimes walked to the Armenian Cloister – a little settlement a couple of miles away from Rostov-on-Don – and there taught Armenian children to speak Russian. The parents paid her with eggs and small cans of milk, sour cream and honey – the usual farmers' goods – but this was only a once-a-month payment and not enough to support so many mouths. So, the golden chain was broken and more than half of it was already sold and 'eaten' during the previous dangerous and hungry years. The Tsar's gift literally helped them to survive.

Victor looked at the remains of the chain and the cross and shook his head.

"Well," he said sadly, "I'll take this cross and sell it now by myself. I know some of my fellow-officers who would be interested in buying it. Some of them have a lot of Tsarist gold coins left, so it

51

would be safer for you to sell the coins later, one by one. If I don't return in couple of days, don't worry. I need to travel somewhere and prepare something for us."

With deep regret, Sonya agreed – she really had no choice. She must concede. Victor was always very smart and creative in his ideas.

He returned home a week later with a pocketful of gold coins, which he solemnly put, along with an envelope, in the middle of the table.

"I see you were successful," Sonya said, happily hugging him. "And what is in this envelope?"

"Two tickets for the very last ship to Turkey, then – on to Paris! I went to the Black Sea port of Odessa and bought them. It's our last chance. We're going to emigrate."

"What?!"

"Sonya, dear, look around you! The White Army is defeated. It's crushed! The Bolsheviks have begun their terror! Everybody is trying to get out - emigrate. Who would want to stay here and be killed?"

"No," Sonya looked at him with horror. "No, Vitya, my darling. We can't go anywhere. You know, I don't really like Russia. I never lived here before. I was born and raised in Warsaw and have a mix of nationalities. My Polish is even better then my Ukrainian, my German or Russian. But, still, my love, you must realize that I have my precious family here. My sick papa... Anya...her kids. Nobody knows if Nickolay is dead or alive. There has been no news from him. If he has been killed in the fighting, how could they possibly live alone – papa, Anya and the children?"

"She could take care of your dad," Victor tried to object. "He's actually her dad, as well."

"No, darling. It's absolutely impossible. Anya is weak, not very cleaver, and has no strength after giving birth. She needs me. I'm like a mother to her little ones and I can't think of abandoning them. If you could obtain seven tickets, all of us could leave together."

"There were no more tickets. I took the last two they had."

"I really love Europe!" his young wife said, slowly. "But I'm sorry, Vitya. Without them I'm not going."

"Sonya, you don't realize how much danger you're putting me in! I know I'm wanted. I'd have to live illegally – underground - here in Soviet Russia. I could still be arrested at any moment."

"I realize that. If you must go – you go, but I'll stay here with my poor family."

"I'm your family now," Victor protested. "You're my wife! We'll have children and live in the free world."

"I know that I'm your wife," Sonya answered bitterly. "Well...I love you, Vitya, but you can go without me. We would be separated. I must stay with my blood family to make sure we all survive. I refuse to betray them. Never! Never!"

They tried to resolve their differences until late at night. Sonya stood firm in her position. Obviously, she had no intention to yield on this critical matter. So, it would have to be Victor who made concessions this time.

"Okay," he said finally, waving his hand in helplessness. "I'll stay here because you know I can't live without you. I love you too much. Anyway, I'd risk my life for you. However, you'll be under threat, as well, because Bolsheviks are arresting spouses of 'traitors' and executing them together. It's your choice.

"We'll live illegally. I refused to register at the Government Registration List as a former lieutenant of the White Army. All my fellow-officers went to register and tried to persuade me to do the same. They said they had been promised a pardon by the Bolsheviks, as well as adaptation to the requirements of the new regime – in job search, in placement to study. Twenty thousand White officers are on the list – those who love Russia so much they don't want to emigrate. But I strictly refused to put myself on their list. I don't trust the Bolsheviks. I really don't trust them – not at all! So, from this time forward, my old friends would live above ground, while we will take to the shadows. It's dangerous but, as I said, it's your choice."

Sonya nodded dutifully.

"Okay," Victor continued, "bring me all your personal documents, please. I must examine them."

She took another wrapped package from under the mattress and opened it. Victor chose her birth certificate, her parents' marriage certificate, her Noble Title certificate, all her father's documents and all of Anya's documents. He only left the girls' Gymnasium diplomas and for Vladimir Diachan his two published Ph.D. dissertations.

"They could be useful if you or Anya decide to study in the future," he explained, "but we can't leave anything here that reveals your mother's royal blood or your father's involvement in the Noble society. The Bolsheviks could barge in and search your flat whenever they felt like it."

They walked out to the back yard. Victor built the fire in the middle and, as the flames rose, put the selected documents into the blaze. They sat on an old log beside the fire, silently watching Sonya's family history reduced to cinders. The pages twisted and turned in the heat, burned brown and then black; the sealing wax melted and sputtered; colored ribbons incinerated and turned into ash on the red-hot coals. Tears slid down Sonya's cheeks and she put her weary head on her husband's shoulder.

"Who am I now?" she whispered in despair. "A vagabond without a past, a vagrant without kith and kin, someone who is nobody from nowhere."

"No," Victor objected, hugging her tenderly. "You're my wife, Mrs. Demina. You're starting a new life in a new society and will build our new identity with our new document – our marriage certificate, doesn't matter that it looks ugly. And you're also a wonderful human being – the woman most loved on the Earth. Isn't that enough for a start? We are come into the world naked and nameless, having nothing. Then, step-by-step, we build our self. That's what we'll do together."

The following day, Victor sold the two tickets to Turkey to a fellow-officer and brought home more golden coins to Sonya.

"Keep this money safe," he said. "It will feed you and your big family. I'm leaving for several months to complete my engineering course in the next city of Taganrog, at the Polytechnic Engineering Institute, where I studied before the Civil War started. I really need to get my diploma now because after all the gold coins are gone, I'll be the head of the family and need to provide for all of you."

Some days later, he left.

When Sonya discovered that she was pregnant, she didn't tell anyone in her family. She decided to keep it a secret and then surprise Victor when he came back with his engineering diploma. That would be in five months time.

For her, life continued quietly until the day Sonya heard a timid knock at the door. Confident that it posed no danger, she opened to find Yura, her 5-year-old nephew standing there, red in the face and breathing hard.

"Auntie Sonya," he begged, "come quickly! My mom needs to see you… really fast."

"Oh, my God! What happened?" Sonya exclaimed, feeling shivers of alarm run down her back. She was very fearful that bad news would arrive about Anya's husband. "Something about your daddy?"

"No. It's Auntie Varya. She came to us, crying. There are soldiers searching her flat."

"Okay, okay, I'll go," Sonya murmured, as she hastily wrapped herself in a gray shawl. She never went anywhere without it, using it as a disguise as an illiterate farm girl rather than an educated young lady. "Okay, give me your hand, Yurik. Let's run."

They skipped three stairs at a time, racing down to the street.

At Yura's home they found Anya and Barbara, hugging one another and crying at the turn of events. Sonya soon heard the whole story: six soldiers had forced their way into the apartment where Barbara was residing with her husband, her parents, her two younger sisters (aged 18 and 20) and two little brothers (aged 6 and 10). Their suite was quite big; it consisting of four rooms – two people slept in each room which was not bad for the war years.

Some of neighbors had grown jealous of all their space, and had reported them to the authorities as 'capitalist and bourgeois' – in other words, an 'enemy of the people.' Such 'scum' should be killed (along with their family) and roomy accommodations should be spread among true 'proletariats'.

The soldiers arrived just as the family was sitting down to their usual meal – the unpeeled boiled potatoes with dark bread and hot water with a trace of tea in it. Their meager meal failed to impress the soldiers, who forced all of them to rise, shouting that they were ready to shot them all.

"Search the suite!" the commander ordered to his men. "I want to know if there is a White Army uniform on the premises."

Luckily, no one in the family was connected to the White Army, so the soldiers' search was in vain.

The commander searched high and low for some proof that Barbara's father was *bourgeois* – the term applied to all educated people. And the evidence was easy for anyone to see – book shelved walls filled with scientific tomes and the classic of world literature. The illiterate soldiers – not knowing any better – were convinced that all these books had made this family too clever to be permitted to live.

"What are all these books about?" the commander shouted at Barbara's father, the chemistry professor, Sergey Pyshnovsky. "Are they teaching you how to exploit the workers' labor? They're fucking capitalists' books, for sure."

The old professor kept quiet because, anyway, there was no reason to answer – nobody would listen or understand if he tried to explain.

The commander approached the shelf, grabbed one of the books and opened it. It was a chemistry workbook for university students, laying out Mendeleyev's Periodic Table of Elements. Mendeleyev was a world-famous Russian chemist, who had discovered this system, so the book focused on his research and opened with his bearded portrait on the first page. This image was familiar to every Russian schoolchild.

However, the commander was illiterate and had never attended school. He looked at the portrait attentively. All he had ever studied in his life was Marxist propaganda.

"Hey, fellow! Look here!" he exclaimed, turning to his soldiers. "Look at this! It's Karl Marx. Yes, yes, I know - Karl Marx. I know him with his bushy beard. So, you're Communist, comrade, if you're reading and keeping Karl Marx's books!" he addressed Professor Pyshnovsky. "You're a fellow Communist! You and your family won't be executed. You're safe, comrade. Don't worry, comrade. Let's go, men! This family is okay."

The Bolsheviks quickly departed, being fooled by their own ignorance of the world.

The old professor felt sensed a horrible pain in his heart and immediately lay down. He was drained of energy and had difficulty breathing. He still couldn't believe that his favorite science – chemistry, had saved their lives. His wife and daughters broke into sobs, brought on by the stress. Barbara's pale husband, Earl Alexei, sat both her little brothers on his lap and hugged them to comfort them. He affectionately petted their precious heads with his shaking hands.

"I must run and tell Anya!" Barbara exclaimed hysterically. "I know she has Nicolay's uniform at home. If they'd come to her place, they'd kill her and the kids for sure!"

So, now she was here, in Anya's suite.

"What should I do, girls?" Anya, pleaded, filled with helpless horror. "I have two of the Nicolay's White Army lieutenant's uniforms – both casual and parade. He left them here because he didn't need them anymore. They are only keepsakes, since he's a captain already. But they are dangerous for us. They are also big and bulky. How can I possibly carry them to the dumpster? There is likely to be a witness. Oh, my God!"

"Maybe you should to wrap them up, somehow," Barbara suggested.

"No," Sonya shook her head. "The soldiers are always stopping to check the people who are carrying suspicious bundles. And if you deposited them close to your house, when found they will easily incriminate you."

"What if we burn them in the yard..."

"No, Varya. They're not paper and will take time to destroy. For sure, someone would notice what we're doing," Sonya objected. "They must be taken far away and disposed of - outside the city. You could just throw them under some bushes, somewhere in a field..."

"But how could I possibly transport them there?!" Anya exclaimed in despair. "To walk with bags and kids?" she broke down in fear and frustration.

"Come on, stop it, please," Sonya said positively. "I have an idea. You wrap them up in some old sheets or old newspapers. I'll walk to the Armenian Cloister and borrow a horse and cart from my students' family. They're nice people and don't speak Russian. They won't understand what's going on and won't ask me any questions. They also wouldn't inform the Bolsheviks against me. They're simple but honest and decent people."

Sonya felt quite confident about this. She had great experience dealing with horses from her girlhood and youth in Warsaw, when she often went riding. The plan was agreed and she set out.

Three hours later, she returned at Anya's with a hay-covered cart drawn by an old quiet brown horse. While the women loaded the wrapped uniforms into the cart, camouflaging them with the hay, Sonya petted the horse's muzzle with white markings on it, and kissed its wet pink nose.

"I love horses," she said to Anya and Varya, "you know that, girls. Her name is Asmik – it's a beautiful Armenian women's name. She knows me. When I come to teach, I'm always petting and kissing her. Yes, Asmik?"

The horse snorted and wiggled its ears.

"You see, she's agreeing," Sonya laughed. "Okay, go home, girls. You didn't see me and you don't even know me, just in case..."

She nestled in the coachman's seat and jerked the reins. Asmik moved forward and then began to trot.

"Oh, Virgin Mary!" Anya made the sign of the cross at her retreating sister's back. "Save her, please."

Sonya's ride through the city went smoothly. The streets were almost empty. Few shoppers and passers-by were seen only towards the flea market, but she was heading in the other direction, out of town. The jogging of the cart began to calm her nerves. The tension of the afternoon was subsiding, and she truly believed that she could complete her mission without bumping into any soldiers along the way.

The mounted patrol – three Bolsheviks armed with their cavalry swords – suddenly appeared out of a small side-street, when she least expected them.

"Hey, young thing!" they shouted, addressing Sonya.

Oh, My God! I don't even have my identification with me, she thought in panic, so she spurred Asmik on. The horse jerked and galloped. However, it was too late to escape. The soldiers turned and followed Sonya.

"Hey, girl! Hey, kid! Wait! Wait, you fucking thing!" they shouted riding up behind her.

The time stood still for Sonya. Her lovely eyes misted with horror, while her insides churned and her teeth began to chatter. The hand of death was certainly closing in on her. She could only pray in desperation and whip the poor horse more and more. Again and again she looked back and saw the horsemen right behind her. More alarming still, Sonya noticed that the racing cart and the wind had displaced some of the covering hay, exposing pieces of old newspaper and even revealing a corner of a uniform.

The death knell was ringing inside Sonya's head, driving her wildly insane. She acted without thinking, unaware that her mission was doomed from the beginning – old Asmik, was certainly no match for three young, strong warhorses.

"Hey, young thing!" the soldiers passed Sonya and halted their horses in front of Asmik, who stopped abruptly and pranced in alarm, nearly overturning the cart.

Sonya let the reins fall and gripped the seat cushions so tightly that her knuckles turned white. She looked up at the commander of the patrol with large eyes peeking out from her shawl-wrapped head. She couldn't make out his face; she only saw his red starred khaki helmet (*Budennovka* in Russian) perched on his head. In every cell of her body she sensed the piercing red spikes from the star boring into her and setting her womb aflame.

"Hey, you! Girl! Where is Semenovka Street? Is it around here?" the commander inquired.

"W…w…what?" Sonya stammered.

"We're looking for Semenovka Street, number sixty-one? Do you know where it is?"

"No…not exactly…Se…Semenovka is right beside flea market. You have to go back and then turn to your left."

"Okay. Thanks girl."

Involved with urgent business, they whipped their horses and vanished as suddenly as they had come.

For a while, Sonya sat in stunned silence; then she slowly slid down from the seat into the cart, dug out the uniforms from under the hay and dumped them right in the middle of the street. At that point, her world went dark and she lost consciousness.

Sonya woke up, feeling someone slightly patting her cheek. She opened her eyes and saw Shoshanna, the Armenian mother of her students.

"Oh, thank God! Dear God you're alive! Miss Teacher!" she exclaimed, crying and murmuring her prayers in Armenian. She fervently hugged the limp Sonya.

Rubbing her eyes, Sonya looked around and saw she was still lying in the hay in the cart but she was surprised to find herself at Armenian Cloister, at the stables beside the Shoshanna's house. She couldn't grasp at first, how she had gotten there, but then realized that faithful Asmik perfectly knew the way home and had brought her there.

In six months, Victor returned from Taganrog, having finally obtained his engineering diploma.

"I'm bringing bad news," he told them dejectedly. "Twenty thousand White officers were executed by our hated Bolsheviks. Those men were the ones who loved Russia the most and wouldn't leave. They were the very ones who put their names on the government lists and who trusted Lenin's promises of assistance. How naive my friends all were! Even Anya's husband Nicolay Obolensky had registered on this list, as well. Someone who knew him said that he did register right in the Army. That means I'm the only White officer left alive here in Russia. How right I was! Remember, Sonya, never trust the Bolsheviks! Never, ever! Even if something happens to me, always teach that to our children and grandchildren. Never trust the Bolsheviks - it must be our family motto!"

On June 25, 1922, as their daughter was born, they discovered, to their surprise, that the baby had a big red-star birthmark on her leg.

... I looked at my mom with amazement.

"They were my Baba Sonya and Deda Vitya, of course," I half-asked, half-established the fact, not being quite sure that it was possible for the people who I knew so well to survive such things in real life and not just in adventures books and movies. To endure all of these here, in Russia where I lived, and not far away in the Wild, Wild West! "And that baby was you, Mom? So, you were marked with a star by the Bolsheviks, weren't you? And so was I."

She nodded as she said, "It's a special mark to remember my father's motto..."

"But, Mom, there are no Bolsheviks today," I protested. "So I don't need to worry about those bad people."

"But, sweetie, you are wrong there. Over the years, they changed their name and became 'Communists'. Today they are the members of the Communist Party of the Soviet Union."

"No, I won't forget!" I promised confidently, inspecting my birthmark. "Here is my small knot to remember – if I want a quiet and secure life, if I want to survive in this country, not to trust the Communists! Are there any exceptions, Mom? Aren't there any decent, kind and good people among the Communists?"

"Mmmm..." my mom thought a bit, "...sometimes...May be, sometimes...but very seldom...Only a very few exceptions! But that's another story. I'll tell you about it when you are much older and mature. For now, just be careful with them. Don't tell any of them the stories about our family, ever."

"Okay, thanks Mom. I will keep our secrets."

The end of the Part 1.

PART 2

FAMILY

I didn't want the second part of this book to be about KGB, Stalin's concentration camps, World War II or the decimated Russian population, losing 60 million lives in the first half of 20th century. The world is already well aware of all these matters.

But those of us in Russia had to survive these horrors, somehow, and they crushed our souls, even in the crib, and continued to cast an ominous shadow above our daily existence from our earliest years.

The evil was there, all right, but I won't dwell on it.

Chapter 5

THE PICTURE OF THE BOY

One of my favorite pastimes was to leaf through our family albums. We had a lot of them – old leather albums - and I was allowed to take them and explore them whenever I liked. They were stored in my mom's bookcase on the very bottom shelf, making them quite accessible for me.

It was easy to see that the albums lacked any organization - they were more like collections. My mom really tried to keep them in order but it was almost impossible – the picture was fixed on the pages, so as additional photos were added on the same subject, they couldn't be reorganized, slipping them in between older ones. So, my mom would start a new page for the recent pictures, and the continuity was broken, and a logical sequence was supplanted without rhyme or reason.

For example, in the middle of the section of photos of 'My co-workers' you would find a snapshot of me ('My daughter'), just as photos of me would be interrupted by the introduction of both mom's latest travel and a portrait of our new cat. Still, mom had striven for some sort of thematic sense.

When I was very little, I only pulled the albums out and onto the floor and built from them houses or castles for my dolls. Some years later, I began to peruse the pages of pictures and to draw big bushy moustaches and beards, or wild hair-dos, or huge ears on the faces. My mom got really upset as she discovered my defacing activities. She spent quite a long time erasing my artistic additions with a regular eraser or, if I had worked in ink in some places, she cleaned them with a wet piece of cotton. If the water didn't help, she used eau-de-cologne or vodka. Anyway, it was a lot off work to fix my mess and I was punished being made to stand in the corner of my room for a couple of hours.

'Being put in the corner' was very popular Russian punishment for children. It was assumed that a child would stand there and think about his or her bad behavior, and repent of what he / she had done.

To say: "Sorry, I won't do that anymore," was obligatory, otherwise you wouldn't be allowed to go free.

I don't know about other kids, but for me 'the corner' usually didn't work. I did spend my time there scratching the wallpaper, investigating its pattern and imaging something interesting there, talking in whisper with my imaginary friends, toys or game partners. My brain, heart and soul were full of adventure stories at this quiet time, but totally absent was any regret for breaking or smearing something. I closed my eyes and daydreamt about travels and adventures in the future, when I'd be all grown-up, but I seldom felt shame about what I'd just done wrong.

However, I did easily grasp the rules of the game and as soon as I was finished with my games with the wallpaper or with my imaginative stories, I felt bored and 'confessed' in a whimpering voice, "Mom, sorry, I won't do that anymore."

"What won't you do?" my mom or Baba asked me sometimes to check the sincerity of my announcement.

"That," I responded, cunningly, because mostly I really couldn't remember what my punishment was all about. It was absolutely not important to me. Much more important was that I created a new game during this hour in the corner.

When I grew bigger, my mom showed me the pictures in the albums and explained everything about them – who the people were, where the places were, and what was happening. She liked to reminisce about her life and tell me stories. And I liked to listen.

A very special place in the album was given to the picture of my grandpa, my mom's father, Victor Demin, erect in his Soviet military uniform. It was taken before he left for the Second World War in 1941, where he lost his life. I never had the chance to know him. My mom dearly loved and admired him. He was her real hero and she spoke about him a lot.

We seldom made it to the last pages of albums; we would both grow tired or bored, or be called away for something urgent. It might also be supper - or bed time. I really had no idea what I would find on the last pages, but one day (I was probably in grade one or two) I finally turned the last page of the album and came face to face with a large portrait of a cute 5-6-year-old boy, with a dark curly hair, dressed in a sailor's dark suit with white-striped collar and tie. He was good-looking like a doll, though his eyes were very deep and too serious for a child. He was staring somewhere far away, propping his chin against his fist and seemed to me unusually wistful. I had never seen him before.

"Who is this?" I asked my mom in surprise.

"This is your father," my mom said. "I guess he's five here."

"Wow! I didn't know that he was such a nice boy. And really... he looks like me."

"Yeah. You look a lot like him, except for his amazing brown curly hair. I dreamed you would to inherit it but, alas! - Your hair is blond and very straight, like mine. It's very ordinary – nothing special. But his hair was very remarkable. He was also creative and talented boy."

My curiosity grew.

I'd never heard much about my father. My mom had told me earlier that my dad had gone away. That's it. And I wasn't particularly interest in this topic; the absence of a father had never bothered me.

Most children of the Soviet Union who were born after World War II didn't have fathers. Thirty million people were killed during the war and most of them were men. The men who survived slept around with dozens of women and had dozens of children everywhere. Mostly, they didn't take care of their children and few knew - or were interested in - the biological fathers of that generation. The mothers raised them alone, without any outside help. This was normal for the Russian demographic situation and was officially recognized – since the decimated population must be replenishment.

Besides, it was a subject for grown-ups, one they knew too well. Since I was only a child, it held little interest for me. I was more absorbed in my toys, games, and books and the people around me (friends, classmates and playmates), than about an abstract, absentee figure, which was all my father was to me.

I knew only that my mom and my Baba were always speaking French when there was news of my father. Clearly, they hoped I wouldn't understand, but why...Why were they insistent on hiding there something from me? I didn't know but I didn't care much.

Sometimes, I would play on the floor with my toys, and mom and Baba were sitting on the couch beside me and talking. I didn't pay any attention what they were talking about. However, I noticed right away when my mom would switch into hushed tones and lean toward Baba's ear, *"J'ai quelques nouvelles..."*

"Est-ce que elles sont de son pére?" Baba asked in French, as well.

"Oui," my mom nodded.

When this exchange would take place, I was immediately on guard. My ears picked up suddenly. Though I didn't know French at that time (I only began studying it in grade 6) but I understood absolutely everything. They continued to talk about my mom's and my dad's work, about some mutual friends – the people who knew both my parents, about some official procedures, some documents, some money, some lawsuits and other things which were completely beyond my sphere of interest. Somehow, I understood language but couldn't grasp the details or purpose - these subjects were so tedious that I didn't want to listen more and turned my ears back to my dolls and games.

But now, coming across my dad's childhood photo, I took a greater interest in the man. I was even amazed that my mom spoke freely about him in Russian to me.

"Could you tell me more about my dad?" I asked.

"Hmmm..." my mom thought a bit. She was visibly hesitant. "Well... okay...I can tell you...a little..."

I climbed on the couch and prepared to receive the story.

...This morning, as usual, little Dmitry was woken up by his grandma, Lydia, who petted his luxuriant hair. She was an old gray-haired woman, the Latvian mother of his father, Vladimir, and the only person who stayed at home and looked after him while both his parents were working. Grandma Lydia loved him dearly and always used pet names for him.

"Dima, Dimochka," she whispered fondly, "wake up time. A magician will come today. It's a magic day. You still have many things to do before the circus. You should have a breakfast; then practice the piano for a couple of hours..."

Dima stretched his arms and hugged his grandma. He was an affectionate child, very kind, warm and good.

"Please, Grandma, let me sleep a bit more," he begged, yawning. "I was having such an interesting dream."

"I know Dima your dreams are always interesting and adventurous, especially when it's time for breakfast. You would be happy to sleep for twenty-four hours. No, I love you too much to spoil you. You must follow a regime. Wake up! Otherwise I'll pour cold water on you."

Dima knew that his grandma wasn't joking. She was serious and strict and he must listen to her. However, he liked that. He felt glad to be guided by a cleaver, strong older woman. It might be that he inherited this quality from his father Vladimir – the readiness to be under a woman's thumb and to be guided by a woman-leader.

So, the charming boy readily jumped out of his bed and ran to their little washroom where, as he knew, the bowl and the jug of warm water, prepared by grandma, were already waiting for him.

Then followed a breakfast which consisting of boiled potatoes and beets with dark bread Dima hated. It had been his daily breakfast fare ever since he'd been weaned from mother's milk. There was nothing else to eat where they now lived – the Russian town of Tver, several hundred kilometers west of Moscow on the Volga River. It was not as fertile as South of Russia (like Rostov-on-Don), but in Central Russia, far poorer and less productive in agriculture-terms.

"Don't make faces," Grandma Lydia said in severe tone, taking in Dima's grimace as he viewed his unappetizing plate. "Today I have some treats for you!"

She poured boiled water into a glass and sprinkled in some dry tea leaves from a teaspoon.

"Tea?!" Dima exclaimed, not believing his own eyes. He was accustomed to always drinking only boiled water and, occasionally, some milk. So tea was indeed a special treat.

"Yes. Tea!" Grandma Lydia laughed victoriously. "And even more – sugar!"

Dramatically, she put a small package wrapped in dark-colored fabric on the table and knocked it. Then she solemnly unwrapped it, opening before Dima's eyes irregular lumps of gray sugar and said, "I dashed this morning to the flea market and back while you were sleeping and, you see, I was finally successful. We have sugar now!"

"Wow!" Dima excitedly stretched his hand to grab some lumps.

"Just one," grandma forestalled him. "And don't put it into the glass of tea, but lick it with your tongue so it will last you longer: one lick – one sip, another lick – another sip. Actually, this way it would be even tastier. You can enjoy it, Dimochka, after you finish your food - especially your beets."

"Uhu," Dima nodded agreement, already having filled his mouth. Tea! Sugar! These were such amazing things that for their sake he would agree to swallow the less tasty items.

Then he was eligible to enjoy his treats. He even didn't finish his precious lump of sugar, refusing to return it to his grandmother, and hiding it in his trousers pocket instead.

After breakfast was his piano practice time. While Grandmother Lydia washed the dishes in a big bowl right here, on the dining room table, because they didn't have a kitchen in their small house, Dima played the piano in the same room. He loved the piano and music, and he even loved what most children hate – exercises for his fingers. He was very hardworking and absolutely ready to repeat even a hundred times, one of the three-four notes configurations that might be difficult to execute, until it flowed smoothly, without a mistake.

Now, he had had music lessons for only two years, but in that time had become a very good student, playing as well as an older child in the fifth grade.

Grandma Lydia monitored her grandson's practice sessions seriously and silently, but her heart thrilled at his persistence. She would happily stop him and reprimand him sternly, if he floundered, but she found nothing to correct. He did play and train himself as a disciplined mature musician, so she felt proud of this amazing little boy. Meanwhile, she listened as she splashed soapy water and lent her own music with a clatter of crockery.

After she was finished with the dishes, Grandma Lydia walked to the next room and did her sewing on a machine there, listening to Dima's music through the open door.

A big Grandfather's clock struck twelve noon, as Dima finished his piano lesson, slid down from his stool and came to see her.

"I'm done, Grandma," he said, begging. "Don't you remember that it's circus time now? Would you please give me money to go now?"

"Okay, okay," she answered, cleaning the multitude of lose threads from the lap of her dress. "Come here, Dimochka, I have something else for you."

Grandma showed him a dark blue sailor's jacket with a big white striped collar and tie.

"Look at this," she uttered proudly. "I have finally finished sewing it for you. It's not bad at all, isn't it? So, you can put it right on and wear it outside to see the circus. You'd look good wearing it. You deserve a reward for all your hard work this morning. You're a good boy."

She kissed Dima's forehead, pullet the new jacket on him and turned him toward the mirror.

"Wow!" he smiled. "Thank you, Grandma."

The jacket was a good fit and looked festive. It was the ideal jacket to wear to the circus today and Dima felt content, especially fingering the sugar fragment in his pocket. He even decided to reposition the lump in the new jacket pocket and he did so furtively.

"Be careful of your new jacket," Grandma Lydia warned him, speaking to his back as he left.

The circus shouldn't be far away – right in the middle of the next side street – so Dima was allowed to walk alone. Actually, nobody was particularly concerned about kids' safety in Russia and they usually walked alone outside, since they knew their address and could return home by themselves, starting at the age of five, or even less. Grandma Lydia stayed at home to cook. She had no time for the circus. Dima's parents, Vladimir and Maria, would be home soon from Tver Pedagogical Institute where were both working on their Ph.D.s, and the dinner should be ready.

Dima walked to the ground alone and, seeing there a lot of children - his neighbors and friends - already seated or standing around on the grass, he approached. They were all waiting for the old magician with a big salt-and-pepper beard, dressed in an oriental costume to get his equipment ready.

The magician had a street organ, hanging on a belt over his shoulder. He had also huge rings, a huge ball, a parrot, a monkey and a little dog. The animals were sitting quietly on the grass; only the monkey was active, scratching the back of its head with a foot that looked like a hand. The kids were amused and laughing, and Dima joined them. He had never seen a live monkey before, only in books.

The magician was now ready and began the show. And what a show it was! The organ-grinder played music; the dog counted to ten, added and subtracted simple numbers by barking; the parrot balanced on a ball and jumped through the rings; then the dog and the monkey jumped, as well. Next, the magician juggled and performed conjuring tricks and the happy-faced children shrieked with delight and applauded energetically. Dima felt the greatest happiness he had known in life.

For a final, the dog, with the magician's hat in its mouth solicited the assembled crowd and everybody threw coins into the hat. Dima gladly offered from his little fist the coin his grandmother had given him. After that, everybody was allowed to come closer to the organ-grinder and make a wish. As they did, the parrot stationed on top of the organ would take from a can a little note with written predictions and hand one to each child, while the magician, with the monkey on his shoulder, kept the music going. The kids lined up for this last trick.

As Dima's turn came, he approached the magician and put his hand out to take the note from the parrot like everyone before him, but, suddenly the monkey hopped onto his shoulder, stuck its long and agile hand into Dima's jacket pocket and grabbed the sugar cube.

Maybe the scent of sugar was so strong that the monkey detected it. Maybe it could just see through the swelling in the pocket. Either way, Dima had no time to dwell on it. He squawked like crazy and clutched the little beast's arm - but it had been too fast for him. Already the sugar had gone into the monkey's yellow-toothed mouth and disappeared.

At the same time, the boy's shriek scared the animal, as well, and as it jerked, it ripped Dima's collar so wildly that his new jacket was undone and fell apart.

"My sugar! My jacket! Oh, my new jacket!" Dima howled, violently threw the monkey off him and ran home, sobbing loudly for all to hear.

Grandma Lydia heard his cries from far away and ran out on the porch to check what had happened.

"Oh, my goodness!" she exclaimed, seeing his torn jacket. "What happened? How come?"

"It's the monkey..." Dima stammered, crying. "This monkey... It grabbed my sugar and then tore my jacket! Wa-a-ah!" The tears began again.

Grandma Lydia hugged him, trying to comfort her grandson.

"Did it hurt you?" she asked anxiously. "It could be rabid and dangerous. Did it bite you?"

"No..."

"Did it scratch you?"

"No..." he said through his sniffles. "Wa-a-ah! It only stole my sugar..."

"I told you to leave it in the pack at home, didn't I?"

"Wa-a-ah! And it tore my jacket!"

"I told you be careful with it, didn't I?"

"I was careful, wa-a-ah!"

"Okay, I'll fix the jacket and sew it again. Stop crying, please."

Grandma Lydia changed him into a t-shirt and carried the dismembered jacket to her sewing machine in her bedroom. It a few days, it was fixed like new again. Dima's parents took him to the photo studio to take a picture of him wearing this jacket to smooth over his unpleasant experience with the monkey.

However, Grandma Lydia didn't forget about it and often grumbled as Dima went for a walk outside, "For this boy, monkeys are always tearing his new sailor jackets." Her words didn't offend Dima. They were just funny, but he always remembered them.

"This is the picture," my mom ended the story. "He forgot and left it in my album. Now your father, Dmitry Belov, is a university professor and delivers philosophy lectures to his students. Some of those attending his lectures told me he uses this experience from his childhood as an example. 'Never conclude anything on the basis of only one single case,' he says. 'Otherwise you'll sound like my Grandma Lydia with her postulate: *For this boy, monkeys are always tearing his new sailor jackets!* "

"I'll remember that!" I promised, seriously grasping the idea. "It's a strange story but a good example. My dad might be a good teacher. Now, I think he was probably a good little boy. No, I'll never conclude anything on the basis of only one case. Please, could you tell me more stories about Dima, Mom? I need more cases...to draw conclusions from..."

My mom coughed a bit, full of uncertainty.

"No," she said. "Not yet. Maybe in some more years. I'll continue them when you're older. Many years older!"

Chapter 6

THE DOLL

It was the last week of December and a few days before the New Year's Eve. My mom brought home a nearly frozen live fir tree and told me, "I guess you're big enough to know that Grandpa Frost doesn't bring children gifts - their parents do. So, this year I want to give you my favorite doll, Sasha, as your New Year present. I have had it since childhood, dreaming that one day I'd have a daughter and pass it onto her. Are you ready to play carefully with this special old doll?"

"Of course," I exploded with excitement.

"If you're ready," my mom said, "we have to open the basement."

"The basement? What's that?" it sounded strange to me because we used to live on the main floor of an old, big four-storey building and there weren't any basements at all. At least, I had never heard about one.

We called Baba from the kitchen where she was cooking dinner and chatting with the neighbor ladies and, together, all three of us moved aside my mom's writing-table. It was quite heavy, with two big sets of drawers on both sides. As we shifted it, we could make out a square cut in our old-fashioned hardwood floor. It seemed to be the lid of a hatch.

"Here is where we enter the basement."

"Wow!" My eyes widened. "Has it always been there? I never knew about it."

"No, it wasn't here when we moved into this suite, in 1929. My dad, as you know, was a construction engineer and he built it by himself to hide some important things and stuff that we seldom used, like New Year tree decorations. Our apartment lacked any closets or storage places, so this underground room was quite useful."

"But we've never opened it all these years!"

"Remember, you're only ten years old," my mom laughed. "We opened it quite often before you were born, especially during World War II, when Moscow was bombed. It was big enough for your Baba and me to hide in during the bombing."

"Really?" I said, because it all sounded very scary to me - almost unbelievable. That horrible time, I've only seen in the movies, was not actually so long ago. I felt that I could reach out and touch it.

"I never saw you take out even our New Year's decorations," I protested.

"Your Baba and I usually took them out while you were sleeping – in order to make a surprise for you," my mom explained. "Now you're big enough…"

"Well," I squatted down and fingered the outlines of the hatch lid. There was no pull handle. "How can we open it?" I questioned my mom.

"I'll show you." She pulled out one of the desk drawers and took out a chisel. Then she wedged it into the narrow space around the hatch door. As she levered it up, a part of the hardwood floor would rise enough for her to reach in with her hand and lift the entire cover easily. She then left it propped up against the table leg.

All I could see was a dark hole in the floor and three small rungs leading into it.

"Do you want go first?" my mom asked, but I shook my head 'No', making a wry face. There was a cool and stale air wafted from the opening, smelling like raw potatoes or beets. It gave me a yucky feeling.

"Okay," mom said. "I'll go down and pass up the things to you and you place them on the floor. I guess Sasha is buried quite deep. We need to empty the room to find her."

Feeling really uncomfortable, I watched as my mom climbed down the ladder and waited, half fearing she would disappear down there. But that was silly, of course. She landed on the dirty soiled floor and still her shoulders and head were stuck out, since the 'basement' wasn't deep at all.

"You see," my mom laughed. "There's nothing to be afraid of. It doesn't go down very deep. When Baba and I hid there, we had to lie down on the floor. It was a bit cold, so we put an old mattress down there. We also arranged shelves around the sides for storage. They have old things on them."

First of all, she took out the boxes with our New Year's tree decorations – they were on the top shelves.

After that, my mom bowed down to retrieve and pass me things wrapped in dusty cloth. They were very old, even antique: a broken Erica typewriter with Latin letters; an old-fashioned box camera that used glass plates to take pictures (also broken); three unused huge Orthodox icons framed in polished wood and plated in tarnished silver (an odd heirloom as none of us was religious); a leather box with silver knives, forks and spoons – half of the set missing and the remaining pieces tarnished and unused, as well. Then, followed stacks of old French books in red leather covers with gold embossed titles. Next, many old German books printed in gothic type. Lastly, bunches of old notebooks, and so on.

I had already created quite a mess trying to arrange everything on our floor, by searching for free spots.

"What's that? And that? And that?" I barely had time to ask, as the next thing appeared. My mom briefly explained them to me and told me why they were there.

She also passed up to me a small wooden box with some golden Tsar coins – what was left from Victor Demin's sale of my Great-grandpa, Vladimir Diachan's, award from the Tsar. They hadn't all been used at the flea market to purchase food. A few were kept as a memory. My mom opened the box for me and I timidly touched them with my index finger, trembling with excitement. They were really shiny and had the Tsar's profile on each of them. And, most importantly, they were REAL!

It gave proof to the family stories she had been telling me for years. Of course, I always believed her, but only on a mental level. Now, with physical evidence before me, I could believe her in my heart and soul, as well. I could see in front of me, touch even, the things which had once seemed almost unbelievable.

Finally, wrapped in old towels, the doll Sasha was located on the very bottom of one of the shelves. I witnessed my mother unwrapping her and my mouth gaped in surprise. Sasha's face was delicately made from fine porcelain and had beautiful, blinking heavy-lashed blue eyes. They were open wide when she was upright, but would close as she was laid down. I had never seen a doll anything like this in my whole life. All my dolls – and those of my friends - had plastic heads and only painted-on eyes.

Her hair was also a living miracle – natural blonde and soft and not artificial at all.

"Sasha is actually wearing MY hair," my mom explained, when I gave her a questioning look. "I was very blonde as a child. Now, as you can see, I'm much darker. But this is my real hair which was made into a wig to repair Sasha after... a horrible accident. I sacrificed my braid and let them cut it off to make Sasha beautiful again."

"I see," I whispered, looking attentively at Sasha's face. "She also has some little scratches on her cheeks...and chin...and forehead. What happened to her? Did you drop her?"

"No, I didn't," mom's voice quavered, "but she was smashed. I'll never forget it."

"Tell me the story please," I begged, kissing Sasha's cold lifeless rouged cheeks and handling her, hoping that she would warm up and come back to life.

...A little Liudmila, (nicknamed Lala) was already sleeping as her father, Victor, brought in a blue fir tree from flea market. It was wrapped in rough burlap.

"I hope nobody saw you," his wife, Sonya, asked, worriedly. Her anxiety was high when they did things that were supposed to be prohibited. "Are you sure?"

"I believe so. The streets are quiet and empty," Victor reassured her as she softly kissed his cheek.

"I think it would be better if we let her decorate it herself, wouldn't it?"

"If she is able," Victor took a deep breath, looking over at sleepy Lala. "It depends on how she is feeling. Does she still have a fever?"

"No, fortunately. Now she is okay," Sonya shook her head. "I hope she will continue to get better in the next few weeks. Look what I've got, Vitya."

She excitedly pointed at the table full of cardboard boxes. "Anya brought her Christmas decorations and candles to us. There are so many things...Really I feel like a child again – so happy! For so many years we didn't have a chance to have a Christmas tree! And for Lala..." she lowered her voice to a whisper, glancing furtively at her sleeping child, "the lady from the French shop brought this doll, finally. It's quite expensive but... look at this..."

Sonya opened a box painted with pink flowers. Inside, Victor could see a special porcelain doll with closed eyes, long eyelashes, pink cheeks and soft dark brown ringlets, lying on a pink silk pillow and covered with a similar coverlet. The doll was beautiful and refined and even the box smelled of French perfume.

"Wow!" Victor said with satisfaction. "It's truly amazing! I've never seen a doll like this. Even when I was a child...Our family was big and not so rich – mom and dad were the village school teachers... My sisters never had such a doll. Good job, my darling! I'm very glad that you found this shop and ordered it. Poor Lala really deserves such a nice Christmas present."

"Yes, she does," Sonya nodded sadly. The thoughts of her sick daughter's two and a half years in bed made her feel especially guilty.

"Okay, okay," Victor hugged her, tenderly patting her shoulders to comfort her. "Forget it! You're a great mother and you saved her life by your excellent care. That's the truth! I'm sure she'll be much better by Christmas."

Lala's health was a major concern for their family.

One day back in 1913, when they lived in Warsaw before the World War I, Sonya and Anya went for a walk and noticed a poster advertising a psychic reader.

"I want to know my future," Sonya said. She hoped, subconsciously, that there might be a new development with Alexander Dedulin, her first love. Maybe something would happened...or...Who knows?

"Oh, I don't want to go," Anya said dismissively. "I really don't care about such things. Maybe I'll die tomorrow! I think it's better not to know! And, besides, those future-tellers are all cheats and thieves."

"Okay, I'll go alone," Sonya suggested and bravely entered a tiny dark shop, leaving Anya outside to wait for her and to window-shop in the neighborhood.

The psychic was a middle-aged woman with a bright red hair and piercing dark eyes. She was most likely a Gypsy. Over her shoulders was draped a traditional floral Russian wool scarf – patterned with bold red roses and green leaves on a black background. Her eyes searched Sonya attentively and she fixed her price. Surprisingly, it was quite low. Sonya fished some coins out of her purse and laid them on the draped table, where she found a seat right across from the psychic.

The woman took her hand and studied the lines for quite a long time.

"Well," she said thoughtfully, "you'll be happily married, not to the man you're thinking of. At the age of forty-eight you'll become a widow. Then you'll live a long life – until around 90. In your later years, you'll, somehow be related to music. Your house numbers will always be 7's. You'll have only one child – a daughter. Take care of her. In early childhood she will be very sick, and could possibly die. That's all."

In truth, we are now living at house number 7, Sonya thought. How does she know? Unbelievable!

Sonya rose and went to join her sister out in the sunlight. The events that were foretold for her she found very convincing, especially with the coincidence of the number 7.

"What did she tell you?" now Anya was curious to learn. "What about Alex?"

"Nothing," Sonya shook her head. "I'll meet another guy."

"I could have told you that myself," Anya laughed. "And I would've done it for free."

Later, when they moved to Rostov-on-Don, their building number on Konkrinskaya Street where they resided with their father was 32, but the apartment number was, again, 7. As the girls saw it, they laughed, remembering the psychic, but soon Sonya almost forgot the other predictions. There were too many everyday happenings and troubles surrounding them; there were already plenty of things for her to worry about.

Sonya married and then Lala was born. Once again Sonya realized that she had a daughter, as the woman had foreseen. But Victor laughed at her, noting that predicting a child's sex was not so difficult since there was a 50/50 chance it would be a girl. About the child's health he was more concerned and ordered a special doctors' examination to certify that baby Lala was absolutely strong and healthy.

For the next few years these anxieties faded into the background, because the family was caught up in many other concerns. Anya's husband, Nicolay Obolensky, was executed by the Bolsheviks and she fell into a deep depression. Then a large epidemic of typhoid fever rolled over Southern Russia, carrying thousands of lives away – Vladimir Diachan and two of Anya's older children were among them. Anya was left alone with only her younger daughter, Galya, born one year before Lala.

Following her father's death, Sonya learned from Barbara Torchinsky the address of the couple Young von Altenburg – Ekaterina and Peter – now living in Kiev. She decided to make contact with her estranged and unknown mother. She had always dreamed about it but didn't want to do it while her father was alive for fear of hurting his feelings.

Anya sharply refused to have any contacts with Ekaterina – she couldn't forgive her mother for deserting her at the age of four. She still had vivid memories of the trauma she had experienced as a little child losing her mother.

Sonya wrote the letter herself and Ekaterina answered. A close relationship didn't develop, but the two women exchanged birthday and holiday cards. Sonya enjoyed getting to know her mom at last and was proud that Ekaterina was stubborn enough to reach her goal and became a successful artist. She was glad to know that her mother was happy with the old baron, Peter, who worked as a Soviet accountant, before retiring.

Her whole life, Sonya was used to only having a father. But now, to discover her mother, as well, even though she lived far away, was an amazing feeling.

Their life started to improve, step-by-step. Anya remarried, this time to a musician. Victor had a good position as an engineer of a big construction site – they were building a huge tractor plant named after the river beside which the city stood – Don. His salary was good enough to buy a small house on a quiet street – two rooms with a kitchen and a full bathroom. There was also a little garden outside, for Lala to play and walk in. When Sonya first arrived at the new residence, she shuddered. The number of the house was 7.

"Vitya, why did you buy it?!" she exclaimed in horror. "Where were your eyes? Didn't you see the number?"

"Come on," and once again he laughed at her superstitious mind. "The house is perfect for us; the neighborhood is quiet, clean and respectful, and the price is reasonable. Don't be silly, please, my darling. Just watch Lala, that's your job."

Sonya did. She really watched. Really cared. Actually, she cared too much. She had a family doctor who checked on Lala every month, just in case.

One summer day, when Lala was about two, they were picking strawberries in their garden and ate a few of them unwashed. As a result, Lala had a little diarrhea, nothing special, just a common child's ailment which would pass the next day.

But Sonya felt feverish about it.

Oh, my goodness! she thought. The horrible prediction might be coming true. My daughter's sick and she could die! I must get the doctor immediately!

Leaving Lala at home with Anya, she ran to see the doctor and to get some medication.

She was sure that their doctor didn't need to see Lala in person. He knew her perfectly. However, her doctor's office was closed and there was a notice on the door that he left for vacation and would be back in a week.

No, we can't wait a week! Sonya panicked. That's too long. It must be fate! Oh, no!

She dashed around the city, like a crazy woman, looking for another doctor; finally, she found one and, nearly hysterical, burst into his office.

"My girl is dying! Diarrhea! Medication!" she shouted through her sobs, all trembling.

Without giving it much thought, the doctor prescribed something to get rid of this woman faster. She didn't even ask how old the child was. Somehow, he imagined the 'girl' was a teenager, and had prescribed an adult dose.

With her own hands, Sonya gave the medication to her little healthy daughter. The effects were disastrous – Lala's bowels were singed. For a week she survived unconscious, with bloody diarrhea; then their family doctor returned and helped a little. Lala's life was saved, but she remained an invalid for many more years. From time to time there were reoccurring attacks of fever and bloody diarrhea. The girl was condemned to a diet of only rice water and dark chocolate for the next ten years.

Feelings of guilt hung over Sonya after that, even though Victor tried his best to soften her self-accusation by stressing what a good mother she was and what excellent care she provided for Lala. He was a really tactful man and loving husband.

However, he was also a loving father and tried to give his sickly daughter special treats. This year, he decided to decorate a Christmas tree, for her to feel happier and more festive.

Before the 1917 Revolution, Russia used to celebrate the Orthodox Christmas on January 7. In those days, New Year's Day had little special meaning. It was a minor holiday, of course, but not as important as Christmas. Even less religious people always enjoyed the Christmas parties, decorated trees and presents. But for children it was extra special - a magic time of dreams coming true. There was something sacred in the joy of the celebrations. They were the victories of more than a 200-year-old Russian tradition, begun by Tsar Peter the First when he borrowed these festivities from the German culture he adored.

But, after the revolution, all the churches were closed, the priests killed by Bolsheviks and the Christmas celebrations prohibited as religious. So, now there must be no trees, no decorations, no presents... Yet, a loved tradition doesn't die so quickly, even if you are trying to kill it. It died slowly. Some people still continued to decorate their trees, especially for children, even knowing that it was illegal and the authorities could cause troubles.

The next morning, Lala was woken up by an amazing fir fragrance reaching her nostrils.

"Oh," she said, sitting on her bed and sniffing the air in her room. "Mom, where's this smell coming from? Is it really a tree? The

79

Christmas tree you told me about? Wow! But I can see it's fresh from the forest."

"We'll decorate it together," Sonya told her daughter. "Decorating is the best job for children to have at Christmas time. It's so much fun!"

"I'm sure it is," Lala beamed with joy and anticipation. She had awakened without a fever, though she was still pale and a bit chilled this morning. Despite that, she was eager to start the day which promised the excitement of new experiences. She noticed the table was piled high with things. "What are in all the boxes Mom?"

"Tree decorations. Auntie Anya gave them to us. She will be coming over today with Galya and we will have a party decorating the tree together. You and your cousin can do it."

On that day the tree was decorated; Lala and Galya played together; even permitted to go outside in the cold to make snow angels in the yard and then built a snowman. It was a happy time. Usually, in Southern Russia there was little winter snow and it would melt right away. If there was a heavier snow, it might stick for only a couple of months. So, it was a special treat for Rostov-on-Don children to play in the snow, and Sonya wanted her daughter to have the pleasure, even though she wasn't completely healthy.

While the kids played outside, Sonya and Anya started to prepare some food for next day's Christmas dinner. About twenty people had been invited – Anya and Barbara Torchynsky and their whole families, and two of Victor's brothers with their wives and kids, as well. It would be quite a job to cook such dinner, but Sonya still felt happy and excited – it was the first time their family could afford such a holiday since moving from Warsaw.

In the evening, when Victor returned home from work, they ate all together, beside the shining, decorated tree which was lit up by the little multicolored bulbs resting on almost every branch.

"Oh, we forgot to close the curtains," Sonya suddenly remembered at the end of the supper. "Oh, gosh! Someone may have seen Christmas lights from outside!"

"Don't worry," Victor said, "our street is too small and there're seldom pedestrians on it. Besides, we have so many trees in our garden that the windows are hard to see from the sidewalk. But, anyway, I can close the curtains now, if you want."

"You better do it, Vitya. There might just be some *militia* (police) patrols, walking around the city to check for Christmas celebrations," Anya guessed, pulling up a scarf on her 5-year-old daughter's head. "Are you ready, little Snow Girl?"

"Uhu," Galya nodded.

They all kissed each other, what Sonya called jokingly 'a kissing ceremony' and then Anya left for her home with her daughter.

After Lala was put to bed, dreaming of Santa's visit that very night, her parents pulled out the box with the doll from its temporary hiding place under their bed and placed it under the Christmas tree among the other presents. Everything was ready for tomorrow's celebration.

Anya and Varya would arrive before the others to help me to cook and set the table, Sonya thought sleepily, hugging her husband. Christmas! Finally! I can't believe how happy I am.

In the middle of the night an abrupt knock at the outer door awakened Sonya and Victor.

"Who could that be?" Sonya whispered, sitting up in bed, only half-awake.

"It might be *them*," Victor guessed in a hushed voice and stood up hastily.

"Maybe it's just our neighbors...something has happened... a fire..."

"I don't think so. For one, they are pounding on our door," he said. The loud bangs at the door continued.

"Should we open then?" Sonya asked, rising, as well, and wrapping herself in a thick flannelette robe.

"We better. Otherwise they'll break the door down. Just wait a second - I'll put the picture up."

Victor stepped toward their wardrobe, and from behind it pulled out a large framed portrait of Stalin and proceeded to hang it on a nail especially prepared for that purpose.

It was obligatory for each family to have a portrait of Stalin; otherwise people could be accused of being an 'enemy of the people'. They could be arrested or even executed, depending on the situation. Of course, the Demins family had had this picture for several years already, just in case. They always kept it behind the wardrobe, out of sight, in order not to look at the ugly, pock-marked mug with a mustache. They only hung it up if strangers were coming to visit. You never knew – each stranger could be a secret police informer. This possibility was always present.

Obviously, now was a time for the picture!

Only after hanging it up did Victor go to open the door. His intuition had been right; there stood a night patrol – one militiaman and two secret police agents (well-known later as the KGB, but at the end of 1920s called the GPU – Government Political Department).

As Victor opened the door, they forced their way in and rushed to search the house.

"Turn the lights on!" they shouted. "Christmas tree! We got you! What are you doing with this? It is not for a proletarian holiday! You must be a White Army officer? Or a bourgeois family?"

"No. I'm a Red engineer from the Soviet plant," Victor objected.

"So, why would you put up this tree?"

"It's only for our dear sick child!" Sonya interjected.

"You mustn't bring non-Soviet influences into your home! This tree should be removed."

Lala had been sleeping soundly, but now she was startled awake by the shouting. She blinked and looked around, not comprehending what was going on.

"Mommy!" she cried. "Mommy, I'm scared. Who're those men? Is one of them Santa?"

"Look!" one of the agents shouted. "Look what's your child talking about! Santa! It's insane, backwards! Such ignorance! Holdovers from the dark Tsarist past! There is no Santa little girl!"

"Santa promised to bring me a present!" Lala whined and climbed out of her bed. Her parents stood motionless, knowing that the most important thing was not to object to anything these power officials did or said. But, of course, Lala lacked such sophisticated political survival skills. Clad in her pajamas and barefoot, she ran to Sonya and threw her arms around her mother's legs, as she cast a wary eye at the three big intruders.

"We have been assigned to root out the survivals of capitalism from people's minds," another agent announced. "You have a portrait of Comrade Stalin. That's good. But this tree should be removed. Take it, Ivanov."

"Yes, Comrade."

With one strong hand, the militiaman grabbed the tree trunk and dragged it toward to outer door.

"My tree!" Lala shrieked, dashed to the man and yanked on the flap of his military overcoat. He pushed her away and continued pulling the tree out of the house. "My Christmas tree!!!"

Victor stepped over to Lala, and tried to restrain her, but she wriggled out of his grasp, leapt up to the man and, with all her might, bit his free hand with her baby teeth.

All this happened so suddenly, that the militiaman howled and dropped the tree. The shiny glass balls fell, smashing on the hardwood floor like mini-explosions. He angrily jerked his wrist free and forcefully shoved the child. She crumpled on the floor, howling and screaming, the hands over her bloody lips revealed that her two front teeth had been knocked out.

"Fucking bastard! Little bitch!" the man shouted, and began stomping the controversial tree, its fragile decorations and the presents with his heavy, muddy military boots. A frenzied rampage of destruction began as the two agents, swearing freely, joined him in his madness.

Protectively, Sonya swept up the sobbing Lala and swiftly carried her to the other room. Victor remained standing in paralyzed shock, awaiting his doom.

"You're arrested!" one of the agents shouted at him and grabbed him under his arm. Another seized his free arm.

"Hey, you bitch," they shouted toward the door, behind which Sonya was doing her best to soothe Lala on her lap. "We're arresting your man. We'll find out who you are and how you're educating your kids."

They walked out, pulling Victor with them.

To hold herself in check, Sonya needed immense willpower. The whole night was devoted to comforting Lala, trying to suppress her fear and anguish, and convincing her that her teeth would, indeed, grow in again. Finally, the little tigress dropped off to a merciful rest.

The situation seemed unbearable. Sonya couldn't simply sit and cry about her husband; she needed to do something to occupy herself. Crying soundlessly, she picked up the smashed pieces of her hopes for a beautiful happy Christmas that year. It was anything but that now.

Holding on to the psychic's prediction, she believed that Victor would return home. She knew that she would not be a widow until she was forty-eight, and she was only thirty-four now.

With shaking hands, Sonya carted the mangled tree and broken things away to a garbage bin, swept and washed the floor and checked on the presents, to see if anything had survived the onslaught.

The doll was in really bad condition; its porcelain face was smashed to pieces, its eyes had lost their ability to open and close and the once lovely curly brown hair had been torn away. The locks had fallen out of the box and been entwined in the fir branches, and had been discarded into the garbage bin already. Sonya went in search of it, but when she identified it, saw that it was impossible to restore.

For days, a dark ominous shadow hung over the once-happy home and family.

Everyday, for the next month, Sonya walked to the GPU offices and begged for information of her husband's whereabouts. She was always told the same thing: there was no news. Still, she figured that was a better response than to be told he was given 10 years *without the rights of correspondence,* which was a code for the fact that he had been executed.

At night, she tenderly put Lala to bed, hugged her and in hushed whispers, talked with her about Victor and her hopes for his early return. To console her little daughter, Sonya told her about an experienced handyman whom she found with the help of the lady from the French shop. The man had promised to fix the special Christmas doll made bald by patrolmen. Sonya cut Lala's long hair which a hairdresser would fashion into a new wig. Lala decided to name her doll 'Sasha'.

"In a few days, your Sasha will be fixed up and return home - like daddy will soon," she said, knowing full well that Sasha would, but that Victor would only if the fates decided so.

Anticipating the return of the GPU officials and the possibility that she, too, might be seized, Sonya faithfully displayed the picture of Stalin every night.

"Who is that man?" Lala inquired.

"He's the father of the Soviet people, our beloved father, Comrade Stalin."

"No," Lala protested, "my beloved father is my daddy."

"I know that. And you know that, but you shouldn't bite and fight with the Bolsheviks if they come again. It was the wrong thing to do and just made things worse. That might be why they arrested daddy. You must pretend that Comrade Stalin is your beloved father, like you're pretending that you're a princess and Galya is *BabaYaga* (Russian witch) in your fairy tales. Or like you're pretending you are both pirates on a ship. Please pretend... just for now. Please, Lala, remember that. It's very important for all of us to stay together and be okay."

"Mommy, you told me not to lie, didn't you?"

"I did, sweetheart. Of course, I did. But this is not a lie. It's only a simple game. The whole country is playing a stupid game now. All of the people are pretending that they love Bolsheviks and their regime. It's a rule of the game. If you want to be safe with mommy and daddy, and all together, you just pretend...pretend and play that Stalin's your beloved father..."

Sonya felt uncomfortable, even horrible, to have to teach her child to be two-faced. But what choice did she have, really? By being open and sincere, Lala had already put the family at risk. Sonya

84

wept over what she was forced to do and hated herself for it. She was filled with remorse for violating her own and her daughter's precious souls.

Damn animals! What're they doing to all of us, anyway! she thought in despair.

But Sonya's lessons weren't in vain. The next time they visited the GPU-department, Lala solemnly announced to the guard by the door and to the officer questioning Sonya, "Comrade Stalin is our beloved father!"

"Good girl," the soldier said and petted her head.

"I think your husband will be home soon," the officer commented. "He was not charged with any crime, except putting up a Christmas tree. But he's already admitted his mistake."

"Thank you, sweetie," Sonya whispered in Lala's ear, kissing her.

Two days later, Victor came home. Sonya even recoiled in horror, not recognizing him at first. He had gained about sixty pounds of weight and become bald. His blonde hair completely disappeared from the top of his head.

"Oh, my gosh!" Sonya whispered, terrified. "What happened? Did they feed you so well that you have gained weight?"

Victor smirked and had no answer; he seemed to be in a zombie-state. Wearily, he showered and lay down on his bed, burying his face in the pillow. And then the tears came.

Sonya lay down beside him, embracing her husband's wasted figure and stroking his newly bald head and well-padded shoulders.

If he could only relax and release the tension of his trauma! she thought.

Before long, Lala entered the room, carrying her newly restored doll, Sasha. She joined her parents on the bed and curled up beside her father. Putting the doll in front of him she said, petting him in imitation of her mother, "Look, Daddy, Sasha is hurt, too, but she's not crying. And look I lost some teeth," she opened her mouth wide for him to see. "So, you see, I was hurt, too, but I'm not crying. Please, Daddy, everything will be fixed. That's right, isn't it Mommy?" She planted a reassuring kiss on Victor's bald pate and affectionately snuggled into his arms. "Daddy, I know why you're crying. It's because you lost your hair, isn't it? Sasha lost her hair, too. If you want, Daddy, we can make a nice wig for you, like we did for Sasha. If the rest of my hair isn't enough for your big head, then Mommy can give some hair, too. Right, Mom? So, everything's okay!"

These innocent and sympathetic words spoken earnestly in a sweet child's voice touched Victor at the deepest aching level, tearing his heart apart. What could she know of the torment he had just been through and why should she have to live in a world of cruelty and injustice? Out of his grief he glanced at the far-from-perfect doll and managed to grin ironically, "Well, Lala, Sasha and I both have disabilities now."

"But Mom and I love you both, anyway. Just the way you are," Lala proclaimed and wrapped her loving arms around his neck.

Only after a few more months did Victor reveal to Sonya what really happened to him in prison.

"They tortured me with an electrical current," he explained, finally. "They guessed that I might be a White Army officer, who hadn't been registered or executed with the others, for some reason. I didn't admit to anything, or they would've killed me on the spot. I endured, but the prison doctor said that the electrical current had destroyed my thyroid gland and it caused me to gain weight and loose my hair quickly. Now, nothing can be changed. I will look like this for the rest of my life."

"It doesn't really matter, Vitya, how you look," Sonya said lovingly. "The most important thing is that you're alive and we're together."

Some time passed quietly, and it seemed to the Demin family that the things were going to improve. Victor returned to his job. However, sometimes Sonya caught him lying awake at nights. He only lay motionless on their bed, hugging her and staring up at the ceiling, thinking. He didn't want to say anything to alarm her, but inwardly he experienced a deep dark fear, as sticky as the glue enveloping his entire being.

The situation in the country worsened every day. Victor purposely hid the newspapers from Sonya that published the new Bolshevik decrees: in the future spouses would be arrested together, without exception, and not only adults, but children of any age were also subject of arrest. Children over 10 could be tortured to confess in front of their parents and those over 12 years of age could be executed.

Lala was just turning six, and would soon fall under these instructions, he thought, feeling feverish. But she is so sick and weak that she won't survive. I have to act now. Maybe divorce is the only way I can save my family?

He couldn't imagine really divorcing Sonya, but there might not be any alternative if he wanted to save his beloved girls. He mulled this over again and again to himself, still not daring to broach the subject with his wife.

About a year later, the Rostov-on-Don tractor plant Don received the Directive from the Central GPU-office in Moscow to arrest 130 'English and American spies' and 'enemies of the people' among its employees. The director of the plant was in horror and despair. He didn't know whom to assign for torture and death in Siberian concentration camps. The whole staff at the plant was paralyzed with fear over what would happen next – would the director follow the new Directive, or would he go to the torture rack himself. It was common for the decent people of Russia to commit suicide in an impossible dilemma. But the director understood that his integrity alone wouldn't save his workers and friends. If he sacrificed himself for them, anyway, the new director, appointed after him, would follow the Directive.

Psychologically, the tension was insufferable. Of course, the Bolsheviks decided to begin with the more-educated engineers first.

One day, Victor came home after work looking sullen.

"Engineer Petrov has been arrested," he mumbled.

"It's starting again?" Sonya glanced at him worriedly.

"It's never really stopped; only now it's much worse."

The next day... "Engineer Katz has been taken."

Then, "Engineer Saakian is seized."

"Engineer Kondratenko..."

"Fedorov..."

"Palkin..."

"Emerashvili..."

Finally, in a couple of the weeks, Victor said seriously, "It's time, Sonya. There are only the two engineers left at the plant – Mishin and I. I have the feeling that my turn is next. They must leave at least one real engineer at the plant; otherwise, it will stop working. So, if I run away, Mishin could be saved."

"Run?" Sonya stared at him in amazement. "Where to, Vitya?"

"Wherever! Somewhere I can get lost! In Moscow! There is a population of six million. There it might be possible to disappear. We don't know anybody there and nobody knows us. No-one has any idea of your family history, nor of my years in the White Army. Let's think out the scenario."

They did talk all night and in the morning, instead of going to work, Victor grabbed a bag with some personal belongings and took the train to Moscow.

A few hours after he left, the GPU agent from the Don plant knocked on door #7.

"Where is your husband? Why didn't he come to work today?"

"I don't know," Sonya sobbed pitifully, utilizing all her theatrical skills. "He's such a villain! He had a mistress! Did you know that? He took a lover and they ran away somewhere together. He left me alone, with our child! OUR child! Do you hear me? Tell me, how am I supposed to live now? Oh, poor me! I have to apply for alimony, but he probably won't pay anything! I need help to live. You must help me. Find Victor and that woman so I can divorce him and get my money!"

Sonya wept convincingly for the agent and he fell for the ruse about Victor's love affair. Yet, at that critical moment Lala appeared from nowhere, with Sasha cradled in her arms.

"Where is your father, girl?" the agent queried, to check the mother's story.

Sonya's heart stopped – she hadn't prepared Lala. In fact, the child knew nothing about her father leaving.

Oh, God, save us! she silently prayed, though she wasn't at all religious.

"My father is there," Lala answered, pointing to her parents' bedroom. The agent walked abruptly to the next room. The girl ran showing him the way.

"Here!" she exclaimed excitedly, directing his attention to the picture on the wall. "Comrade Stalin is my beloved father!"

"Well," the agent smiled broadly and patted her head. "That's a good girl!"

Then he left quietly.

A couple of weeks later, Sonya got the expected telegram from Moscow, "I am happy with Natasha. Bye forever. Victor."

This, their pre-arranged signal, meant that Victor had found a new job and a place for them to live. As planned, Sonya sold the Rostov home and furniture as soon as possible, packed some things into her huge suitcase from Murex & Mary-Lisa; then, with Lala, carrying her notebooks and pencils in a little backpack and pressing the doll Sasha to her chest, Sonya took the next train to Moscow. It was accomplished quickly and quietly, without a word to anybody, even to Anya and Varya, about where she was going.

While in transit, Sonya wired Victor her reply, "Go to hell with your Natasha tomorrow. Sonya." - for him to know when to meet her train from Rostov-on-Don. So the family was reunited in Moscow at the end of the year 1929.

In January 1930, a new Communist policy was put in place requiring everyone to register their place of residence with the militia.

In Russian this registration was named *propiska*. Throughout the whole Soviet Union, each person was restricted to this address and no changes were possible. National passports were issued as well, each carrying a stamp indicating one's registered location. Of course, these measures were used by the officials to find and pick up anyone they wanted to interrogate or arrest. Living without such a *propiska* became a criminal offence.

Now the whole terrorized country was turned into a kind of prison, fixing people in their homes and providing an address for every person.

This was especially true of Moscow, the bustling capital. It was nominated as a 'closed city' and *propiska* access was limited to those with GPU authorization. If Victor and Sonya had stayed in Rostov-on-Don a bit longer, they would not have had a chance to relocate in Moscow. Luckily, they had just arrived in time.

"Okay, Vitya. Will we be living in apartment number 7, again?" Sonya asked Victor her very first question, clasping her clever husband at the Kursky station in Moscow, as they exited the train.

"No," Victor laughed, "apartment is number 1..."

"But the building was – and now still is - number 7!" I shouted excitedly. "Mom! Was it really this very suite?! The one you and Baba have been in ever since?"

"Yes," my mom nodded, smiling. "Actually, you know, another important thing happened that very year -1930 – as well. Lenin's wife, Nadezhda Krupskaya, who survived her husband for many years, insisted on one more new law – this time, fortunately, a happy one. Traditional Christmas things, like a decorated tree, parties and presents from Santa, were allowed again, only moved to New Years day. They just changed the names from 'Christmas tree' to 'New Year's tree' (*Novogodnyaya jolka* in Russian) and from 'Santa Claus' to 'Grandpa Frost' (*Ded Moroz*), and gave him a granddaughter, as well, 'Snow Maiden' (*Snegurochka)*. This way the Communists were happy because it was not religious, but only a sweet fairytale family and children's winter holiday and the people were happy to have such a celebration back. And that's what we still have to this day."

"And we have Sasha with us, which is my New Year gift, today," I concluded, kissing the doll and putting it on the couch. "Thank you, Mom. So, let's clean up the mess, close the basement and decorate the tree. It's not frozen anymore and I can smell the fresh fir needles like in the forest. Hurray!"

Chapter 7

THE YOUNG MAN WITH GLASSES

On my birthday, I was awakened early by the smell of roses. When I turned on my side, I saw a vase with a large bouquet of soft pink roses sitting on the chair right in front of my nose. A thick envelope rested beside it.

"Mom! Thank you!" I shouted. I knew that it was present from her – my Baba Sonya usually gave me her presents later, after breakfast. Since Baba was a survivor of three wars (WW I -1914-1917, Civil War 1918-1922 and WW II -1941-1945) as well as three revolutions (1905, 1917-February and 1917-October) her priority was that the meal should come before anything else in life.

"You're welcome," my mom answered, appearing from the next room. "Good morning, my birthday girl!" She sat beside me, hugged and kissed me, sharing the usual birthday greetings. "You have very special present today," she added, pointing to the envelope. "Can you guess what's there?"

"I don't know," I shrugged. "It looks too fat for a card or money. No idea."

"Open it!" my mom urged impatiently and gave me a wink. "Go ahead!"

I did. "Wow!" It was money but a bigger wad than I had ever seen in my life. "Gosh! So much! Where did you get it, Mom? Is it your salary for the last five years? Or did you rob a bank?"

"No," my mom laughed. "It's yours. This is your last royalty – a quarter of the payment your father got for publishing his eleventh scientific book. Now you're eighteen and his payments are finished. But I think we should buy a country house with this. Don't you think it's a good idea?"

"A country house? Our very own dacha?"

"Yes, a dacha to spend the whole summer in the country and to breathe in fresh air. Here, in Moscow, it's barely possible to survive because of the pollution. It's still tolerable in winter, somehow, but in summer, especially when it's hot, I feel like I'm dying. I'm tired of looking for dachas to rent each summer and having difficulties with nasty owners. It's better if we have our own. It would be your present today."

"A present from my dad, you mean," I replied.

"No, a present from the state. Your dad always tried to avoid paying child support from his royalties, but the officials usually caught up with him and sent the money to you...actually, to us."

"Did he? Hmmm..." I didn't know that. "Why didn't you tell me about this before?"

"You weren't old enough to understand."

Mom's answer offended me a little. Yet, I wasn't greedy about money and didn't have any interest in the matter, so I wasn't very hurt by the news.

"Okay," I agreed, "let's buy a dacha. Are you sure this is enough money?"

"Yes. The Union of Composers gave vacant lots to its members – that's us. There will be an entire street of composers' houses in the forest, fifty kilometers out of Moscow. This money is enough for a new building. We'll buy materials and hire construction workers. The rest of the money is for you to have some fun with your friends."

I nodded, "Sounds all right." Then I asked the question which interested me much more than money. "Is it true that my dad authored eleven books?"

"Yes. He's a very productive and hardworking man. He's also career minded. At forty-three he's already a professor and corresponding member of the Russian Academy of Science. There's only one step left for him to reach Academician level - the highest position in science in the Soviet Union."

"If he's such a remarkable person, why did you divorce him?" I asked not quite understanding.

My mom shook her head sadly.

"I didn't, actually. He just left me when you were six weeks old."

"Why? That would be mean and make him a bad person. And I've never seen him at all. Why? ...Usually, children from divorced families meet the fathers..." I added, noticing my mom kept silent in her uncertainty. "You told me one story about his childhood – about the little boy and the monkey, then another story about his parents and the rug. I honestly need 'more cases to summarize' about him. I remember that you told me - not to judge something or someone on the basis of one single case, like he taught his students. However, that was ten years ago already and I haven't heard any more since then. I still don't know anything exactly. I'm already of age, Mom, and I want to know more about my dad. Maybe I would like to see him."

"Well," my mom hugged me, "you weren't big enough to hear about some stories before. Now, as you're eighteen, I can finally tell you... Plus, I wasn't sure that you would be happy about what I have to say."

She stood up, approached the bookcase and took an album from the bottom shelf.

"I know," I outstripped her, "I already saw his childhood picture in the sailor's jacket..."

"But I want to show you something else," my mom opened the well-known page, lifted the corner of the picture of the boy and drew out from behind it another picture, a much smaller one.

"Here he is, at the age of twenty-three, when I met him."

"Was this picture always sitting there, behind? I didn't notice it!" I exclaimed, taking the old black-white photo from her hand and studying it attentively.

There was a tall young man, slender, with dark curly hair, wearing glasses. He was very handsome, as handsome as a movie star or model, but with glasses... This was surprising to me. Not many people in Russia wore glasses at a young age, especially in those years. There was no TV, no computers, and no chemicals in the food – so a young man wearing spectacles was quite a rarity.

He stood in front of the main entrance of the Moscow Conservatory of Music, under the pillared canopy, unsmiling and serious, looking somewhere far away, into the void. His thoughts, probably, floated high in the sky at that moment. The young man's expression was as thoughtful as the expression of the 5-year-old boy wearing the sailor's jacket...

"He looks romantic," I commented.

"Yeah...He was the most handsome and clever man I've ever known – he did study for two Ph.D.s at once – at the conservatory as music theoretician, and at the university in the Philosophy and Fine Arts Department. When I met him, all the girls around were crazy about him and were almost dying from love..."

"Were you in love with him, too?"

"Not at first. We were just class-mates. I didn't know anything about him..." my mom paused and took a deep breath.

"Now you know?" I teased her.

"Oh, for sure! Even too much. I wish I knew less..."

...Dima dropped his hands following the last cord and sat still for some seconds, not daring to look at their teacher Alla Petrovna. She was really exacting, and he knew very well that, in some places, he missed the mark and fumbled. He was sure she wouldn't be pleased with his performance.

He glanced sideways, at Lisa by the next grand piano and saw her lowering her hands as well. Her head was bowed and he saw the dark hair ringlets at the back of her neck – the charming soft ringlets he was drawn to and would like to kiss.

Lisa...she was his best friend and class-mate, the musical partner and his first love – a pretty, smart and talented girl. Nice and devoted, Lisa was only fifteen, awhile he was already sixteen.

"Good job!" Alla Petrovna finally exclaimed after the pause.

For Dima and Lisa this praise came unexpected. She usually criticized them quite often.

"Good work! I even can't believe it. It's a great accomplishment. The piano concert by Edward Grieg is a difficult thing even for adult pianists. Of course, it needs more work in some places...I noticed everything, Dima!... but we still have some time. You're on a good level to pass your graduation exam next week. Then we'll have about two months to prepare you for the exam to enter the musical college in Moscow. Even now, I can't believe my own eyes and ears but you did it!"

Dima and Lisa exchanged looks, smiling. They were still a bit stressed – the tension of their serious performance was great and they needed more time to relax. All their inner power had been mobilized to work hard during the last school year preparing for this concert.

Of course, Alla Petrovna had adapted for them her own edited version of the concert score, dividing the pianist's and orchestra's parts for two grand pianos. She also made a more simplified arrangement of the music for her teen students, but, anyway, it was still a challenge and both, Dima and Lisa, were successful. Now, their strict teacher's praise inspired them and made them proud and motivated to work even harder in the future.

After the rehearsal, they had some tea with cookies at Alla Petrovna's house, discussed the future schedule of their additional after-school classes and then, Dima saw Lisa home, as usual.

They had been friends for the last two years. After they went to the movies, walked in the park, or did their homework together, he always saw her home like a gallant gentleman. Some times he dreamed of the chance to put a 'good night' kiss on Lisa's cheek, but never dared to do this in reality. He never even got up the nerve to touch her hand – Lisa was like an angel: innocent, sweet and pure. They were very close spiritually and mentally but Dima didn't really know what to do about his sexual feelings. He wanted to express his love but he couldn't imagine how to begin.

It was a warm May evening. The apple orchards were blossoming around the city, shedding white and pink petals over the fences right onto the sidewalks. It was spring; it was time of Love which Dima felt in every cell of his strong, young body.

They walked and talked about their coming exams, their future travel to Moscow and study at the musical college. Finally, upon reaching Lisa's house, they stopped in front of the entrance.

"Bye Lisa," Dima said shyly, handing her the bag with sheet music which he had carried for her the entire way. He stepped back a bit from her to quench the temptation to kiss her.

"Bye," she responded quietly, gazing at him with her dark brown begging eyes, and took the bag. "Good night Dima! See you tomorrow!"

"Good night!"

He hastened away, dreaming only to reach his home, to dive under his blanket, to bury his head under a pillow and drown in his desire. He wanted her; he dreamed about her and even awakened with erections from wet dreams, like a normal teenager. But, at the same time, he felt as if he were dying; as if something very special was happening to him and he was plunging into an abyss without any idea where he could turn for help.

It was 1939 – a scary and difficult time for the Soviet Union. Nobody in the country gave a thought or taught about problems of sex, love and feelings. Teenagers had no sexual education at school and were assigned to only sterile, political books by contemporary Soviet writers lacking in all personal feelings. Classes focused strictly on edited classic literature, where any material related to relationship between man and woman outside of work were removed.

No kisses were shown, even in movies; only Stalin's speeches filled the radio airwaves, along with the heated political meetings denouncing 'enemies of the people', accompanied by military marches and patriotic mass songs. This was like a straitjacket for teens, who were supposed to put all their energy into sports, being good soldiers, and take in the media delirium like robots.

The classical music of some composers which escaped censorship offered one of the few narrow cracks in which educated, intelligent and sensitive people (like Dima's and Lisa's families) could breathe. Music mostly remained a neutral, non-political subject, like philology of the Russian language in which Dima's parents, Vladimir and Maria, completely immersed themselves at work. They were the Russian language teachers at the Tver Pedagogical Institute.

Lisa's father was a surgeon and her mother - a math teacher at school. These were neutral subjects as well. Only people with such useful, non-controversial professions could survive in Russia during this period somehow, without losing their minds and souls. But, still, no questions of love were discussed anywhere, especially regarding teenagers.

What do I have to do? Dima thought, feeling helpless about his first love. Tell mom and dad that I love Lisa and I want to marry her in two years? They would only laugh at me and say that I'm silly. Ask Granny Lydia? She would only get very angry and say that I must think about my exams and studies, but not about girls. Ask friends at school? That would be a shame! They would surely tease us, call us names and humiliate us. They were also likely to abuse her, and might even beat me or both of us. It's better to keep silence.

Finally, he decided to talk to his next closest person – his music teacher. Alla Petrovna was knowledgeable, respectful, understanding, and she knew both, he and Lisa. She had also been married for more than twenty years and had an adult son who was now studying at Moscow University.

Alla Petrovna must know what to do if someone is in love, and might give me good advice, Dima thought and concentrated on the idea to give himself courage.

The following evening, Dima had an extra music class. Alla Petrovna was a very enthusiastic teacher; before the exams she always trained her students after hours and never charged this extra time. It was her pride to produce the best pupils of all.

After the class finished, Dima must go home, but he stood beside the door in hesitation. It looked like he didn't want to leave.

"Do you want to tell me something, Dima?" Alla Petrovna asked, sensing his confusion. "Did something happen?"

"No," he shook his head. "I mean, yes."

"Something to do with your parents?" she knitted her brows in concern.

"No. They're okay."

"Oh, you did scare me. You know... now so many bad things are happening to people..."

"I just want to talk to you... I need some personal advice," Dima finally blurted his words out.

"About your work? About music? You mean some teacher's advice?"

"No, not really...I mean a friend's advice."

"Well," Alla Petrovna looked at him in surprise, still not grasping what he was driving at. "It's nice of you to consider me a friend, Dima. Let's talk. Just come back inside and sit on the couch. It's not the best place to have friendly discussions right by the door, you know."

They returned to the living room and Dima lowered himself bashfully onto the edge of the couch. Then he put his trembling hands awkwardly in his lap. Alla Petrovna sat next to him and looked at him expectantly.

"Alla Petrovna," he said with a struggle, biting his lips. "I don't know how to say this...I have a problem. I love Lisa."

"Lisa Ginsburg?" she looked puzzled and Dima nodded, feeling doomed. "Have you fallen in love with her?"

"Yes."

"Does she know about it?"

He shook his head, looking at the floor. He couldn't even guess what she would say next.

"Do you know, Dima, that she is Jewish?"

"Yes." This was the last thing he would've expected to hear and he leapt quickly to Lisa's defense. "What's wrong with that? What's the difference? Our family is very international. We have never had anything against Jews."

"It's okay," Alla Petrovna agreed thoughtfully. "Now I see that you love her. I don't have anything against Jews, either, but my point is that we all live in Russia. This country has always been jingoistic and suspicious of anyone who is not ethnically Russian. It could be dangerous for Lisa one day, and for you, too, if you'll marry her. I have already had such a bad experience myself, you see," her voice quavered nervously. "I don't know if I can talk about it, Dimochka. It is too painful of a subject for me. But I'll try to explain.

"My husband was Estonian. Our family name was Kiaru. After the Baltic countries – Latvia, Lithuania and Estonia – didn't get along with the Soviet Union and became separated, all the people of these nationalities, who were left in Russia, were declared enemies. My husband was arrested and shot. I even was forced to divorce him after his death and to change back to my Russian maiden name, Golubeva, which you know now. This was the only way to save my life and my son's life. He was ordered to change his last name to mine, as well. Otherwise, my son couldn't get permission to attend the university," she fought back her growing tears, trying to hide them from Dima. "Many people from the Baltic countries perished during those years. Did you know that?"

Dima looked at her with horror.

"I did hear something on the radio about this..." he whispered. "But my Grandma Lydia...She is Latvian, too, and nobody touched her."

"It might be because she was married and changed her last name to her husband's Russian name, so it went unnoticed by the officials. But you shouldn't tell anybody, Dima. It could be dangerous for her even now."

"I won't," he promised, still terrified.

"Then..." Alla Petrovna took a deep breath, "look at the situation now. Because of the tense relationship with Germany, all Germans – including Russian-Germans who have lived here for centuries - are in trouble. They're arrested one by one and I'm afraid, will all finally be killed."

"My mom is half-German, half-Ukrainian," Dima exclaimed desperately. "My dad is half-Russian and half-Latvian. As a result, I only have one-quarter of Russian blood. So, who I am? What left for me?"

"Nothing wrong with that. Just keep quiet about it," Alla Petrovna put her arms around the boy. "Just be very careful, Dimochka. Nobody should know about your nationality mix. So, as I said, I'm afraid that one day soon, great danger will come for Jews and talented and nice people like Lisa could find themselves in big trouble. I just thought that if your wife were to be Russian, you could feel a bit more secure in the U.S.S.R. You're too special and too talented a young fellow to lose your chance and your possibility for a great future just because of your wife's nationality. But, anyway, it's nothing but my opinion based on my own life experience. It may be that I'm wrong. Actually, it's not the point. The point is - why are you telling me about your love for Lisa? What business is it of mine? How can I possibly help you?"

She looked into his eyes, smiled and hugged him affectionately. The moment of sadness passed and Dima shyly smiled back at her.

"I...I don't have anybody to talk about this...I just guessed that you might know what I have to do. Could I kiss her, or would she get angry? Could I hug her...somehow... or would she protest and run away, and I will lose her?"

"Dima! Haven't you ever kissed a girl?"

"No," he blushed almost to tears.

"Well," Alla Petrovna laughed. "Poor boy! Russia has always been too judgmental about educating teens. I was raised at Estonia and there was much more freedom to experiment and express those feelings. No, my dear, it's too sad but you can't touch Lisa in any way because she is only fifteen. She is a legal minor and it would be a crime. You could be arrested and go to prison, even if no politics are involved there. In our communist country, there are more than political prisoners. We have real criminals, too. You must wait three years until she becomes eighteen. Then you can marry her."

"Three whole years! But it is way too long," Dima protested heatedly. "I love her now."

"Whatever!" Alla Petrovna stood up, approached her china cabinet and took out a flat bottle and two small liquor-glasses. "Let's celebrate your patience, my dear boy," she said, pouring wine into them. She carried the glasses over to the couch where Dima was sitting and handed one of them to him. "Try it! It's cherry liqueur, very sweet and light. You're already sixteen and could drink a bit. There is nothing wrong with it. So," she raised her glass clinking it with Dima's in a toast, "for your love, my sweet boy!"

Dima drank the liqueur bravely. He already knew that his grandmother brewed homemade cherry brandy and they usually drank it at New Years celebrations or on their birthdays. It was pleasant and made him flushed.

"One more?" Alla Petrovna suggested and he nodded readily – why not, if it was so tasty and she was offering it. They drank a second glass.

"Actually, you know, Dimochka," she said, smiling playfully, "I don't see anything good in your idea to marry Lisa in three years. Both of you are naive children with no experience at all; neither of you would know what to do with each other in bed. I don't think you would be happy. In marriages normally at least one of the spouses should have some previous intimate experience to pass it to the other."

"Well, but how could I gain such experience if you said that I have no right to touch her?" he objected.

"Just find another girl...temporarily...until Lisa matures."

"It's difficult. All of them at our high school are the same age, plus or minus one year difference. I don't know anybody else."

"Well..." Alla Petrovna poured the third little glass for both of them and clinked with him once more. "You told me that you consider me as a friend. Is that right?"

Dima nodded certainly, "You're doing so much for me..."

"I can do some more... I can teach you a bit," she moved closer to him on the couch and put her hands on his shoulders. "You know I'm your music teacher, my sweet boy, but you know, as well, that I'm a really unhappy and unlucky widow. I'm still relatively young enough and need to be with a man, but I lost my husband about four years ago and haven't slept with anybody since. You, Dimochka, are already suffering for love - maybe the last year or two, and you know how painful that suffering is. Well, I've been suffering twice as long as you - and ten times sharper because I'm experienced. You don't know exactly what you are missing, but I know exactly what I need and what I want. Let's help each other like friends, like very close lovers. I'm sure we could be happy for some time. And then you'll marry Lisa if you want to. Okay?"

Dima's heart stood still. He felt hot and excited from the liqueur and, at the same time, from his close proximity to an arduous woman. The very thought made him lose his head and his mind which, anyway, had no clue as to what to do in this situation.

"We have our music classes every evening..." he murmured, trembling, not knowing what to say, just to utter something.

"...and we'll have our love classes after that...every evening, as well," Alla Petrovna finished his thought, tenderly kissing his cheek.

Dima didn't dare to look into her eyes; he just closed his in order not to see her aged, long-nosed face with saggy, soft skin which hung loose on her neck. Alla Petrovna was quite far from a beauty but she wasn't ugly. He wanted a woman so badly that he silently agreed to everything, tried to imagine that it was Lisa who was with him now and let her kiss his lips as a prelude. Then, his first sex class started.

In the beginning, Dima was confused and scared and didn't feel much. Then, after some nights, he grew accustomed to Alla Petrovna, became more bold and confident, and finally, after about two weeks of daily exercises he was able to enter the realm of real sexual pleasure. In about a month, he had learned all about a man's lust and delight. His personal transformation from a teenage to a man, took place in secret.

But there were bodily changes, as well. Over the summer, Dima noted that his shoulders and neck grew larger, some hair appeared on his chest and the hairiness of his legs and arms grew thicker. He even began shaving his face.

It seemed strange to Dima that not only his physical condition was changed, but his whole mentality and way of thinking, as well. He became more career minded because Alla Petrovna repeated daily to him that he was almost a genius and must go really far in life. That pushed and inspired him even more. He stubbornly played his piano the whole day because the school year was already over.

Then, Dima not only ran, but flew, to his evening class with Alla Petrovna and then stayed at her house until late at night. He came home tired but slept like a baby the rest of the night. That gave him enough time to regenerate his lost energy inside his young, healthy and strong body.

He really had no time to see Lisa; no time was left for walks, for movies, for talking on the porch or sitting on the bench and watching the moon, like they did before. That was back in his childhood and was not interesting for him anymore. Those things were now left far behind.

"Where is Lisa?" Grandma Lydia asked him once, "I haven't seen her for a long time. Why isn't she coming to visit us? You used to spend almost every evening with her..."

"No time... Exams," Dima barked in response as he dashed off.

"Well, study is okay, but...what about your friendship?" Grandma Lydia shook her head, surprised, and didn't get an answer. It seemed strange and quite rude to her – she had never seen her grandson so obsessed about anything before. He had always been a good, nice and polite boy.

A few days later, she met Lisa in a grocery store where they waited together in line to buy sunflower oil. The girl looked sad and tired.

"Lisa, what happened?" Grandma Lydia asked her. "Why don't you come by, anymore? You used to play with Dima the concert for two pianos..."

"You know, Lydia Yanovna," Lisa said wistfully, "the situation has changed. Alla Petrovna called Moscow Musical College and talked to the director. He said that they only enroll someone over the age of sixteen. So, I'm too young and can't go to the college this year.

"Another thing, the pianists are eligible to take entering exams only if they play the pianist's part, but not the orchestra part, as I did in my duet with Dima. Now, Alla Petrovna gave me a big job to study the pianist's part of the concert which Dima use to play. It'll take me the whole school year, and then, next summer I'll go to Moscow, too."

"Good for you, Lisa. So, both of you're too busy to walk," Grandma Lydia concluded. "That's okay. But I was worried because it looks to me like you're not friends with Dima anymore. It would be sad. I did like your friendship."

"No. We are still friends," Lisa assured her dolefully, "but friends who're too busy to see each other."

At home, Grandma Lydia sternly demanded an answer from her grandson, "Why didn't you tell me that Lisa is not going to go with you to Moscow?"

"What's the difference?" he shrugged indifferently.

"How'll you play the concert without her?"

"Alla Petrovna will play the orchestra part on the second piano. We're practicing together every evening."

"Well then, please tell me why you're always so late?" Grandma Lydia grumbled unpleasantly.

"Because there's not enough time during the day and my entrance exams are coming so soon."

"Well," she shook her head suspiciously but didn't say anything else.

When it came time to travel to Moscow, Dima's parents were very busy at work and couldn't go with him. Grandma Lydia didn't feel well and couldn't travel, either, because of her arthritis and heart problems that bothered her from time to time. But Dima explained to them that Alla Petrovna would escort him to Moscow, anyway, because she had to accompany him in his try-out in Lisa's place. His parents were grateful that a serious and responsible adult would support their boy on the trip to the big city and help him get enrolled in the college.

However, Grandma Lydia continued to feel uneasy and suspicious – she didn't know exactly what about; she only felt that something was seriously wrong with the arrangement.

It was a hot day at the end of July, as she went to the train station to see Dima off. It didn't matter that her heart wasn't very good that morning. Grandma Lydia entered with him his train compartment. She had checked attentively how comfortable her dearest grandson would feel sitting for about five hours on his dirty and stinky wooden bench. In those days, the trains in Russia were always ugly and particularly unpleasant; most train travel was a torture.

"Don't worry, Lydia Yanovna," Alla Petrovna said assuring, with a handshake and a smile. "Dima will be okay with me. Of course, it's not comfortable here, but he is enthusiastic, full of high spirits and happy now. And he's ready to fight with his competitors. He's feeling great. Am I right, Dimochka?"

He nodded, grinning and threw his arms around his Grandma.

"I'm going to my future, Grandma," he announced proudly, "and I'll be back in two weeks. It's not a long time for you to wait."

Grandma Lydia hugged him and kissed him 'bye'. Then she climbed out off the train, dried her sweaty face with a handkerchief, waved back to Dima and Alla Petrovna who were returning the fare-well through the window, and slowly and heavily walked away from the platform.

But before Grandma Lydia left the station building, she suddenly remembered that she had forgotten to give Dima the little bag with pies she had baked for him to eat on his way – it was still in her hand.

"Oh, my God! What am I thinking?" she blamed herself and hastily made her way back to the about-to-depart train.

It was not so easy to find the right car – so many people were crowding around and shouting to the windows and waving crazily. Even more difficult was to recognize the right window. The train had already started moving very slowly and the platform crowd walked along with it, faster and faster.

Finally, Grandma Lydia saw the two of them behind one of the windows. Her teen grandson and his middle-aged teacher were standing beside the window, embracing romantically and kissing passionately.

"What!?" she exclaimed in total disbelief. "What?! Dima! Dimochka! What're you doing?!" She has suspected something like this deep inside her heart; she had sensed something amiss, but then had abruptly convinced herself that those were crazy thoughts. However, now the evidence floated right in front of her eyes and disappeared down the track, while other windows flashed by the platform.

"What're you doing?! She's a bitch! The old bitch! Dima! Dimochka!" tail end of the train passed her swiftly and in a minute Grandma Lydia was left alone on the station platform, her mouth open soundlessly, trying to gulp more air like a fish out of water. Her heart was knifed with a piercing pain and her forehead broke out in a cold sweat. Everything went dark in front of her eyes and she collapsed on the asphalt, lifeless. Her bag with homemade pies fell out of her limp hand.

Some people noticed her crumpled figure and gathered around. Someone called an ambulance, but it was too late – Lydia Yanovna was dead of a heart attack.

Dima only learned of this tragedy when he returned from Moscow in triumph. He was now a student of the biggest and most prestigious musical college in the whole country. Now, he had a two-week break to say goodbye to his family. Starting from September 1.1939, he would study in Moscow and live on the campus there.

He took his dearest Grandma's death very close to heart. He walked to the cemetery, brought flowers to put on her grave and sat on the bench beside it, thinking about his wonderful Grandma who had cared for him throughout his childhood. He began crying.

Dima didn't have the slightest idea that her death was somehow related to his relationship with Alla Petrovna and his departure for Moscow on that day. He, nevertheless, felt guilty and sad, knowing full well that nothing would be the same again and he saw off forever his Grandma and his childhood, all together.

For almost two years Dima studied at Moscow, residing on the campus. Alla Petrovna visited him persistently every weekend and they spent hours in bed while his roommates took walks or went to the movies. He visibly matured and his studies included many successes. He had big plans. On May 23, 1941 he had his eighteenth birthday which Alla Petrovna invited him to celebrate at a restaurant.

In a month, on June 22, Would War II started for Russia and Dima was exactly of draft age for a military service. He was tall, strong and healthy and could be a good soldier.

"No," Alla Petrovna protested loudly, "never! I will never let you go to that hell and be killed. You're a genius! You're super-talented and to be killed or handicapped is not your destiny."

"How can I avoid it?" Dima asked despairingly. "They're only making exceptions for sick people, or for men with bad vision, wearing glasses. But you know there aren't so many of them. It's a rare thing."

"That's the point," Alla Petrovna said. "I know the secret. I know how to deal with that. I've already done this for my son, even before the war began. He has bad eyesight now. I made him need to wear glasses - just in case! And I was right. The communists took my husband and killed him. I hate them and I'll never let them take my son or conscript you, my love. Better to be a half-blind than dead."

She taught Dima a secret trick, how to exercise his eyes, how to look at the light in a special way to quickly ruin one's vision - in only a couple of the weeks. He started to work on his very good eyes as ardently and enthusiastically, as he played piano every day.

In about ten days, he was called to the military station for a health check to be prepared to go into battle – German troops were advancing and had already reached the middle of the Ukraine. They were heading straight for Moscow, so it was a time of crisis.

"How come you have such bad vision and still aren't wearing glasses!?" the doctor exclaimed in surprise. He prescribed them right away. Than he filled out the special exemption form for Dima: "Not liable for call-up (even for reserve duty) because of very poor eyesight."

Dima bought glasses right away and was unpleasantly startled seeing himself in mirror. He thought they diminished his good looks. But anyway, he would remain at home and stay alive.

However, Alla Petrovna had to let him leave her clutches. Tver Pedagogical Institute was evacuated to Siberia, along with its whole staff. Both of Dima's parents, Vladimir and Maria, were professors there and were relocated, as well. Dima, as a handicapped young man, was allowed to follow them. In this way he escaped the war as a draft dodger.

Out in Siberia, since there was little to do, Dima decided for the next four years to study at the same Pedagogical Institute. He missed his piano and music classes badly, but not as badly as he missed his erotic life, which Alla Petrovna had accustomed him to the previous two years before war. So, he met a nice 18-year-old student, Vera, and married her.

He found some relief for his sexual tension however they only had sex for fun. There was no real love between them and they had little in common. As the war came to the end, Dima and his parents made plans to return to Tver. Dima and Vera easily decided to divorce, just as they'd easily decided to marry.

The departure for the West happened so fast, that there was no time to run to the registration office and officially put the divorce seals into their passports. Vera moved somewhere else with one of the demobilized front line soldiers, and Dima returned to Tver with his passport still registering him as married.

Where should I look for Vera to finalize our divorce? Dima wondered. Then he light-headedly tore the page with the marriage seal out of his passport.

He was sure Vera did the same...

"Oh!" I said shaking my head in dismay as my mom finished the story. "Oh-oh! Such a kettle of fish for a young man! Was it the bigamy when he married you? And avoiding the military draft! And deliberately damaging his eyes! And betraying Lisa's friendship! And sleeping with his music teacher as a teenager! Were all of these crimes?"

"I guess some of them were," my mom nodded sadly. "Some things weren't legal crimes but more mental - and moral crimes, for sure. He told me about them only when we had been married for two years and, by then, I was already pregnant. What could I do? I cried a lot about Vera. I was scared that our marriage wouldn't be considered legal if someone knew about it. But Dmitry just laughed and told me that it was only the bureaucratic formality to get a divorce seal in one's passport. It didn't mean a thing to him. Really, where he should look for Vera to get a divorce? He finally convinced me. Of course, he didn't want to die in the war as thirty million Russians did. As my father did!" my mother raised her voice in anger, offence, and shame over her cowardly young husband.

"It wasn't a matter that my father was overage – the call-up was only until the age of forty-five, but my father was already forty-eight. He went voluntarily, as a construction engineer, to help to build the military fortifications around the Moscow and he was killed. Same as Lisa's father who served as a surgeon at the age of fifty - he went voluntarily, too, and worked in a field hospital in the front lines. He lost his life, as well."

"How do you know about Lisa?"

"I met her. She was studying at the Moscow Conservatory after the war, like we did."

"What about Alla Petrovna? Did she bother her *dear Dimochka* anymore?" I asked sarcastically. "Wasn't it a crime what she did to him? He was underage, after all..."

"Alla Petrovna died of cancer during the war. Of course, officially it was crime that she slept with him, but a crime only on paper. Nobody cared in those years about morality and about teens. Millions of people were in concentration camps and many thousands of them were teenagers or kids who were arrested along with their parents. The guards used them all, boys and girls, as they wanted – in every possible and even impossible ways. It was 'normal'. It was very scary. So scary to live through that, that it turned most of the people in our country into mentally sick persons. I'm not angry about Alla Petrovna. I just felt pity toward her.

"However, still, it was wrong what she did to Dima. She used him and taught him to meanly betray Lisa and his first love, to betray his health and to betray motherland. And to later break the law with Vera and not get a legal divorce. These poison seeds fell on the fertile ground, I'm afraid – Dima's adventurous and careless character. They yielded a great harvest later."

"Gosh! Such a kettle of fish!" I repeated, shaking my head in disbelief. "You were right, Mom. I'm not really sure I would want to meet him, knowing all of this."

"I suspected that," my mom commented, taking a deep breath. "It's sad to say, but that was not the end of the story. All of these things were nothing compared with what was yet to come..."

Chapter 8

THE FAIRYTALE NOTEBOOKS

While I was sick in bed, I usually read or drew something when I grew tired of playing with my dolls or imagining something in the exotic carpet hanging above my bed.

My mom always brought me the best world classic books from the Composer's Union Library. It was a very good and well-stocked library that was restricted to union members. My mom, as a music specialist, was among them. Luckily for me, she belonged to the cream of society.

Getting a hold of good books was a problem in the Soviet Union, as well as food, clothes, footwear, furniture, cars and so on...everything, actually.

However, during my childhood, following the death of Stalin, the Soviet economy had substantially improved over the period when my mom was growing up - the 1930s. One day, feeling that my breasts were starting to bud, I asked my mom what size of bra she wore when she was fourteen.

She only laughed, "I can't answer your question. There were no bras produced in the Soviet Union in those years."

"How come?" I was surprised. "How did women live? Baba Sonya... you... What did you wear instead?"

"We usually tore up old bed sheets and sewed bras for ourselves," my mom explained. "I think most other women did the same. Everybody knew perfectly well how to sew. You couldn't possibly imagine what life was like in the thirties! Now it is much better. Sometimes, you can even find bras of three different sizes in the shops today, if you're lucky. To me it seems unbelievable!"

I could compare such things, grasping little snippets of conversation between adults, here and there. I knew, for example, that in the thirties my Baba Sonya could only buy butter after standing for sixteen hours in line. Now, we could buy same butter after only a half an hour wait.

However, all of these things were exceptional for Moscow – the capital, but also a restricted city. In the provinces – throughout the country itself, there was never anything at all to buy, except vodka, herring, dark bread and potatoes (in both the thirties and the sixties).

'Not for everybody' – was the basic reality of life in the Soviet Union. Restricted medical clinics and hospitals, restricted sanatoriums and health resorts, restricted libraries, stores and closed cities reserved dignitaries - governmental, intelligence agencies, the militia and army; top scientists and cultural figures, sports stars – in short, for the elite. In their closed world, the best services and products were available, mostly from abroad. But for ordinary folks, who were living outside this exclusive realm, only low-quality goods existed – or shortages. They had to steal. There was no other choice for them.

The majority of the Soviet population was workers and collectivized peasants. They were treated like garbage in a society which officially proclaimed itself as the "Workers' and Peasants' State". What cynicism! What a big fat lie! The lie which my great-grandpa, Vladimir Diachan, grasped from the first word of Lenin's address on the armed-car back in April 1917, when this Bolshevik Head made his famous speech which every student in the U.S.S.R must study! The result of the Bolshevik Revolution was the same as my great-grandpa had predicted, as well. 'Each kitchen maid' didn't rule the country – far from it! She was treated like garbage by the rulers. The old, stable, traditional Russia was being undermined and corrupted. Something new and scary had replaced it – the Empire of Evil.

However, I was a young girl at this time and wasn't interested in politics at all. I lived in my own world filled with the characters of Alexandre Dumas, Walter Scott, Jules Verne, Victor Hugo, Daniel Defoe, Mark Twain, James Fennimore Cooper, Jack London and Charles Dickens; next to this were heroes of many fairytales – we had in our home a whole library of folk fairytales from almost fifty different countries of the world.

In the thirties, back when my mom was a child and then - a teenager, her father, Victor Demin, every weekend visited Rostov-on-Don or later - Moscow flea market and bought for her world famous classic books published before revolution. Possibly, they had been confiscated by GPU-soldiers or stolen by neighbors from the home libraries of arrested educated people. The thieves sold the books because they were more interested in the money than the contents – they didn't read and didn't care to educate their own children, and they needed the extra money for vodka.

In the sixties, there were no more flea markets as they had been closed down. So we had to get our books somewhere else. My mom always bought books when she went to Congress of the Composer's Union as a delegate. Those gathering hosted members of the government and communist bosses, as well as leading cultural lights. During session breaks, people left the auditorium and gathered in the halls and foyers for refreshments. Among the tables laden with tea, coffee, soda pop, cookies, cake and fruit, there were also books laid out for sale. My mom always took a lot of cash in her purse when she prepared to go for the next congress.

"I'll buy more books for you!" she always told me happily, looking forward to the opportunity. She usually added, in a conspiratorial tone, "and I'll also bring two pieces of cake for you and Baba."

The books she could purchase at these congresses were, of course, Russian classics: Alexander Pushkin, Mikhail Lermontov, Anton Chekhov, Leo Tolstoy, Fedor Dostoevsky; adult French classics – Honore de Balzac, Guy de Maupassant, Gustav Flaubert, Edgar Poe, Anatoly France; or German classics: Friedrich Schiller, Erich Maria Remarque, Friedrich Durrenmatt, Thomas Mann, Heinrich Boll and so on.

Especially interesting, according to the publishers' Russian names, they were all printed in the U.S.S.R, in Moscow. Yet, these very books were never available at ordinary bookstores and so were treated treasures of cultural wealth shared only among the elite during professional and political congresses (like the one my mother attended) or subscribed to academicians on a special closed list.

Our home library grew, thanks to my mom, though I was lazy to read myself. Mostly my mom sat on the edge of my bed and she read the books aloud to me. I loved to listen. These were my best hours with my mom, replacing the earlier intimate and special bath time we shared.

My mom always commented to me what she was reading, pointing out the writing skills that lay behind this or that professional writer's wonderful story.

"Look, how he is describing this!" she exclaimed sometimes. "Look how he is building the plot! This line expresses that idea perfectly! This detail is just amazing. It creates the entire image of the character! Note this, please. Pay attention to these details."

I did take note. I became a student of my mother's once more. I felt very happy and excited while we were studying literature together. I especially loved my mom deeply and always understood her completely when we were working like this; I was very happy from her encouraging glances and I needed no words at all.

One day, I was, as usual, sick with the flu and had nothing to read. All that I was allowed to read, I had already finished. Only some of the adult books were left unread, but my mom didn't want me to read them at the age of thirteen, so I was lying in bed, bored to death. I whimpered, "Mom, give me something to read, pleeeease!"

"You know," my mom said seriously. "I'm really busy these days and have absolutely no chance to run to the library for you. Every one of my minutes is booked, but...well...I have one idea," she checked her watch. "Stand up, please, and help me move the table. I have something you can read in storage. But we have to get it quickly."

"What? Those old German or French books? Oh, no!" I begged. "They are too complicated for me. I don't want them."

"Wait a second. I promise you'll like what I get for you. Just let's do it faster. I have to go soon."

I jumped from my bed, looking forward to having some fun. For me, the basement always contained mysteries – things that were unusual and unexpected. We shifted the table, raised the lid and my mom entered to pass me the stuff which was on the top. She quickly found what she was looking for – two big batches of notebooks bound together by cord.

"Take them," my mom said. "You take a look at them. I think you will find them interesting. These are my fairytales."

"Yours? Really?"

"Yes, mine. I started writing after I learned my letters at the age of three."

"Wow! Why didn't you tell me about them before?"

"I wasn't sure they would appeal to you. Try them now. Sorry, but I really have to leave for work at the moment."

She closed the basement; the table went back in its place and my mom went into the hallway, leaving me with the dusty notebooks. They were even covered in some places with cobwebs and gave off the distinct smell of a musty, unused basement, like raw potatoes.

"Yuck!" I reacted to the unpleasant odor. I swiftly took a pair of old underwear, which served me as a duster, wet it in the kitchen, and then returned to clean the layer of dust on the tomes. I untied the cords and put the fat notebooks on the table one by one. Each bunch contained twelve notebooks of assorted sizes and colors.

"Mom!" I shouted down the hall at her retreating figure. She was now dressed in her winter coat and had just fastened her boots. "Why are all of your notebooks so different? Couldn't you write on similar ones?"

"Ha-ha," my mom retorted. "I was lucky if I even got the chance to buy a notebook at the flea market, or sometimes - very seldom - at a store. There was hardly any stationery to buy at that time anywhere. Believe me - it was very difficult to write without paper or pencils. Okay, bye. See you tonight," she shat the door and I heard her hill clacking across the foyer tiles. Then, the outer door of the building banged shut and I was left alone with the notebooks...

...The first thick velvet notebook Lala had gotten as a present for her third birthday from Auntie Anya.

"I'm sorry I couldn't find anything better for a child than that," Anya said, apologizing. "I've spent about half an hour searching flea market, but there weren't any toys and I didn't see anything that would be reasonable for a child. Maybe you can use it somehow, sweetie. Draw your pictures or something in it..."

"Thanks, Auntie," Lala kissed her cheek and turned to Sonya, "Mom, could you show me the letters, please?"

"Letters?" Sonya was surprised. "What for? You'll be taught them in school when you start. For now just draw something."

She knew that Lala would not be very well for the next ten years and might not enter school until she was twelve years old. Sonya understood that she would have to educate her daughter for the first four grades, but she didn't see any reason to begin such study so early. Nobody did it in the Soviet Russia. At that time, children usually went to school at the age seven or eight, without preliminaries or learning the alphabet, numbers, colors, and shapes.

"I could draw," Lala explained, "but each picture needs to be signed. There should be some writing under the pictures. Look at my books. Under every picture is a caption. I want to do the same. Otherwise, my creation won't look like a real book."

"You don't need to create books yet, Lala," Anya laughed. "Just draw some nice pictures. That's what kids usually do. It's enough for now. You're too little to do more."

"It doesn't matter," Lala objected heatedly. "I want to be a writer. I'll write children's books."

Sonya and Anya looked at each other in surprise at this assertion. Their smiles were filled with misgivings.

"Well, sweetie," Sonya agreed, "right now I have a visitor – Auntie Anya, but this evening before you'll go to bed, I'll show you some letters. You draw the pictures now and leave some empty space under them to write later what you'd like to put there."

"Okay, Mommy," Lala sat on her bed and took out her box of colored pencils.

Anya and Sonya walked into the kitchen, where they proceeded to sit drinking tea and sharing confidences. They knew full well that Lala would be occupied for some time, so they could relax together and enjoy their conversation. Sonya fully expected that Lala would forget her unusual lesson request during the course of the afternoon drawing. After all, she was only 3-years-old, and a very sick girl, at that.

However, it didn't happen that way and, as soon as Anya departed, Lala pestered her mother to teach her. Sonya showed her 'A' and 'M' before putting the child to bed.

Early the next morning, Sonya woke up to make a breakfast for Victor and to see him off to work. She was more than astounded to find Lala up, sitting on the chair by her little table in her blue pajamas, writing away in her new notebook. There were already several lines of "A's" and "M's" as well as an additional line of the repeated word "MAMA". Of course, Lala's fingers weren't strong enough and her hand coordination wasn't developed yet – some letters were too huge, while others were undersized; some were straight, but some dropped to the right or sunk below the writing line. It would've looked like poor work for a child of six, but for a 3-year-old the results were impressive.

"Good morning, Mommy," Lala said, smiling proudly. "Look at my work! I need more letters to write 'daddy' and my name. And some letters for the word 'princess'. Please, teach me more!"

"Will do, sweetie," Sonya whispered, with eyes full of tears from happiness as she kissed her daughter's forehead to check for fever. "After daddy leaves for work, I'll change you, give you your rice soup and then we'll have another lesson."

It seemed peculiar to Sonya that Lala was still too little to dress herself, but here she was learning to write already.

And that was how they proceeded, on days that Lala felt good enough. Of course, everything stopped when her bouts of illness returned. Then she would lie in bed, feverishly hot and sweating, almost unconscious. Sonya would sit beside her, holding her little hand and from time to time changing the cold wet cloths on her forehead. And always Sonya suffered from the feelings of guilt and remorse.

Some days later, as the attack subsided, even though Lala was weak and pale, she would open her tired eyes and whisper tenderly, "Thank you, Mom. Okay, what will our next letter be?"

By the time Lala reached four, she was already making up her own fairytales, with a series of labeled pictures. At the age of five, she wrote out simple stories and illustrated them with one or two pictures to the page. When she reached six, there were 3-4 pages of text for every picture drawn. Her growing pile of notebooks already resembled children's picture books. As the Demin family was leaving Rostov-on-Don for Moscow, Lala carefully packed her precious notebooks in her rucksack.

Now in Moscow, Sonya taught her daughter at home until she recovered her health once more. Lala could once again eat normal food (with a special diet) and felt strong enough to enter school and to mix with other children. She joined the fifth grade class without any difficulties because her mother had prepared her well. Lala not only fit in academically, but also socially, thanks to her calm, easy-going and sociable character.

But her new circumstances didn't in any way alter her passion for writing. Everyday, upon returning home from school, she ate dinner, did her homework speedily and then took up her pencil at her desk to write. Such a preoccupation concern Sonya, who feared Lala wasn't getting enough outdoor exercise and playtime.

"Lala, stop writing and go for a walk," she said one day to her daughter.

"I don't want to, Mom."

"Well, I really think you need to get out more. Go for a walk or something. Anything to get more fresh air and exercise."

"But Mom, I exercise every morning, and I go to school and back. That's enough, Mom," Lala objected.

"No. It's not. I'm insisting that you go out for a walk right now," Sonya asserted her authority as a mother.

"Mommy," Lala protested with a whimper, "I really want to finish this chapter. You don't understand how important this is. I might forget what I was going to write by tomorrow if I leave now."

"No," Sonya uttered sharply, putting her will against her stubborn daughter's. "I'll close your notebook and take it away, if you don't go out for a walk this minute! Look how nice the weather is. We don't often have such amazing days. It's a crime not to take advantage of it and spend it outdoors..."

"Well...Where should I go? I don't know..." Lala finally conceded. She usually was an obedient child.

"Walk to the *Pokrovsky* Boulevard and back," Sonya suggested, knowing well that the way to the boulevard took about half an hour and that would mean Lala would have an hour's walk. That would be enough in Sonya's opinion.

"Okay, just don't touch my notebook. I'll be back soon," Lala answered, putting her light jacket on and running out.

Twenty minutes later, Lala returned all hot, sweaty, with matted hair and almost breathless.

"What happened?!" Sonya clasped her hands in dismay, looking at her daughter with horror.

"Nothing...I just ran...to...boulevard and...back...to please you... Mom. I did it...for you... Can I finish my writing now?"

"Gosh," the astounded Sonya replied with tears in her eyes. She wrapped her loving arms around her poor overloaded child, petted her wet hair and listened with compassion to Lala's young strong heart pounding forcefully under her unzipped jacket and moistened sweater and t-shirt. "Just go change! Sorry, my dear. Sorry, my sweetheart. I didn't know...I didn't understand that your writing was so very important to you."

Once again, Sonya must yield to fate. She realized that there was no alternative and that Lala's writing was much more than just a simple pastime. It seemed to be a real serious calling from above – perhaps her destiny.

However, Lala accepted music lessons and her private piano teacher trained her so well that after only a year she was ready to enroll in music school in the fifth grade. But, for all of her success, she didn't take her music as seriously as her writing and considered it merely a hobby.

But she did love music - especially opera - and often visited the *Bolshoi* Theater performances with her parents or her school friends. In the 1930s it wasn't such a problem to get tickets – you could even purchase them right before the show started. In case the theater was sold out for the evening, you could slip a small amount of money to the door woman who would allow you to enter and sit on the stairs in the upper balcony. It was not very comfortable, but you could see and hear everything, the same as those patrons sitting in the lodges.

Lala usually attended the opera once a week, and grew to love them dearly. She couldn't exactly say what she liked the most: the music, the stage decorations, the acting, the singers, or the stories themselves. In fact, she found the whole more than the sum of its parts and deliciously wonderful taken all together.

And her opera experiences were reflected in the pictures draw in her books. She freely borrowed ideas from operatic stage décor, both the design of the rooms where her characters dwelt and the costumes they wore. These varied impressions mixed together into a heady brew in her youthful head, yielding creative results. Lala became a bright and polished young lady, a teenager who was talented, as well as well-educated and broad-minded.

One day, in the mid-thirties, Victor brought a couple of tickets home from work.

"They are offering a special excursion," he said, "to the Armory in the Kremlin. There is the exhibition of Russian National Treasures. I guess we could see many beautiful things there. But I only got two tickets, so, you girls must decide which of you will come with me. I can't give both of them to you to go instead of me because it's from my work and all my co-workers will be there and expecting to see me."

"You better go, Mom," Lala suggested. "You're always at home and it's good for you to get out, sometimes. For me, it is actually better to stay at home this evening and to write some more."

So, Victor and Sonya went on the excursion. Entrance into the Kremlin was very restricted in those years. All of Victor's co-workers gathered outside the Kremlin Wall, on the Red Square (in Russian *Krasnaya Ploshchad*), in front of the gate *Borovitskie Vorota* – the main gate through which government vehicles came and went. The group, followed by security guards, entered a little door beside the gate. Everybody had a passport that was carefully checked and all the people were searched before entering. No purses or briefcases were allowed at all.

In this way the group followed the guide to one of the Kremlin's main buildings, feeling quite uncomfortable and anxious as if they were about to be taken prisoner. Sonya couldn't even understand how this tour group was permitted. It was strange and unusual for simple people to be allowed to enter *the Holy of Holies* where only *the High Priests* could go. But then she recalled that Victor had explained that the government earned money this way by charging a lot for the tickets; Soviet employees were obliged to buy such tickets.

Of course, they didn't exactly enter the Kremlin Armory that tourist visit today. Instead they came into large hall in the conference building, where some antique things were placed on the long tables in the middle of the room and covered with unbreakable glass. The line of the sightseers slowly circled each table display. People were gawking in amazement and disbelieve at all the fantastically beautiful things, arrayed on black velvet. Among the items were pieces of jewelry, little statues, all kind of imaginable fretted clocks, Easter eggs, dishes and china, lockets and snuff-boxes made from gold, silver, porcelain, ivory and crystal, studded with multicolored gems and diamonds. There were also icons in gold settings, with gems, crosses, censers and other Orthodox Church apparatus, followed by vases.

The guides, in hushed tones, explained to each visiting group the sort of things on display and in which century they were produced – the 19th, the 18th, the 17th, or even earlier.

The huge quantity of such expensive and beautiful things overwhelmed the onlookers, leaving them absolutely dumbfounded. It was way too much for ordinary people to digest, so the groups walked softly and speechless in the presence of such beauty and wealth, awed by the power of these divine art works.

Startled, Sonya couldn't even begin to guess where all these items came from and whom they had belonged to, before they were looted by the Communists. Where were the people who had owned all these treasures now? Possibly, her father's award from the Tsar, with its cross and diamonds would be on the table, if it hadn't been sacrificed, piece by piece, to be sold and eaten. It helped her family survive, but it was obviously tragic and undeniable that the former owners of these treasures hadn't survived. These things had outlived the people. They served as fitting memorials now. There was something funeral about the room.

Suddenly, a strange feeling of recognition pierced Sonya. Her glance fell on something very well-known, very familiar, very close to her - the pink sparkling crystal with an enormous gold letter Ɛ ...The vase...That vase which stood at her bedside through twenty-one years of her life. The Empress's vase which Ekaterina left with her daughters, when she ran to the city! The vase which Sonya left behind in her bedroom, on the second floor of their country house *Vysokoye,* in Poland, a hundred kilometers away from Warsaw! The vase, which she had told Victor so much about!

"Look!" she exclaimed unconsciously, pointing to the middle of the table with vases. "Look, Vitya! It's my vase! It's my! My vase!"

Her voice rang out so unexpectedly and so clearly in the quietness of the room that all heads turned toward her. Victor squeezed her hand and covered her mouth with his other palm.

"What? What did you say?" the guide asked suspiciously, approaching Sonya.

"Sorry," Victor answered for Sonya, digging his elbow into her side, "she means that we did have a vase from a cheep glass which looked similar to this. It was accidentally smashed last year and we threw it away. Right, Sonya?"

She nodded, incapable of pronouncing a single sound from the horror of it all. If Victor hadn't graciously stepped in to save her and wouldn't be such a great actor, her unwise outburst could've spelled their doom.

"I'm sorry to hear that," the guide smiled. "Of course, your glass vase could have only a distant resemblance. This vase was produced in 1764 by a special order of the Empress Catherine the Great. We have two of them absolutely identical but we're only displaying one. The other is in the depository. This is a historical mystery – why the Empress ordered two of the same vases. Our historians tried to solve it, but they were unsuccessful."

"Have these vases been in the Kremlin all this time?" Sonya asked in a husky voice and coughed a bit to clear her throat after her spasm of fear.

"No, they were found by the Russian Army during the World War I, somewhere in Poland."

"How did they get there?" Sonya wanted to know.

"That's another historical mystery."

"Thank you for the explanation," Victor ended the conversation. "It was very interesting to talk to you."

"You have such an amazing knowledge of history. It's so patriotic of you," Sonya added and they moved ahead, rushing to rejoin their group, which had moved on to the next table.

Later, back home and still feeling the stress of the evening, Sonya revealed to Lala the story of the vases and the separation of her parents. Her daughter heard these for the very first time in her life and was completely intrigued.

"If you become a writer later on," Sonya suggested, "you might want to write our family history... of course, many years from now, if the political situation drastically changes."

"That's not a bad idea," Lala agreed. "I'll think about it. I like Baba Ekaterina and her paintings. Maybe, one day she could illustrate my books."

She saw Ekaterina and Peter Young von Altenburg once, a year ago, as the Demin's family went to visit the elderly couple in Kiev. But she hadn't known Ekaterina's story before. Now, she tried to weave it into what her impressions of Ekaterina were. It was certainly a precious family legend to keep.

Now that Lala was twelve years old, she lost interest in writing short fairytales. They were for kids, but she wasn't a child anymore. She outgrew them and envisioned a bigger effort that would begin as a fairytale but expand into a whole novel.

'One upon a time there was a King who ruled the North Kingdom,' Lala started to write her more ambitious new story. 'He was very nice, kind and everybody loved him. He ruled his country politely and carefully.

'The King had two sons – Prince Dodon and Prince Gvidon. He loved them both dearly and decided that before he died, he would divide his kingdom equally and apportion it to his sons as their own kingdom. It seamed to him a good and just plan.

'However, one day, walking through his palace, the King overheard his sons fighting over some toys or a turn in a game, actually about inconsequential details. But they were still very agitated and angry with each other.

"When I'M KING," Dodon shouted, "I'm going to start a war with you."

"Of course," Gvidon answered, "when I'M KING, I'll go to war with you, too, and I'll size your whole kingdom. Then I'll kill all your soldiers."

"No you won't! I'll kill all of your soldiers and kill you. Then I'll be the ONLY KING," Dodon continued in rage.

'Their father, the King, was dumbfounded. He certainly didn't expect such ugly threats and thought from his sons. He was very peaceful man and didn't want any war, especially a civil war between the two halves of his kingdom.

'The King called both his sons into his throne-room, asked them to stand straight in front of him and said sternly, "I'm really upset about you, my sons. I raised you to be best friends and future neighboring Kings, but already you're prepared to strike each other. You're too carefree and too spoiled. Even though you are grown, you Dodon are already20 and Gvidon is 18, but your behavior is immature and too childish. It's not serious. I don't want my country and my folks suffering because of your stupidity. Neither of you will be worthy to be king until you go and study what real life is about.

"Tomorrow morning, both of you will leave on a three-year journey: Dodon will head west and Gvidon will head east from here. Upon your return, I'll test the two of you to see what you have learned from the School of Life Experience. Only then will I decide who is worthy to rule our country. Farewell, my sons!"'

This was how Lala's major project began. There were the twelve notebooks of Prince Dodon's travel and adventure, followed by twelve notebooks of Prince Gvidon's travel and adventure stories.

The first part, Dodon's story, took Lala three years to write begun at the tender age of 12. It was still a fairytale, mixed with romantic historic fiction of the Sir Walter Scott or Alexandre Dumas variety. The tales were filled with knights' fights, horse chases, and kidnapped princesses.

This novel was the product of the fantasy of the sensitive and talented child. It was a long, involved tale full of interest and adventure. It was surprisingly well-written for a young teen's first story and might even have been published, if such a thing were possible in the Soviet Union at that time.

For all of her talent, Lala was modest about her skill and considered Dodon's story as a mere warm-up exercise. She pressed on with writing the second part.

Now, the story of Gvidon took on a life of its own and practically became a separate book. Lala worked on it from age 15-18, finishing it in the spring of 1940, as the Second World War was already raging in Europe, but Stalin and the Soviet Union pretended it had nothing to do with them.

Because the author was now older, Gvidon's story was more mature and serious. Lala had left fairytale magic, witches, giants or dwarfs behind. Her characters now were all real people dealing with their feelings, ideas, sufferings and problems. It was closer to a blend of "The Three Musketeers" and "The uncle Tom's cabin".

Traveling east, Prince Gvidon came to a country named Panula which had been sized and occupied by another country named Valenadia years earlier. The Panulians were turned into slaves. They created an underground organization and plotted to liberate themselves and their land from Valenadians.

There, also, Lala begun her tragic love triangle, mixed with war, politics and romantic adventure. She put a lot of psychology, painful experiences, ecstatic love, betrayal and doubt into the twists and turns of the tension-filled story line.

Truly, it was an action-packed, insightful book which could be published in a free country. It was a serious romantic fiction of good quality and Lala felt confident enough to take some of her best and strongest chapters to the entrance exam at the Institute of Soviet Writers. She wanted to study to become a professional writer. In many ways, she had already taught herself. However, she felt that she needed to have more education and to get her master's degree and be published in the U.S.S.R.

Lala finished the book when she was nearly an adult, a high school graduate ready to be enrolled into The Soviet Writer's Institute named after the famous communist writer, Maxim Gorky. She filed her application for the Institute in 1940 and then visited the Institute's Open House meeting. This was a disaster for her.

The members of the examination board – three famous Soviet writers – looked through her work apprehensively, shaking their heads.

"What are you talking about here?" one of them asked. "A war for freedom? The only true war for freedom was the *Bolshevik* Revolution of October1917! That brought true freedom!"

"Who are your characters? Kings, princes, princesses, countesses, generals...What are they? Reactionaries? Aristocrats? Bourgeoisie? Imperialists?" added another.

"Do you realize that you are writing about enemies of the state? This is unacceptable!" contributed third one. "If we even suggested publishing such a book or recommended you for our writing courses, we ourselves would come under fire as disloyal citizens. We think you have no understanding of the mission of a Soviet writer, Comrade Demina.

"This is probably your first mistake, so we will let it pass. There is no need to involve the GPU at this point. But if we ever hear of you writing this kind of trash again, you'll be arrested, for sure," he torn out Lala's pages and threw them in the wastepaper basket. "Forget it!"

Another writer, probably more sympathetic, calmly advised the tearful Lala, "If you want to be a writer in our Communist society, my dear, you must write nice stories about the happy life of workers and peasants in our country, about their love for their motherland and loyalty to Comrade Stalin, to our beloved Communist party, and to the greatest genius in history, Comrade Lenin. I see from your pages that you have enough talent to do that. You could write such books that would make you a good and famous author. So, next year, please bring us your new stories, filled with the Communist spirit and ethos, and you'd be enrolled, I'm sure."

"If you need more dramatic subjects to tackle," first panelist joined in, "you have many Soviet heroes to work from: Red Army soldiers or hero workers in factories. Or why don't draw a picture that compares the happy life of our workers and collectivized farmers with the horrible existence they lead in countries such as Germany and America? You can criticize their capitalist governments as much as you want, but don't forget to add clearly that our Communist government is always honest, sincere and filled with concern for the ordinary person. Bring your stories to us next year. But for now, please leave the building as quickly as you can."

He forcefully pounded his palm on the table, indicating that the interview was definitely over.

Lala could barely get out an inaudible, "Thank you," and hastily made for the exit. The world around her was closing in a total blackness. She stumbled forward and couldn't remember how she managed to reach home.

"My heavens!" Sonya exclaimed in alarm when she saw her daughter's paper-white face. "What happened?"

Lala was still in shock and humiliation, her dreams shipwrecked on jugged boulders blocking her future. She collapsed on her bed and sobbed like a little girl with a broken heart. Sonya rushed to comfort her devastated child and did her best to calm her heaving sobs. Only after an hour of convulsive crying, Lala could master her emotions and give her mother an account of the crisis she was in.

"I can never be a writer," she wailed, her tears smearing her pillow chocked words. "I will never, ever write about subjects they said I must. All of them are pure lies! I just can't fabricate what is politically correct in order to be published! My soul and my heart are at stake! The good writer expresses what is inside him or her and cannot be dishonest. Lies kill both his soul and his gift. I will never write for them – ever! But I can't live without writing. I'd rather not live than give it up. I'd better commit suicide."

Sonya held her daughter tight and kissed her, despite the horror she felt in her heart.

She had seen for herself over the years what writing meant for to her daughter and could understand her, but she was desperately frightened to lose her only child in this way. She had already saved Lala from deadly illness but she couldn't figure out how she could possibly save her this time.

When Lala's father arrived from work, she calmed down a bit because his presence brought strong and positive energy into the house. Victor Demin always had creative and compassionate ideas how to apply to resolving many sticky situations. He suggested they all share dinner together, and that Lala begin by telling about her recent visit to the Writer's Institute as calmly as she could.

"We shouldn't cry, sweetie," he said seriously, as she finished her story. "We should examine the issue to make a decision. Your mom pushed me into a tough corner when she refused to emigrate almost twenty years ago. If we had gone to America then, like my fellow-officers did, you would be the writer, for sure. But, since that didn't happen, we must now think what to do in the present situation and develop a course of action."

"There is no way here," Lala protested.

"No, my sweetheart, there is always some way out. Just we must find the right doors. What do you love second to writing?"

"Nothing," Lala sniffled. "...You? ...Mom?"

"No. I mean interests...activities, not people."

"Music?" she said with hesitation. "Operas?"

"Okay," Victor smiled. "Can you see a way now?"

"No. I can't be opera singer. I have no voice."

"Well. I didn't say you should be a singer. We're talking about the writing now. I guess that operas are the only art form in the Soviet Union where your favorite characters – the kings, princes, princesses, fairies, knights – have a legal right to exist..."

"Are you suggesting that I write plays for operas?" Lala exclaimed, beaming at her father with her excited, still moist eyes.

"Close, but not exactly, my dear. The operas you like are the classical ones – written a hundred years ago. Modern Soviet operas suffer under the same rules as modern Soviet novels – they must be communist-orientated. There is no difference. But...," Victor gave Lala a wink and a meaningful smile, "... why don't you become a musical critic - a musicologist who writes historical books about composers of the previous centuries and about their creations – fairytale operas? Someone who would write composers' biographies? Who would study their creative procedure and describe how these geniuses composed their beautiful operas?"

"I don't know..." Lala shrugged filled with doubt. "I've never studied anything about that."

"You have to study. There are other places of higher education besides the Writers Institute where is possible to obtain an education in writing – the Conservatory of Music, for example," her father asserted, and then continued his explanation, "Having this profession, Lala, it would be possible to pretend that you're working this way for the communist society – to summarize the classical musicians' experiences and to teach the Soviet composers how to write operas about even Communists subjects. There would be nothing illegal in this work and, at the same time, you wouldn't go against your heart and soul, against your integrity and yours believes.

"Classical operas are considered neutral subject, which is good for you. In our country, it's possible for decent people who want to keep their consciences clear to only work with non-political subjects. Writing fiction in this day and age is no longer neutral, but classical music and operas still are. Everything magic and beautiful would be permitted and acceptable there. I think you would be satisfied and happy to write about what you do love. How is that?"

"I'll think about that. Thank you, Daddy," Lala nodded. "It's good advice because, you know, I really don't want to live, if I'm not writing. Maybe you're right - it's the only way. Maybe it's my chance to live. Maybe..."

Full of excitement and gratitude, Lala hung on her father's neck and kissed his cheek.

A month later she was enrolled in courses at the Moscow Musical College, the program she must complete before attending the Conservatory of Music.

As the Second World War drew closer, Sonya became concerned about her mother and Baron Peter. She had had no word from them for a long time and she guessed that they might be sick, or even dead because of their significant age. After searching, she finally found the phone number of the management office of the building where they were living in Kiev and placed a call. The officer explained to her that Ekaterina and Peter were arrested *without right of correspondence* two years ago because they were considered to be foreigners and 'Germans' and could be spies.

At the time of their arrest, Ekaterina was sixty-six and Peter – ninety-one. Both of them had grown up in Poland, spoke Russian at home, and didn't even know the German language that Ekaterina's mother language was. They ran from Europe in 1914, to escape the German advance, and considered themselves Russians. And Russia – in the cloak of Soviet State – murdered them, an old couple full of love and trust. They hadn't hidden or changed their names. They hadn't even bought false documents to protect themselves from suspicion. They had truly loved Russia and believed in it. This devotion Russia never forgave.

On hearing the painful truth, Sonya shed tears of horror for the country she was living in. What other country world take its seniors out and have them shot? However, Stalin's paranoid state got what it deserved: a year later his 'friend' Adolph Hitler took his 'little war' to the Russian border.

The start of the war was even more horrible for Sonya than for other people. She had just turned forty-eight and knew, only too well, that this was her year of widowhood, according to the psychic.

...It was already late evening when my mom returned home and found me completely absorbed in her notebooks.

"Did you read the whole day?" she asked surprisingly. "Did you eat anything?"

"Yes, Baba gave me something. I don't remember. Don't interrupt me, please!"

My mom laughed, "Why? Is it so interesting?"

"It's the best book I ever read in my life!" I exclaimed, sincerely. "It's true, Mom. It's not a flattery. It's really amazing! My God, what humanity lost! You would've been the best writer ever! I'm so sorry you weren't able to fulfill your dream!"

"Yes," my mom took a deep breath. "I know. I just console myself that my current occupation is not so bad at all. Anyway, I'm the author of twelve books about the opera and composers, and I completed my Ph.D. on the opera, as well. Besides, I have a good salary and can always get free tickets to the *Bolshoi* Theater and sit in the special media box with you and Baba. And I'm true to my own heart and soul. I write honestly what I think and about what I love."

"Well," I said with conviction, "I've made my decision today. I'll study from you, Mom, and I'll be a writer. I love music and opera, but I won't write about music. I'll be an author who writes about life, about adventures, about true tragedies and true feelings. Do you think it's possible in the Soviet Union of the 1960s-70s?"

"Hmmm..." my mom considered my question and then shook her head, "I think not yet," she confided to me. "For sure, it's better than in Stalin's time - but not much. The restrictions on writing fiction are nearly the same today. Any hint of the truth is prohibited. Official writers must still spout the same old lies, even though they are a little better decorated these days..."

"Anyway, I'll be a writer," I announced stubbornly. "And if there's not enough freedom for my work, I'll correct my Baba Sonya's mistake. I'll leave my motherland and seek out a free country."

Chapter 9

A CANDLE FOR COLONEL
KALOSHIN

The summer, following my eighteenth birthday, we started to build our dacha right away. Of course, it was almost impossible in the Soviet Union to buy wood and hire construction workers in the open market. All personal goods and services were produced by the state in limited quantity and then immediately hidden under shop counters or in desk drawers for dispensation to family, friends or for a 'fee'. This developed as the special Soviet form of nepotism and favors. The whole country participated in this system to get things (and get things done). If one didn't have well-placed relatives, then bribes would be necessary to obtain something.

Some of our neighbors advised us to contact a man working at a lumberyard. So, my mom did. This man helped us buy the lumber we needed, though at double the official (but un-obtainable) price. The difference he simply pocketed himself – a perk of his position.

We were forced to go this route, as were our fellow citizens. Anyway, the size of my windfall was large enough to cover even those exorbitant costs.

Then, my mom hired some workers from the same warehouse to construct our dacha from the lumber. More than money, they required payment in cases of vodka, which proved to be a more popular currency in the 1960s than rubles. At that time, there were no U.S. dollars in circulation in the U.S.S.R, except for a few black marketers who risked getting caught and faced the death penalty for their 'terrible crime'. The media always splashed such cases across the headlines to deter anyone from even considering such a move.

So, most laborers preferred vodka as payment; it was the most convenient for them. Since all of them were alcoholics, it proved a better incentive than money.

When the construction of the dacha was in full swing, my mom brought home two airplane tickets and announced happily, "We'll take a trip to the Crimea for a month. I booked a room at resort there, right on the Black Sea coast – two beds, a big balcony and amazingly beautiful sunsets and sunrises will fill the horizon out our windows. You're excited, aren't you?"

"Fantastic!" I exclaimed. The very idea was so unexpected and thrilled me. "But how could we desert our construction site? If we will leave our workers alone, they will only drink the time away. Someone should watch them."

"We will leave Baba Sonya to deal with the workers," my mom answered. "Anyway, neither of us is particularly useful at this point in the process. I'm getting really tired because of this damn construction. Baba is more experienced in this area. You know, she grew up in *Vysokoye*. She always helped her grandma, Stephanida, to run the estate and to deal with tradesmen and laborers. You also heard all her stories about their Polish manager, Zbignev Pshesinsky. He taught her the basics of business management while he helped her to rule the estate in her teen years, after Stephanida's death. Believe me, she knows what to do."

"Did you ask her? Has she agreed to it?" I wanted to know.

"Of course. I rented a comfortable room for her next door at the neighbors on our village street. She really prefers living at the country and will be happy to manage the dacha construction the way she wants. So, my sweetheart, go and pack your stuff."

"Right now?"

"Yes, right now. Our flight is tomorrow morning but tonight we still have many things to do. We should visit one place before we go."

"What place?" I inquired.

"A very special one you've never been to before – the church."

"The church?!" I was shocked by her proposal. My mom was certainly full of surprises today.

Nobody in our family was religious. We kept the two wrapped icons in storage, only for historic keepsakes - and I had no idea what they represented to us. None of us prayed, lit candles – ever. In my family no one was baptized or even wore crosses, except for my Baba Sonya during her distant childhood when she was baptized as a baby in the 19th century. However, when Sonya was a teen, she refused to wear a cross or attend church because she had no feeling for religion in her soul. To decorate a Christmas tree and to paint Easter eggs were for her mostly ancient Russian national traditions and not religious expressions.

My mom and I were both born in the Communists era and there was no consideration of us being christened. It was severely prohibited and there was no reason to agitate the authorities for an act that held so little meaning for us.

So, now at age 18 I had never entered a church and had no interest in it at all.

"The church?!" I repeated uncertainly. "What church? Weren't they all closed down after the revolution?"

I had faint memories of walking with Baba as a little girl down streets and we sometimes saw vacant, destroyed and neglected churches. They were usually headless, colors washed away by rains; some trees and little bushes had sprouted on their roofs between remains of beautiful stucco moldings; birds made their nests there. I recall the huge gates out front were either locked or barricaded with logs. As a curios child, I quite often came as close as I could to these mysterious and frightening giant towers and peered inside through cracks at the gates. Mostly they were empty – I could maybe see a gray stony floor. But some of those buildings had been converted by the government into warehouses or, if the gates were not blocked, people from the streets used them as toilets and garbage bins. As a result, they were dirty and stinky and full of excrement inside.

In these cases, my Baba always pulled me away quickly and announced strongly,

"Come on, Katya. Let's go. Go! It's all yucky!"

Since this was my image of Russian churches, my mom's direction to visit one was really incomprehensible to me. I looked at her questioningly.

"All the churches were closed," she answered my suspicious gaze, "but in the middle of the World War II, some of them were re-opened. Stalin probably realized that the war was almost lost. He must have thought back to his own education in an Orthodox Seminary and understood that the only way to improve morale and give people something to fight for was to open some churches again. He did it; right after that, the course of the war turned around – Russians rallied to defend their country. Religious people believed that it was somehow connected, spiritually."

"Maybe it was just a coincidence?" I knitted my brows skeptically.

"Maybe. But maybe not. Nobody could say exactly. Maybe this is a superstition, only, but, you know, I was turned a bit superstitious after some moments in my life. I can never fly in a plane, without first visiting a church and lighting a candle."

"Honestly?!" Her confession stunned me since I had never heard a word related to church candles from my mom. "You do travel a lot, don't you? You fly almost three to five times per year on business trips. Do you always light candles?"

"Yes," my mom admitted. "It might sound silly to you because you were educated without religion… But if I know that I had lit a candle before going, I felt quiet and confident on an airplane. It comforts me and I can sleep quietly and not to feel worried. I still don't believe in God but I believe in fate. It feels right to buy its good will with a simple candle. I've convinced myself that fate will give me its protection in return."

"Yes," I nodded, quite understanding her. "I'm scared of airplanes, too. I do remember Uncle Gleb's stories. If the candles will help me feel safer, I'm ready to go - even to the church."

I had not yet traveled in a plane, but I had heard plenty of scary stories about plane crashes from one of our neighbors, Uncle Gleb. He was an airplane construction engineer and a member of the government board which investigated each crash in detail. Most crashes were caused by technical errors, and technicians were trying to prevent future accidents. Then at home, in the kitchen, while waiting for the pot of tea to brew, Uncle Gleb shared these stories with us, his neighbors, who listened with a mixture of curiosity and terror.

Of course, I agreed with my mom – knowing well all these stories. It was absolutely necessary to visit the church, even though I wasn't religious, especially since it was my first trip on airplane so far away from Moscow.

The little Holy Trinity Church was hidden between huge high-rises on the small side street in downtown Moscow. It was fully renovated and looked shiny and festive, reminding me of the picture from glossy albums about Old Russia. My mom often bought such coffee table books to present to foreigners on her business trips abroad.

"Wow!" I exclaimed. "It doesn't look like it was opened during the war by Stalin. It's quite new and fresh!"

"Yes, this church was renovated and opened just recently, by the order of Yuri Andropov – the new KGB head. It was in all the newspapers that Andropov gave permission to open more churches."

"Why? What business is it of the KGB?"

"Quite a lot, actually. An opposition underground has started to emerge in our country. Have you heard anything about 'dissidents', people who are against the Communist regime? Andropov wants to catch all of them."

"Are those people in churches? I don't get the connection. Why isn't Andropov closed churches instead?"

"No. Dissidents are not usually religious people, of course and not related to the church at any ways. But Andropov wants to open more churches. He can then use the priests as his agents. When believers come and make confessions to the priests – something required by the church – they might pass on some useful information about the activities of these opposition activists. He decided to use the churches and priests as his new spy-web around the country."

"How do you know about that?" I went on, bewildered.

"All my friends and co-workers are talking about this. All educated people know. The grapevine travels everywhere. You know, some people have friends or relatives who are working for KGB. Not all of them keep quiet about what they are up to, about all their secrets. The truth leaked out of their circles and many people know, somehow. However, simple folks don't know anything and really trust their priests. But you shouldn't worry about that. Today's service is finished and the priest – at least a major or a colonel of the KGB has already gone. We won't even see him."

"Hmmm," I said meaningfully as we entered the church.

It was dreadfully gloomy inside, lit only by hundreds of flickering tapers arranged throughout the sanctuary on circular candleholders placed in front of icons of different sizes. Most of the icons were gilded and studded with colorful gems, often obscuring the figure hidden behind it. The walls were fretted and painted gold, as well. The aroma of burning lamps filled the space from their positions on long hanging chains in front of the major saints. It gave off a special strong smell which nearly caused me dizziness.

I recalled that my Baba Sonya stopped attending church because she fainted there a couple of times. Now I understood why. I found the aromatic atmosphere suffocating and she probably developed a reaction to it.

Candlelight, mystical gloom, shimmering gold and gems and the soft mumbling of the chanted prayers – all of these looked like an alien world to me. It was scary and repulsive, making me dizzy and echoing dark olden days of antiquity, former centuries which I had only seen in movies. From the perspective of the living and boisterous Moscow's streets outside, we had entered a time machine which had carried us back 200-300 years. I was dumbfounded. I felt very uncomfortable and a little fearful in these surroundings. I sensed no attraction to this sort of religion.

Here were few people left in the church, only some old, bent-over women garbed in dark clothes and black scarves on their heads. As we entered, those praying turned to us and cast short angry glances at us as if we were interrupting something and didn't belong there. I was surprised at their hostility and contempt. Why did they judge us? I hadn't done anything wrong. We'd only come to take a look at their world. Who knows, maybe I would like it and would turn religious? If they want to spread their faith, they should welcome newcomers instead of giving us looks that could kill. I couldn't fathom it at all.

"Oh, my gosh! We forgot to put scarves on!" my mom whispered and took out from her purse two little gossamer scarves – blue and pink – that she usually decorated her black English suit with. She covered her head with the kerchief and put the other on me. "It's obligatory," she murmured.

"What a narrow-minded stupidity!" I unhappily commented in a hushed voice. "What's the difference if I wear a scarf or not? It should be more important if I believe in God or not. What's inside my soul is far more significant, than what's on my head."

"You must understand, the Orthodox Church has very restricted traditions," my mom noted. "If they knew that we don't believe in God at all, they might even try to kill us."

"Well, then, we're on a dangerous adventure!" I whispered excitedly. "Like in the movies! We're walking on the edge of a knife. I'm going to enjoy it!"

My mom headed to a small counter at a corner where a similar woman in black kerchief was selling tapered yellow candles. They all were long, but of three different sizes – thin, medium and thick. The prices were appropriate, so we bought five candles – the thinnest and the cheapest – not because of the price but because they were more elegant and delicate looking.

Then we walked around, looking at the images on the walls.

"Where shall we put our candles?" I asked in hushed tones – there were dozens of candleholders to choose from.

"Here," my mom indicated, pointing to an icon of Christ. "He's the boss here. I usually prefer to deal with him. I guess he should be more responsible." She lit her candle from a burning one, melted some wax on the bottom end, and placed it in an individual holder at the top of the flaming tier. "This one is for my protection, so I can fly to the Crimea without incident. The second is for my safe return. Now, light yours two the same way."

I repeated the ritual faithfully, and then, realizing we had one remaining candle, gave her a puzzled look.

"Is this one extra? What is it for? You probably messed up and bough too many."

"No," she shook her head. "This one is extra special. I always light it in memory of one man who saved ours lives already – yours and mine – and sacrificed himself for us. I just want for his spirit to know that I will always remember him with great respect and gratitude, even admiration for his courage. I'm sure you would, too."

"Why should someone save us? Was there a fire? An accident? I don't remember anything like that."

My mom wistfully shook her head, "You have no memory of it. You were only two months old at the time. It was much worse than an accident. MUCH worse. Both you and I were scheduled for KGB arrest and deportment to a concentration camp."

"Me! At the age of two months?! It's crazy! It's unbelievable!"

The other women in the church were upset by our speaking so much, so we stepped outside, into the bright daylight, to continue our conversation.

"It happened to many people in Stalin's time. There were even special children's prisons and camps in Siberia."

"It sounds horrible!" I exclaimed. "We could have died there!"

"Of course," my mom nodded. "Millions did. There was cold and hunger, beatings and shootings, and physical and sexual abuse of women and children of all ages. A real hell, for sure, and many did not live through it. But fate sent us a savior...after Baba lit a candle for us..."

"I would like to listen to this story," I implored, as my mom had already stirred up my interest. The day was full of new sensations and revelations and I was open to them all.

"Okay, let's go over and sit on the bench beside the church gate. I'll share this story before we offer the final candle."

...Lala Demina met Dmitry Belov at the Moscow State Conservatory of Music at September 1945. World War II just ended and some survivors – much of what was left of the population of the Soviet Union - dragged themselves to the capital city to start a new life. Moscow remained a restricted city, so the only way for young people from other regions to live there was to be granted student status (a kind of internal visa).

Ten years later, officials added a worker status during the period in which Khrushchev made a campaign of rebuilding Moscow, a task which required more working hands for construction sides.

Actually, Khrushchev was the first Soviet leader to be at all concerned with ordinary people, to provide a better life for them. Unfortunately, leaders in the previous decades had thought only of their subjects in terms of milking and exploiting them and found them expendable enough to kill for very little reason.

Now, Khrushchev began bringing people out of darkened, rotten basements which were the only available post-war housing crammed with three-five families a room. By quickly throwing up cheap apartment buildings throughout the city, these survivor families were now awarded for free a one-family flat in a five storey block. True, the rooms in the *Krushcheby* (Russian slang name of those buildings) were small, but no longer had communal kitchen and bathrooms they had to share with neighbors. Depending on the size of the family, they were given one or two rooms of privacy and balconies if they were not on the ground floor.

It was unbelievable! It was fantastic! After suffering the exhausting and tormenting ravenous eras of Lenin and Stalin, Muscovites felt on top of the world at such 'luxuries' they had never expected to see.

But I'm getting ahead of myself. For the present, nobody could even guess that something like that could ever happen in the Soviet Union. Stalin still had about eight years to live and the current situation in the country was the same as Orwell described in his well-known novel '1984'.

During the four years of the war, Lala studied hard at Moscow Musical College. She took musical sciences as her father had advised her and, at home, continued writing her novels.

Dima, himself, had just returned from Siberian evacuation with his parents. His piano technique had, sadly, been lost through four years' disuse, so he couldn't pursue a career as a professional pianist right away. Still, he was good enough pianist to be enrolled into the music sciences courses.

In this way, Lala and Dima became classmates. There were ten girls and only two men at the course. One man, Vasily, was an older war veteran, around thirty-five, and handicapped. He had lost one leg in battle, wore the Order of the Red Star on his chest and walked on crutches. He was a real hero and the girls respected and admired him, but nobody fell in love with him, perhaps because he wasn't very intellectual or talented, and rather plain looking.

Dima, who was quiet the opposite, was a star. At each point he was outstanding, except maybe for the glasses he wore, but he tried to use them as little as possible, mostly for reading, and often took them off. Every girl was in love with him and he felt himself a king inside a gorgeous flower garden, or an oriental sheik surrounded by his young lovely harem. There was a serious competition between the girls to win his attention.

However, Lala was the only person who stood apart from the Dima-worship. She was still a virgin and wasn't interested in men at all. Her love, passion and even sexuality were spiritualized and imagined and found a satisfying outlet in her novels. She had yet to love a man, but this didn't concern her at all. Her heart belonged in another world – the world of her creations. She was in love with her characters and was devoted to them.

Dima didn't have much interest in her, either, though he certainly unconsciously noticed that Lala was beautiful and unusual. But he was surrounded by adoring young women who all wanted him.

He dated one girl, then - another, then – a third one, but couldn't find happiness or satisfaction with any of them. They were all dewy-eyed ingénues, and he was not motivated to initiate them into the mysteries of the body. His first lover, the aging Alla Petrovna, had spoiled him for furtive juvenile fumbling and groping; he was now accustomed to mature, sophisticated love-making and this is what he was looking for. Since his fellow students were miles behind him in this department, he just kept changing partners and enjoyed their youth and charm.

At the same time, Dima worked hard at his studies, learned a lot in sciences, spent most of his time in libraries with books and a couple of nights a week attended operas or ballets at the *Bolshoi* Theater or symphony concerts at the Big Conservatory Hall. One of his female classmates usually accompanied him.

One day, Dima bought two tickets to the theater but his current girlfriend came down with the flu and couldn't escort him.

O, shit! Who should I take this time? he thought frustrated, as she broke the news to him. Well...Let me see, who is next in line?

Dima closed his eyes and opened his phonebook somewhere in the middle. Then he glanced at what was in front of him. On the page were listed Lala Demina and her phone number.

"Wow!" he laughed. "It might be fun! Lala is so damn beautiful that she must be quite an experienced bitch. Well, we will see!" and he dialed the digits.

Playing that evening was the 'Mermaid' by Dargomyzsky at the *Bolshoi* Theater. Lala had, of course, already seen it many times before. But they were presenting a new cast and Lala wanted to hear some advanced singers. She had been writing that afternoon and, as she finished one of her poems, sensed that she needed a little break and was free for the evening. So, Lala agreed to go to the theater with Dima, though the opera and not Dima himself was the draw for her.

Surprisingly, they both appreciated the stimulation of the other and enjoyed their theater-going partnership. They choose not to take the *Metro* (Russian subway) home from the theater, but walked for two hours - all the way from downtown to Lala's home. The evening amazed the two of them and they continued talking one more hour, standing beside Lala's foyer entrance. They both felt they could talk forever and it was hard for them to say, "Good night".

A few days later, Dima invited Lala to a concert and, after that she became his constant theater-concert-mate for the next year.

After the each show, they walked for hours and discussed what they had seen, and talked about their music studies, as well as mutual interests in poetry, history, science and psychology. They were on a similar intellectual level, could communicate spiritually and had never tired of strolling and conversing. They also were young and good-looking and created a very attractive pairing – a tall, slender curly-headed brunet and petite blonde with inspired blue eyes.

The unspoken gap between them was that Dima dreamed about sex but had no idea how to bring this subject up because it was noticeable that Lala had no interest in it, whatsoever. She seemed to be flying so high on a heavenly plane, that he couldn't imagine how to turn her back to the earth. So she was both close to him and unreachable at the same time. Her beauty and purity were like a Greek statue of Aphrodite or Madonna by Michelangelo. Dima admired her but felt a bit intimidated, too; it brought back echoes of his first love with Lisa at age sixteen. Lala resembled Lisa, too, in that she was a precious soul mate – a woman from the sky. There was something sacred in their friendship.

Sadly, Dime realized that he was completely mistaken when he had had dirty thoughts about Lala from the start. However, he was in love and understood that the only way to get Lala was to marry her. This situation continued for more than a year.

Finally, when Dima proposed to Lala, she happily agreed. She was in love with him, too, admired him and felt very proud to win such a special, clever and handsome man at a time following the war, when even ugly, stupid or deformed men were considered prize catches by lonely men-starved women. Statistically, there was about one man per hundred women left in the Soviet Union after the war. The women suffered horribly and many turned crazy without sexual partners. Lala unconsciously needed a man, as well (she was already twenty-four years old) but didn't recognize it. She never even came down out of the clouds to think about bodily needs and sex. She was just unbelievably happy and mentally and spiritually in love with Dima.

The wedding was simple and small. In attendance were only relatives from both sides and classmates who knew Lala and Dima at the Conservatory. They had a good feast since now it was 1946, and more goods were available in the shops and at the farmer's market. Lala's mother, Sonya, prepared a Russian salad, fried fish and baked small pastry - cabbage and apple pies.

The Wedding Party was filled with happiness, laughter, jokes and dancing. There were even some wedding gifts; friends and relatives brought what they could find in the shops for the young couple – flowers, dishes, some furniture, some clothes and some shoes. Everything was gratefully received. People were so extremely poor at this time that they weren't fussy or impractical – every present was important and useful.

Lala became especially excited about the bolt of pink satin which her aunt, Anya, bought for her at the flea market. These years, in Moscow there was no chance to find quality fabrics at all, so this pink satin would be nice to use to make blankets, sheets, clothes, swaddling-clothes and nappies for their future children.

Lala dreamed about children and wanted to have at least two – son and daughter, or maybe more. She always regretted that she didn't have any siblings. When she asked her mother, why she hadn't had more children, Sonya wistfully explained, "We were living illegally, you know. Your dad was a former White officer. We could be arrested at any time. With one child was easier to move somewhere and to hide. Who could guarantee that, if we'd have five or six kids all of them wouldn't meet a painful death somewhere deep in the forest, in a camp in Siberia. We didn't want such a fate for them."

Lala totally disagreed with this philosophy.

"If you don't want to endanger your children, then you certainly should have emigrated all those years ago, as daddy suggested," she objected. "But if you stayed here, you must have more children to give your family a better chance to survive somehow. Look at Anya! How good it is that you have a sister! How much both of you love each other and help each other! It's amazing to have a sibling!"

"Of course. That's why I didn't emigrate," Sonya commented dolefully.

"I will have many kids, for sure," Lala pronounced. "It doesn't matter that the political situation in our country is not good. Now, my daddy perished in the war and became a hero so our family is in no more danger."

One and a half happy years passed in the life of the young newlyweds, but there still was no sign of pregnancy. Dima and Lala's wish for children was in vain. Their relationship continued to be amazing and their spiritual bond strengthened. They never fought, even had almost no minor disagreements at all.

Dima and Lala were each other's best friends, sharing all their thoughts, hopes and dreams. They shared even dark personal and family secrets. Lala told her husband all her family history, starting from Ekaterina von Wilde and her vases. She related that Sonya had some Royal blood and that her dad, Victor, had once been a White Army officer. She even confided in Dima about her red star birthmark when he noticed it.

In turn, Dima told her about his parents' counter-revolutionary past and how he was saved - being an embryo, with his mom together - by his father, who wrapped them into the rug, fooling the Bolsheviks. He even brought the rug from his parents' house and put it on the wall in their bedroom which he shared with Lala every night.

They trusted each other in full, so Dima even confessed to Lala about his first love, Lisa, and 'episodic affair' with Alla Petrovna, his brief first marriage, and even why his eyes been sacrifices to escape military service.

They were completely open to each other and loved each other dearly, though Lala was disconcerted by many of his confessions and cried a lot, anxious that further revelations of dirt and dishonesty would soil forever her once-admired love.

But loving him so deeply, she was able to forgive him and hopped that he had changed forever from a lust-seeking coward. It wasn't hard for her to convince herself that they were all in the past and now best forgotten.

Their mutual love and understanding would have been total bliss – a never ending honeymoon – if, somewhere deep in his soul, Dima didn't have unconscious desires that were not fully satisfied in his married life. It came back to the same old point with him – he hungered for more adventurous sex.

At her age of twenty-five, Lala was an innocent in bed. He tried to teach her but she wasn't a good student in this subject. She wasn't mature enough to feel the pleasures and passions he wanted reciprocated; she was stuck on the dutiful wife level. She lacked sensuality and the play of seduction; she agreed to sexual relations out of obligation and a longing to give birth to Dima's children. For her, sex was the worst part of being a wife, but she obediently tried her best to make her husband happy.

Then, one day, the dream for child came true in this union.

Dima had grown up in the city of Tver, in the middle of the

Russian woodlands. His grandma, Lydia, quiet often had taken him into the forests to pick wild mushrooms. They were a big and important part of their simple and poor family's menu during the hungry decades stretching from the twenties past the forties. Grandma Lydia knew mushrooms very well and taught Dima from his earliest childhood to identify them. He was a real mushroom expert and was also good in orientation. He never failed to find the best path, even in an unknown forest.

Every summer Dima and Lala rented a dacha and walked in the forest for hours, harvesting pails full of mushrooms. Then they fried them, boiled them, dried them on threads, marinated them or salted and canned them. In this way, the young couple always had a lot of protein to last through the winter months.

Lala was raised in Southern Russia, where there weren't so many mushrooms and weren't any forests, either. So, she never learned about mushroom picking and cooking before. Now Dima quickly educated her and she was a willing and successful student.

One summer's day in 1947, they walked quite deeply into the forest and were surprised to find themselves in an amazing pine grove they had never come across before. The trees surrounding them were used for ship timber. Stretching their necks to view the treetops, Lala and Dima could see the soft pine branches contrasted with the piercing blue sky. The trees were topped in pink and infused with gold and orange sunshine.

Initially, dumbfounded by the divine beauty of nature, the couple remained silent, listening with wonder as the pine boughs rustled from an elevated light wind. Then they looked down.

The earth at their feet was covered with bright green moss and strewn with dried tan needles and dark, open cones from tall conifers. The soil was a thick, soft carpet, as resilient as a spring mattress under their feet. The springiness was fun to explore, and Lala and Dima exchanged playful looks and began to laugh. Before long they had temporarily abandoned their half-filled mushroom pails and began to play tags, like little kids, and toss pine cones at one another.

They were so happy and so full of merriment that, when Lala accidentally stumbled over a root and fell, she couldn't rise again from laughing so hard. Dima lowered himself on the moss beside her, found her girlish side more attractive than ever and covered her with kisses. She answered him readily and pleasantly, inspired for the first time in their married love. There, in that lovely pine grove, on their mossy mattress, they shared the deepest love they had known and conceived a child. The symphony accompanying them was the twittering of the birds and the whisper of the wind. It was a triumph of love and nature! It was the beauty of life!

In a few months, Lala visited her doctor and he confirmed her pregnancy. In her heart she was pretty sure that she would have a son. She and Dima were on top of the world over the news and even chose a name for the boy – Sergey (Russian nickname – Serezha). Lala's doctor later assured her that all the scientific signs pointed – one hundred percent – to the child being a boy. He even gathered a group of students during one of Lala's visits and gave them a chance to hear the baby's heartbeat by pressing the stethoscope to her tummy.

"Come over here, everyone, and listen," he called. "Here is a good sample – an absolutely typical heartbeat of a male – so strong and healthy."

The students came and listened attentively in turns and nodded and then congratulated Lala, who felt incredibly content.

During Lala's pregnancy, Dima had already completed his courses and begun working as an editor in a musical publishing house. They published the scores of classical music. In the evenings, he worked on his graduate project at home or went to operas and concerts. However, Lala could no longer accompany her husband in public because her physical condition was showing.

The Russian mentality in those years decreed that pregnant woman hide at home and not show their expanding stomachs in public. For Lala to attend concerts or theater during this period was out of the question. She was sure it might cause a scandal. The audience would certainly be distracted from the show and may even point the fingers at her in disgrace.

"Look, look! She is pregnant and still she had the nerve to come to concert! Ha-ha-ha! What a shame! She must be crazy!"

Lala, understandable didn't want to hear these kinds of remarks and preferred to stay at home.

Such a hypocritical outlook was based on a disingenuous rationale by the communist regime which officially announced, "In our country, we have no sex!" They were all ready to humiliate and slap in the face a shy young wife who was happily with child, but at the same time, look the other way while debauchery and lewdness on the level of prostitution, flourished on all levels of society - especially at the highest. And so the dirty and sick of society tried to shame and ridicule those who were clean and spiritually healthy. The country was turned mentally upside-down and inside-out and resembled a madhouse.

Knowing well the situation, Lala bound her tummy tightly, while attending the courses, in order to hide her condition, but at home in the evenings, she relaxed and gave her baby more room to move, turn, jump and to punch with its tiny fists on the walls of her womb.

"Our Serezha is so active," she told Dima, showing him the baby's knees or elbows which jutted or stuck out sometimes under her stretched belly. "He is playing there, running and wiggling. I guess if he were in the theater listening to music, he would be inspired to start singing. Shame that would be! You'd better go without me."

However, she didn't want Dima to attend the concerts with any of their class-mates, knowing well that all of them were still in love with him and possibly would try to seduce him in spite of his married status. She trusted her husband...but...just in case...

"I could probably invite my boss from work, Tatiana," Dima suggested. "She is professional, loves music and she is not a threat to you since she's fifty-years-old, short, fat and ugly. Her hair is always matted. She can carry on an intelligent conversation, like we usually do. She may even be inspired to increase my salary in the future, so it would be not bad to bribe her a bit with such an invitation."

"Does she have a family?" Lala queried.

"She is divorced, but has two sons – twenty-six and thirty years old – both older than we're," Dima convinced his young wife. "She is like a mother. And she is also well-connected with the people from the highest level. This could be useful for my career to establish close links with some people on those levels. You don't have to worry, honey. I'll do this for us, for our future and well-being."

This sounded reassuringly to Lala and she wholeheartedly approved the idea, completely forgetting about Dima's teen adventure with his forty-five-year-old music teacher, Alla Petrovna. The situation seemed so different now – he had a wife and a child on the way.

Yet, the more evenings at the concerts and theaters Dima spent with Tatiana, the more excited he became about her. Being the director of the publishing house, she was twenty-five years older and had twenty-five times more experience in life, science, art, music and personal relationship at the top of Soviet society. Tatiana was a Communist party member, of course, otherwise, she wouldn't be in the position she held, ever. She was on the same intellectual level as Dima and Lala, but not as spiritual as Lala, however, much more practically experienced.

She could give a good advice to Dima, sometimes, in areas in which Lala couldn't, and the thought that she was much clever that his young wife began to grow in Dima's mind. First, from time to time, and then, more often, he started to turn to Tatiana, instead of Lala, as his adviser in all situations, even family problems.

Step-by-step, he fell fully under Tatiana's influence since they were constantly together, working side by side full-time during the day and then visiting the theaters three to four evenings per week. She always praised Dima, told him that he was a genius, that he was special and would have the greatest career imaginable, especially with her help, but...but the one factor working against his future career would be the expected baby - one who would be crying day and night, disturb his sleep and work, and rob him of chances to do truly creative books. The coming child would be sure to wake him up early, be sick or teething, troubled with diarrhea or rashes and full of annoyances like the smell of dirty diapers. In short, the little one would prove to be a huge pain in Dima's ass which would interfere with his professional advancement.

"The best thing would be, if you wife would have an abortion," Tatiana suggested.

When Dima proposed the idea to her, Lala was dumbfounded. First of all, they had dreamed of having the baby for two years of their marriage. It was their life, their future and their love. Another point was that Lala was already about six months pregnant and the time for an abortion was long gone. And finally, abortions were prohibited by the law after the war in order to increase the population of the U.S.S.R. Exceptions were made only for woman who were very ill and might not survive childbirth.

However, Tatiana explained that she knew a doctor who, for a sum of money, would sign such a paper confirming that Lala was severely ill. Besides, she argued, even at six month it would be possible to perform illegal surgery at home, them to dismember the fetus and dispose of it. If they're short of money, Tatiana, as the best friend of their family offered to pay the underground abortionist for his services.

When Dima announced this representing it as his own new idea, Lala flatly refused, burst into tears and, in disgust, slammed the door on her husband.

"But fatherhood would disturb my career," he tried to argue.

"Many people who had successful careers had even many kids," she insisted, sobbing. "Remember Mozart, Bach, Schumann, Wagner, Liszt...I would be with the baby – not you. My mom will constantly help us. Dima – just forget it! I'll never give up this child! OUR child!"

When he reported back to Tatiana about Lala's stubbornness, she only shrugged, "Well, it's her choice," and pursed her lips, pretending to be offended. "But you, Dimochka, forget about your career under the circumstances. I have much sympathy to you, my poor guy. What a horrible situation you're in, my dearest friend! A crying baby and a scandalous wife! For sure, she can't give you good sex with such a huge tummy, can she? You're so unhappy and unfulfilled, my poor boy. Why don't you come by my suite after concert this evening? You need to relax."

"Lala would notice if I came home late," he anxiously replied, yet experienced recollection of Alla Petrovna's unsurpassed skills in bed. He anticipated, based on his intuition, that Tatiana would be even better.

"Okay, then let's leave after the intermission and go to my flat, instead of later. That way you will be home on time and not arouse any suspicion from your difficult wife. Tell me, how you can live with such a woman?!" she looked at her handsome escort and future lover with compassion. "I really don't see how you can put up with it."

After his first sexual encounter with Tatiana, Dima felt that he had found exactly what he needed – a strong woman who could guide him in life, back him up and advance his career, combining his bright talent with her high level connections. She was also, at he same time, absolutely amoral and into debauchery – the kind of playmate he dreamed of and missed. After his time with Alla Petrovna, this was very important to him.

From this time forward, the two of them left their concerts or last act of the operas early to romp in bed together, especially as Lala had a difficult last month of pregnancy and had to be hospitalized. Her kidney didn't function because of inflammation, endangering both her life and the baby's. Her mother, Sonya, stayed with her all the time and failed to notice when her son-in-law returned home from the theater.

In the mornings, before his work, Dima sometimes visited Lala at the hospital, even bringing her flowers and suggesting that if their 'boy' turned out to be a 'girl' that they might name her Tatiana.

Lala flatly refused once more. "If our child is a girl – something, by the way, our doctor says is impossible - she will be named Ekaterina, or Katya, after my dear grandma. And certainly not after your 'old witch'."

"No, no, I didn't mean that," Dima stepped back not to offend her. "I just mean it's a popular name. Every second girl in Russia today is called either Tatiana or Natasha."

"Well," Lala snapped back. "We're going to be different! It will be MY child, and I will be one to name it. You were happy for it to go in the sewer! You certainly won't be one to name it!"

"No, no," Dima reddened with shame. "It was only a proposal to abort the baby. I care too much about your health, and you are having problems carrying the child. I only love you so much!"

Dima was really caught between the two women in his life and didn't know what to do. He needed help and advice. There were no psychologists in the Soviet Union in those years because the Communist Party Secretary or board was supposed to handle such cases and give ideological rather psychological guidance. Tatiana as a communist boss was Dima's psychologist and she was in a position to advice him. But of course, she had her own motives in this triangle.

Since they were lovers and co-workers, he openly shared with her all his family secrets, including Lala's family history, as well as his own parents' involvement with the *Left-SR Party;* the failed plot against Lenin and his own escape from Bolshevik guards along with his mother, with the help of the rug. He decided he couldn't live without Tatiana anymore, and depended on her in full. Yet, he still dearly loved his sweet, pure Lala, even though his sexual tastes ran more along the lines of Tatiana's sensual exploits.

Lala had very difficult and dangerous delivery. A baby girl, Katya, was born with no crying or breathing. But still – there was a strong heartbeat and this gave the doctors some hope. They put a pipe into the infant's lung and pumped in air.

Suddenly, a weak and an almost unconscious Lala heard one of the nurses laughing, "Look at this! Such a child! She is still not breathing, but already eating!" And everybody smiled seeing Katya sucking the pipe even before she took her first breath.

"This strong-hearted eater will live!" doctor announced joyfully.

While Lala stayed – the last month before and two weeks after the delivery - in hospital, Dima openly lived in Tatiana's suite. Once Sonya met him, when he returned home to pick up some stuff, she said, "Congratulations, Dima! You're a happy father now!" and hugged him warmly. "Why haven't I seen you much these days?" she queried him.

"I'm staying with my parents in Tver," he explained. "They're feeling very bad and extremely sick. They need my help. I hope you'd be able to manage to help Lala and the baby by yourself."

"Of course, I will," Sonya assured. "Just say 'hi' to your parents for me. I hope they will recover soon."

She was confused. She didn't hear anything about Dima's sick parents. A week ago she had sent them a card about their first granddaughter's birth but didn't ask a thing about their health. She felt uncomfortable.

Two days later, Sonya got a phone call from Dima's father, Vladimir, who wanted to congratulate her and Lala.

"How are your and Maria's health?" Sonya asked by the way.

"Just great, never better," Vladimir answered, surprised. "And where is Dima? Don't you have any idea why he didn't call us and didn't show up here for so long? Of course, I understand, he is too busy with his new baby..."

"Yeah," Sonya murmured ironically, as she hung up. She realized that something bad was going on behind everyone's backs. However, she decided not to say anything to Lala who still was struggling to retrain her health and some days hung somewhere between life and death. Such horrible suspicions could easily undermine Lala's progress; this was a burden that Sonya must carry alone, at least for now.

As Lala and Katya returned home, Dima finally put in an appearance. He filled the role of happy father and husband so casually, as if nothing was amiss. The contented family life picked up where it had left off. Dima had decided to stick with Lala and continue his liaison with the 'other woman', Tatiana, on the side as long as he could. It suited him perfectly. Lala should nurse the baby now and couldn't go to the theaters and concerts for some time. Everything was settled once more, as it was a few months before baby Katya's birth on April 30, 1948.

However, Tatiana had other dreams. She didn't want have a young married lover who could possibly dump her at any moment and return to his family hearth. She felt a need to force things to ahead. She studied Dima's character long enough to discover how to capture her prey.

Every day, Tatiana asked Dima how Katya was doing but his answers didn't satisfy her. The baby was very calm and quiet. She was always full because Lala had a lot of very healthy and concentrated milk and Katya slept almost twenty-four hours a day, with a few short breaks, only, to be fed and changed. Dima didn't have a crying, sick infant at home, but rather a happy and smiling one. She was, in short, one of the last troublesome babies in the world.

This angered and disappointed Tatiana, who had hoped to separate Dima firmly from his growing family by playing on his complaints.

A month later, finally, she boldly proclaimed to her young lover, "I want you to leave your family and marry me."

"You know..." Dima weakly objected. "I still love them, too, and there is no reason. Why can't we leave things as they are?"

"Here is the reason," Tatiana announced angrily. She took a piece of paper and pen, sat at her desk and started to write.

"What are you writing?" Dima asked worriedly, because the expression on her face told him she was up to something.

"I'm writing my report to the KGB," Tatiana explained, narrowing her eyes, with a cruel smile. "I'm a secret informer for the KGB and my duty of honor is to let them know about your parents' anti-soviet activities. They should be arrested and executed immediately, the same as you, because you shouldn't cover for them. You, as a young Soviet citizen should have been the first to report about your parents many years ago and turn them in to the authorities. You know that. It's correct action under Communist morality. If you cover for such enemies - your parents, you will be executed along with them. So, you decide. If you choose to leave your wife and marry me immediately, I'll throw this report in the garbage. If you refuse, I'd finish it and deliver it to the KGB right now. It's up to you!"

At first, Dima thought Tatiana was teasing him with a silly joke. He didn't believe her. But then he realized the situation he was in. His talkative mouth, his naïveté, his open heart and soul gave Tatiana a chance to use the personal information he had shared with her to blackmail him, to corner him and claim him as her property. There was no way out for him. Only, to kill her, but he was a gentle man, not even capable of killing a fly.

The whole evening Dima spent pleading desperately with Tatiana to pardon him and his parents. He was on his knees in front of her, kissing her knees and hands and sobbing, but she was adamant. She demanded from him that he must divorce, immediately, the next morning, to save his and his parents' lives. She completely set him up.

This way they spent the entire night and in the morning took a taxi and rode to Lala's apartment to pick up Dima's belongings.

Lala didn't even notice that her husband wasn't at home that night. She was sleeping quietly, tired of waiting for him in the evening, cuddling her baby and experiencing a lot of sweet dreams, happy and content.

She was awakened by Dima fussing around their room, packing his stuff into a suitcase.

He had no room or time for the aristocrat's carpet, so he left it hung on the wall.

"Good morning, darling," Lala whispered. "What are you doing?"

"I'm leaving," he grumbled.

"A sudden business trip?"

"No, I'm leaving you, Lala."

"Are you going to see your parents?"

"No. I'm leaving you forever. I'm going to get a divorce."

"What?!" she sat up abruptly in her bed and stared at him, blinking sleepily. "Sorry, I can't grasp what you are saying. Who's divorcing? Surely you don't mean you and me? But why?? What are you talking about? Are you joking?"

He knelt down in front of her and took her hands, as she realized with horror that his eyes were tear-stained and swollen.

"I love you, Lala," he said, stammering from chocking sobs caught in his throat. "I really love you and the baby. But I have to leave you forever. This is the political situation in our country. Remember, this is not about our love; it's only about politics. I'm trapped. Here is my application for our divorce," he took the paper from his pocket and handed it to her. "You put it in motion, please. And forgive me. I'm innocent, just a stupid idiot! It's my mistake, only, and I should pay for it."

Lala reacted with total bewilderment, as he picked up his suitcase and exited. He had no more time to talk to her – Tatiana was waiting for him outside, in the taxi.

Soon baby Katya woke up, hungry, and began bubbling to herself and smiling, Sonya entered the room and found that her daughter had fainted.

Many trying weeks followed that fateful day. After the startling bolt from the blue, Lala was in mental and emotional shock, and the days passed by in a blur. Her thyroid gland reacted at her calamity the same way as her father, Victor's, gland had under KGB torture – she gained 20 pounds in only a week and a half. She also lost her milk. It curdled and turned sour.

Lala didn't know at first what happened with her milk and allowed Katya to suckle, so the baby, who was only six weeks old, became sick and suffered diarrhea and stomach pain. She cried constantly with hunger, even having seizures and began to lose weight day by day.

Sonya dashed from doctor to doctor in despair, alarmed that both of her dear girls were losing their health at the same time. Finally, the doctors found for Katya some manufactured baby food and her life was saved, but, anyway, her perfect health was undermined for the future. Everything collapsed in the family, in their life, in their home.

However, Sonya found a minute to write a letter to Dima's parents about the tragic news. Vladimir and Maria came to Moscow immediately and tried to make Dima change his mind and return to the family, but Tatiana (who was even older than them) openly explained her threat that if their son ever left her, their lives would be in danger. So, they shut up in a moment and retreated back to Tver without a word. Nobody wanted to die.

It looked like Tatiana had won; it didn't matter that all their friends and relatives, co-workers, Dima and Lala's classmates and teachers and even Tatiana's two sons, along with their families, were against her marriage to Dima who was twenty-five years younger. Everybody was shocked by the pairing, but no one (except Dima and his parents) knew the real reason. This spousal union was a mystery to all who knew about it.

In spite of her victory, Tatiana realized that her happiness was quite fragile. Stalin was already about seventy years old. He could die any minute and the national political situation would, most likely, by altered by his death. When this occurred, it was very possible that Dima would be free to leave Tatiana and return to his family.

So, naturally, Tatiana looked for a guarantee that Dima's young body and money would belong to her alone. She was certain that his mind and gifts would eventually assure him of reaching academician status. He was well on his way now, working full-time and brilliantly studying for two PhDs at the same time. Not every young man could carry such a demanding load, especially going through a painful divorce.

If Tatiana could have her way, Lala and Katya would disappear (die, perhaps) following the divorce, but they both recovered their strength. This meant they were still potential rivals for Dima's affection. So, she decided to take another drastic step, to forever prevent Dima's from crossing the bridge back home.

She wrote another letter to the KGB, informing them that Lala's father had been a White Army officer and that her mother had inherited some royal blood from the Empress Catherine the Great. These were things Dima had foolishly revealed to her in confidence, as well. She asked Dima to sign the letter together with her. He refused, at first, but then, she threatened him again and he put his signature, finally, on the document, tearfully knowing full well that Sonya, Lala and Katya would be sent to the concentration camp. The women would be executed and baby would be housed in a children's prison to be indoctrinated and raised by the Communists, which meant, for most orphans, beating, hunger and sickness often leading to death.

Two weeks after Dima's betrayal, Lala received a notice from the KGB, inviting her to come in for questioning because they had received some information which accused her of being an 'enemy of the state'. This was very unusual. The KGB never 'invited' anybody anywhere. They always came in full force, grabbed a person, threw them into a car, and took them away to who knew where. But they were never heard from or seen again.

Whatever the form of communication, Lala felt she was condemned. Once the divorce had sunk in, she had felt things couldn't get any worse. Now she was way beyond tears or outrage. She was just convinced that this was the end of the line for her and she might as well accept it.

On the day of Lala's encounter with the Secret Police, Sonya took the baby and went to Barbara Torchinsky's suite to be harder to find - just in case. Barbara was, by now, widowed by the war and had moved to Moscow to study at Medical Institute in spite of her advanced age. Of course, Sonya knew that it was impossible to hide anywhere from KGB, even in another country, but in Barbara's flat she felt a bit more protected and secure for the moment.

"We have one church opened not long ago in our neighborhood," Barbara told her. "Let's go there and lighten a candle for Lala. It's just possible she'll have a sympathetic KGB interrogator."

"A sympathetic, decent person? At KGB? What are you talking about?" Sonya shook her head in disbelief. Still, she knew it couldn't hurt and she and Barbara, carrying Katya, walked to the church.

Meanwhile, full of trepidation and dread, Lala entered the dismal KGB Headquarters. She never expected she would walk out these doors and ever see her mother and daughter again. A sullen guard followed her to the office on the third floor and even opened the huge oak door for her. She came in and saw a middle-aged man in a gray civilian suit, white shirt and tie, sitting by the large table. Framed portraits of Lenin, Stalin and Felix Dzerzhinsky (the founder of the KGB) hung on the cold, painted wall above his head.

"Good morning, Comrade Demina," he greeted her casually and pointed to the chair across from him. "Sit down, please. I'm Colonel Kaloshin."

Lala bashfully lowered herself onto the edge of the chair, tense as a string, expecting any minute to be seized and beaten. She didn't have the courage to look at her accuser.

"Well," he said calmly. "I wanted to see you because I have quite a serious letter with accusations against you. It is signed by your former husband and his new wife. They brought the letter here, in person. I did talk to them. I saw them," he paused.

Lala lifted her head and, finally, glanced at him. The man looked very ordinary, with a plain Russian face, gray eyes and little smile, hidden somewhere in the corners of his mouth. His gray hair was cut short. There was nothing about him that said that this was professional 'secret agent', or a horrible KGB executor and killer. He could be a farmer, a teacher or an accountant, a locksmith or even a plumber – an unremarkable person in society.

"They claim that your father was a White Army officer. Is that true?"

"No," Lala shook her head slowly. "He was killed in the war as a hero."

"We know that," the colonel nodded. "They also claimed that your mother has lineal connections to the tsar's family. Is that true?"

"No," Lala murmured again. "My grandma, Ekaterina, was a peasant woman. My mom was raised in the countryside."

The colonel laughed.

"We must investigate these reports, you understand. Your ex-husband's claim sounded a bit absurd," he uttered with a smile. "It seems to me that he and his new woman are villains who want to get rid of you, using our government system. You're so young, exhausted, weak, and sick and they seemed to be really disturbed by you. He dumped you and she wants to finish you off. She must be afraid he'll dump her and come back to you."

"I'll never take him back," Lala angrily replied.

"Of course," the colonel nodded, agreeing with her, "but this shameless woman with no soul and no morality doesn't know that. She is scared of you and she wants you dead. And she wants your baby dead, as well, so he won't need to pay alimony. It's obvious to me. They're abusing our system." He took a deep breath and then continued, "However, I have no right to ignore their letter. According to my duty, I have two options: first, to believe them and to arrest you right away; or the second, which is to check their claims.

"I'm sure that each of my co-workers would use the option number one because it requires little effort – you just press a button. But I have compassion for you and I can't just snap my fingers to decide you and your child's fate without substantial evidence. I'll check these claims. I'll make enquiries in all the places you or your parents lived, studied or worked before. It will take me about two month to get all the answers. Then, I'll invite you for a second meeting.

"So, now you can go, Comrade Demina. See you." And he signed a pass for Lala to exit the building.

She even forgot to say 'thank you' or 'bye'. She silently stood up and walked away, feeling her legs were like rubber and wouldn't be support her weight. It was unbelievable! No one who was accused by somebody exited the KGB building, ever! This man was a godsend for her. He was her lifesaver! It was a miracle!

When Lala shared the story with her mother, Sonya assured her, "Don't worry, there aren't any documents or evidence anywhere to be found. Your dad burned all the documents imaginable in that fire in our backyard after I refused to emigrate. There is no record left. But you are now paying for your own mistake. You should never have told Dima anything!"

"I trusted him, Mom," Lala sniffled. "My daddy was so good. I couldn't imagine that a man could be different than him, that the man who loved me might betray me."

In exactly two months, a second letter arrived with an appointment scheduled at the KGB offices. This time Lala felt better and more confident, knowing that she had one protector there who went out of his way to be kind for no reason. Possibly, it was due to his heart of sincerity. But how could such a man work for the KGB, and a colonel, yet! It was hard to understand.

Colonel Kaloshin met her in the same office, with the same portraits, by the same table, wearing the same suit. A big pile of papers filled the table in front of him.

"Congratulations, Comrade Demina," he said, warmly. "My investigations have yielded the same results – no information at all. I can tell you what. I have two options, once more. 'No information' could mean that your parents were a White Army officer and a countess and they successfully hid all the evidence; or, then again, 'no information' could mean that they were simple Soviet people devoted to Communist Party, but their documents got lost somehow through the chaos of bombing and fires of the revolution, the Civil War and the World War II during the German occupation of Rostov-on-Don.

"Again, each of my fellow investigators would choose option number one. However, I prefer to choose option number two. I can't arrest you without evidence and I'm saying 'no information' equals 'no guilt.' So, I'm closing your file. You're free to go and raise your child."

He stood up, approached Lala, shook her hand and handed her a signed pass.

"Forget your bastard ex-husband and his witch forever, Comrade Demina," he added, smiling. "This nightmare is finished. There is no danger for you anymore in our society."

"Thank you," Lala said her voice choked with gratitude and her eyes tearing with relief. She didn't linger another minute in that awful building.

When she learned of Lala's second appointment, Sonya was convinced that her prayer candles for God helped. How else could they possibly explain the fact that Lala was being protected by a kind-hearted and hardworking officer in KGB Headquarters? This colonel Kaloshin was one who saved their lives and Lala had even forgotten to find out his first name. He was stranger who saved them, at a time when Dima, the closest family member was working to destroy them. How could such a development be possible? It was truly an inexplicable mystery!

However, the time of testing wasn't over yet. The Communists' evil eye never rested; it was always out any signs of decency, fair-mindedness, and compassion in the people's souls in order to root out such impulses. Lala received a third letter from the KGB the next month. She must, once more, go to *Lubyanka* (the square where the KGB building was located) for questioning. On her arrival, she was unnerved to encounter a different man in Colonel Kaloshin's third-floor office.

"Where is Colonel Kaloshin?!" Lala exclaimed disappointedly, as she entered.

"Kaloshin is dead. He didn't do his work properly," the man barked back. He failed to offer her a seat, but she perched on the edge of the chair on her own initiative. "Forget him. I want you to work for us, to be our secret informer."

"What?!"

"It's very easy job but extremely well-paid," the man continued. "You're alone with your child. You certainly need more money. Every month you'll get an envelope with cash added to your regular salary and nobody would know about our agreement. You'll be allowed to travel abroad, even to capitalist country. You'd have a lot of beautiful dresses, shoes, cosmetics; you'll also attract many men. Besides, we'll give you a car and your own flat without nosey neighbors. You'll be able to live like the elite in our country with only a little bit of effort on your part.

"Every month you should write a detailed report about your

class-mates, co-workers, friends and relatives: what they are saying and thinking about our Communist regime, the Communist Party, Comrade Lenin, and Comrade Stalin; about our communistic future and so on. It might only be a couple of pages long.

"It's quite an easy job. In fact, it's the perfect job for a poor, single woman – like you. You'll easily advance your career, you know."

He gazed at her attentively, pausing for her answer.

Lala knew perfectly well that everyone she knew hated such political topics; ridiculed the party and its leaders and certainly didn't trust them at all. What could she possibly to write in her reports?

It was clear as day – all of her friends would be arrested. She would be asked to betray them – something she would never do. If she tried to fill the reports with lies, the KGB would still uncover the truth, as there were usually at least two informers in each company, class, office, for them to check one another. So, such a strategy was doomed to failure and the KGB wouldn't take kindly to her clumsy attempts to fool them. They had little mercy for traitors.

While the promises of success and money were tempting, Lala knew the job would be impossible. 'Don't trust the Bolsheviks, ever!' she heard the motto of her father echo in her mind.

The KGB promises could be false, since they just want to nail me. That's it', Lala said to herself. Anyway, in each office, class, group everybody knows who the informer is. People have a special feeling and instinct to identify someone 'watching' them. Naturally informers are universally vilified and mistrusted.

He proposed that I be an official snoop, hated by everybody, for a good salary... she thought. No! Never! I'll never sell my soul, my honesty, my friendship for money or privileges. No career, travel, wardrobe, cars or flat are not worth my own self-respect and my soul is not for sale. My mom and my child would never forgive me if I were to do such a horrible thing. My dad's spirit would cry out from his grave at the thought. Don't trust Bolsheviks! Don't work for them! I already refused to be a writer in order not to compromise my conscience! How could I possibly agree now to become a sneaky dog licking their boots! The very thought is totally absurd!

In her most diplomatic voice Lala said politely, "Thank you very much for your suggestion, but I can't do this job. No. I refuse."

"Well," the professional agent took her refusal as an insult. He angrily retorted, "Well, if you don't want to work for us, that must mean that you're not devoted to the motherland person!"

He followed his opening salvo with two hours of threats, trying to intimidate her with fist banging on the table and unpleasant hissing in her face. Soon, Lala was crying and quivering, emotionally drained once again. Of course, she was scared, but still stubbornly refused. In fact, after all the abuse hurled at her, at this point she was completely adamant. Her will-power was forged of iron and, finally, when his tirade failed, the KGB agent gave up. He realized that this woman, recruited as an informer under such inhuman pressure wouldn't be a good informer, anyway, so he let her go. But he hurled a final threat at her retreating back, "Just be ready. You and your family will be exiled from Moscow. People like you don't deserve to live in the capital city. You are only fit to live in the provinces deep in the Siberian forests!"

As Lala reported to her mother about what had happened, Sonya sighed, "Well, in the distant provinces, people live, as well. Let's pack our stuff, my dear child. You did well, refusing a sordid proposition. I'm proud of you!" Then she hugged Lala and cried, "I'm so sorry that I didn't emigrate thirty years ago and unknowingly condemned you to such a horrible life. Your dad was probably right. But I was trapped, as well. I couldn't desert my dad who was ill and Anya. Just like you are unable to betray your friends and co-workers now."

"I had to remain true to my soul, Mommy," Lala insisted, hugging her back. "Same, as you had done."

It turned out, however, that the final threat of the KGB was a false threat. Lala and her family remained in Moscow, undisturbed, in the period after her last visit to the secret police.

Bit by bit, Lala regained her equilibrium, worked hard and completed her Masters in musical history and then got her doctorate. She became a member of the Composer's Union and published about 100 books on operas, classical music, about famous singers and composers – both Russian and foreign. She attended dozens of international symposiums (though in East European countries, only) and delivered her speeches which were published in Soviet and foreign publications. Some of her books were translated into other languages and well-known abroad. She became a famous musical scientist and was even listed in The New Grove Dictionary of Music and Musicians; she considered that a great honor.

But her career inside the U.S.S.R was limited and she never held a top position in any department because she remained outside the Communist Party and refused to serve the KGB. Everybody knew that and respected and liked Lala – she had a lot of friends.

The only thing she really regretted was the fate of Colonel Kaloshin, who clearly lost his life trying to help her, as most likely, others as well scheduled for prison or worse. It was remotely possible, even, that this saintly man joined the KGB in order to save others. He did that until one day he was finally caught and killed. He sacrificed himself for them, for the innocent, for those suffering, for the Russian people and the future of their children in the motherland that would one day be freed from Communism. Maybe he sensed, too, that these few survivors, the ones he had rescued, would live on and remember him. In Lala's eyes, Kaloshin was a real Russian hero, even if she didn't know his full name!

She was so deeply thankful to him that she desperately wanted to thank him somehow, but didn't know how she could express it.

"You better go to the church and light a candle to his memory," Sonya advised her. "Don't be surprised that I'm saying this. You know, I'm not religious, but the first time you went to see Kaloshin, Varya Torchinsky pulled me to church and there we lit one for you. It might be superstitious, but it helped. Fate brought you directly to Kaloshin that day, but not to the other wicked man. Now, it's our duty to light candles in his memory every time we visit a church. It might not be very often, I grant you, but it should be done, sweetie."

"So, that's why I'm lighting candles for Colonel Kaloshin always when I visit a church to offer candles for airplane flights," my mom concluded her story. "It's our family tradition now, and it would be good if you'd continue this. Our gratitude for the brave people, for our rescuers, should be passed on and honored by all our generations because their memory is holy. They gave us a chance to live."

"Well, I will, of course," I responded, overwhelmed by her tormented narrative and shook my head to return to reality. "Let's go then and offer this candle... for him...I just want to know one more thing first - about my dad. Is he still with that horrible woman, Tatiana?"

My mom nodded.

"She's probably seventy already, but he's only forty-three!" I exclaimed in disbelief.

"He has no choice," my mom explained. "He tried to come back to me right after Stalin's death, in 1953, as she couldn't threaten him anymore. But I kicked him away from my door, like a homeless hobo, even quiet rudely, and said that I would never forgive him. Then he tried one more time, ten years later, with the same result. Nobody respected him after this story, nobody wants to know him; so, he even was forced to change his profession and go far away from music and the conservatory. He is now teaching students about art

152

and philosophy, writing scientific books and became a famous academician in an area where nobody knows about his past..."

"... and about his despicable secrets – how and why he traded us for an old woman; how he tried to throw his young wife and 2-month-old only daughter into the Stalin's concentration camp, how he wanted us to die," I added, feeling abused and totally betrayed. "I'd never forgive him, either. Now I understand why you didn't let me visit him as a child. He and his wife would possibly poison me, or throw me out the window, pretending that it was an accident in order not to pay alimony."

"Exactly," my mom confirmed. "I knew that, I felt that and tried to protect you, not telling you anything about him and not letting him to see you. You were too little. I didn't want to disturb your child's soul."

I took a deep breath.

"It's sad that such people exist, but even sadder, that they are somehow related to us. However, it's amazing that the most unlikely person was there and saved us. Let's go then and thank Colonel Kaloshin for our happiness! We'll go to the Crimea! We'll tan, swim in the Black Sea, and walk in the parks, thanks to him! I'm an adult now; I'll be married and have kids! I'll live! I'll always remember him and pass this special tradition on to my children! Please, give me this candle, Mom. I'll do it myself!"

She handed me the waxen taper, as we rose from the bench and re-entered the church.

The end of the Part 2.

PART 3

ME

I didn't want to include in this book the hatred, abuse, humiliation and insanely toxic mentality which broke personalities and turned them into slaves. Once again, all these things are quite well-known around the world.

But how could we, ordinary Russians, possibly escape them?

This was the compost and muck on which, sometimes, the most beautiful flowers were miraculously able to flourish. Anyway, I'll omit the unpleasant elements of the story as much as I can.

Chapter 10

MY HOME

It was a beautiful summer evening in San Francisco, California, nestled on the Pacific Coast. A peaceful atmosphere surrounded a newly-built, modern house, set in a large, lush yard. I was with my 10-year-old granddaughter, Alina. We were sitting on the steps of the cedar patio and enjoying the view of the endlessly playing ocean waves, the fragrant smell of the deep pink flowering oleander bushes beside us and the smoking BBQ at the other end of the patio. My American son-in-law was our outdoor chef.

On the side lawn in front of us, my husband was playing catch with our curly, red-headed 3-year-old granddaughter, Natasha. They were both laughing with delight, and Natasha shrieking when she tumbled down and then was lifted and then thrown high up over grandpa's head. It looked like she was flying in the sky for some seconds, holding his hands and bubbling with happiness.

Our daughter, Rimma, still was busy inside working on the computer – there was a deadline tonight for her to complete and enter her short story in an Australian International Writers' Competition. She promised to join us later as dinner was served.

"Do you like our house, Baba?" Alina asked looking at me with her big, brown eyes, full of life, inherited from her mother; Rimma, in turn had gotten them from my husband's side. The bright, blue eyes of Empress Catherine the Great (and Ekaterina von Wilde) were lost somewhere at the mist of time. However, Alina favored my Baba Sonya in her lips, and my mom Lala in her nose, both from the Empress herself. It was something which only I knew and could identify from memory. But anyone who had Catherine's portrait handy could easily come to the same conclusion.

"Yes, I really like your house," I assured her and gave 'my dear little future' a big hug. "Of course, I do. I even don't know what to say and how to express this. I'm just so happy for you."

"I'm happy, too, that all this construction around is finally finished," Alina admitted. "I was so tired of it! I even began to write a new story about myself. Do you know how it started? 'Once upon a time there was a girl named Alina. During all her life she was sur-rounded by nails, screws and construction machines..."'

"Really?" I was amused.

"Yes. Every time I went outside, I found nails and screws in the mud on the ground. Now, at last, we have lawn all around... And those bulldozers and excavators were so noisy..."

"It's funny that these made such an impression on you that you even wrote it down... 'She was surrounded by nails, screws and con-struction machines...' What an amazing beginning for a story! It's very unusual! Good for you, Alina!" I kissed her forehead.

"Do you like it, Baba? Okay, I'll read it to you later. Just tell me now, what were you surrounded by? I mean, during your childhood. Was there something yucky, too? Or was it something nice?"

I took a deep breath.

"It was something very different, my darling. I can tell you what I was surrounded by. Would you like listen to the story?"

"I do," Alina begged. "I really want to, Baba. I don't know much about Russia."

"I do, too," interjected my son-in-law, Charles, who was cutting up sweet peppers, tomatoes, onions and pineapples for the BBQ. "I don't know much about Russia, either. I hoped one day you would tell us..."

"Didn't Rimma tell you something?"

"Not much. She was a teenager when you all emigrated, and probably only remembers a few things."

"Okay," I agreed uncertainly. "Let's begin with what I, as a child, was surrounded by."

...“O, gosh! What're you doing, Tina?" I suddenly heard my Baba Sonya shriek. I looked up, curious to find out what was the matter.

Tina, an older woman from the Caucasus – the mother of one of our neighbors - stood in the middle of the kitchen and brushed her long black-gray hair. She was catching lice and nits from her hair and pinching them between two fingers. Then she threw them down towards the cat and I, who were nearby.

While my Baba cooked in the kitchen, I usually sat on the wooden kitchen floor and played with a big gray cat named *Pushok* ('Downy' in Russian).

The cat belonged to one of our neighbors, but mostly it lived in the kitchen because his owners worked full-time and came home very late. *Pushok* wasn't locked in their room so he roamed freely around the kitchen, hallways and other neighbors' rooms. That why he never suffered boredom or hunger. My Baba and I were at home most of the time and took care of him. Sometimes he hunted mice in the kitchen corner where there was a hole next to the rotten molding on the floor.

Usually, *Pushok* crawled close to the hole and sniffed the darkness. I didn't know what he sensed there, so I crawled after him and tried to smell, too, but couldn't identify anything except for the usual underground smells – raw potatoes and beets. He obviously sensed much more – a tasty lunch – and was ready to sit patiently beside the hole for hours. Sometimes, he was successful and got a mouse.

"Don't you see the child and cat here?" my Baba continued to shout at Tina in her irritation. "The lice could jump on them! You shouldn't throw the nits around the whole kitchen, but just squeeze and kill them all."

"It is not good to kill anything," Tina said, shrugging. "God created lice and they should live. In our village in the Caucasus everybody has lice. It's no problem if your child or cat has them, too. It's okay. I'm actually doing this every day here."

"O, gosh! I didn't know that," my Baba grumbled, knowing full well that to lecture on hygiene was a futile exercise since nobody would take it seriously.

Baba pulled me (then around 3 years old) into our room, changed me, and put all my clothes into a big pot to boil. Then she checked my head carefully and was terrified to discover that it was full of nits and some lice were even crawling in my hair.

My Baba, a survivor of three wars and three revolutions, knew well the danger of lice because these parasites could carry bacteria from person to person and potentially spread an epidemic of typhus – a deadly, feverish disease. However, what could she do to protect me while we lived with others in a cramped, dirty, poor communal flat?

She seated me on a chair, took a razor, shaved my head and smeared my bald scalp with kerosene. I whined a bit, but didn't cry. It wasn't painful, only stinky. I just screwed up my eyes to prevent the kerosene from coming in. Then, Baba wrapped my head with a towel and left it there for the next half hour, while she prepared a bowl with warm water. Then, she finally scrubbed me all over. All the parasites were killed and Baba used a tweezers to pull their carcasses from my naked scalp.

Pushok was covered with lice, as well, but his fate was much worse than mine. His owners took him to the vet and put him to sleep because nobody was able to clean him. In this dreadful way, I lost my first best friend of my early childhood and the very first animal I knew and loved.

Our municipal apartment was located in an old building which stood on the biggest and noisiest of Moscow's streets – The Garden Ring Road (in Russian - *Sadovoye Koltzo*). The building was constructed in the opening of the 20th century and seemed to be perfect at that time. It held two enormous luxury suites on each floor.

Before the 1917 Revolution, one family had lived in each suite that contained a living room, dining room, master bedroom, children's bedrooms, nanny's bedroom, kitchen with a little room where the kitchen maid slept, and storage. *Sadovoye Koltzo* at that time was a ring of boulevards which encircled the whole city and created a nice restful area full of trees, bushes, flowers, alleys, benches and playgrounds. So, the building was situated in a quiet and prestigious district.

Following the revolution, the family who had occupied our suite was possibly killed or, if fortunate, had emigrated and the suite was then stuffed with eight families – some rooms were divided by light veneer walls into two, or even three, sub-rooms. One family lived in the storage and another had to make do with the attic storey over the kitchen.

My grandpa, Victor Demin, when he escaped from Rostov-on-Don upon his arrival in Moscow at the end of 1929, was assigned the 'living room' in this suite due to his work as a construction engineer. With his own hands, he built a veneer wall and partitioned the room into two smaller spaces – one bedroom for him and Sonya and the other for daughter, Lala. He also constructed 'the basement' in one of the rooms. The family settled into the flat, knowing well that the *propiska* system didn't allow people to freely move around and, most likely, several generations of Demins would reside here for the rest of their lives.

In the mid-1930s, by Stalin's decree, all the boulevards on *Sadovoye Koltzo* were eliminated and all the trees and bushes cut down. Stalin's paranoia grew worse and worse, and he began to fear 'enemies' not only under his bed, but also hiding in the trees and bushes who would try to assassinate him as his car passed along the street. As a sad result, the once lovely Ring Road was paved with asphalt and became stony and dusty.

I was a child in the early fifties and, by then, the street had involved into a wide motor artery for the city. Seven lines of traffic passed in one direction while seven lines of cars and trucks moved in the opposite, making such a noise that the windows of our rooms vibrated and shook in nearly non-stop commotion. In truth, living on the main floor of the building, on *Sadovoye Koltzo,* next to the Kursky Train Station was equal to a home in a hell. No one could even remember the once glorious history of the beautifully named roadway.

In this suite I was raised – it was my world where I learned my lessons of life.

The hallway between the rooms in our apartment was dark and dingy. Greased dust, in great flocks hung under the fretted antique ceiling which was about four meters high, like in a palace. Nobody ever cleaned it, nobody even noticed it and, anyway, nobody could reach so high. To clean or to paint the ceiling would take a special very high ladder and a brush with very long handle. Nobody in the building had it, nobody could buy it anywhere and, anyway, nobody had money to do it. As a result, nobody cared.

So, this layer of filth always hung above my youthful head when I walked along the wooden oak hall floor which was ancient and shrilly squeaked underfoot. Even the light weight of a child was enough to produce those horror house sound effects. Believe it or not, I used to like to sit on the hallway floor and gaze up at the ceiling; I was probably the only one person in the suite who paid any attention to the lofty grime. Still, I easily convinced myself that that was completely normal way how hall ceilings should look.

Adding to the atmospherics, one little greasy light bulb of about 20 watts hanging down from a wire, guaranteed a dim gloominess. But due to people's poverty and stinginess, it was often turned off in order to save a few kopecks from the monthly electricity bill. Residents were ready to bang their heads against the walls or listen for the squeaky floorboards signaling that somebody was walking to meet them, than to pay monthly 3 to 5 cents more for electricity.

But, at this time, noise came not only from the traffic lines outside or the floorboards inside. There was something else, much scarier.

We had four windows in our rooms. Two of them, from one room, faced *Sadovoye Koltzo* and the two others, from the other room, looked onto a little side street around the corner. There, right under our windows sat a giant barrel full of beer. A woman wearing a once white – now very dirty - apron sold the beer the whole day long.

A large crowd of men, usually workers of the Kursky Train Station, train depots, and the local gas plant behind the station, gathered there and drank beer from morning till evening. Of course, they left for work for some hours but then returned. The place was always crowded.

This was, possibly, the worse place in Moscow – the noisiest, ugliest and very stinky. Because of the constant clamor and fetid smell, we couldn't open our windows. They were always closed, even when the weather turned very warm and suffocating. We also feared burglary, as well.

Sometimes, when my Baba was cooking in the kitchen and talking with our women-neighbors, I had nothing to do and climbed on the wide window-sill and sat there, watching the doings in the street.

I could see the workers wearing greasy overalls, drinking, talking loudly and laughing coarsely, swearing, and yelling at each other. They brought vodka from liqueur stores and deftly added it to their tall glasses of beer, making a special Russian cocktail called *yorsh*. This guaranteed they would reach a drunken state sooner.

And once they'd attained their favorite condition, they would shamelessly pee right there in public, behind the barrel, throw up on the ground, and boisterously smash empty bottles against the walls of our building, right under our windows. Sometimes they started to argue and beat each other and as they became more and more agitated, began striking each other's faces, often bloodying them.

In these cases I became scared and ran to the kitchen, shouting. A couple of times, my Baba called the *militia* but they seldom showed up, unless someone was killed.

Many times these drunken men walked around the corner to the main door of our building, entered the lobby and collapsed there to sleep. Some even used it as a toilet. We were supposed to step over them to come to our flat. Baba usually lifted me up and carried me over the sprawled figures. It was tolerable to walk over them during the day, however, in the evenings there were difficulties. Most often the light bulb in the foyer was broken and in the darkness it wasn't very pleasant to step over a loud, snoring drunk. Especially if you were never sure he wouldn't suddenly wake up and grab your foot.

Sometimes, the homeless men would walk the whole way around our building and enter the back door to sleep the drink off. The back foyer was even smaller than main lobby, and full of coal. In the corner, there was a little door that led to the boiler room.

In winter, our caretaker, Tatar Shamil, usually opened this door, shoveled the coal and threw it into a fire-box. This heated the building up and it worked fine, as we were never cold.

The alcoholics liked to sleep there in winter to be warm, too, or to heal their wounds from the fights at the beer barrel. When my Baba took out the garbage through this back door, she once again had to step over them quite often. Once, she discovered a strange, dirty, motionless figure sleeping there for three days in a row. She immediately called *militia*.

On that occasion, I saw three uniformed *militia* men walking through our entrance door, through the dark hallway (Baba turned on the light for them), into the kitchen and grouped near the back door. I (about 5-years-old at the time) was mesmerized by their red cap-bands with golden stars on the gray hats they were wearing. Their black peaks were shiny. They looked impressive to me and I watched them in awe-struck wonder.

"Take the child away!" one of them ordered loudly.

Baba wanted to lead me into our room but I refused to go and, instead, hid under the long folds of her home robe, peeking out curiously.

The *militia* men opened the back door, roughly picked up the limp body, lying in the foyer by his arms and feet and carried it out through our kitchen. I saw the head of a man drop back, revealing a filthy, slim neck with a big Adam's apple. There was a long deep gash across his throat, marked with dried cherry-red blood. His opened, lifeless eyes looked like they were made of glass. His long, dark hair brushed our kitchen floor when he was being removed. Somehow, I sensed that he was dead but, surprisingly, I wasn't scared at all. He didn't look real to me. I was sure, deep in my heart, that he was a mannequin – just a dirty, smeared doll which I wasn't allowed to play with.

My Baba wasn't happy about my presence and curiosity and chastised me. Then, she locked the door behind the *militia* men, poured some chlorine into a pail and began to wash the floor to disinfect it and remove the stains and smell.

"Was he dead?" I asked her.

"Yes."

"Why?" I insisted.

"Someone cut his throat."

"Why?"

"How should I know?! Go to the room, Katya!"

"Will the *militia* investigate who did it?"

"I'm sure they won't," Baba barked in annoyance. "Go to the room, now, you, naughty girl!"

"But...Why won't they?"

"Because it's not important to them. He wasn't a respectful man."

I didn't really understand what she meant but the scene didn't upset me much and I quickly forgot about it. The whole thing had been so matter-of-fact that people used to take it as a commonplace in their everyday life.

Sometimes, though, our littered and fouled entrance lobby was cleaned. A neighbor everywoman, Pasha, cleaned several buildings throughout the district and our turn came round by-weekly.

Pasha was a widow, with two daughters, schoolgirls, and her salary was so small that it wasn't even enough to keep food in their mouths. Pasha had a chronic cough, as well. At the end of each month she would appear at our door apologetically and, with embarrassment would softly say, "Auntie Sonya, would you mind, please, lending me a ruble until tomorrow? I'm so sorry but we don't even have bread for today. Tomorrow is my payday..."

Baba Sonya always gave her a ruble and even extra bread, if we had any left and, to tell truth, Pasha always kept her promise and returned the money in time. She was kind, honest, hardworking and extremely poor – a typical, uneducated Soviet woman.

I usually observed these scenes silently and saw my Baba pitifully shaking her head, as Pasha left.

"Why hasn't she got enough money?" I once inquired, finally deciding to clear the situation for myself and to satisfy my curiosity.

"Her salary is too small, though she is working hard. Her job is so heavy and dirty, oh, my goodness," Baba explained full of compassion toward Pasha and, in her face, toward millions of poor people in the Soviet Union.

"Why do we have more money?"

"Your mom is educated. She was graduated from high-school, from musical college, from the Conservatory of Music, which is like university, and then she completed her Ph.D. She was studying nonstop for over 22 years, but Pasha is only a peasant woman from a village, barely literate.

"She and her husband were arrested by the Communists as *kulaks* (so-called rich farmers) and exiled to Siberia. Her girls were born in a concentration camp, and her husband died there. Then they were let free because the government officially recognized that it had made a mistake about them – they weren't 'rich farmers', after all. Pasha even got a permission to live in Moscow, if she would work at the Gas Plant. This was dangerous job and her lungs were burnt by the poisonous gases and made her invalid. So, she can't work at the plant anymore and now she is cleaning foyers for living, however, it's not enough, as you can see. But she doesn't have any other source of income to help raise her girls.

"It's a good lesson for you, Katya. You should always remember, sweetie, that the education is the most important thing in life. Does it make sense?"

"Yeah," I grumbled unhappily because I didn't like to study a lot, especially music.

What I really liked to do was to draw. I was usually drawing, seated at our dining table while Baba read books aloud to me. Mostly they were books about animals because I really liked them. We even had an old zoological encyclopedia which my grandpa, Victor Demin, had bought at the flea market in Rostov-on-Don. Baba 'read' it to me, mostly showing me the pictures and explaining about the animals in her own words because the encyclopedia was written in a scientific language, quite difficult for a child. However, it was still very interesting. Some animals looked scary and I studied the pictures, terrified.

The worst, in my opinion, was the octopus, especially after Baba told me that it was capable of killing a person by squeezing its prey with strong, long and flexible tentacles. I always drew it as a circle with big eyes in the middle and eight arms-legs sticking out all around. It was a symbol of horror to me.

Sometimes, my Baba listened to radio, while I drew. I listened, too, together with her and made, by the way, pictures illustrating what I had heard. Of course, I didn't understand much because there was mostly political news, but from announcer's expressive voice I grasped easily - who was who, who was good and who was bad.

"What are these?" Baba asked me one day, noticing two quite similar pictures, one next to the other. "One is octopus, of course, as I see, but who is this?"

"This is Truman," I answered.

"What?! Who is Truman?"

"Harry Truman. He is definitely a bad guy, so, I guess he must look like an octopus."

Baba laughed until she almost cried. Typically at that time, the U.S.A president Truman was painted as the number one negative figure in all the Soviet news broadcasts, yet most of the population had no idea who he was. Like me, they had a childish view of the world.

Another thing that happened in my fifth year, I saw my mom

and Baba sitting on the couch discussing some matter in hashed voices.

"What happened?" I wanted to know. "Has Truman done something bad, again?

"No, sweetie," Baba Sonya shook her head. "Stalin is dead."

"Dead?" I asked in disbelief. "You mean like that man by our boiler room door? Did someone cut his throat, too?"

"No, no, no. Don't say such things, Katya!" Baba exclaimed. "He was very sick!"

The news surprised me, but I wasn't in the least touched by it. If one of my toys had broken, I would be much more upset. I just never guessed that Stalin, who was not a person to me, but only a picture or statue, could become ill and die.

"We're wondering what will come next," my mom tried to explain me. "Who will follow him as ruler? Will our life become better, or worse? Nobody knows. It has been bad, but you never know. It could possibly get even worse now."

I didn't understand her explanation. I was sure that our life was okay and had no idea what could be better, but I imagined what could be worse. If we wouldn't have enough bread sometimes, like Pasha, or if somebody would take away my toys, or if the drunks by the barrel would smash our window and climb in into my room, or if the capitalists would come and exploit me (I didn't know what 'exploit' meant but I heard it every day on radio and realized that this was something quite scary) – all these would be worse and would make me cry. But how this was related to Stalin's death, I couldn't grasp.

However, the next day was exciting. I walked outside with my Baba and all our neighbors. We stood in front of our building and heard the farewell whistles which the factories, plants and steam-locomotives of the whole country should blow at the same time in Stalin's honor. It was very loud and very special and continued for about five minutes. Some people around were in tears, but not my Baba. After observing the faces, I decided to join my Baba and have fun. Really, where or when else would you possibly hear such a loud concert in the entire country all at once? So noisy, so loud, so long and so much fun!

Unexpectedly, Stalin's death made my life more exciting. The next month after the funeral, the Moscow City Government began to plant trees all along the streets, starting from *Sadovoye Koltzo*. The Planting of Greenery Program was set in motion because nobody was any longer scared of enemies hiding behind trees. It was possible to return to a psychologically normal life and to make the city look attractive again.

I was able to watch the show seated on the window-sill of our second room. First, the pneumatic hammer broke up squares of the asphalt in the street. Then, the excavators dug deep holes. When they were ready, a truck appeared, loaded with the trees from the forest. A crane lifted the trees with clods of dirt hanging onto the roots and placed them, one by one, into the holes.

So, now there were heavy construction machines, as well, in front of my windows. They were noisy, too, but this was a happy noise. The trees were lindens. They were amazing; they grew quickly, soon became luxuriant and blossomed every year with little yellow flowers full of honey. The nice fresh honey smell wafted to our windows, as we opened them sometimes, in spite of the street noise. Now I understood what it meant to see life improve.

"Yeah! Baba, I watched, too, as our trees and bushes were planted," Alina exclaimed, full of understanding, "those hawthorns, junipers, oleanders, hydrangeas and poplars. Look! They are nice, aren't they? They have blossoms and are full of aroma, too, but not like a honey. Could we, probably, plant some lindens next year, Daddy? I would like to have some honey fragrance in our yard, too. What do you think, Daddy?"

"I think, we could," agreed Charles, but I saw his face was quite sad. The earlier part of my story made much stronger impression on him, than the happy ending which Alina emphasized. Maybe, it was her childish unconscious self-protection of the soul and I was happy that she had it. I didn't want to disturb her comfortable and secure little world, but I wanted to relay the truth about my childhood, as well.

However, suddenly Alina hugged me and kissed my cheek.

"Poor Baba," she said, petting me, "I'm so happy that you're living in America now."

"Dinner is ready," announced my son-in-law. "Alina, would you mind calling your mom, please?"

Chapter 11

"ONCE UPON A TIME, WHEN THERE WAS A GREAT STORM OVER THE OCEAN..."

Over dinner, Rimma, our beautiful dark-haired, brown-eyed daughter, told us about her business which she began recently as a photo journalist, translator, editor and writer. She also shared about her website, publications and writing competitions. As we finished the meal and thanked Charles for his amazing BBQ, she presented us with two books she was proud of. One of them was a fiction anthology, including one of her novellas; the second was a photo album of the fifty best U.S.A. photo journalists which embodied one of Rimma's works - a photography contest winner. Her own book – short stories collection she authored – was at the time already in the publishing procedure.

They were each a major achievement for an immigrant girl and made me happy and satisfied for my child and for myself, as well. I felt that I had made the right decision, pulling my family out of Russia. Life in America had opened up many possibilities for my girls, as people around the world realize, and both my daughter and granddaughter started to grasp them right away.

When we first arrived in the U.S.A, Rimma completed her high school, while working part-time for the Sears and, occasionally, doing some modeling. Then she was drawn to journalism. She was fortunate following her graduation, to become a newspaper correspondent for several years. When she gave birth to her second daughter, though, she decided to work from home.

Then, her husband, Charles, was transferred to California and I didn't see my darlings for quite a while. But, at long last, my husband and I had found the time to visit them. We came from New York where we have been residing since arriving in the U.S.A.

Our daughter was a very good mother and selflessly gave her time to her family - not only to Charles and the little one, but especially to Alina. My oldest granddaughter read plenty of books, watched a lot of movies, from the age of two played computer games, and from the age of five could research topics on the Internet. Besides attending school, she also took creative writing and painting classes, played soccer, played the guitar, skated, danced tap and ballet, studied French and Russian and composed stories in English - definitely her first language – on the computer. Oh, I would have been so happy to have even half of these activities in my childhood, instead of the damn piano!

I had also brought to San Francisco presents for my beloved family – my two page-turner books, published in the U.S.A. and Canada – "Stolen" and "Deadly Paradise". They were strikingly beautifully designed. I wish, my own mother, Lala, could have seen them, but she died in Moscow, before we emigrated, almost 15 years ago. My Baba Sonya had also died twenty-five years earlier and never knew that we would finally correct her mistake and emigrate from Russia.

"Wow, Baba!" Alina exclaimed, opening the glossy cover of my book. "You're also a writer! Just like mom and me! It's amazing! What are these books about?"

"They're about quite adult subjects, sweetie," I noted. "You and Natasha can read them later when you reach age eighteen. But, anyway, I'm sure you would like them. I wanted you know our family history and many other immigrants' stories which could teach you something about another world, from where we came, and as a result, from where you appeared."

"Did you write anything in Russia?" Alina asked, looking at me curiously. "I mean, in your childhood, as I'm doing?"

"Yes. I wrote my first story at age 7, when I was in first grade. But I never finished it."

"Why not?"

"I don't know," I shrugged. "I got stuck, somehow. Nobody could understand what I want to say. It looked to me, like I had a kind of misunderstanding with the whole world...."

"Well, we're going now for a walk to the coast," Rimma said, preparing some small, empty bags for shells which the children liked to collect. "Let's get ready to go and when we're there, Mom you can tell us the story about your first creations. Okay?"

"Okay," I laughed as I began to reminisce about those episodes of my youth.

"What is so funny, Baba?" Alina wanted to know.

"It's funny that my first book started at the ocean coast, though, at that time, I had never seen it."

"Tell me, tell me, Baba," Alina begged, then took my hand and we walked down the patio steps, following my husband and Charles who had already gone ahead. They were holding Natasha by both hands, while Rimma caught up with us, carrying on her shoulder a bright, multicolored bag with children's things.

...I was seven years old when I decided to write my first story. I didn't know why. At that time, I didn't hear a thing about my mom's writing and hadn't seen her notebooks of fairytales which she presented to me when I was thirteen. I just decided to write my own book, and that was that.

I thought about it in the evenings when I lay in bed before sleep and always imagined an amazing picture which would be perfectly good, in my opinion, to launch a story.

In the picture I saw in my mind's eye, it was night. It was very dark and stormy - raining cats and dogs. The site was the seacoast, not far from a sandy beach, but you couldn't make it out in the darkness. Everything was soaking wet and the waves sloshed, making it feel more like a swamp than a beach, because again nothing was visible in such darkness.

The ocean was furious and wild. Gigantic waves flew up to the sky and mixed with the falling rain. It was a dramatic and terrifying scene and I wanted to describe it first, before some of characters entered my story. I thought a lot about the exact, particular words which I should use to describe this sublime and scary natural phenomenon.

Then, one sentence formed inside my head – the most beautiful sentence I ever heard:

"Once upon a time, when there was a great storm over the ocean." I repeated this sentence many times: I tasted it, I savored it, and I enjoyed it. It sounded like some magical music inside my ears. Oh, gosh! It was amazing – "Once upon a time, when...!!!"

After some nights of pondering over it, I took a large notebook to record my God-given opening sentence with enlarged, dancing letters. Then, I showed it to my Baba Sonya. She just petted my hair, kissed my forehead and said, "Good, Katya. Continue, please."

However, I was so full of pride and so pleased with my sentence that I wanted to collect the opinions of my loved ones about it. I guess I expected more support, not just a kiss and advice to continue. I already knew myself that it should be continued. After all, it was only the first sentence of my story. I wanted to hear an enthusiastic response that would feed my very soul.

Sadly, I concluded that my Baba was no literary specialist, so, she had no way to estimate the true worth of my creation, and I next took it to my mom.

"Well," my mom said as she read it, "I'm afraid the grammar is wrong."

"What?" I was shockingly disappointed. "How come?!"

"Yes," my mom explained. "You don't need a word 'when' here. You should have put 'Once upon a time there was a great storm over the ocean'. That would be more correct."

"No!" I exclaimed, feeling like I had been stabbed in the heart. "When - is the most beautiful word in this sentence! It determines the whole flavor of the piece! I could never take it out!"

"Okay," my mom conceded, "you can keep it, but in that case, you must continue the sentence. Once, blaa blaa blaa, when, blaa blaa blaa, the boy walked out of the house..."

"What boy are you talking about?!" I yelled. "There weren't any boys at all, and any houses either!"

"Well, find something else. Maybe something like,'the wind whistled wildly', or 'the trees were uprooted', or...I don't know. Just find something to continue; otherwise the grammar is wrong."

"What it is – blaa blaa blaa?" I demanded with burning resentment.

"O, gosh!" my mom took a deep breath and looked at her watch. "It's just something to take place of your original words to shorten the sentence. I'm sorry, but I'm really in a hurry right now. Can we talk this evening? Or during our bathtub night?"

I felt disappointed. She seemed to me too educated and too full of grammar to see the beauty of my sentence. I intuited that, as a writer, I could dispense with the formality of grammar and needed only the sounds, smells, and tastes of words to 'paint' my pictures. When! The word sounded divine to me. It even smelled divine! I decided to try for a third opinion.

The next person closest to me was my teacher at school – Raisa Alekseevna, a twenty- year-old woman just graduated from a two-year Teacher's Collage. In my eyes, however, she was a serious and responsible, mature middle-aged lady. She was very kind, quiet, and shy. Maybe this was due to her character, or maybe because her pale face was covered in big pink pimples.

To me, this seemed normal; again, this was because it was

what it was. I just loved her, respected and admired her. She was my Goddess.

One day, I brought my notebook to school and, while we were writing some class work, I called Raisa Alekseevna by raising my hand. She approached me on tiptoes and asked in a whisper, in order not to distract the other kids, "What do you want, Katya?"

"While we're writing, would you mind reading my book, please?" I whispered back. "I would like to know your opinion."

"Okay," she said, took my notebook and returned to her desk, sat down and started to read immediately.

She took her time reading it. I did my class work and glanced at her from time to time, and always saw her pouring thoughtfully over my notebook. Her lips were moving soundlessly. Possibly, she was trying to understand my message and searched for something meaningful in her little student's story.

After the class ended and other kids had gone home, I advanced to her desk and stood anxiously awaiting her judgment.

"Very good, Katya," she said, returning the notebook to me. "I would only say that you need to finish out your sentence. It strikes me as incomplete. You placed a period at the end, but it really needs a comma instead, and so you can go on to tell what happened during the storm. What was it? Something special? Perhaps a ship was sinking? Or the moon penetrated suddenly through the dark clouds. Or...what?"

She had a romantic streak, as I grasped later because of her suggestions, but at the time I felt very upset.

"There was no moon, and no ships, at all. Only the ocean and the rain. Is it hard to understand?"

"Not really," she responded kindly, trying not to hurt me, "but in that case, you should take out the word 'when'."

"Oh, no!" I even moaned. Why the heck, was everyone so stuck on getting rid of the most beautiful word I ever heard!?

"Thank you," I murmured disappointedly and grabbed my notebook. "There would be no continuation. My book will stay like this forever! It's complete enough."

I went home, hid my notebook and never returned to the story. I decided that creative work had no meaning, if no one could understand a writer's feelings and images and wanted to change things. There was no reason to write anymore. It was sad but I had a lot other things to play with and to think about, so I soon let my first unsuccessful foray into creative writing fade away.

My second book was started when I was about eleven. I was just after I read "Quentin Durward" by Walter Scott, which had stirred my imagination. In the book, Quentin, always wore a small, blue hat on his head. I liked that. So, I decided to write an adventure story about an English knight who always wore a blue hat, too. I named my character Anand (an East Indian name which I got from one of the Indian movies that were very popular in the Soviet Union at those years). The last name for him I did found somewhere in English fiction – Newrfold. To my Russian ear it sounded amazingly beautiful.

This time the story developed more smoothly. I already knew some grammar, which we were studying at school so I was able to write properly.

The story was long and interesting for a child: there were horse rides and chases, but especially kind princesses, kidnapped by wicked magicians who needed the brave Anand to rescue them. I drew many illustrations, filling almost every page, to picture the events in color as well as in words.

One evening, my mom's cousin, Helena, with her husband, Mikhail, came for a visit. They were both younger than my mom, but about fifteen years my seniors. They were students of art. Usually, they would play with me, tell a lot of jokes or draw funny caricatures of all of us and I loved them. This time I decided to share with them my happiness and proudly presented my story of Anand finally finished and filling three thick notebooks. I proposed that I read some chapters to them and they agreed readily.

However, as I started to read, Mikhail began to make fun of it right away and laugh at each my sentence, though, the grammar was all right. Helene hissed at him and slapped his hand again and again to get him to stop, but he ignored her and continued to poke fun of it. Especially funny for him was the last name of my knight.

"What?! What?! Newrfold?! Newfoundland?! How do you pronounce that? O, my gosh! The real Newfoundland!" he yelped almost to tears in amusement.

The name 'Newfoundland' was known in the Soviet Union at that time only as a name of a breed of large dogs'. Possibly, those famous dogs were really bred in Newfoundland and then spread around the whole world. The name only identified the place of origin. However, in this context it sounded to me (and to everybody around me) like a synonym for the word 'dog' and nothing else.

Mikhail purposely stressed that he considered the name of my knight character as a dogs' one. I felt very offended and hurt by his taunts, even humiliated, especially when he mocked me.

"Stop it! Stop it, please!" I tried to demand, but he didn't listen and went on teasing and laughing. Finally, I threw down my notebook and run to my room all in tears.

I collapsed on my bed and buried my face in my pillow, sobbing. I didn't want to see anybody. After our visitors left, my mom came to me and petted my head.

"You better not read your stories to adults, sweetie," she said fondly, "even better, to anybody, except me and Baba, ever. People are jealous. Mike is simply an idiot. He and Helene dreamed of having kids, but after ten years of marriage didn't. Helene went to doctor and found out that Mike is not able to father children. That's why he is angry now about all the children he knows and resents them. It's just envy that was behind his attack on you."

When I retrieved my discarded notebook in the living room, I noticed that Mike had written under one of my illustrations 'Newfoundland' and an arrow pointing to my knight. It made me really mad. What right did he have to spoil my book that way? My creative work! I took thick black pencil and quickly scribbled the word forcefully.

I hated Mike from then on and, when he came for visits later on, I usually went to play with the neighbor's kids or my school friends. I tried to avoid Mike because every time as he saw me, he always asked with a mean smirk, "How is your Mr. Newfoundland doing? Is he barking a lot?" It must have pleased him to continually deride me and nobody shielded me from his hurtful remarks since mom and Baba thought it was nothing very serious and I should just ignore Mike's stupid comments. But I couldn't. My soul was wounded and I learned, for the very first time, what it meant to have a personal enemy.

I still didn't know how to behave with enemies because I had never encountered one before. So I continued to talk with Mike when it was impossible to escape the situation but I constantly hoped that he might change and be nice to me. But, I'm afraid he was never able to treat me right.

One day, one of my mom's co-workers brought me a mechanical pencil from France. In Russia, nobody had ever seen a mechanical pencil at this time, and I was happy and proud to have this present. When a lot of guests came for my Baba's birthday, I craved to share my happiness with everyone and showed the new pencil to each guest in turn.

"Good for you, Katya," my senior relatives congratulated me as they patted my head.

When Mike had a chance to look at it, he took it, studied it from all sides and then inquired, "What is this stupid thing for?"

"It is pencil for drawing," I explained sincerely. "Look at this button on the end. It moves the pencil lead in and out. And if you unscrew this button, there is a pencil sharpener inside."

"No," Mike said, casting an angry glance at me. "That's impossible. It's not a sharpener but just a button."

He was an artist who drew using techniques with pencils! He was professional! Poor thing – he was born in Russia. That's why he had never seen such a pencil.

But now he saw that a little child had it as a plaything. This thought was murderous to him. He got so angry that couldn't even talk but only hissed at me, "It's not a sharpener!"

"It's a sharpener," I insisted, because I did already sharpen the pencil using it many times and knew that it worked perfectly.

"Well," Mike suggested. "Let's try it. If it isn't a sharpener, I want you to stand up and announced to all the guests, 'I'm a fool! I'm an idiot! I'm a stupid girl!' Okay?"

"Okay," I agreed, knowing full well that I would win, though my voice quavered with offence and I had to fight back my tears.

Mike unscrewed the button. Three small metal petals appeared from inside.

"Now, you put the graphite end of the pencil between them and turn," I taught him with trembling lips.

Mike did it and the light shavings of lead flew as the pencil was sharpened.

"Oh gosh! Amazing!" he muttered in total awe.

"So!" I explained happily. "Now you should stand up and admit publicly that you're the fool!"

"No!" Mike shook his head. "I'm the smartest person in the world. Adult are never the fools. Remember that, you, mucus!"

Mucus (in Russian – *soplya*) was a very popular epithet used in Russia by adults to express disdain for children. "Shut up, you, *soplya!*" many grown ups would callously say to put a child in his place when he (or she) asked a question or (unbelievable!) offered an opinion. In common Russian mentality, children were not precious darlings, or even human beings, but only disgusting blobs of mucus.

At home I never heard this ugly, insulting word since my Baba and mom never used it, but I heard it from other people and, being a child, was on the receiving end of it a lot, especially from Mike. I knew I could expect it from him anytime. It seemed strange to me that an adult was always losing and unleashed his hateful abuse on me time and again.

His wretched jealousy (since I, *soplya,* knew and had much more than he did) made him loathe me all the more and spout his venomous dislike toward me out of all proportion. For years, I couldn't fathom why he behaved like this. I only felt his ugly enmity chill my bones and intimidate me so I subconsciously tried to evade any contact with people like him.

Perhaps they sought to kill my enthusiasm to create and prevent me from developing my talents, like Russians usually did. This frame of mind was more widespread, than you might expect.

However, I stubbornly continued to grow, spending all my after-school free time with my pictures, stories and music (I had recently started composing, too). I loved these three subjects so much that had trouble choosing between them my future profession: writing, painting or composing.

Around the age of twelve, I was impressed by *Pictures from an Exhibition* by Mussorgsky. I started to write short stories, draw illustrations for them and then compose some music appropriate for them. I made a whole album of water-colored pictures with stories on the bottom of each page and with musical notations on the back of each page. This was perfect activity for my age and my mom was happy and proud of me. But she strongly advised me not to show the album to anybody, not even my own friends, and especially not to let Mikhail or Helena see it.

"Why?" I asked sorrowfully, already anticipating her answer. "I want to share it with someone."

"You can share with me, and Baba, and your music teacher. But others will most likely be envious and will try to hurt and mistreat you. That's for sure," my mom warned me. "It's sad, but true, that creative work is the subject that has produced more green-eyed monsters in this world than anything else. You have to read Pushkin's *Mozart and Soliery* to better understand this. You can't imagine how the composers in our Composers Union hate and resent each another. There is an old proverb in the world: 'A person toward another person is a wolf'. So, our composers even created a joke about themselves: 'A person toward another person is a wolf, but the wolf toward another wolf is a composer.'

"I'm so lucky that I'm not a composer but merely a musicologist," my mom related. "That's why I'm no competition for any of them; so I can have many friends and feel myself secure."

I read the *Mozart and Soliery* but at my age was still unable

176

to grasp what jealousy really was. I understood it in my mind, in theory, but I really couldn't sense it in my heart. It was honestly a totally alien feeling to me. I never experienced jealousy and greed. I had everything I needed and wanted in my life and, if someone else had more than I did, it certainly did not bother me at all. I absolutely didn't care. I was completely satisfied with what I had.

In fact, I felt the opposite of envy for someone who had more, knew more and could do more than me. They served as a perfect role model in my eyes and inspired me to go ahead, to accomplish greater things, and, by effort, to achieve the same success and to work hard for this purpose. Those who advanced always produced very good feelings in my soul; I admired them and loved them; I dreamed to learn from them, to be like them in the future, and I tried.

I really didn't understand what purpose it might serve I hate them, to resent them or to attack or ignore them, like my Uncle Mikhail did toward me. This defensive mentality was alien to me. However, before long, I was faced with this ugly social phenomenon once more.

In 1963, I was fifteen and already enrolled in the Moscow Musical College, exactly the same college where my parents had come to study before the World War II. Dima came in 1939 to study piano, and my mother, Lala, entered the next year to become a musicologist.

One day, my teacher gave our class composition homework. We had to create musical works which were variations on an ordered theme. He assigned us all the same short melody and gave us two weeks to complete our work of 8-10 variations. I decided to use styles of the composers I knew. Of course, as a teenager myself, I hadn't developed my own style yet, and the best way to learn was to try to mimic what musical geniuses had done.

I used the style of Haydn's sonata, Bach's polyphony, Mozart's minuet, Beethoven's scherzo, Chopin's prelude, Schubert's impromptu, Liszt's fantasy and finally, back to Russia – the famous concerto for piano and orchestra by Tchaikovsky. I worked hard on my assignment those two weeks and my variations seemed to be good, especially the final one, which sounded solemn and impressive. It was just like the beginning of Tchaikovsky's concerto, as I intertwined the melody in similar way between passages of cords ranging across the whole keyboard. I even had difficulty learning how to play it. It took me a while, but by the day it was due in class, I was ready to perform it myself.

My work was shocking for everybody because most of the students only produced short 2-page compositions, which was the minimum requirement to pass the exam and nothing more. My variations were my show; on the other hand, they were my creative outlet, the breath of my soul, and the culmination of my ten years of musical study. The last thing I thought about was an exam mark. I was excited and only dreamed to express myself.

Our teacher was so impressed that he couldn't help but show my variations to everybody: to all the students, all the teachers and even the administration staff of the college. He asked me to perform them in front of each class and on the stage in the concert hall. And of course, he gave me the highest mark on my exam and increased his demands on the other students. While I was happy and proud of myself, I suddenly realized that all my fellow students now hated me. Because of the excitement our teachers felt, the students reacted with anger and resentment.

They no longer talked to me in a normal, friendly way, but made faces, while glaring at me. They mockingly hissed as they minced with airs, "Of course, you have a composer's talent but we are just ordinary students. We're nothing compared to you. Honestly, we aren't even qualified to be in the same college with such a genius! Ha-ha-ha!"

No one smiled and quipped, "Hi, Katya," like they did before, but only smirked, "Hi, genius!" or "Hi, talent!" and even showed, fawning, that they bowed before me.

I felt really upset and crushed, which served to darken the delight I should have had over my perfect exam mark and teachers' admiration. My only hope was that my 'friends' would soon forget about it all, but it didn't happen; the persecution even grew worse. They stopped talking to me or inviting me to join their parties. When I inquired why I had been excluded, I was told with great irritation, "Geniuses aren't in our circle. We're simple people!"

"But I'm not a genius! I'm a regular girl!" I tried to remind them.

"If you're a normal girl, how did you possibly compose such music!" they demanded.

I found this rejection and isolation so painful, that I decided never to compose anything after that. It wasn't enough that my mom, Baba and all my teachers begged me to continue composing. One of my teachers even proposed that I have extra composition classes for free because she insisted that I should develop my talent. I baldly refused, and refrained from writing any more music. My interest and love in composing, which were just developing, were thus killed in the bud by crashing jealousy. And I was sad to tears.

After that, I returned to my writing because it was possible to hide my notebooks, whereas music needed to be performed in public, needed to be heard and couldn't be hidden under a mattress. I decided to keep my promise to my mom and to become a writer. However, knowing about her tragic experience with the Writers Institute, I planned to follow her course and after college graduation, to become a student of the Moscow Conservatory of Music named after Tchaikovsky.

It was no surprise to me then, when, after eight years of study, the chairman of the professors' board awarded me with the best mark on my final exam, but added, "I have to say that this work seemed strange to me. I have never seen such a thing before. Formally, your paper is about opera, about music, however, in reality it's a work written not by a musician but by a writer, historian, dramatist, and philologist. Out of one hundred and twenty pages, only ten are really about music."

This old man was experienced enough to see through things, and he grasped my core interest well. After that, I never worked as a musician but spent my time by raising Rimma, my daughter, writing fiction books and traveling with my husband around the world.

"Really! Baba!" exclaimed Alina, sitting beside me on the white, sandy beach stretching out to the Pasific Ocean. "You kept your promise to your mom and you're a writer now. And what's more, you're living and writing in a free country."

"Yes, I did," I agreed with a smile. "And yes, I do. It wasn't an easy way to keep my promise, but I was persistent enough. But look, sweetie, our bags are already full of shells. What will you do with them?"

"I use them for crafts," my granddaughter explained readily. "First I clean them, and then coat them with varnish or paint. And then, I attach them to the lids of little boxes and covers of notebooks. I'll show you. They are beautiful, though I don't have many notebooks. Mostly, I've been writing on my computer. But first, Baba, when we return home, we'll go to my room and I will read you my stories. It will be our story time together."

"Thank you, my darling," I said shifting my weight on Alina's arm in order to rise from my position and brushing the sand from my jeans. "I am impatient to hear them. I'm sure it will be the best evening imaginable."

Chapter 12

<u>STALIN'S GRANDSON</u>

The next two days were school holidays and two of Alina's girl-friends came to play with her in our backyard – a Chinese Rebecca and a Kosovar, Buyana. This American mix of nationalities always excited me. I had been raised only among Russians. This was prob-ably the thing that I was subconsciously missing in my childhood – the influence of different cultures and mentalities, some new spirit and fresh air; these qualities which, in America and Canada are in abundance.

Charles was at work and my husband and Rimma had gone shopping. Now I was enjoying the company of my little granddaughter, Natasha, babysitting her in the playground. I was a little startled to hear her chant a traditional Russian children's rhyme:

"Goosie, goosie - ga-ga-ga"	(Geese, geese, - ga-ga-ga)
"Yest hotite? - da-da-da"	(Do you want to eat? - yes-yes-yes)
"Nu letite - nyet-nyet-nyet"	(So fly home, - no-no-no)
"Sery wolk pod goroy	(There is a gray wolf under the mountain.)
"Ne puskayet nas domoy!"	(He doesn't let us go home!)

Natasha recited it so enthusiastically, full of excitement, and pronounced the Russian words exactly as they are written here, with such a cute accent that I couldn't help but smile to myself.

"Good for you, sweetie," I said in Russian, petting her red curls. "Who taught you this rhyme? Mom?"

"No," Natasha answered in English. "Alina, my big sister. She is always pressing my nose at the end. Just like this," she reached out her tiny hand and poked my nose with her index finger. I knew it was not part of the Russian version, so I supposed it was most likely one of Alina's own interpretations.

Around noon, Alina's girlfriends went home and I took my little ones into our house from the yard playground to serve them lunch.

"I'm really glad that you have friends, Alina," I offered, as I poured chicken soup into small bowls for them and cut their sandwiches.

"Not many," Alina answered sadly. "My mom is not very happy that we're living where many rich people live. Most of the kids at school are millionaires' children, very snobby and arrogant. They are spoiled and not so polite. But these girls are good. They are from intelligent immigrant families. Rebecca's father is a computer engineer, just like my daddy, and Buyana's parents are doctors. Their diplomas aren't recognized here, so they can't have a professional job. They opened a house cleaning business and are working as cleaners, though they are very educated people.

"Next year all three of us plan to transfer to another school – the French Academy of Arts. I went already there for an Open House. It's a perfect school with a creative program, though quite far away from our home. But, anyway, mom will drive me."

"Good for her," I said, feeling proud of my daughter and the way she was managing her kids' education. I felt completely satisfied that what I had taught her was not in vain. On the new American soil, she chose to follow our Russian family traditions and that made me happy. "And what's especially good that your friends will be at your new school, too."

"Yes," nodded Alina, "I like them. Did you have many friends in your childhood, Baba?"

"Yes. I had plenty of friends at school. In Russia, people were mostly very poor and very simple. Nobody was arrogant and snobby in the area where I lived. But my very best friend was not at school at all, but in our communal apartment. It was a boy, the same age as I was, only one month older, named Alexander. His Russian nickname was Sasha or Sashka, as I called him."

"Did he live next door? In the next apartment?" Alina didn't understand me and looked questioningly.

"Not in the next apartment," I corrected her. "The next room in our apartment."

"Two families in one apartment?" she raised her eyebrows in surprise.

"Not two but eight families in one apartment," I laughed, seeing bewilderment in her eyes. Obviously she couldn't grasp it. Thank God! I was happy that she couldn't grasp it. I wished she would never experience something like that, but still I wanted her to know and to imagine my childhood – its positives and negatives. One real positive was - having a best friend in the same apartment, for example, if you didn't have any siblings.

"Could you tell me more about your friend...about Sashka?" Alina inquired, finishing her sandwich and beginning to load the dishes into a dishwasher. "Baba, please..."

"Okay," I agreed, taking our drowsy little one from her highchair and wiping her face. "Please, clean the table, Alina. I'll put Natasha to sleep and then we'll talk."

"Tooty-toot-toot! Tooty-toot!" I heard a sudden noise coming from the hallway behind my door, pretended to be a blaring trumpet call. "Tooty-toot-toot!"

"Baba!" I exclaimed with joy, sweeping aside my toys, games, drawings or anything else which had been occupying me. "Sashka has arrived! I'm going to play now! Bye!"

I ran out of our room without even cleaning up my mess. I had no time. I was too impatient to see him.

My 6-year-old friend was standing in the middle of the dark hall and trumpeted with his two fists which he pressed to his mouth, producing a blaring bugle. Sasha wasn't tall for a boy; in fact he was the same height as me. His whole appearance was quite unusual for a Russian child; he had coal black straight hair and a face with prominent cheek-bones which made him look almost Chinese. Still, his skin was white and eyes were green.

Usually, Sashka wore beautiful Chinese sweaters – bright green, blue or red with embroidered dragons or pandas on the chest - which his mother brought him from abroad. I never had anything like that in my childhood, until, one day, his mother, Nina, gave me a similar sweater for a birthday present. Mostly, Sashka wore short pants and knee socks, making him look like a classic obedient boy. But he was much more than that – he was a fountain of ideas.

"Hi," I said, gazing at him in admiration. "What will we play today?"

"Marshal Hierbel," he answered boldly. I had already known he would offer this, so I wonder now why I bothered to ask. We were always playing 'Marshal Hierbel'. It was Sashka's invention and his own scenario. I was always the subordinate in our games but I never minded. It was fun to be under such a smart, active and creative theatrical director.

Hierbel was the name of an imaginary German marshal. There was also Soviet marshal, Voroshilov, a lot of different generals, a brave Soviet woman spy, Vasilieva, and many other characters involved. We changed the roles all the time; however I always got to be the woman spy.

Actually, it was a war game. All Russian kids were playing war-games in those days because the recent experience of the Second World War strongly left its mark on everyone in the U.S.S.R. Unlike popular war-games, Sashka's version was not at all violent or aggressive. It wasn't on the level of battles – rather, we focused on the operations headquarters staff, marshals, generals, spies, secret agents, diplomats – the people with whom his mother worked. Sashka knew such people quite well by her descriptions and narratives. He even visited them with her.

"Our Sashenka is Stalin's grandson," I sometimes heard his grandmother, Baba Nadia, whisper in the kitchen to my Baba Sonya. This news was not for my ears, but they (my damn ears) were so cunning; they always pricked up and turned into anything around me that was told in a whisper.

However, I just couldn't make any sense of this information. I knew Stalin was a marble statue at our *metro* (Russian subway) station.

How would it be possible for a statue to have grandchildren? I wondered.

I knew Sashka's physical grandfather, Baba Nadia's husband, Grandpa Mitrophan, who lived in our apartment, as well. And that was it. For any Russian child to have even one grandpa after the war was a luxury. I, for one, didn't have any, so Sashka was lucky, compared to me.

The fact that he didn't have father didn't bother me at all – I was in the same boat. I was only interested in our games which were amazing.

We had built military forts and bunkers from chairs, couches, blankets and pillows in our or Sashka's grandparents' rooms. We crawled under the tables and armchairs, pretending that we're forcing underground tunnels; we jumped down from the chest of drawers or book shelves or even my piano, pretending that we're parachuting out of the skies. And we had ministerial-level summit talks as if we were marshals or heads of governments.

Sometimes, Vasilieva, the spy, was captured by Germans. Sashka, playing the role of marshal Hierbel, bound my hands with a scarf or kitchen towel, put the ruler to my neck and asked in a booming voice, *"Would you be to be my wife?"*

"No!" I responded, bubbling with laughter and jerking my feet. "No-o-oh!"

He glared at me with big eyes and shouted more aggressively, *"Would you be to be my wife?!!"*

"No!" I wailed, roaring with laughter until the tears came. I didn't know why he invented such a phrase with strange grammar, but it sounded very funny to me and we laughed about it a lot.

"Okay," he usually stepped back, as our giggles came to an end. "I'll give you one day to think it over and if you *wouldn't be to be my wife,* you will be killed."

Then marshal Hierbel left the scene, but the brave Soviet general appeared and helped Vasilieva to escape from the jail to the kitchen cupboards or to hide behind the stove.

Among the four children in our apartment, who mostly were babies or toddlers, Sashka was the only child who didn't constantly live in the building. It was the residence of his maternal grandparents, Baba Nadia and Ded Mitrophan. He and his mother lived in a room in another communal apartment building in downtown Moscow, close to the Ministry of the Foreign Affairs, where Nina used to work.

However, she quite often had business trips abroad – for a week, a month, three months, six months, and even a year. During those periods Sashka lived with his grandparents who took care of him. So, he was my neighbor, but not always next door. Sometimes we played daily, sometimes – yearly. It was a very special treat for me to play with Sashka and he probably treasured my friendship as well because he was always very nice to me and we had never ever argued. We really missed each other, but never had any contacts when he left his grandparents to return to his mother. We didn't talk on the phone. We didn't write letters to each other and didn't visit each other. We only remembered each other and waited patiently until Nina would leave on her next business trip. Then, our happy time together resumed.

Nina was a highly-qualified English teacher. There were few specialists in those years. In the thirties the whole country was preparing for war with Germany. Stalin officially announced that everybody must know the language of the enemy; so German was the only foreign language children learned in schools. There was no choice, of course.

During the war, Nina was studying philology at Moscow

University. Somehow, she chose English in the Department of the Rare Languages. And it was a right choice. After the Second World War the Soviet Union found a new enemy – America, and now everybody was supposed to learn English but there was a great lack of English teachers and specialists. So, Nina who was fluent in English got a very prestigious assignment – to teach this language to Soviet diplomats, members of the government, as well as the military and communist bosses. She also taught Soviet diplomats right on the spot – in the Soviet embassies around the world. Her usual assignments were in China and Viet-Nam, where she traveled quite often.

When my mom, Lala, arrived in Moscow from Rostov-on-Don in 1929, Nina was already living in this communal apartment with her parents. The girls became friends and went together to the same school across *Sadovoye Kiltzo*. They kept their close friendship for their entire lives, so it might be that both Sashka and I inherited our fondness for each other from our mothers.

Nina was a short, dark-haired woman with very plain looks. Added to this was the fact that when she was only two years old, back in Byelorussia, she accidentally crawled under a horse and touched its foot. The horse was frightened, and kicked her right in the face. She was lucky she wasn't killed. Her life was saved at the hospital, but ugly shapeless scars permanently formed on her chin, cheeks and forehead. It led to a tragic womanhood of disfigurement, condemning her to being unattractive to men. Even for beautiful women of this period, there were not enough men in the Soviet Union.

In spite of that, Nina developed an amazing personality. She was kind, polite, honest and warmhearted; plus – highly intelligent and talented. I remember her as being full of fun and burst with laughter. She was not just a woman but a bright fountain of happiness and love of life; she was an outstanding individual, capable of melting ice in cold men's hearts with her beautiful character and soul, instead of a pretty face.

And her inner attractiveness was appreciated. One spring day in 1947, Stalin's adopted son, a young general in the Soviet Air Force, Artem, became her student. They both fell in love with each other, were very happy and, soon, Nina discovered that she was pregnant. (There was no contraception in the Soviet Union those years, at all, and even abortions were prohibited.)

When Artem brought the question of his possible marriage to Stalin, the infamous tyrant didn't approve it. He explained to his son that Nina didn't belong to their circle. From earliest childhood,

Artem was expected to marry the daughter of the head of Spanish Communist Party. There were rules in the international Communist world - not to allow outsiders into their circle – similar to the rules of royal marriages between different countries. So, Stalin demanded that Artem immediately marry the lady from Spain without any objections. Otherwise, the pregnant Nina would be arrested and killed together with the baby in her womb.

It was sudden and horrible shock for the young lovers. Broken-hearted, they were separated. Gritting his teeth, Artem steadfastly agreed to his new marriage without love to save his beloved's and their child's lives. He only insisted in front of Stalin that Nina would keep her job to have enough money to raise his child alone, as single mother.

Stalin 'generously' accepted this because he loved Artem very much, possibly even much more than his official children – daughter Svetlana and sons, Jakob and Vasily. Why? This was an historical question to which I didn't know the answer at the time when my mom revealed the story of my dear friend Sashka's birth.

Later, after Stalin's death, when I was already teenager, my mom told me the other part of this story which was a top secret in Communist circles. Nina told my mom after hearing it from Artem himself.

Before the October Revolution, Stalin was an ordinary Bolshevik organizer with another name, 'Koba'. He was arrested by the Tsarist Secret Police because of his revolutionary activity and exiled to the northern Siberia village of Turuchansk. Next door to him lived a fellow Bolshevik exile, Fedor (alias 'Artem') with his family – his parents and younger sister Anya. They belonged to a native Siberian population and had oriental looks – dark hair and eyes with prominent cheekbones. Koba became person number one in this family - the best friend of Fedor (Artem) and lover of Anya who was only thirteen years old. The girl considered Koba a hero and was completely in love with him, too.

Some time later, Anya gave a birth to a son whom she named Artem in honor of her brother Fedor's conspiratorial name. Then, Stalin escaped from Turuchansk to continue his revolutionary activity, promising Anya that he would always take care of their baby. When Anya died from pneumonia, her brother, Fedor, adopted his nephew (and Stalin's son) Artem and, following the Bolshevik Revolution, brought the boy to Moscow.

Soon, Stalin rose to head of the Soviet Russia and Fedor continued to be one of his best friends. Nobody had known why Stalin always publicly stressed his brotherly fondness for Fedor.

However, some years passed and Stalin's cruel nature began to betray Fedor. Stalin's pattern was to eliminate anyone who knew him and his secrets. An accident was engineered and all of a sudden Fedor was killed in an airplane crash. Stalin, fighting back his tears during his speech at Fedor's funeral, promised his party comrades that he would never forget 'Bolshevik Artem' and decided to adopt his teenage son, Artem.

In this way, Artem was returned to the family of his biological father and officially filled the position of 'Stalin's adopted son.'

This story showed that my friend, Sashka, really was Stalin's grandson, as his Baba Nadia revealed. There was hardly any evidence of it; however, I had little interest in the story.

The fact that both Sashka and I had came into this world in tragic circumstances where our mothers survived the two together their pregnancies and deliveries, meant not much to me. However, this point probably subconsciously united us and fastened our childhood friendship. We were two who had survived the malice of the Communist regime and we were both the victims of it. Thanks to fate, we didn't perish; thanks to our luck, we were living victims. And more than that, we were educated, well-provided (compared to others), yet still victims!

But we were both too young to take it all in.

I was far more excited about our games with Sashka and the presents which his mom, Nina, always brought to me, on her return from China.

Those were usually little glass duck figures. Their bodies were glass balls (the size of golf balls); their necks were glass pipes, their heads – another glass balls with big eyes and a long yellow sparkling nose. They had multicolored feathers on their heads, on their sides (like wings) and on their tails. They had also long feet in huge boots, to stand properly.

I took a little saucer with water, bowed the duck's head and wet its nose. Then, I released it and duck began to bob back and forth, back and forth by itself. I didn't know how these toys were designed, but this was fantastic and looked miraculous to me.

One day, Nina brought to us a little fretted red lacquer with a picture on it of a Chinese pagoda and some Buddhist monks in national dress.

"This is a jewelry box," she said to my mom. "I want you, Lala, to keep it to remember me by. Stalin is dying. Nobody knows what will happen to us now. I'm really worried. Everybody in the Ministry of Foreign Affairs knows about my story with Artem, and everybody knows, as well that Sashenka is his son. It's so obvious since Sashka looks so like his dad. They're similar like a doubles! I'm scared. After Stalin is gone, many people who hated him may try to exact revenge on us."

Interestingly enough, Sashka and his two half-brothers, Artem's sons from his legal wife, were studying at the same privileged school and looked almost like copies of each other. All the teachers and staff knew that they were brothers, but the boys themselves had any faintest notion about that and never noticed their likenesses.

Fortunately, nothing really bad happened to Nina and Sashka after Stalin's death because everybody at the top level believed the version that Artem was adopted. He still had the last name of his uncle, Fedor, and his young mother, Anya. The dead Bolshevik Fedor was a very nice and sociable man towards his Party comrades and all of them loved him. So, nobody did anything bad to Artem and his Sashka or to Artem's official family.

However, both of Stalin's legal innocent children (the oldest, Jakob, perished in the war) were harassed a lot after his death and faced enormous difficulties and problems. Finally, Vasily was driven to his death and Svetlana escaped to the U.S. (through India) to save her own life. Stalin's former friends, co-workers and admirers wreaked their anger and hate toward the tyrant on those unlucky offspring. It was so typical for the Communists!

Luckily, Nina lost only her abroad trips but continued to teach diplomats English in Moscow so Sashka didn't need to live with his grandparents anymore. He could from now on always stay with his mom. Grandpa Mitrophan died and Baba Nadia was left alone in our apartment and kept her friendship with my Baba Sonya.

Sometimes, late in the evening, we would hear a quiet knock on our door. Then, it opened crack and we saw Nina's brown hair and sparkling eyes appear and whisper, "May I come in, friends?"

"Yes, yes, of course!" all three of us exclaimed, even if I was almost sleeping, my mom was writing at her table and Baba was listening the weather network on our old-fashioned radio. We were happy to put aside all the things we were preoccupied with in order to spend time with Nina over a cup of tea.

"I have a lot of news today," she continued to whisper. "Guess, what happened..."

Nina came to visit her old mother weekly and every time she dropped in at our place to share 'high society news' with my mom and Baba. Mostly, I was also included, unless there was a discussion about sex or politics, and then I was ordered out. Of course, I cunningly listened from the other room, pretending that I was busy with something there, or sleeping.

All of Nina's students shared their family secrets with her because she was full of compassion and understanding. However, they didn't know that Nina was a big gossip. She played the role that the modern media is playing today. In the Soviet Union all the personal 'news' were kept out of the official media, but from Nina we could learn everything that happened in the living rooms, kitchens and even bedrooms of the elite of the Communist society. And it was a lot of fun and entertainment.

Sashka very seldom came with her. We didn't play together anymore. Our childhood was finished.

"How is Sasha doing?" I asked Nina sometimes.

"Studying," she always answered. "Doing lot of homework for school and I'm also giving him a lot of extra homework in English. Plus, he's playing chess in a professional school, and we go skiing every Sunday. So, he's very busy, but asked me to say hi to you."

"Well," I answered sadly. "I'm very busy, too, but I remember him as well. Please, tell him hi from me, too."

We were both growing up and I saw my friend only couple of times during all these years but I was sure that the meetings with Nina would continue forever. And they did, until one day (I was already eighteen-years-old) I opened my door to the same accurate quiet knock that Nina used and was startled to see a strange man in front of me.

It was Sashka - and it wasn't. It was his face, his eyes, his hair, his height, everything was his but the only difference was that the man was over fifty.

He wore a light gray, silky full military uniform with lots of decoration. The golden oak leaves were embroidered around his collar and each leaf had an acorn in a tiny pimpled cup. I didn't know why this small and probably unimportant detail caught my attention. Maybe it attracted me because the man was just a bit taller than me and his collar with the leaves and acorns was parallel to my eyes. I stared at him in shock and confusion - who was this man and why was he at our door?

"Hello," he simply said, introducing himself. "I'm Artem – Sasha's father."

"Oh, gosh!" I gasped in amazement. It was a lieutenant-general uniform that he wore.

It was such an unforeseen surprise to see a person of his importance in our poor, dark, dirty communal apartment. It was a miracle and must mean that something extraordinary was happening to lead this fairytale prince into our lives. Knowing well the legend of Sashka's birth, I always took it as some kind of tall tale, so now I had trouble believing my own eyes, seeing in front of me, in the flesh, the center of the whole story.

"Sorry to bother you," Artem continued, noticing my stunned facial expression. "I bring you very bad news – Nina died unexpectedly. The horse kick she suffered in childhood produced a brain aneurism. Sasha came home from university and found her on the floor, dead. He called ambulance but it was way too late. Then, Sasha called her work. They notified me and I came to help him."

"Oh, God!" I whispered, burying my distraught face in my hands. Who would've expected such a turn of events? "Where is Sasha?"

"He stayed at home with her. I came here to pick up Nina's mother for her to see her daughter for the last time. But I don't know how to bring up the subject in front of the old lady. She is over eighty and could possibly die of shock from the horrible news. I know you were her friends. Maybe your Grandma could come and talk with her for me."

Of course, we did help him and my Baba gently broke the news of the sudden tragedy to Baba Nadia. But it was so difficult to realize that someone whom you had seen some days ago in good health, a good mood, laughing and bubbling with life could now be dead. I felt such grief and despair, but it was tinged with some inner satisfaction at the same time that Sasha had gotten, finally, his father.

Later, Artem helped Sasha to get his internship in England for one year, before his university masters degree was completed. Such an international internship was almost unreachable for ordinary students, so his father's help and connections with the top Soviet powers were priceless in this situation. Returning from England, Sasha visited his Baba Nadia weekly, continuing his mother's tradition, and sometimes came to visit me. I was already married and once he spent the whole evening drinking tea with us and telling me and my husband about England.

It was an unbelievably interesting narrative because at that time (early seventies) it was very difficult to know something truthful about capitalist countries. All information was restricted and we knew absolutely nothing about how people were living in England, except for 'the workers there were suffering under capitalist exploitation as much as everywhere in the western world'. Andropov, the notorious world terrorist, had just been appointed head of the KGB (1967) and all the screws began to tighten on the common people.

Then, our building on *Sadovoye Koltzo* was rebuilt to become a military Headquarters, so all of us - the neighbors of my lifetime - were relocated to separate apartments in newly built-up regions of Moscow. Sasha's Baba Nadia, who was by now over ninety, wasn't given a flat but was instead placed in a nursing home. Sometimes we did visit her there and she told us that Sasha continued visiting her weekly, like he always did. He married a fellow student, nice girl, Galina, and his father found him very prestigious position in the U.S.A.–Canadian Research Institute in Moscow.

"Oh, it's nice that Sasha has such a good relationship with his father," I commented, feeling really happy for my special childhood friend.

"It's already finished," Baba Nadia said sadly. "Artem's family found out about his helping Sasha and became furious. So, they don't see each other anymore."

This was the last doleful period at the end of the story of Stalin's illegitimate grandson who, even with superior education and good appointment was still not acceptable in higher Soviet circles. I never saw Sashka again or heard anything more about him. Baba Nadia died soon after and I went traveling around the world with my husband. So, Sashka and I totally lost track of one another.

"Did you ever meet him later, Baba?" Alina asked disappointed, as I finished my story.

"No. But I might guess that he, too, could have found himself somewhere on this North American continent – in the U.S.A or Canada. Many talented Russians chose to emigrate and we are quite often learning that our old friends are now over here. But I had no time to look for Sashka. I was busy raising you, studying English, working, writing, publishing my books.

"However, I always remember him and I even brought you two little things for a future memory."

I opened my suitcase and took out a small bright green sweater with an embroidered dragon on its front and little fretted red box with a pagoda on it.

"Wow!" Alina exclaimed. "They're beautiful!"

"These are our presents that Sashka's mother brought me from China. The sweater would fit Natasha now. It's brand new. I wore it only once for a big celebration and then I outgrew it. But I kept it as a nice memory about my childhood and even brought it with me when I emigrated. And the jewelry box is for you. It's the exact Chinese box that Nina brought as a gift for my mom and it became our family's jewelry box. There are golden earrings inside which belonged to our Baba Sonya. I would like you to wear them in memory of our family. There are also other gold jewelry pieces for you, for Natasha, for your mom and even a fat gold chain for your daddy. It was a Russian tradition to wear gold, though I never had any during my life in Russia. But now we can return to it."

"Thanks, Baba," Alina hugged me and kissed my cheek. Then she excitedly poked her nose into the jewelry box. "Wow! Wow! Wow!" she shrieked, trying on the bracelets and chains and hanging around the mirror. She was truly a little lady and I felt content that my presents pleased her so much.

Later that evening, when I came to Alina's bedroom to kiss her good night, she asked me suddenly, "Baba, are you sure that this story about Artem's parents is true? Was Sashka REALLY Stalin's grandson?"

I sat down beside her and stroked her head now sunk in her pillow.

"I guess so, sweetie," I said. "I didn't believe the story when I was back in Russia. But here, in America, I've had a chance to study many books about Soviet history which were prohibited in the Soviet Union, or which were written later by different American and English historians. I found in some documents that Stalin (Koba) really was exiled to Turuchansk. It was true that there he had a relationship with a 13-year-old girl which was illegal even a hundred years ago. There were some documents that said that the Tsarist government wanted to increase his punishment in prison because of that. However, Stalin promised to marry the girl and she claimed to love him, so the Tsar's guards left them alone, realizing that it was not a rape, but a love story."

"But it was still illegal, Baba," Alina reminded me. "It was child abuse."

"I know, sweetie. But for the Bolsheviks, it was normal behavior. They often did immoral things from the human point of view. They accepted all kinds of crimes and labeled normal things like freedom of thought, speech and existence 'crimes'. Their mentality was turned upside-down and inside-out. They made the whole country live in their perverse reality. Do you think the Bolshevik Revolution, which killed millions of people, was legal? Or the Civil war when brothers killed brothers, or fathers killed sons was legal? Or concentration camps for innocent people of all ages, starting from babies? Or a constant surveillance around you? Or bugged phones? These were all horrors we lived through. But we couldn't change anything then. It was what it was and what your ancestors were forced to survive. It was the truth of our lives. And it was the real tragedy of Russia."

"Oh, Baba," Alina murmured, scared. "I'm so happy that I was born in America."

"Yes, sweetie, you're very happy and I'm happy too," I answered, kissing her forehead to calm her down. "When your mom was a little girl she often cried and asked me in hopelessness, 'Mommy, why did you have me? I don't want to live in such a country!' though it was already Brezhnev's time, a time easier than Stalin's, but, anyway, there still was a twisted mentality and a lot of disgust and horror. I'm happy and proud that I made my dream come true – my daughter and my granddaughters are living in a free country. But, our family history and world history should still be known, sweetie. You must never forget the experiences I tell you about. So, go back to Artem, Sashkas's father.

"Here, in America, I also discovered documents that Bolshevik Fedor (Artem) was involved with Stalin baby's adoption – the child who was born in Turuchansk and named Artem. I'm considering it as evidence. That's all about the deep past. Now I know for sure that it was true.

"The later events – Fedor's death in a plane crash, Artem's adoption by Stalin were officially well-known in Soviet Union. There was no question that it was true, as well.

"And the ending of the story – Sashka's life – I knew myself very well. I saw lieutenant-general Artem with my own two eyes standing in our doorway. I remember clearly that, above the tiny golden oak leaves with acorns on the collar of his military uniform, was the face of an older Sashka."

"But how come, Baba, Sashka was such a good boy, if he was that monster Stalin's grandson?" Alina asked. "Didn't he inherit anything bad from Stalin in his genes?"

"Inheritance is not always so direct, my dear," I explained. "It's well-known that Stalin's daughter, Svetlana, is very warmhearted and kind woman. Maybe those kids took after their mothers? Who knows?"

I saw Alina's big eyes shine in the dim light of the cozy bedroom, as she listened to the story that touched her heart. I felt satisfied that I had paid off my debt for the following generations of my family and opened for her a little personal door into the Russian past which I myself witnessed in my childhood. Now I knew for sure that our Russian history would not be lost and Alina would surely pass it on to her future children and grandchildren.

Where are you now, Sashka? I thought.

Chapter 13

UPS AND DOWNS AT MY DACHA

The following weekend, Charles suggested that we go fishing at the lake by their vacation home. He had already gotten the license for fishing and my husband excitedly supported the idea.

We were surprised to discover that Rimma was an avid 'fisherwoman', too. Maybe she remembered the beautiful time when we were living in the Middle East and she used to go fishing with her father in the Red Sea. The Sea was warm, around +36 degrees C., and small funny schools of fish swarmed around 5-year-old Rimma. She enjoyed picking them up and called them 'sailors' because of their yellow and black stripes.

Now, in America, the grown-up Rimma liked to fish, as well. The main reasons that they bought their second home at the lake was their mutual love of fishing and Alina's special love for horses, since there was a horse farm next door.

The house was about thirty years old. Like the homes of American pioneers, it was a log cabin structure with the interior done in unfinished wood. This looked unusual and created a special atmosphere of life two hundred years ago. However, modern kitchen, shower, bathroom and heating system were added.

The house stood on the top of a hill and had good-sized acreage to set it off. There was a garden, but Rimma kept it simple – just a couple of apricot and cherry trees, and only perennial flowers, except for a lawn. Trees from the forest surrounded it, not requiring any human care. Our daughter wasn't a big gardener and really had no time for that.

There was also a playground for children in the yard and an outdoor fireplace, with a glass-top table and chairs next to it for patio suppers or a light drink, sometimes, by the night fire.

But especially beautiful was the view – the silver surface of the lake reflected the mountains on all sides and magnified the feeling of natural beauty. It was both glorious and awesome.

They had also a little moorage on the lake with a special lift for their new motorboat.

After dinner I opened my travel bag and took out a roll of a gray rough canvas.

"Here is a family present for you," I said, unrolling the canvas. "It's something special for all of you. I supposed it would go well with your country retreat. This is *The Boat On The Pond* – the painting that my great-grandma Ekaterina painted 110 years ago."

"Wow!" Charles exclaimed. "It must be valuable at an Antique Auction!"

"It would be, but only maybe. You see, it's not finished. However, I brought it for you - not to sell. You just need to buy a new antique-like frame for it and keep it here, in your cabin, on the wall in the living room.

"When we emigrated from Russia, I took it with me, though it was quite difficult to get round Soviet custom, but we succeeded, perhaps with the help of fate. Rimma knows the story well. Right, sweetie?"

Our daughter nodded, smiling, as she noted, "Oh, it was one of a kind..."

"I think that fate wanted this painting kept in the family," I continued. "It's a long family history and I want my grandchildren to know it and pass it on to their grandchildren."

"Well, I'll buy a frame, an old-fashioned one, and the next time we come here, I'll bring it," Charles agreed, scrutinizing the painting. "You're right. It really fits our old bungalow. However, even here, it looks quite gloomy."

"It's Russian life, my dear, always gloomy and tense," I explained. "Ekaterina was a very talented artist and she was capable of deeply expressing it in her painting. In Russia, you never knew what would collapse on your head at any given minute. You never felt free or fully happy. Always, even when you are excited and on the top of the world, you feel an ominous shadow looming behind you, not giving you a chance to savor the moment and relax. It was a scary life – always was, and still is, and, I'm sure, will always be. That's why I ran away from there and pulled my family with me. Now I'm finally feeling secure for all of you."

"Thanks, Baba," Alina said, hugging me. "Mom told me Ekaterina's story. I'll keep the painting, I promise."

In the evening, Charles and Rimma, my husband and Natasha went fishing on their boat. I refused to go because I didn't like water much and, as a true Taurus, preferred to stay on land. Alina decided to spend the evening with me and we sat on the steps of the patio together to gaze at the serene lake-side view.

"I heard, Baba that you had a dacha in Russia. Could you tell me about it?" Alina inquired. "What did you do there in your childhood? Did you have friends to play with? Did you have some animals, horses, or...dogs, cats? I want to compare your experiences to mine."

I took a deep breath. What could I really say? Our experiences were totally different but my dear girl wouldn't be able to take it all in and I did want to try to lift the curtain to another world for her get a glimpse of my life.

"We built our dacha, sweetie, when I was eighteen," I said, "but we always rented dachas in my childhood. Moscow was a metropolis, a crowded city with cars and trucks chasing round-the-clock. There were also polluting factories, hazardous chemical wastes, and military radio-active plants right in the city. The air was so dirty to breathe!

"Summers were usually quite hot and it seemed that even the asphalt was melting under your feet. In addition, the atmosphere stank from the smell of oil and gas from the cars. There was little green shrubbery and few trees when I was very young, during the Stalin period, to take a breath without gagging. It was a kind of hell, so my mom always paid big money to landlords who had their own dachas, to rent a small room from them to send me and Baba Sonya somewhere in the forest, in the fresh air..."

"...between the bushes and flowers," Alina continued, smiling. "Right, Baba?"

"Yeah," I uttered hesitantly. "There were some bushes and flowers, of course, but there were many other things there which you could never imagine. I can tell you a story, if you want."

"I definitely do," Alina nodded and put her head on my shoulder, "please, tell me, Baba."

...The chickens' cluck woke me up in the morning. They walked under our house, looking for rain-worms because the gloom underneath was always moist. Though the house stood on 2-feet-tall brick foundation blocks, the clay soil below never dried out.

Once I tried crawling down there to explore the space, but I didn't find anything except for lots of mud which got all over me. Then Baba Sonya blamed me for giving in to my curiosity, especially since it was difficult to wash me without a bathtub and launder my clothes. We had only a wash-basin and a pitcher in our room, so my Baba had to draw water from a distant well, and carry it back in two big pails. I helped her as much as I could, and carried my little pail and small watering can full of water in both my hands. However, my portion was barely enough to fill just our little teapot.

It was not easy work for an old woman and a young girl.

So, although I was outdoors and theoretically 'free', I had to be careful not to get dirty. The goal was for me to be limited to a weekly washing, but that meant that I couldn't really go exploring much. It was impossible for me. Not allowed to go exploring in a new place?

That morning I had been awakened up by the rooster's crow, and I rolled over on my tummy on my squeaky cot and looked down through the narrow cracks in the floor, where the damn chickens were visible. My worst enemy, the rooster, was there, of course. I reached my hand over and scooped bread crumbs from the floor under the table and dropped them down the crack to give the chicks something different to eat and try to befriend them a little. They reacted immediately - dashed to the crumbs, fighting, flapping their wings and cackling in great agitation.

My relationship with the rooster wasn't good, so far. His bellicose manner made him quite a terror to everyone residing in this dacha – six families in all. There were four rooms downstairs, partitioned by thin veneer, one – on the second floor and one located in the outer storage room in the yard. The owner of the dacha tried to make as much money as possible on his old, tumble-down house without running water, toilets and electricity.

It was illegal, of course, and he would be arrested and his dacha confiscated by government if anyone reported his private money-making. However, he was lucky. Nobody informed because everybody wanted spend their summers outside of the city, even in crude accommodations like a hundred years ago, but, nevertheless, in the fresh air.

We had had only one very stinky, wooden outhouse located quite far from the house, in the back corner of the yard behind a bush. To reach it, people had to cross the whole yard, taking a path between vegetable patches.

When it saw someone approaching, the rooster was already on guard as if he was destined to protect the toilet as his dearest property. He quietly stole between the rows of potatoes and then suddenly attacked people from behind, sharply pecking at their heels, sometimes with a bloody result.

When heading towards the outhouse, the adults always had to carry a branch of hazel bush in their hands and check around carefully. They had to begin beating the rooster as soon as they saw him, before he got a chance to attack. It was a real war that continued the whole summer.

Sometimes, angry tenants complained to the owner and asked him to restrain the rooster in a cage during the day time, but he refused. He locked his poultry up only at night, but in the daytime he wanted them to walk freely and feed themselves on worms, so the owner could save on their food. Yet, the tenants were advised to be patient and leave the rooster alone. The war escalated as the hate intensified on both sides.

One day, the rooster caught me on my way to the toilet. Before I went, I checked the path to be sure it was safe. However, when I had already run half of the way, the damn aggressor appeared from out of the blue and began pecking my feet. I screamed but had nothing with me that I could use to strike him. I could only run, but the rooster easily chased me.

Suddenly, near the outer storage shed I saw a 3-ft.-long chunk of wood. My fear empowered me, so I up-ended the log and climbed up to safety. There was barely enough room for one foot on the end so, holding the other out, I maintained a balancing act worthy of a circus performance. Since I desperately needed to get to the toilet, I balanced on the log with difficulty, yelling crazily, "Help! Help!" while the rooster tried to attack and went on, jumping and pecking the top of the log just a few inches away from my foot exposed in my sandal.

My foot soon became numb and I thought my torment would continue for eternity, until my Baba at last ran from the house with a broom in her hands, shouting angrily at the rooster. She pushed him away and I was delivered from assault.

Ever since that day, I really hated the rooster and was always scared of him. My Baba became especially worried about me because I was only five at the time. I was short, and the rooster could easily fly up and peck my eyes, blinding me. The owner would never take responsibility for such a tragedy.

From then on, my Baba with a hazel branch in her hands usually followed me and fought with the rooster while I went and did my business in the outhouse. But she mostly decided to sit me on a chamber pot, and then rinse out the contents under a big, wild rosebush planted by the porch. All the slops from the kitchen and dirty water after our washing and our laundry ended up in the same place, and the happy rosebush, fertilized with all these things, blossomed and grew fantastically.

Now, watching the rooster through the floor cracks, I realized that it was good time to go for a walk – my enemy was completely busy with his breakfast.

"Baba," I begged. "Can I get up now and go outside?"

"Okay, you can get up. But first, before you go outside, sit on the pot, then wash up and then you'll have your breakfast – hot wheat cereal."

"Oh, yuck," I wrinkled my nose. "Lumpy cereal!" and I retreated under my blanket.

I hated such food, called in Russian *mannaya kasha*. It was tasteless, gray and always full of lumps because my Baba couldn't cook it properly on her little, stinky kerosene-stove right here, on the table above my camp-cot. To be tasty, kasha should be made creamy, without lumps and boiled with milk, but there was no milk in our country shop – there was only dark bread, herring and vodka.

At the beginning of the summer we had one local milkman who owned a cow illegally and every morning, about 5 o'clock he brought a 2-liter can of fresh milk and left it on our porch. Baba usually left money for him under a doormat. However, to own cattle privately was prohibited by the government, so, somebody informed on him and his cow was confiscated, he was arrested and we lost our chance to have milk the rest of the summer.

On weekends, my mom usually came out from Moscow to see us and to have some rest, too. She always brought two huge bags full of food, including a half-liter bottle of the milk. The bottle was made of thick, heavy glass so she could only carry one at a time. It was barely enough for me alone for the whole week.

If the weather was hot, the milk sometimes soured because my mom had to travel a long distance. She carried the food bags on a bus, then on a *metro*, then a local train, followed by a two-kilometer hike under the scalding sun from the train station to our dacha.

For these reasons my kasha was mostly boiled with just water, and was tasteless. Nevertheless, my Baba was absolutely convinced that it was nutritious for a growing child and forced me to eat it every morning. If some lumps were in my spoonful, I had the horrible feeling of wanting to throw up from utter disgust.

"Stop, Katya," my Baba harshly reprimanded me as I was hiding under my blanket. "I don't like these games when you're pretending to vomit. My kasha has no lumps at all. It is the healthiest and tastiest food in the world."

"Baba, can I have an egg instead?" I pleaded from my cocoon, feeling judged for rejecting what was good for me. Eggs were my favorite. I was crazy about them and would like to eat at least a dozen everyday. This was possible because the landlord of the dacha was always ready to sell us fresh eggs from his hens.

But Baba's dietary wisdom was to interfere with such happiness.

"No, you had one two days ago," she double checked on the wall calendar. "Yes, on Tuesday."

"Can I have one more today?"

"No, no, no. Don't be silly! You know that eggs are not healthy. They are giving you red spots on your face. It's an allergy, for sure. No, you have to wait until next Tuesday."

So, I had almost a week left to dream of my next egg.

While reluctantly downing my kasha, I glanced furtively at Baba Sonya who was peeling potatoes on the table right beside me. She looked concerned.

"You know, Katya," her tone was unpleasant, "you're always creating problems. I'm about to keep you indoors …permanently. Do you have a headache?"

"No!" I strongly insisted. "I haven't had one even right after my fall!"

"Okay. No dizziness?"

"No, Baba."

"Okay, no nausea?"

"No, no!"

Baba's concerns were understandable. She was worried that I'd suffered a brain concussion because of my falling from the second floor of the house four days earlier. As far as I could tell, except for plenty of scratches on my behind, nothing serious had occurred.

It was an accident, of course, and no fault of mine. My friend, Lucy, and her mom used to live up there, in a small room under the roof. Lucy was a nice girl one year older than me and we enthusiastically played dolls every day. We built houses for our dolls under the beds and chairs, making furniture from pieces of paper, wood, clay, little stones, and cones. We decorated the dolls' beds with grass, leaves and flower petals.

Sometimes, we glued some pink petals with our saliva to our fingernails, pretending that we had nail polish on, and walked proudly holding our hands up, with outspread fingers. Our games were so interesting and so gripping that I was often unwilling to stop them and return home, downstairs.

On the day of the accident, I suddenly felt the urge to pee during our game. I was brave and stubborn enough to endure it for awhile, squeezing my legs and keeping the game going. So, it continued like this for another 15 minutes, until I finally realized that I couldn't hold it anymore and told Lucy, "I'll be back in a minute!" as I ran downstairs.

The stairs were wooden and quite steep – about twenty-five steps with one landing in the middle. I tried to run down as fast as I could and, of course, had missing stepped on one of them. My little leather sandal slid from the edge of the step and I suddenly found myself flying through the air and flipping over, head over heels, again and again. I really didn't understand what was happening and wasn't even scared. I could only see the cement wall on my right side twisting and twisting in front of my eyes, and felt with horror that I couldn't hold back my pee anymore and it gushed around through my panties.

When I came to the bottom of the stairs, I hit the dry, dusty ground with a thud, and began wailing loudly. I jerked my feet, to straighten myself and stand up, but my efforts only mixed my flow of urine with the dust, smearing me from head to toe with a newly formed mud. I wept from shame and horror, seeing Lucy scared to death, watching me from the top of the stairs and my Baba running toward me from the garden where she was sitting and talking with the neighbors.

"Are you okay, Katya?" Baba cried, terrified and clutched me to her to comfort me. I didn't see any problem with my fall, except for the dirt and shame of peeing on myself but, of course, she was worried because in reality it was a serious fall. As I found out later, many people had died from just such a fall down steep stairs.

My Baba and neighboring ladies quickly gathered round, asked me to stand, to bend, to turn my arms, my feet and legs, checked my spinal cord and then Baba carried me home for a thorough washing. Luckily, I didn't even get one bruise, or any broken bones. I just had some scratches on my bottom that my Baba smeared with iodine to disinfect. Still, grandmothers are grandmothers, and she promptly put me to bed for a couple of days to be sure that there were no brain injuries as well.

It was so boring lying in bed in the middle of summer, only reading books as if I were REALLY sick! I was whining all the time and begged Baba to let me go. Finally, she yielded.

Two days after the cartwheels down the stairs, I walked outside and found some new interesting things. While I had spent two days in bed, the owner of the dacha bought a full truck of wooden boards and now they were stored, one on top of the other, beside the back fence and looked like a huge pile. In some places they looked like steps, so it would be easy to climb up onto the top of the pile. And, from there, it would be easy, by holding on to the branches of the fir tree, to step onto the fence, walk along the top toward the shed and climb up on the roof. It was so clear, so inviting, and so challenging that I found it hard to believe that no one had done it already! It seemed to me a fantastic adventure so I promptly began my climb.

I soon discovered, to my dismay, that what looked like a stable pile of lumber was actually a jumble. It was an uneasy business - to climb up on the top of the plank mountain. They were angled this way and that, and constantly shifting under me, but carefully I mounted the pile. Once I'd successfully ascended, I proudly jumped onto the roof of the storage shed and sat on the edge, with my legs dangling down. From the height, I surveyed the neighbor's garden below. Before long I spotted my friend, the 8-year-old Andrew, who was standing beside two talking men. Andrew was holding his German Shepard, Lorka, by its ear.

"Hi Andrew," I waved to him. "How are you?"

"Hi there," he responded and whistled from excitement, "Oh, how did you get way up there, Katya? It's great! I wish I do that, too! Great job! Do you want to come over?"

"I do, but Lorka is there..."

Their dog was very aggressive and when I came to play, Andrew's father always locked it inside their house.

"It's okay," Andrew said, "Daddy is here, you see. He is busy talking with Uncle Ivan, but he is controlling Lorka. He orders her to sit quietly and she does. Don't worry, come down the step ladder."

There was an old wooden step ladder leaned against the fence between our yards and we always used it for climbing over to visit one another, to avoid walking a whole block to reach another gate.

I couldn't say that I was best friends with Andrew, like I was with Sashka. He wasn't nearly as smart or creative as my friend back in the city. He could even be quite silly at times but, anyway, he was better than nothing in my summer boredom. We usually played ball on a lawn in Andrew's front yard and it was a lot of fun.

"Okay," I agreed and returned carefully from the roof to the top of the fence, stepped in the direction of the stepladder and proceeded to climb down into Andrew's yard. "Let's go and play ball," I suggested, approaching the group of four in the middle of the yard – Andrew, the two men and Lorka.

It wasn't matter that the dog was sitting – its terrifying head seemed to be all teeth in an open mouth on a level with my childish face, just inches away. Lorka was panting, perhaps from the heat irritating its coat on a summer's day. Dog's long pink tongue hung from its mouth and, from time to time, the slobbering saliva would drop into the green grass underfoot.

Lorka's black nose was wet, as well.

"Let's go play ball," I repeated to Andrew, feeling very uncomfortable beside the dog, though it didn't pay me any visible notice.

"Wait a minute. I haven't finished the game I'm playing with Lorka," he explained. "I play with her that I'm torturing her to get her to confess. I am a brave KGB investigator and she is an American spy and an 'enemy of the people'. I want her to confess, so I can justifiably kill her after that. Look what I have," he showed me a black plastic gun and, with one hand, pressed the barrel against Lorka's neck.

With his other hand, he reached for the dog's nose, made a circle with his thumb and index finger and jabbed his fingernails into the sensitive, wet muzzle. The dog jerked from pain but then, continued sitting without resistance.

"Confess!" Andrew said sternly and thrust his nails in once more.

"What are you doing?!" I exclaimed indignantly. "She is jerking! It's painful! You shouldn't hurt helpless animals!"

"She is not an animal. She is an American spy," the boy objected and inflicted the agony yet once again.

"Don't abuse her! She has feelings!" I begged. "My Baba taught me..." I even didn't finish my sentence as Lorka jumped up with a mad bark and leapt on me, pushing her sharp-clawed paws against my chest. The shove was so strong that I fell over backwards and the dog pounced on me. Its terrifying muzzle full of angry bared teeth appeared for a moment in front of my face, as she was ready to size my childish throat. I didn't even have time to cry or close my eyes. My wide eyes took in the snapping teeth just inches form my cheek. Then, Lorka's body ascended as Andrew's father grabbed her by the collar and lifted her, rescuing me. Then he dragged the dog, still barking angrily, toward the house to lock her away.

The other man, whom Andrew called Uncle Ivan, helped me to scramble to my feet.

"It's okay, girl," he said in an unpleasant voice, "don't worry. Nothing happened! You just go home. You shouldn't have come here when Lorka is loose. It's actually your fault."

I was in such a petrified state that I couldn't even cry, or say, or do anything. Dazed, I walked like a zombie to my fence, slowly dragged up the ladder, stepped over the fence on the wooden pile of planks in our yard, and only then, in a kind of delayed shock, began to take in the reality and my gripping fear led to fits. I plopped on the top of the wood pile and wept loudly and shrilly to the whole world. As I landed, however, the lumber began shifting and sliding and, before long, I was toppling from the height to the ground, along with the falling wood structure that collapsed and buried me deep under the planks. I was a mountain climber caught in an avalanche!

I went under with such a piercing howl, that it brought my Baba form her kitchen in a dash to see what I'd gotten into and to dig me out. It wasn't an easy matter, I tell you, to uncover the boards one by one to free me. She was in frenzy herself, aware that I might be badly injured or even handicapped from the fall. However, I went on to be incredibly lucky once more, with only some scratches on my sides. So Baba, once again, painted me with iodine.

The terror I experienced with the dog was much longer lasting than my fall. Ever after that, I was always scared of dogs and began to hate them all. I've had that traumatic memory with me my whole life.

Baba once more, lectured me on my reckless ways, and ordered me to stay in bed for a couple more days, just in case.

The days passed boringly and now, finally, my moment of freedom had nearly come.

"Baba, I'm done," I begged, finishing my kasha, even licking the plate with my tongue to show her that I was an obedient eater.

She took a deep breath.

"Well, I don't know what to do with you. Would you mind playing properly with the other kids instead of climbing and jumping all over the place? Could you do that for me? I'm tired and one day will probably have a heart attack because of your foolhardy behavior. There are about ten kids nearby and none of them are falling down from anywhere, none has been attacked by the rooster or dog. You are the only one who is always in trouble. Promise that you'll behave like a proper child, at last."

"Yes, I promise," I nodded confidently. "I won't go climbing anywhere without your permission, and I'll only play with the other children."

"Okay, then you can go," Baba sighed more deeply than before, put a pink sundress over my head and sat a white panama hat on my head.

"I don't want the panama," I whined protesting, but Baba insisted firmly, "If you won't wear this hat, then there is no way I will let you go out."

"Well, then..." I yielded unhappily, making faces and finally left the house.

In our front yard, on the grass, some boys and girls were gathering to make some weapons. Andrew, Lucy and other children I knew were among them. There were also some new faces - the neighbors' children from the farthest ends of our street, whom I had never played with before.

All of them were 6-10 years old (older than I was) and wore only shorts and sandals. None of them had hats, of course. Wearing my pink sundress with frills and a panama, I stood out and felt uncomfortable. In the Soviet society everybody should look the same; any sign of difference or individuality seemed to signal dangerous or capitalistic tendencies, which I probably unconsciously sensed as a child because it was in the very atmosphere. Probably, that's why I always protested against beautiful dresses and hats. I fought them instinctively, while my Baba stubbornly tried to dress me elegantly and spent hours with a sewing machine to make something new and charming for me from her or mom's old skirts.

Now, I held back on our porch, seeing that all the children in the yard had plastic guns, sabers, rifles, automatic guns and knifes. It seemed not enough for them and they were bending hazelnut branches, tightening them with strings like bows and preparing arrows. Some of them had just sticks which they pretended were rifles or swords.

"Hi, Katya," the children greeted me. "Come on. We're going to play war! Don't you want to join us?"

"Yes," I shyly nodded. Of course, I wanted to play with them but I didn't have any weapon among my toys and had no idea how to play war. "Would you mind giving me a weapon, please, or teach me how to make one?" I asked, approaching them.

"Of course," Andrew agreed, "you can hold my gun, for now. Watch how I am doing the bow..."

He tightened a string on one end of a stick and began to bow it, but then stopped and looked at me critically.

"Hey," he noticed, "what a silly hat you have on! What stupid idiot put it on your head?"

I wanted to say, "My Baba," but the words stuck in my throat. I couldn't pronounce that and admit that my Baba was this *stupid idiot*. I didn't want to hurt her and utter any bad words about her, though I had completely disagreed about wearing the panama on my head. Still, I really appreciated my Baba's concern for me. I knew she loved me more than anybody in her life and I loved her, as well.

So, I just silently grabbed my hat, crumpled it and put it into the pocket of my sundress, feeling really offended. The children laughed.

"Okay," Andrew said, "that's better. Well, hold the stick."

I put his plastic gun into the other pocket of my sundress and held the other end of the bow with both hands. Andrew tightened the string on the other end of the stick and shouted, "Ready! Are the arrows done, private Vasya?" he asked a red-headed boy with a freckled nose.

"Yes, comrade general!" readily barked the boy.

"So, we can start! Let's count turns."

Everybody gathered in a circle and Lucy, standing in the middle, began to count every child, rhythmically reciting special children's counting rhyme, pointing to each child's chest. The person, on whom the rhyme ended, would be out. The one who was out early was lucky, because the last one in the chant would be the *Fascist*. All the others would be the brave *Red Army*.

I was eliminated early and stepped back, as everybody did and sat on the grass, waiting.

At that moment, Lucy messed up in her counting and the kids began arguing. They shouted at each other, called names, blamed each other, swearing coarsely and shoving. It became so noisy that my Baba opened our door and looked out to check on what was going on.

"Katya, put your panama back," she shouted unpleasantly. "It's too sunny! You may have a sun stroke!"

My first instinct was always to obey her, so I silently pulled a crumpled hat from my pocket and placed it on my head, again. Then Baba disappeared inside the house, satisfied.

The children finally stopped their argument and decided to count once more from the beginning. However, suddenly Andrew's gaze stuck on me and he shouted, "Hey, look at Katya. She is so different. Her dress and hat could be a fascist's uniform! She will be our Fascist!"

"Yes! Yes!" everybody unhesitatingly supported him. If they agreed, they would be safe from playing that hated role themselves.

"No! I don't want to be a fascist!" I protested heatedly, jumping to my defense, but nobody was listening to me anymore.

"Kill the fascist! Kill the fascist!" they chanted excitedly and dashed toward me, holding their weapons up and, in reality, ready to attack me as a mob. "We're the brave Soviet Army! Kill the fascist!"

I screamed and ran, but the crowd, being older and stronger than me, easily chased me, brandishing their assorted weapons above their heads, angrily.

I had no time to think about where to run; I had completely

forgotten about the rooster in the back yard and also about my own door on the porch that could serve to shelter me. I just ran, crazed with fear. The horror made me blind, deaf and brainless.

In this pandemonium we twice circled the whole yard and house, jumping over rows of potatoes and vegetables, stumbling over gnarled tree roots that stuck out in spots, and tearing through the blackcurrant and raspberry bushes. Someone had already beaten me with a stick on my back, but, luckily for me, the end of the stick only slid down over my skirt and didn't hurt me. However, I lost my panama hat somewhere in the bushes right at the beginning of the chase, along with Andrew's plastic gun which fell out of my pocket.

Finally, like a crazed hunted animal, all shaking and choking with sobs, I dived into the middle of the rosebush beside our porch. Now, my sobs turned to deafening wails as the rose thorns scratched my tender skin and the smell from under the bush reached my nostrils – all the yucky, stinky black mud from our waste and sewers greased my hands, knees and pink fancy skirt.

The children gathered around the rosebush and went on shouting and beating me, but the rose branches were springy and took revenge on them, protecting me from the blows. The rose petals and beaten leaves drifted down and coated my back while I was crouched there on all fours.

As my howl reached my Baba's ears, she ran out on the porch and begun to shout at the children, driving them away from me. They became quiet and spread out momentarily, carrying away their weapons, but Andrew hid behind the porch and we didn't notice him.

Lamenting, Baba pulled me out the bush, grabbed my hand and wanted to take me home to comfort, wash and dress my wounds. But before she could, Andrew snuck up closer and threw white, fat worm – a grub of the May-bug (cockchafer) – under my collar, so it fell down my back and disgustingly tickled my skin under my dress. I screamed in crazed fear of the creepy thing. To me, the grub was the ugliest thing in the world and I was understandably squeamish of it.

"What do you think you are doing?!" Baba barked at him, but he just grinned broadly and ran away.

The yucky grub finished me off. I wept inconsolably the rest of the day, resisting all of Baba's efforts to calm me down. I felt both humiliated and devastated.

The rest of that summer I spent playing in our room or in the front yard with my Baba sitting beside me.

"You're an impossible child, Katya," she complained unhappily.

"You need to be watched around-the-clock. I can't grasp how all the other children can play normally without incident - but you, within just five minutes have gotten into a fix of some sort."

When my mom came on the weekend, she tried to talk to the parents of the other children about abusing me, but they assured her that everything was okay, that nothing serious had taken place – the kids were only playing. During children's games, it's usual for one child to be the fascist beaten by the Red Army, or a dragon attacked by knights, or a rabbit eaten by the foxes, or a wolf being hunted. This is how all children play.

Andrew's father explained to my mom that the grub dropped into my dress was only a joke that Andrew did to support me and lift my spirits. He also asked her to replace his son's missing plastic gun that I had lost out of my pocket in my panic to escape. We tried to look for it around the yard but it had dropped from sight.

"Anyway, I guess that the next summer we should move to another country village," my mom decided. "This place certainly isn't working out for Katya."

A week later, when my mom brought a new gun for Andrew from Moscow, my Baba asked her, "Was it difficult to find it?"

"No," my mom laughed. "It was unbelievably easy. Guns, swords and rifles are plentiful in every toy store and they cost almost nothing, so everybody can afford them for their kids."

As I finished the story, Alina's eyes were enlarged and full of anxiety.

"Gosh! It wasn't much fun for you, was it, Baba?" she said dolefully, hugging me. "My poor Baba! Everybody treated you so badly! And you were only 5!" she kissed my cheek affectionately and took a deep breath. "How could you stand such thinking and rudeness? Didn't people even apologize? It could never happen here!"

"It was certainly an upside-down world," I commented. "My mom and I never asked for apologies. That's why I always disliked my country and since I turned 8, decided to emigrate as soon as I could. However, it took me another forty years. But, finally, I did it. I did it for you, Alinochka, for you, my dear sweetheart, to live in a free world and in a free mind. I always dreamed for you to feel safe; for you to love animals; for you to have nice feelings toward people and to receive smiles from others around you. I wanted you to enjoy your life, instead of enduring suffering from your earliest childhood."

"Why had Lorka attacked you instead of Andrew? He was the

one who torturing her," Alina asked in her incomprehension. "It was so unfair. You tried to defend her..."

"Don't you understand Andrew was her owner's son? He was her family member. She couldn't bite him, but she was so irritated and so hurt that she unconsciously wanted to wreak her pain and anger on somebody and I, a weak little stranger, was perfectly fitted for that role. The dog was obviously trained to attack people.

"As I was a child, I didn't understand much, but years later, I guessed who those people really were who kept such a big, ferocious dog as Lorka. The dog needed at least a kilogram of meat, daily, plus a lot of other food at a time when the whole country had almost nothing to eat. People could only afford for themselves and their children just the simplest food – potatoes and bread. Most of the population had never even heard about good meat, much less had it on their dinner tables. It was possible to buy some meat only at the farmers' markets, but nobody could guarantee its quality and nobody could be sure where the 'mystery meat' came from. There were sometimes cases of cannibalism in Russia because of a mass hunger. And criminals also made money this way. Anyway, very few people could afford the market prices of the meat.

"Now, thinking back, I'm absolutely certain that Andrew's father, a big and strong man, had had this aggressive and well-trained dog as his working dog and the money to keep her fed. It could be that he was one of the KGB concentration camp guards or something like that. These people shaped our life and mentality; they decided what was good and what was bad. We, the intelligent, kind and simple people, had only one choice – to get away, if possible."

"It's so sad and scary," Alina uttered thoughtfully. "Wasn't there something nice and sweet in your childhood, ever? Except for your creations?" she asked then with a voice full of concern. "Can't you remember anything like that too, Baba?"

"Yes, of course," I smiled, "there were many nice things, as well, but I will tell you about them tomorrow. Not now. It's getting late. Look, our dear ones are already coming back from fishing. It looks like they were successful."

I pointed down the hill, to the darkening lake that reflected the deep orange colors of the sunset, where the boat was already approaching the coast.

While Charles jumped out on the moorage and tightened the chain, we saw my husband gathering up their spinning rods, and Rimma held Natasha who was standing in the middle of the boat. My youngest granddaughter was displaying a good-sized fish in a plastic pail and shouting in excitement, "Baba! Alina! Look what I got! Look what I got! Myself!"

"Let's meet them!" Alina proposed mischievously and jumped up from the steps where she was sitting with me. "Come on, Baba! Give me your hand! Let's run!"

Chapter 14

SOMETHING NICE...

The following day, Rimma and Charles got a phone call from their friends who lived not very far away, over the next property and had three toddlers who were Natasha's friends. My daughter and son-in-law hadn't seen their neighbors for quite a while and today choose to go over for a visit with our youngest granddaughter.

Alina proposed that she and I walk down the road to the horse farm, so she could show me her beloved animals. My husband preferred to stay at the bungalow and watch a soccer game on TV. By the way, he promised to cook a traditional Russian supper from our childhood. It was decided that before 5 o'clock all the family would return home and have this remarkable dinner together.

"What will DD cook for dinner?" Alina asked curiously.

"It's going to be a surprise," I said. "But for sure, it will be the tastiest things I ever ate as a child. And we want you to judge the dishes."

"Oh, it sounds like fun! I hope it wouldn't be just eggs!" Alina teased me, remembering what I had told her about my passion for eggs when I was small.

For me, in my turn, was delightful the way Alina called her grandfather 'DD'. She had made up this special moniker for my husband.

When we were raising her in New York as a baby and toddler, we taught her to talk a bit of Russian and, exactly, to call me, her grandma, *Baba* and her grandpa, *Deda*. Since *Baba* consisted of two similar syllables and was very easy to pronounce with her inexperienced baby lips, she had no problem. But the name *Deda* made from two different syllables, with different vowels proved to be more troublesome for Alina and she automatically simplified it to *Dede*, equalizing the vowels.

Two years later, as most American children did, Alina began to study letters through games and songs on TV and surprisingly discovered that latter 'D' already had the vowel in its name; so, as she began writing, she shortened grandpa's name to 'DD'. It was a brilliant stroke for his name that was, in fact, David. This improvised childhood name for my husband stuck forever, even Natasha had repeated it after Alina. This was a lot of fun for all of us.

The weather today was sunny and hot, so Alina wore a cap with a long peak in addition to her short sundress. I placed on my head a straw hat with a big yellow flower on the side, and wore shorts and a T-shirt. We both donned our sandals because the asphalt was almost melting from the heat and it was impossible to walk bare-footed.

"Gosh! Baba!" Alina exclaimed as we walked out of our driveway onto a country road. "We certainly should exchange hats. You look so sporty and need a cap, while I would be more stylish in your hat. So, I propose we exchange and set things right!"

"Well," I chuckled, amused at the thought of Alina's new-found fashion sense which Rimma had probably tutored. "Let's change!"

So, while walking along we traded headgear, laughed and chatted merrily. It was such a lovely day and we were surrounded with the beauties of nature. Alina looked like a real young lady in my straw hat with a big brim and she assured me that, wearing her cap, I appeared much younger, like a teenager instead of a grandmother.

The horse farm was about a mile away, so we reached it before long. It was a vast meadow dotted with ox-eye daisies. It looked like a white-yellow sea, swaying ripples on the warm wind, bordered by old-fashioned wooden fence – just gray posts and couple of long planks between them, enough to keep the horses at home. There were so many daisies in the meadow that it even smelled like honey. Bees and wasps happily buzzed, zipping from flower to flower.

It was such an amazing picture – a bright blue sky, daisy-dotted pasture, and aging gray fence - I regretted that neither Alina nor I had inherited Ekaterina's talent for art and couldn't capture this landscape on canvas. When I shared my lament with my granddaughter, she laughed and took her cell phone from her sundress pocket.

"Don't worry, Baba, I have a digital camera here, so I'll take pictures when the horses come in view. We won't lose the beauty of this moment. For now, we have just sit and wait."

We settled comfortably on the opposite side of the road on a grass-covered knoll abundant with hidden tiny wild strawberry bushes. A cool, shady forest of fir trees rose behind us. Actually, I was happy to sit in the shade. Though our way hadn't been so long, I felt tired and dizzy from the sun. I sensed that my usual heart problems, which were reoccurring in the last few days started once again. But I didn't want to spoil Alina's day or worry her by mentioning it.

"It's a good place," Alina explained to me. "I always like sitting here when I come to visit the horses. You can even snack on some strawberries while waiting. Enjoy! The horses are coming soon."

"Aren't they always here?" I inquired.

"Yes, they are. They just ran around the meadow, so we can't see them yet, but they will appear soon. Just be patient Baba."

"Oh, I can wait," I agreed, picking tiny strawberries. "It's so nice here that I would be happy to sit here with you the entire day."

"Yeah... nice," Alina nodded. "By the way, Baba, yesterday you promised to tell me about some nice experiences from your childhood. I heard from you so many horrible things that I started to dread your stories. Wasn't there something nice for you in Russia? Something very nice...You can tell me now while we're waiting, eating strawberries with the whole day ahead of us."

"Okay," I agreed favorably. "I'll choose a very good memory which will help us both feel better."

...In the middle of the night I was woken up by the hollow, resonating beating of a big drum. It sounded like there was music as well, but strongly muffled and almost inaudible. The whole building was shaking and windows were rattling from the heavy machines passing by. For a stranger it would seem like an earthquake was underway, but I already knew those sounds well and wasn't scared at all.

It was a parade rehearsal, I realized with glee. The May First Festival! Again!

I climbed out of my bed and tiptoed in my pajamas to the window to peer out. It wasn't easy to move the big flowerpots on the windowsill and to shift a huge wooden shutter aside, not making much noise and not wakening my mom and Baba. But I succeeded.

Without shutters and curtains the music became louder, however I couldn't see anything clearly in the darkness. The gloomy light of the street lamps offered me only some shadowy figures of drummers, drum major, soldiers and many militia men. Behind them, I saw the giant, heavy military ballistic long-range missiles that were placed on the long truck-beds and moved slowly along our Garden Ring Road towards Red Square.

I knew that now these rehearsals would repeat every night during the week or more because in daytime it would be impossible for such procession to move on busy streets. Major preparations would be made to assure that the military parade would look precise and impressive in front of the whole world. My mom had already been in Red Square during the parade, once. She stood on the guests' rostrum of the Mausoleum with some foreign musicians and news cor-

214

respondents who shot photos. She told me that their faces filled with horror as they watched those missiles parading before them; each designed to carry nuclear warheads.

However, I wasn't scared of the missiles at all. I felt just the opposite. Really, even now, in the darkness of the night, the missiles looked so imposing that this made my childish soul bear with pride that my homeland was so strong. I felt safe and secure that that evil octopus, Truman, or even the next villain, Eisenhower, couldn't do anything cruel to me – take away my toys for his capitalistic children, or even to exploit me. Since I was only in Grade 3, I had no idea what exploitation meant, but I knew that it would be something harmful and maybe indecent that I needed to guard against.

After the first rehearsal, I usually began my impatient wait for the May Feast Days. They would be the happiest and most enjoyable moments I've ever experienced, and I and all my friends were looking forward to having a lot of fun at the feast.

Every night I went to bed before 10 p.m. but couldn't sleep right away. My Baba Sonya was a fan of a weather broadcast and religiously listened to the final evening news program in the next room. She turned the radio up quite loud because she was getting older and was gradually losing her hearing. The weather for the next day followed the last news at 10:25, so I had to suffer form tiredness and usually fidgeted in my bed until 10:30 without sleep.

I asked Baba Sonya many times to turn the radio off, but she adamantly refused, claiming that it was most important to know tomorrow's weather. She rated this knowledge as the second valuable thing in our life, after food. So, drowsy but disturbed, I had to be patient until 10:30 when the flat would at least be quiet enough to sleep.

But as soon as Baba's damn radio turned off, I began to hear through the thin veneer walls a modern TV - with a tiny screen and a big water-lens over it - that Sashka's Grandfather Mitrophan used to watch. Such new technology had only just appeared in Russia and were hard to buy and expensive. My family couldn't afford it, but Sashka's mother, Nina, had bought it for her parents and I always had permission to come and watch a half an hour children's show that was on once a week. When Sashka was there, we usually watched it together.

However, his Ded Mitrophan was even deafer than my Baba, so he turned evening TV news program extremely loud and it didn't finish until 11 p.m. I could do nothing about it, except to wait obediently until things quieted down enough for me to sleep.

Then, the nicest thing in the world began - in the stillness of the night I could clearly hear the sounds of the huge *Kursky* Train Depot, located right behind our building. There was something mysterious about it. Through my curtains, I saw the multicolored lights, flashing in the darkness – deep blue, green, red, and dark yellow. They were accompanied by the long, sad, mournful blasts of the locomotives and the soft, distant, monotonous knocking of the wheels, crossing the joints of the rails on the tracks.

They were truly my lullabies. They made me quiet, calm, content and carried my dreams away to some enigmatic world, to the moon, to the endless and bottomless heights of the universe. I was flying along somewhere, and I slept.

The noises of the trains became the most pleasant sounds in my life; even as I grew older, I continued to love them. Many times it happened that I ended up living in different cities, in different countries, next to the railways and the landlords always spoke apologetically, saying, "You know, it's quite noisy there because of the railway..."

"It's okay! It's just great!" I usually exclaimed enthusiastically, but no one could believe that I would really prefer such a noisy location. No one could understand it. They guessed I was only being polite, but my first choice was always to be able to hear train noises. They put me in a relaxed state ever since my childhood near the station lulled me to sleep at night. I still remember that hauntingly beautiful night magic.

During the daytime, I took pleasure in my philosophical conversations with Baba. They usually occurred while I was sitting on my little chamber pot. The toilet in our communal apartment was cold; it wasn't clean enough for a child, and mostly occupied. So, my Baba preferred to seat me on the pot in our room.

But the floors in our rooms were too cold and too drafty – there were too many cracks, broken moldings, lop-sided doors and loose-fitting parquet wooden pieces. For this reason, Baba placed my pot on a chair. While I was sitting on it, she wrapped my naked legs and bottom with a shawl and I felt cozy, warm and was ready to spend hours in this manner. This comfortable position always disposed me to meditation and philosophy, though I was merely a toddler or preschooler at the time.

Baba Sonya used to sit next to me on our old couch, knitting something from wool – maybe socks, mittens or scarves, sweaters, or even pants. It was time for me to ask my questions, which seemed sometimes unexpected and shocking to her.

She usually answered me honestly; however, her words and

thoughts were often hard for me to understand. She had no special gift for explaining things easily and clearly, like my mom. But I loved her explanations and didn't forget them, sometimes grasping their meanings only many years later.

One day, I surprised her with a question, "Baba, what is it - a revolution?" Obviously, I had heard the word on the radio.

"It is a movement when the poor people come and take everything from the rich ones," Baba said.

"Oh, it's when Pasha comes and takes a ruble from you, isn't it? Is that a revolution?"

"No. It's not," Baba chuckled. "It would be revolution, if Pasha would come and kill me and then take everything in this room."

"And my toys? And my pot?" I was shocked. "But it would be dishonest! Not fair! It would hurt. Wouldn't it be a crime?"

"Yes, that's what a revolution mostly is. You just should never, ever say that aloud to anybody. You know that, but keep silence. And you shouldn't worry about it. There are no rich people left in the Soviet Union, after our last revolution. Now, all of us are poor, just some are extremely poor, like Pasha and her kids. Others are poor, but manage to survive, like we do."

"Are some people, somewhere in the world, rich? Maybe Truman is?"

"For sure, he is," Baba grinned again.

"Could Pasha go and take...his children's toys...or pots... or everything from him?"

"Definitely not. He is protected. And Pasha is a nice, kind woman. Leave her alone, please. She's not a proper example. Forget it. You'll understand this later."

"Okay," I agreed peacefully, feeling a bit confused and willing to drop the subject that now seemed boring to me. "Another question, Baba. Do you know who God is?"

"God? Why do you ask?"

"Actually, I heard this from Pasha, as well. One day there was a thunderstorm and lightening. I came to play with Pasha's daughters, but they all were hiding under the bed. Pasha said that she is scared of thunder because it means God in the sky is angry with us. The thunder is how he growls. They insisted that I crawl under the bed with them."

"Oh, come on! You shouldn't listen to fairytales of such uneducated peasants as Pasha is," Baba exclaimed. "She's not talking about God and religion – but only superstition."

"They told me that God is a grandpa with a big white beard, who is sitting on the clouds and sometimes he becomes angry if children don't behave well," I continued confidently to explain. "That's why the thunderstorms happen."

"Okay," Baba concluded. "I won't detail the nature of thunderstorms right now. Your mom better can do that during your bath times. But I can tell you, what God really is. He's definitely not a grandpa and not a person at all. In fact, he's not a material substance..."

"What is it 'material'?" I interrupted curiously.

"Something you can touch. But you couldn't touch God. It's an idea, a feeling. It's really your conscience. That's what God is for me.

"It must live in your heart, in your soul. You have to treat people, animals, plants and the whole world around you nicely; help them all, and love them all. Give the world as much love as you can, and this would mean that you have the God in your heart. Can you understand that?"

"Yes, I can" I nodded with certainty, though I wasn't really certain. I couldn't imagine an immaterial being living inside my heart. I pictured a tiny charming elf with dragonfly wings, like Thumbelina from Andersen's fairytale. It could possibly live inside my heart and make me full of love for the world. I couldn't touch it for sure, but then again, I couldn't touch the ceiling of our room, either. Could it be immaterial, as well?

However, I had no time to ask about the ceiling because Baba went on with her spiritual explanations, "I don't like religions," she continued. "Religions are only church traditions and don't always have a lot of love. There have also been many religious wars in history, when people killed each other in the name of God, only because they are praying, or fasting, or making sign of a cross differently. It's stupid nonsense! It's a lie and all politics. A person who has the God in his or her heart would never, ever kill, or even abuse or hurt others. Remember, Katya, it is very important. I wish you always have love in your heart, even if no one else around you does."

"I do," I tried to assure her. "I love everybody and everything, even the octopus, though it is quite scary. But...how about bad guys? How about Truman or Eisenhower? Should I love them too?"

"Yes. They are people, the same as you. There must be some reason why they became different and sometimes it's not their fault. And sometimes your love may change them for the better. Even a tiny drop can change the world, if it is a drop of goodness; in other words, a drop of love – a drop of God."

I remembered the wisdom Baba shared with me, though I never

saw a lot of love in the surrounding world, but I tried always to keep it in my heart, and, as much as possible, to share it with others – people, animals, plants and even inanimate objects. I have always loved things and machines, imagining that somebody produced them and put a lot of heart and soul into them during the creation process. I used to do everything I did with my heart full of love toward my work and I guessed everybody in the world did the same.

Yet, as I grew older, I realized that it was not true and many, if not most, people were usually doing things in a heartless and careless way. They had little interest in doing a good job and just wanted money. It didn't make any sense. Anyway, I never changed and always acted only with love. It was my way; it was how I practiced my Baba's philosophy until it became ingrained in me.

Baba Sonya herself really followed her own dictum, too. Sometimes she brought people home from the *Kursky* Station. They were mostly women who had been robbed on the train while traveling, or their purses had been stolen when they did a little shopping on a stopover in Moscow. She usually found them sitting and crying at the station.

Baba fed them, talked to them, and let them spend the night safely on the floor beside the couch where she slept. In the morning she fed them again, gave them some money and helped them to buy a ticket and go back home or on their way.

My mom always laughed about her charitable acts and used to say, "One day, you'll bump into someone who will kill or robe all of us in the night. It's not safe to bring strangers home, Mom." However, it never happened.

Many of those people, whom my Baba used to help, sent her thank-you letters or became her friends later. She always responded and even went to visit them, or invited them to visit along with their families. Some of their children came to Moscow to study and used to stay in our rooms with us, as students. Of course, Baba never charged them and even gave them some money from her tiny pension which she collected as a widow of the Second World War hero.

It was fun. I wasn't bothered by the crowdedness and, instead, learned from my Baba a tradition of helping and caring for others. Those were the beautiful imperceptible lessons for me and really nice memories of the warmth of the human relationship that my Baba treasured. And I drank in some of it.

One day, (I was probably in the Third Grade) I walked into our classroom and saw the kids gathering in the corner very agitated.

"Doughnut! Doughnut!" they shouted, jumping and pointing

their fingers at a new girl. She was big with fat pink cheeks and was trying to hide her double chin behind her hands in the corner. Even her fingers were funny – short and fat like little sausages. Her tears and sobs clearly demonstrated how scared she was by her reception at her new school.

With all of my experience at the dacha, I knew quite well what it felt like to be chased.

I was often enough abused there because I was the youngest one. Now this girl was being picked on because she was the fattest one.

"Hey, everybody!" I shouted, shouldering my way through the crowd toward the girl. I pressed my back to her and turned my face to the angry children who were enjoying their power over the weak one. "Stop it! Go away!"

I knew that my class-mates would listen to me.

"Look at her!" I screamed, pushing the children away by shoving at their chests. "She is crying! Shame on you! Get out of here, you, chicken brains! You, idiots! What did she do to you? You don't even know her!"

I wasn't tall and strong enough to fight, but I used to be respected in the class because, being the best student, I always allowed the others to crib my essays and math homework from my notebook. Everybody knew that if he or she, even once, abused me, they would never be permitted to copy my work anymore and would only get low marks at school. So, my knowledge gave me the power which I was able to use sometimes in good ways – for example, to protect the crying girl.

The kids stepped backwards under my pressure. I took the hand of the sobbing new girl and pulled her to my place. "She'll sit with me!" I announced. "And never touch her anymore. What is your name?"

"Na-adia," she whispered, still breathless.

"Okay. Remember, guys, Nadia is my friend!" I pushed her to sit, took her hands away from her face and dried her cheeks with the edge of my black school uniform apron. "I'm Katya," I represented myself to her. "Would you like to be my friend?"

She nodded, sniffling.

This way we became friends for the next few years at the elementary school, until I was transferred by my mom to another school.

My friendship with Nadia was the nicest memory of my childhood. I soon discovered that she was fun, and always laughing. She was very active and ran and jumped even much more than others, so I couldn't quite grasp why she was so fat. Then I learned why when

I visited her home. Her whole family was overweight. Her mom, dad and little brother, Petya, looked similar - like fresh baked pies. The plumpness was Nadia's heritage, along with a good character of kindness and caring.

I liked to go and play with Nadia for one more reason, as well. She lived in very unusual and special place, right beside our school, and I, surprisingly, didn't know about this place and didn't notice it until I met Nadia.

There were two high-rise residential buildings on the street which were standing very close to each other, separated only by a tiny door and a huge black metal gate for trucks. "The Mechnikov Institute of Vaccines and Serums" read a small sign on the door. It didn't look significant because of its size and I was sure that nothing interesting lurked behind this tiny door. I knew only that Mechnikov was a famous medical scientist but it meant little to me because I didn't really like doctors.

However, I was surprised when Nadia invited me to come over into her place to play and asked me at what time exactly I would appear.

"What's the difference, if I come at 6 or at 7 p.m.?" I wondered.

"I should know the exact time because I will stay by the door and wait for you. You would never be permitted to enter on your own," Nadia explained. "I live inside the Institute."

This was unusual. My curiosity was peaked. An Institute? Among all the people I knew, nobody lived in 'an Institute'. No one, ever!

I came at 6 p.m. and met Nadia on the street beside the gate. She took my hand and we entered a tiny door into a security booth. There were a couple of uniformed armed men and more iron-barred doors behind them. It looked impressive and scary - like a prison that I might imagine from classical books.

"This is my guest," Nadia told them seriously, like she was an adult, and all of them nodded in agreement and put the time in their logbooks, my last name and address. Then they let us enter the iron-barred door and, surprisingly, I found myself in the driveway behind the huge metal gate, which I saw every day from the outside, as I passed by on the way to school and back to my home.

We followed a long driveway between the buildings walls and all of a sudden a huge square opened in front of us – an amazing park, full of fountains, bushes, flowers, trees and big cement bunkers, hidden between the greens.

"Oh, my gosh! What's that?" I exclaimed in disbelief, like I was entered in some fairytale garden of a princess' palace.

"This is the Institute," Nadia clarified. "The bunkers are off-limits to us. They lead down into the underground labs. But we can play 'hide and seek' in the park, or play ball, or play races here. Or we can also go to my home, take the dolls and carry them outside and play with them in the park. Look, here is my house," she pointed far away where an oval-shaped three storey residential building was barely visible between the trees.

It was an antique house with fretted balconies, pillars and arches over the doors and windows. Definitely, it was a mansion of an aristocrat before the Revolution. The Communists had turned it into an institute. Some of the rooms were rebuilt like offices and some became apartments for staff who lived and worked here around the clock in shifts. They were growing and breeding different kinds of bacteria which were living creatures and needed a constant care.

During the springs and autumns we used to spend most of our out-of-school time in Nadia's Institute, playing outside – in this amazing park. There were about 5-6 other children who also resided at the Institute, as well, and who joined us in our games. They were always friendly and we had lots of fun together. These moments were my very beautiful and nice memories of my childhood. I would have been happy to stay in the city and visit there everyday, instead of being condemned to move every summer to the yucky dachas I hated so much.

However, sometimes I noticed that after visiting Nadia's park, I had a headache, but my Baba convinced me that it only happened because I was out in the sun without my panama hat.

One day, while playing 'Cossacks and Robbers' (more interesting and developed version of 'hide and seek') I hid behind a cement bunker that was standing in the middle of some lilac bushes. I had already heard the footsteps of the kids running after me, so I decided to hide more and opened a lid of a big plastic container that stood beside the bunker door, possibly for garbage.

"Wow!" I exclaimed, seeing inside so many interesting and unusual things which I never saw before. There were test-tubes, syringes, retorts - some of them broken – and lumps and clots that resembled cotton, but were shinier. "Wow!" I jumped up, leaned over the edge of the barrel on my stomach and stretched my hand inside, trying to reach those things.

"No, Katya, no!" I heard a sudden scream behind me, feeling Nadia yank my feet back to the ground. I barely had time to withdraw my hand as she slammed the lid of container. "You shouldn't open that!" she explained, still breathlessly from running. "Never! And never touch anything here with your hands. It's dangerous! There is fiberglass. They are almost invisible. They can penetrate into your fingers and really hurt you. It would be horrible! My mom taught me never approach to the bunkers. Let's run to my home. You have to wash your hands and face with soap immediately. Then we'll play in another area."

"Why should I wash?" I inquired on the run. "I didn't touch anything there. I'm not dirty."

"It doesn't matter. My mom said we must do this right away, if we accidentally came close to the bunkers or bins."

Nadia sounded so alarmed, that I obediently washed my hands and face with soap - even three times, not quite understanding why I had to do this. Nothing happened to me later, except for a small headache, again, so I soon forgot about the incident.

An interpretation of this little scene came to me thirty years later, during Gorbachev's *perestroika* and *glasnost* era. All the newspapers began trumpeting the existence of long-hidden secrets of previous Communist governments and one article, in particular, caught my eye and grabbed my attention. There was a description of the institute where Nadia lived that I could easily recognize - surely, it was one of the most beautiful and happiest places I remember from my childhood. It was mentioned in the article that this institute was the precise place where in the post-Stalin's period (right at the time when I was playing there) Soviet bacteriological weapons were created, research and even put into production.

The paradoxes surrounding it were completely in the Communist spirit – toxic material located in the center of Moscow, next door to a school, residential buildings, and where the children played in the lovely park right on the top of the underground labs. With such total disregard for the welfare and safety of ordinary citizens, it came as no surprise to me that the *Chernobyl* tragedy occurred, though many years later. It's all the more astonishing, that an epidemic of the plague didn't ever break out in Moscow.

But we were growing happy and careless not knowing anything, according Russian proverb, "The less you know, the more baby-like you sleep."

Nadia, in turn, always came to my place during the First of May parades because they were marching right under my windows. It was supposed that people would go to the parade to demonstrate their love and loyalty to the Communist government and it was obligatory for most working people to attend them in Stalin's time.

However, when I was a schoolgirl, the population of Moscow had grown – arrests and executions almost stopped following Stalin's death – so, there were too many people to go to the demonstration passing through Red Square at one day. The government leaders had now become old, weak and sick. They didn't want to stay on the Mausoleum rostrum and great parades the entire day, like Stalin did. They were more worried about their own well-being and comfort and thought of demonstration parades as mere formality. In contrast to Stalin, they understood better the real value of people's *love and devotion* for them and didn't care very much to reciprocate it publicly.

As a result, government decided to cut the time of parades from10-12 hours to 2 hours and for this reason did not require all the workers' attendance at parades. Many people stayed at home or only watched from the sidewalks with us, kids. With the introduction of TV, most of the population began to watch the progression of the parade, lying on the couch at home and drinking vodka, as a sign of celebration.

With Nadia, we usually sat on the window-sill and watched a bit, too. Then, my mom gave us some money and we were allowed to walk outside.

It was great fun, as well. On our corner, the parade usually stopped because there they had to change direction and turn left onto *Chernyshevsky* Street that headed into Red Square. Thousands of the people crowded our Garden Ring Road. They were carrying flags, artificial flowers and banners with the names of their plants, factories, institutes, labs emblazoned on them. These were meant to separate one column of the march from another. While waiting their turn in the rearrangement of the columns, people were laughing, chanting, singing, joking with each other; or playing tag and buying things from *babushkas* standing on the sidewalks from the earliest morning.

The *babushkas* were wearing white scarves on this holiday, instead of their everyday black or gray. They sold homemade candy canes, yo-yos, tin whistles, artificial flowers, and wax swans which were empty inside and could float in a bowl of water. These were all special treats, never available, or even seen anywhere, except for May Day. Some people had helium tanks which inflated balloons. Children would line up impatiently, waiting for their balloon to be blown up.

We really enjoyed joining the crowds and walking on the streets with candy canes hanging from one side of our mouths and a whistle on the other. At the same time, we played with yo-yos, clutched big red flowers in the other arm and had our pockets stuffed full of extra candy, yo-yos, whistles and even wax-swans which sometimes melted inside. The balloons were usually tied with thread to the buttons of our coats and jackets because our hands were too full to carry them. Sometimes, people let go of their balloons and they rose in the sky, creating a funny multicolored spectacle against the bright blue background. The music played deafeningly from street loudspeakers hanging on the tops of the electrical posts – the Party songs about people's devotion to the Communist party, Lenin, Stalin, and the government. But nobody listened to the words – we thought it was funny, holiday music that created a very good mood in our hearts and filled our souls with joy and happiness.

The whole day out proved exciting, then Nadia and I returned home to have a special feast made from leftovers from my birthday celebrations the night before. These usually were delicacies: Russian potato salad, cabbage pies and smoked sprats in oil, as well as sausages and cheese – things which were affordable only during holidays - the tastiest dishes in the world.

Later, that evening, Nadia and I, along with other school friends, went outside to view the spectacular fireworks. Although the streets were crowded, the mood was subdued, as people strolled, mostly drank. They cheered with approval at every brilliant explosion of the fireworks against the dark sky. They continued waving their flags and fake flowers, laughed and joked, and seamed to be enjoying themselves. We, kids, certainly were.

These were some of the highlights of my Russian childhood. However, all of the above were quite routine celebrations that repeated every year. None of them can compare to the happy shock that I experienced when I was about 8-9 years old.

One evening, my mom bust through our door and right away turned on the radio.

She leaned her ear to it and listened attentively to the voice that penetrated with difficulty through the noises and static. Her face was so excited and had such an inspired expression that I quickly realized that something important had happened.

"What's going on?" I wanted to know.

"Pst, pst!" my mom waved to me. "This is 'Voice of America'. It is always jammed. Be quiet, I can't hear well! This is Khrushchev's speech to the 20th Communists Party Conference."

I was very surprised. I knew my mom had no interest in Communist Party meetings or any other activities and never listened to them on the radio or even read in newspapers. In fact, to the contrary, she always tried to listen to 'Voice of America' to discover the truth about our life, but those attempts were usually not successful.

Now, her nervous state demonstrated to me the importance of the events and immediately put me on guard.

"Mommy, is it good or bad news?" I asked in hushed tones.

"Very good!" she showed me her thumbs up and continued to listen.

"What is good?"

"Stalin is dethroned!"

"But he has been dead for 3 years already, hasn't he?"

She nodded.

"So, who is dethroned?" I couldn't grasp what she was saying.

"His spirit. His mentality. His cult."

I was totally bewildered by her words, but I could see from mom's expression that she was unable to explain anything to me at the moment. So I left her alone and returned to my drawing that I did at her desk. I knew now that for the next few hours my mom wouldn't ask me to move over so she could use her desk.

Khrushchev? I thought. Well! I can draw him beside Eisenhower.

And I made a big pink pig next to the octopus. I knew that Soviet people always called Khrishchev a 'Pig' in their jokes and anecdotes because he was short, bald and fat.

"The whole our life will change now for the better," my mom suddenly insisted, with her ear still glued to the indistinct radio broadcast.

I shrugged and thought, what could be better? It had already changed to the better – after Stalin died and linden trees were planted outside our windows. What else could be better?

I found out later.

After 1956, when Khrushchev in his historical speech broke down Stalin's cult of personality, it first became possible for more people to travel abroad. Not often, of course, and certainly not for everybody (especially simple people), but step-by-step the 'Iron Curtain' began rising just a little.

Some months later, my mom's friend, Marina, was sent as a Composer's Union delegate to Belgium for a week. Excited, she brought a lot of presents back not only for her own family, but also for her friends and their relatives. My mom got a French perfume by Christian Dior 'Lily of the Valley', my Baba received a can of instant coffee and concentrated milk with sugar, and I was gifted with three ballpoint pens, black, blue and red and a little handkerchief. They may seem like simple things, but they were unknown luxuries for us.

The handkerchief she brought me was special, as well. When I touched it with my girlish fingers, I could tell it was made from fine cotton, so sheer I could see through it. Wee poodle designs, the size of my pinky nail, were spread on its surface, embroidered in silk – black or bright green. Their diminutive figures looked exactly like any properly treated poodle would – a trimmed body with a great mane of a lion, a long tail with a brush on its end and shaved legs with brushes on the feet, as well. Those tiny figures were perfectly done and easily seen, in spite of their size. I was so impressed with quality of the embroidery. And it smelled of Lily of the Valley, indeed, because was packed along with my mom's perfume.

Oh, Gosh! Almost breathless, I took the kerchief. I unfolded it. I looked through it. I smelled it. I pressed it to my face. I petted poodles and talked to them. I wrapped my dolls in it. I placed it on my pillow. I flew, sang, laughed and slept with it. In fact, I almost turned crazy, completely obsessed with this kerchief. I was truly in seventh heaven!

"Why didn't we have these kerchiefs before?" I demanded from my Baba.

"It's foreign," she answered. "I used to have many similar kinds of things in Warsaw, when I was young."

"Does everybody in Belgium have something like this?"

"Of course," Baba laughed. "Not only in Belgium but everywhere in Europe: in France, Germany, England, and also in America... everywhere, except for the Soviet Union. Here the communists are not developing any consumer products - only building up the military. They aren't trying to make ordinary people, like you and me, happy. Instead they want to build more missiles to conquer the whole world and to consolidate their power over other nations."

"So, they want the other countries to become poor, like we are?"

"Exactly. But you shouldn't worry. They won't succeed, I'm sure. The people of the world would stand against them."

"Who, for example?"

"Maybe Eisenhower."

"Oh!" being already 8 years-old, I got it. "That's why he is always called a bad guy on the radio. Now I see."

I pondered over the subject a lot, keeping my handkerchief on my chest and, some time later, asked, "I just want to know, Baba how I could move to another country and live there forever."

"It's called 'emigration'," Baba explained and shrugged. "I have no idea if it is possible now, somehow. But anyway, it would be good for you to study foreign languages, to learn more geography, to know about other countries, about the Earth which is our real home. If you start from these, they will give you a good base for the future. You'll become a teenager, then an adult; you'll analyze the political situation and find some way to emigrate. Just don't tell anybody anything about it. Let's keep it as our personal secret – yours and mine."

"Yes, I promise," I said excitedly, kissing my kerchief. "I'll do that. I'll emigrate because I want to always have things like this and I want my future children have them."

Since that day I became obsessed with geography. I studied maps in my free time; I began study German at school and French at home and was the best student in these subjects. My geography and language teachers always praised me; I often won awards and school-wide and city-wide Olympiad competitions in those subjects. I became brilliant in those, having the straight-forward goal of desiring to explore and prepare for the world I would emigrate to.

I also began to collect foreign postage stamps. My mom used to work as an editor for the well-known magazine 'Soviet Music' at this time. Since correspondence with foreign countries was now officially permitted, there appeared the opportunities to the people who were interested in Russian culture and hungry to know about. So, my mom's editorial office of the magazine was flooded with foreign letters. She used to cut out the stamps from the envelopes and bring them home for me.

She also bought me many foreign dictionaries that began bit-by-bit appear in our bookstores, to help me to read the words on the stamps. So, in addition to German and French, I learned a bit of Italian, Spanish, Hungarian, Check and so on. My Baba taught me a little Polish and Yiddish which she still remembered from her early days in Poland. The only language I was not exposed to was English. I don't know why. Possibly because I always asked my dear friend and neighbor, Sashka, Stalin's grandson, or his mother, Nina, to translate for me, if there was something in English.

Thus, my learning, my skills, my stubbornness, my focused dream to emigrate one day - were all the sweet things that supported and inspired me spiritually during my childhood. Of course, they were quite adult things, but they helped me to mature faster...

...The sudden clatter of horses' hoofs interrupted me.

"Sorry, Baba!" Alina exclaimed, jumping up. "They are coming!" She grabbed her cell phone from the pocket and positioned it to film the horses.

It felt like the earth was quivering, as three flying figures appeared from the depths of the sea of daisies and raced around the meadow along the fence – three supernatural creatures, three choice, magnificent animals.

"Those are Appaloosas! Look at them, Baba!" Alina shrieked and I stood still, full of excitement, believing her, knowing full well that she had learned about breeds of horses. This was her passion.

The horses were ivory colored on their backs and almost white on stomachs and muzzles. They were covered with beige spots the size of apples and had the dark brown tails and manes. They were divine living things which Alina was crazy about. She dreamed to devote herself to them and to become a jockey or circus rider. Her parents were somewhat aware of this and hoped that her enthusiasm would be redirected into something more professional, like a veterinarian or zoologist as she grew older.

I watched, mesmerized, following retreating animals with my eyes. I began to understand my little darling.

"They're amazing," I admitted, smiling at her.

"Yeah, Baba. Now you saw them. Those are the nicest things of my childhood."

I sighed. Here was nothing comparable between Alina's and my childhoods. But it wouldn't be hard to draw parallels with my Baba Sonya's youth – she also had loved horses and had knowledge of them. It was the old Armenian horse, Asmik, which had saved Sonya's life and had given us all a chance to appear in this world.

Later, back home, we shared the special Russian family dinner my husband had prepared. On the menu was boiled potatoes in their jackets, dark, *Borodinsky* bread, unrefined sunflower oil (with a special smell and sediment) and Baltic sprats (little fish) in tomato sauce. Everything, except the potatoes, we had brought out from New York City with us. We purchased them in a Russian store on Brighton Beach, the famous Russian neighborhood. We brought them because they were the tastiest things of our childhood and we wanted our grandchildren and Charles tried them. We were quite sure that trying the provisions would give them a better understanding of how we used to live.

Of course, they ate this strange, new food because everybody was hungry after a whole day spent in the fresh air; however, we were surprised to see by their reactions that our dear Americans weren't happy. Of course, Rimma remembered having this meal, but she only smiled ironically and didn't say anything.

"Baba, did you really like these sprats?" Alina asked cautiously, dipping some potato into the tomato sauce. "It's quite bitter and really not very tasty."

"I thought you might say that. Now you see. They were our favorites because we haven't there so many choices, like you have around you."

"However, this pumpernickel bread is considered delicious, even here," added Charles, trying to fix the situation. He feared that we would feel offended by Alina's forthright remark and cast a disapproving fatherly scowl in her direction.

"Don't worry, Charlie," I replied, placating him. "It's okay that she gave her honest opinion. We're not hurt by that. Quite the opposite. We're happy for our grandchildren and their life. Aren't we, DD?"

My husband nodded.

"But I love these fishes," Natasha suddenly said, looking at me mischievously and put her little hand with a fork out to take seconds.

"You see!" Charles laughed. "It means that your life in the Soviet Union wasn't really so bad, as we thought, and had something nice in it," he concluded, giving Rimma a reassuring wink. "Don't you agree, honey?"

Chapter 15

A CURSE

The next morning, we returned to San Francisco because the weekend was over and Charles had to go back to work. In his thirties, he was a boss of a quite significant computer company and that really surprised me. In the former Soviet Russia, all the enterprise bosses were always over fifty or even sixty at a time when the government officials were mostly more than that - over seventy or eighty. Youthful career possibilities in America I found particularly exciting; especially since Rimma had married Charles because she was madly in love with him as a poor twenty-year-old student, mowing lawns.

My son-in-law completed his education, though he was already married and had a baby daughter, Alina; exactly like my grandpa, Victor Demin, who was studying when his baby, Lala, was on the way. My Baba Sonya always told me, "You have to marry only for love. Money and career will come later. A loving couple can achieve everything together." All of us followed this simple natural wisdom and family tradition. David and I accomplished everything together, as well as Charles and Rimma now had.

After lunch, Rimma planned to show us some local historical sights of the city: the Golden Gate Bridge, the Presidio Park that was rich with history and activity and the Russian Hill. However, I felt a little dizzy and experienced my heart pains again, so I decided to stay at home with the children who had already seen the marvels of San Francisco many times.

"Don't worry DD, we'll watch Baba," Alina assured my husband, and he and Rimma decided to go together to make a film for me.

I made myself comfortable on the black leader couch in the living room. Natasha brought her doll house and sat down on the thick blue rug next to me on the hardwood oak floor. It was a hot day, so Alina lay down to sun on the patio with a book.

A peaceful atmosphere surrounded me. I was lying quiet and relaxed, enjoying Natasha's billing and cooing, as she talked with her dolls. I plunged into thoughts about my past, pondering whether I had done the right thing to reveal our family history to my grandchildren and bring them mementos to connect them to the history. Had I told Alina everything significant about my Russian childhood? Did I complete the story? Was she even interested in it? Would she be able to remember it, like I had my Baba Sonya's story? I hoped so.

About one hour passed and Alina returned from the patio, wrapped in a big yellow towel with brightly-colored fish on it.

"How are you feeling, Baba?" she asked.

"Better. Much better. I'm okay now," I responded weakly.

"I got too hot and decided to cool down a bit in the pool," Alina explained, drying her hair with the towel. "Would you mind, Baba, if we went to a big playground now? It's only one block away from our house."

"Yes. I think I feel well enough to go with you."

"Yeah!" Natasha shrieked readily.

"You clean up your toys, first, and then we'll go," Alina demanded strictly. I smiled, noticing how seriously she was playing the role of an older sister.

When Natasha left the room, carrying her doll house into the playroom, Alina hugged me and asked suddenly," Baba, do you love Natasha?"

"Of course, I do," I was surprised by the question.

"You know," Alina said, amused, "I was your only granddaughter until she was born. I was your Granddaughter Number #1 and I want to continue to be Number #1 always. I don't want to share your love with anybody."

"Oh, my darling!" I hugged her back and stroked her wet hair, being moved by this confession of love. "But I have to explain. Of course, you were my Granddaughter #1, but, from the start, you shared my love with your mom and your DD, and even your daddy, though he is not my natural son, but only my son-in-law. I love all of you. We're family and when Natasha joined us, she really deserved her portion of love as well.

"It's just very sad that fate has us living in different cities now and I didn't have a chance to raise Natasha, as I raised you. I guess that she won't be seeing us very often and won't know us as well as you do. But you will know, remember and love us, even after we die, because you were with me from the first seconds of your birth until your 4th year of life; then you moved to a new house. Then we lived in the same city until you were 9 and we saw each other quite often. So, now you're the one keep our family memories and to share them with Natasha in the future. It's a big mission, believe me, sweetie. However, you were my first granddaughter and you will always in my heart be Granddaughter #1, though I'll continue to love Natasha and all of you dearly as long as I'm alive.

"You and Natasha are not competing in any way for my love. You're sisters, you're growing together and you always have to love each other and care for each other, like Sonya and Anya did. It's amazing to have a sister who is the closest person to you in the world. I always regretted that I didn't have one, same as my mom, Lala, regretted it. Wait a minute I'll give you something else."

I kissed Alina's cheek, stood up and walked to the guest bedroom to bring a picture from my purse. It was an old black-and-white photo with Anya and Sonya sitting side by side, with their hair beautifully coiffed, wearing their ball dresses. It had been taken when photography was a very new art, but, nevertheless, it still kept its quality and was clear.

"Look at this," I said, handing the photo to Alina, "and compare the faces. You look really like Sonya, except the color of your eyes. But, anyway, it's a black and white photo."

"Yes, I do," she exclaimed, beaming. "Does Natasha look like Anya? I guess not..."

"She definitely doesn't. She took after Charles, but there's another surprise there. Your mom strongly resembles Anya, again, except for the eye color. Isn't it fantastic? Anya is Rimma's great-grandaunt – the fourth generation. These genes are making such a convoluted course.

"Every four or five generation sees a repeat! One more example from our family history can prove this idea: Ekaterina von Wilde looked exactly like Empress Catherine the Great, though she followed five generations after her. In fact, the same as you after Sonya. Isn't it interesting?"

"Wow!" a clearly awed Alina remarked.

"You, please keep this photo, sweetie. You'll be able to show your own children how our family's bloodline has developed."

"I'm ready to go!" Natasha announced, appearing from upstairs with her hands full of sandbox toys. She had already a panama hat on her head.

"Okay, can you walk with her, Baba?" Alina requested. "I'll change clothes, lock the house and join you." She took the precious picture of Sonya and Anya and ran to her room upstairs.

"Good," I nodded, "I'll just take my straw hat and we'll go ahead."

The new, perfectly designed playground really wasn't far away. Two young neighbor women had already brought their three children of about Natasha's age to play there. Alina pushed Natasha a bit on a swing and then all the little ones began to play with sand and build pies and castles. Their mothers were watching them. I sat with Alina on the bench in the shade of the oleanders to have a rest because even after such a short walk, I was already tired again.

"Tell me, please, what do you think about your life," I asked her. "Are you happy?"

"Yes," she nodded. "I'm a very happy kid."

"How do you know? Why?"

Alina shrugged, "I don't know how to explain. I just feel that."

"That's good. I wasn't so happy at your age. Though, being a little girl, I was glad to be alive and absolutely sure that everything was just fine. However, as I grew, year-by-year, I began to realize that something was wrong. Then, as a teenager I already felt despondent and understood that I didn't have a very happy childhood. But when I once said that to my Cousin Helena, she became very angry and shouted at me that I'm an 'ungrateful pig' and such and such words. She claimed that my childhood had been perfect – I never knew hunger, I wasn't beaten by my mom or Baba, I never had sleep on the street, was never a child in a concentration camp, like many other children were.

"Of course, I never experienced all those horrors, but I never had daddy, I never had comfortable life, I was always sick and I was constantly mentally abused and hurt.

"At that time, I didn't know anything about concentration camps, but maybe I subconsciously sensed that I always was somewhere near the edge, and about to tumble in. I really had an unfortunate childhood, as I understand now. And all of this was due, not to my family, but to the country of my birth, where I even suffered shocks as a baby. That's why I'm especially happy about you sweetie, and about Natasha, and about your mom that you're living here."

"What do you mean by 'the shocks'?" Alina wanted to know. "The rooster? The German Sheppard, Lorka, that scared you? Or... what?"

"I can tell you now, if you want," I took a deep breath because these painful memories were hard for me to recount, and would surely strain my heart. Yet, I needed to finish the story for her.

...The sunbeams made fantastic patterns on the fretted ceiling of the room. Pieces of dust danced in the rays. Baby Katya woke up and lay still in her crib, watching them and smiling. She was concentrated on her feelings and sensed happiness; it was warm and quiet around.

The sun shone through the window not only onto the ceiling - its beams penetrated through the net of the crib and tenderly caressed Katya's cheeks. Somewhere behind the closed door she heard her Baba's voice, talking with the neighbors in the kitchen, while cooking. This created a secure image of life – peace in the room, but, in spite of that, Baba was always in the background, not far away.

Katya wrinkled her nose and screwed up her eyes, trying to escape the bright lights; then she freed her hands from the covering blanket, yawned sweetly, stretched herself and yanked her feet.

It felt comfortable to explore the surrounding world once more and she touched a string net, bordered her old metal crib from the room. The strings felt rough but stable and it seemed to be reasonable to stand up, holding onto the fencing, then trying to climb over it.

Nine-months-old Katya turned on her side, then rose on all fours and struggled to lift her head. She was surprised to find something blocking her way, preventing her from moving up. She pulled and jerked her head with no success. It was certainly stuck somehow and, continuing to tug, the baby began realize with horror that it would be impossible for her to stand up.

After many unsuccessful attempts to free herself, she discovered that something was suffocating her and held her neck in a vise-like grip. Katya shrieked and wept huskily, almost strangled, seeing her total hopeless situation punctuated with flashes. She was already starting to slip into scary darkness and lose consciousness when, luckily, Baba Sonya raced in from the kitchen and rescued her. The trauma was only of a few minutes duration, but for her whole life, Katya never forgot the total panic of being endlessly trapped and never being able to free her head again.

It was her first shock and she always remembered this feeling, without understanding what had gone wrong. Only many years later had Baba explained to her that dangerous event.

It was a warm blue nightcap with ribbons which were tied in a bow under baby Katya's chin. Katya always slept wearing it because the rooms were usually quite chilly. There weren't any baby clothes in the stores during those years in the Soviet Union, so Sonya had sewn the cap from her old blue pantaloons. To make the cap a little more beautiful and attractive, she placed a big pearl button that she had found by chance, on top of it.

One day, when Katya wanted to stand up in her crib, she turned her head to the side and the pearl button on the top of the cap accidentally got caught between the intertwining of a string net. Then baby yanked her head, the ribbons under her chin pulled tighter and began to cut off her oxygen.

...."Even now, fifty-eight years later," I said, "I can clearly recall my feeling of utter horror when I pulled and twisted to free my head from strangulation. This is quite strange because normally children wouldn't remember anything so early, but I do. That's what pushed me later to think that it was a shock - otherwise, it would've been forgotten."

"Oh, gosh! Baba!" Alina exclaimed in amazement. "It looks like your Baba Sonya didn't know anything about child safety. Weren't there any classes for pregnant women that your mom should attend and then share information with her mother who would be babysitting?"

"Of course not, sweetie. Who cared about babies at that time? If there weren't baby food and baby clothes in the shops, why would they be concerned about the safety of little children?"

"It was neglect, for sure" Alina pronounced judgment. "My mom attended classes with Natasha on the way even though it was her second child."

"In New York, while carrying you, she also took a course. But you wouldn't know that," I added smiling. "But it is different country, my dear, and even more – a different century. It's another world. In the world of my childhood, there was very little protection for the weak ones."

"So, it's even miraculous that you survived, isn't it?" commented Alina. "It was only your good luck."

"I think so. My good luck to live and to bring my three dear girls – Rimma, you, and Natasha - into this world."

"So, we're chosen by fate to live. It's great!" Alina announced happily, but then timidly asked, "Was there another shock, Baba, that you successfully escaped?"

"There was. But the second time I didn't escape. Do you want to hear?"

Alina nodded silently, looking at me with her big eyes.

... "You are a big girl now, sweetie, so you should behave well and be quiet and patient," my mom told me one day when I was five year old. "We'll go now to see a doctor who will perform surgery on you."

I tried to protest, but my Baba insisted strongly, "Otherwise, you'll be sick during your whole life. You always have a cold and a runny nose. It's because of adenoids. This affects your glands and you had quinsy with a high fever many times. Then the noises in your heart began to appear. You're almost on the way to have a serious heart disease. If that happens, you can die."

This explanation didn't scare me. I felt myself perfectly well and was absolutely sure that I'd never die. I was already accustomed to the word 'adenoids', hearing it everyday. It became something familiar and close to me; it even lived with me, like a pet.

But quite the contrary was the idea of surgery; I felt intimidated and I certainly didn't want it.

These discussions continued many times. What I didn't know was that my mom and Baba had already booked the surgery day and the goal of the discussions was only to prepare me mentally, not to secure my consent.

Finally, the day came. My mom promised that she would buy me ice cream after the operation, on condition that I cooperate.

The ice cream was a kind of rarity there and always played a role in my dreams. Being constantly sick, I in fact, never had a chance to have it.

The normal stores didn't carry ice cream. Soviet ice cream was produced in three different, very simple varieties – milky, creamy or fruity bricks with waffles on both sides. Usually, it was sold in the booths beside train stations, or by carriers inside the electrical trains which we took when we went to dachas. There was possible also to have ice cream in restaurants which I had never been inside, being a child. It was out of question according to Soviet mentality. If you tried to take a child into a restaurant, the doorman would never let you in, even for a bribe.

The Russian ice cream was quite good quality and served as an item of export. Many years later, my mom told me, after visiting the Czechoslovakia and Eastern Germany that she even saw special stores offering "Moscow Ice Cream" which were very successful.

However, when I was little child, I didn't know anything about quality. I tried it once and liked it, and then craved more, but Baba always prohibited it because of my adenoids.

It seemed reasonable now – to have this surgery, remove the adenoids, and then have ice cream every day which would be easy, since we were living next to the train station. Reckoning about that point, I agreed to go see an ear-throat-nose specialist.

The clinic was nestled in an old building with a huge waiting hall where about hundred people were sitting on the chairs around the walls of its perimeter. Between the chairs, there were many doors that led into doctors' offices.

We found the one we needed; Baba and mom sat down and handed me over to the nurse. The big woman in a white medical coat pulled me by my hand inside the doctor's office, where I went most reluctantly. It was big, cold and scary.

There was a desk beside the door, but the rest of the room was covered with tiles. It contained a large metal armchair in the corner and a small metal table beside it where on a large, white napkin the surgeon's tools were already laid out.

I didn't notice them at first, but then the nurse sat down in the armchair, forced me to sit on her lap and held me tight, encircling my stomach with her strong, huge arms. In this position, I found the table with surgical instruments right beside me. My glance fell, by chance, on this fearful equipment. Most of it was sharp and looked like knives or forceps.

Another woman, a doctor, wearing her white coat, came close to me and put a band over my eyes, but one second before she tightened it, was enough time for me to realize that those scary tools were designed to cut my throat. I wailed like a crazy frenzied animal, jerked and with all my might pushed the standing doctor in her stomach with both my feet. She hadn't been expecting it, so she collapsed on her back. When she fell, her arms and feet flailed around and turned the instrument table upside down, scattering the sterile tools all over the room. The nurse let me free for a second and jumped up to help the doctor return to her feet again.

At that point, I slipped away to the door, abruptly opened it wide with a thunderous cry and ran out into the hallway. There was a great echo in the waiting room and my screaming startled the people slumped on the chairs. Seeking protection, I dashed to my mom and Baba and crawled under the chairs they were sitting on, to hide.

"Help me! Save me!" I wept, grabbing mom's and Baba's feet, from under the chair. They both jumped up and pulled me out from my shelter. I hung on my mom's neck and growled, steadfastly refusing to return to the horrible place of execution. I trusted her, I hoped to be protected, but I was betrayed. My mom cuddled me to calm me down, petted my head, kissed my wet face and cleaned it with a handkerchief, but as soon as I was more composed and stopped crying, she and Baba took both my hands and carried me into the office, where the two professionals had already tidied up the mess, lifted the tool table and organized the knives on it.

"You'll have ice cream. You will! I promise!" my mom insisted, seeing that I began protesting and cry again. But this time it didn't work. I didn't want anything, including ice cream, except to run as far away as possible.

The doctor called one more nurse for assistance. And then began the nightmare. There were five adult women against one little child and all of them together really raped me. They secured my hands behind my back. The first nurse grabbed me around my waist again and sat me on her lap, holding me. My mom and Baba sat down on the floor and strongly held my feet to prevent them from jerking. Each of them held one my feet with difficulty, amazed at the power their little girl could muster.

The second nurse put a bandage over my eyes and then opened my mouth with the metal forceps. I don't even remember anything clearly, except for a lot of metal in my mouth and in my throat, unbearable pain, a lot of blood that streamed down my lower lip on the rubber apron that they placed on my chest. I also remember the horrible sounds of scraping, echoing in my ears with a terrifying recognition that this was my flesh being cut. I don't know how long it continued; I was almost mad from pain and horror, weeping uncontrollably. I had been suppressed and subdued against my will. Not only my body was assaulted, but also my spirit had been subjugated.

When the surgery finished and I was cleaned up, my mom and Baba carried me home, exhausted and humiliated. I hopelessly sniffled with my bloody nose and begged in a husky voice, "Ice cream, please! Don't forget about the ice cream!"

However, this was my unlucky day. When we passed the ice cream booth by the *Kursky* station, we saw it was locked. "Ice cream is sold out. Next delivery on Friday," read the piece of paper on its door. Friday was three days away. My expectations were in vain; I was completely cheated and devastated.

Of course, later I could eat a lot of ice cream, but it was too late. It couldn't fix anything and couldn't help. This unhappy day stuck in my memory forever, like a horrible shock. It wasn't exactly the physical shock of pain and fear, but more the emotional shock of fraud and betrayal of my loved ones. I trusted them, but they didn't help me and didn't protect me. They condemned me to suffering and I could never forgive such traitorous behavior.

Only many years later, when I was already an adult, could I finally understand that what they did to me was their way of caring about me, their desire to give me health, and their love for me. But the way they did it was awful. They couldn't even buy the ice cream before and keep it ready for me because it was a summer and there weren't any refrigerators in our flat. This was not their fault, of course, but as a child I didn't grasp it. For me, it was the most hurtful shock in my life and, subconsciously, I couldn't forgive my mom and Baba for it for many years after it happened.

...Alina hugged me silently and put her head on my shoulder. She was in a little shock, too, and didn't know what to say or how to express her feelings, except for hugging and kissing me.

"Wasn't there any anesthesiology?" she asked finally.

"I don't know. Possibly they gave me a couple shots in my throat, but these just worsened things. They didn't help much and were lost somewhere in the flood of horror. It wasn't what mattered. The surgery wasn't performed like medical care, but like real child abuse, and this hurt me deeply. I hated doctors and nurses since that day and couldn't tolerate even seeing medical coats anywhere after that. Exactly, as I hated dogs after Lorka's assault."

At this moment, we noticed that our two young women-neighbors had already picked up their toys and were about to leave with their children. They waved us 'good-bye' and we waved back.

Natasha approached us and asked for a drink. Alina took out the cans from her backpack and handed one to each of us. They were still cold. Then Natasha started a new sand castle by herself and we continued our sharing.

"Are those all your childhood shocks, Baba?" Alina asked in both dread and anticipation.

"I guess that I can tell you about one more and then we'll go home, too, and prepare something for dinner. Okay?"

"Yes," Alina agreed, looking at her watch, "we still have a couple hours until mom and DD return and daddy will come from work. Go ahead, Baba! Tell me the scariest story, please!"

She definitely considered my stories like thriller movies, tickling her nerves and she listened with wide eyes, full of horror and excitement, sometimes holding my hand.

"Well," I shook my head, being uncertain if it could be something worse than my adenoid surgery. However, there was one even more ugly thing of my childhood left to recall that seemed important to me now...

...The most popular Soviet transportation was the metro – the subway. For the children under school age it was free.

Usually, the metro was overcrowded during the rush hours, but there were moments in the middle of the day when it was relatively quiet and free of working people. My Baba always used these calm hours to go with me somewhere far away – to a farmers' market, or to supermarkets, or to visit some of her friends.

Sometimes, we saw dirty and scary homeless people on the trains and I knew already that they were begging for alms. My Baba usually gave them some change, but this didn't happen very often, only if they were able to sneak accidentally inside the metro. The militia was always after those people and entering the metro was strictly prohibited for them.

The beautiful underground stations looked like palaces and were supposed to demonstrate to the people beauty and might of the Communist regime. Those were things which the Communists were proud of in front of foreigners, the same as world-class ballet, figure skating and astronautic successes. So, there wasn't any space in the metro for the unsavory sides of Soviet life, like poverty, homelessness and vagrancy. Everybody in the society was supposed to pretend that these things didn't even exist.

On one cold winter day, being about 3-years old, I was riding somewhere with my Baba in the metro train. I was dressed very warmly, wearing small felt boots, *valenki,* and my little fur coat that Baba sewed by herself from my Grandpa Victor Demin's military sheepskin overcoat – it was sent to her after his death by the military command where he was killed in the Second World War. On my top I was wrapped with a big gray shawl that my Baba had knitted for all of us. If my mom or Baba wore it, the size was just okay, but for me it was too big. However, the day was very cold and I really needed to be kept warm, so, Baba Sonya put the shawl on me. She crossed its ends on my chest and tightened them behind my back. It felt nice and comfortable.

There weren't many people around in the metro train, but all the seats were occupied. We were sitting, too, but then stood up and approached the door because the next station would be ours and we were prepared to exit. Baba was holding my hand.

Suddenly, I heard a strange sound – like a rolling of small metal wheels over the floor. I turned my head and saw an alien creature that I haven't ever seen in the whole my life. It was very dirty and scary man, but what surprised me most was that, instead of a whole man, it was only half a man.

Having no legs, he was perched on a board that was placed over the little metal wheels. So he moved along the carriage, pushing the floor with his fists covered by filthy tarpaulin gloves. His chest was decorated with medals and orders, but his greasy military shirt stank from his stale sweat and grime. His face was almost black from dirt and deformed with an angry and aggressive grimace. Even while he was begging for charity, his expression didn't change. He didn't ask please or thank people, but forced them to throw some money into his cap which was lying on the board in front of him. He hostilely blamed everyone and everything with a husky and rude voice.

I had seen this kind of person many times, but they always had legs and walked on their own feet, though, sometimes one foot was made of wood and they used crutches. However, this one was in another category – an exceptionally angry and bitter legless man.

"Baba, look!" I exclaimed astonished. "Why doesn't that man have any legs?"

My clean and sweet child's voice sounded so clear, piercing the noise of vibrating train that everyone heard it and gloomy, tired people around lifted up their weary heads and sullenly looked toward me. The monster definitely heard it, too. He abruptly turned to me and shouted madly, shaking his fists above his head, "I damn you, little bitch! Be cursed!"

I looked at him, paralyzed by horror, unable to move an inch. I didn't grasp the meaning of his words because I'd never heard anything like that and didn't know what it meant. I only saw his toothless black mouth with absolutely dark blue tongue which seemed fearful to me.

"Be damned! Be cursed, you, the little fucking creature of hell!" he wailed, spitting his stinky saliva around. Everybody seemed to be scared of him and didn't even try to stop him. My Baba was only person who stood up for me immediately.

"Shame on you!" she shouted back at him. "You're an adult, serious, responsible man! You must be a hero, according to your orders and medals! Don't you see that she is a little child? She is an innocent toddler! She is only asking what she is seeing! Shame on you for even pronouncing such ugly words to the child! Children are our life and our future!"

"I'm cursing that life and that future!" the beast growled, completely losing all control. Luckily for us, the train stopped, the door opened and we stepped out, leaving him behind to yell and curse in front of his silent, wordless listeners.

At the station, Baba sat me on the bench and took a handkerchief from her pocket.

"Oh, my gosh! Oh, my goodness!" she whispered hastily and began to clean my face, which surprised me because I was sure it was clean. "You should always clean your face when you encounter bad energy which is coming from bad people," she explained, since I looked at her with uncomprehending eyes. "Better to wash it, but we have no water here."

Not understanding anything of what had happened I flooded her with wads of questions. Who was that man? Why didn't he have leg or feet? Why was he so angry? Why had he assaulted me?

"He is an idiot," Baba said, "or mentally ill. Forget about him! Maybe he was in the war and saw a lot of horror and pain; maybe his family, his kids were killed and this grief twisted his mind. However, maybe he is only a criminal, who fell down under the train, being drunk and lost his feet in such an accident. Or maybe he stole those military decorations and was using them to make some small money. Anyway it doesn't deserve your attention and you have to forget about him right away. It's not your childish business."

"Okay," I assured her readily and really forgot about this incident quite soon. I wasn't scared anymore and the initial feeling of squeamishness forced me to stop thinking about this dirty monster. Possibly, it was my subconscious instinct to protect myself.

"This memory only came back to me last year," I finished the story for Alina, "here, in America, watching the psychological TV-show 'Dr. Phil'. This is an adult show, so probably you don't know about it, but I like it. It's very useful for me to understand American life and psychology. It helps me a lot.

"So, one day there was a case about racism on the show. Dr. Phil noted that anyone who would blame a 3-year old child of the opposite race, shout at the child and threaten him would be considered an abuser and thought of as a criminal. Then, I remembered my monster from the Moscow metro and realized that in reality he, too, was had been abusive towards me. Though, I was of the same race as he was, still I was a charming, happy, clean and innocent child - like a fine bud of a flower and this irritated his broken psyche destroyed by the harshness of Soviet life. He had probably suffered a lot himself, maybe even lost his children, but none of that was related to me and absolutely not my fault. Why should I be abused by him for nothing? It wasn't fair, but I lived in a country where no laws protected the helpless and little care was taken for children. At this time, even war veterans and handicapped people had no pension that provide for them and dissuade them from despair and madness making them ripe to commit crimes.

"It was jealousy, again. He must have thought why am I suffering when this child isn't? He wanted me to suffer, too, and wished for me that shared miserable condition. It was very mean.

"But, anyway, this mad and frenzied cripple subconsciously became, in my childish mind, an apt symbol of my country: broken and in pain. To me, he characterized Soviet Russia, and maybe this was what unwillingly pushed me to leave, as well."

"Oh, Baba," Alina sighed, embracing me once again. "I can only repeat my thanks that we're living here. You childhood was so scary! I hope this curse didn't affect your life in any way."

"For sure, not. I was too little to understand it and to take it seriously. The bad energy that he sent my way was deflected like a tennis ball off a wall. I was shielded by my utter naivety. I had very happy life when I became an adult. And, even as an unhappy girl, I was very lucky at the same time, too. If I hadn't been so lucky, I wouldn't have survived all the dangerous situations I found myself in. Well, I guess, now it's our time to go home."

I stood up from the bench, but suddenly became very nauseous. Pain in my heart really sharpened and I felt dizzy. Inside my head things became cold, creepy and sparkling and an unbearable weakness filled me.

"Sorry, Alinochka," I whispered with difficulty, sensing my throat squeezed by a spasm, "I'm feeling terrible."

"Baba, you're so pale!" she exclaimed, looking at me now with genuine alarm.

I lowered myself back down onto the bench, dropped my head back, feeling suffocated and dark, almost flying from dizziness…

Alina was surprised to see her Baba slipping off the bench onto the lawn, motionless and unconscious.

"Baba! Baba!" she shouted, fussing around the limp body, lying on the ground. "Are you okay? Baba!" Crying, she knelt and touched the senior woman's face, her eyes, tried to listen to her pulse. Then she grabbed her cell phone form the pocket of her shorts and dialed 911. "Please, lady," she begged, tears streaming from her eyes, "my Baba fell down. She is not breathing! She is dying!"

"I'll connect you with the paramedical department," the strong voice reacted immediately.

Then came hastily questions, "What is your name, girl?"

"Miss Alina Wonderstein," she spoke up through her fear.

"How old are you?"

"Ten."

"What is your address? I can't see it on the display."

"I'm calling on my cell phone. We're at a playground now. Winter Crest...Right on the corner of Winter Crest and Green Boulevard. Please, hurry. My Baba is not moving. Help, help, please!"

"The paramedics are on the way," the woman assured her. "Are there some adults around you, Alina? Could someone perform CPR on your Baba?"

"Nobody is around. But I can!" Alina exclaimed, remembering suddenly that she had first aid at school and she had had a CPR course just couple months ago.

"Okay. Try it," the voice from cell phone supported her. "I'll give you the commands."

Still sobbing, Alina put her phone on the lawn, folded her palms, one over the other, and pressed on her Baba's chest.

"One, two, three!" she heard voice from the phone.

Scared, Natasha abandoned her toys in the sandbox and wearily approached her sister.

"Natasha, please, blow into Baba's mouth!" Alina shouted. She was really too small herself to reach it while she continued pressing her Baba's chest.

Natasha crawled up to her Baba's face, trembling and terrified.

"I... don't know... how," she cried, tearfully and shaken.

"Just open her lips with your fingers and blow inside with all your might, when I stop pressing," explained Alina seriously, still sniffling from her tears. "One, two, three – blow! One, two, three – blow! Good girl! Thank you! Good job! One, two, three – again..."

...Oh, how their Baba would be proud of her little granddaughters! How happy she would be to see Alina's willpower, strength, bravery and knowledge put to such service! How excited she would be to know how mature and courageous her dear girl was in such a difficult situation!

But there was all darkness in front of her eyes and she couldn't see or hear anything, even when the paramedics arrived in five minutes. Then, some images appeared before her out of the void.

She saw Ekaterina - a young woman walking on the dusty country road, carrying her baby in her arms against the background of an August sunset...

She saw Sonya - a young lady in the shell pink ball gown with roses, dancing the Mazurka on the shiny hardwood floor of a huge hall...

She saw Lala - a 5-year-old blue-eyed girl, cuddling a doll in her arms under huge, framed portrait of an ugly Soviet ruler wearing a mustache...

And then came into focus a very familiar blonde toddler, clutching a gray shawl with a look on her face that was both frightened and disappointed. A little startled, she recognized that she was the little girl, Katya – herself in her childhood. The circle of existence finally closed and this was the finish of her life course. A final blaze flashed inside her brain and then came a total darkness – the end of the life. The end forever...

The end of the Part 3.

Printed in the United States
by Baker & Taylor Publisher Services